# THE BITTER ROOT INN

A Jamison Valley Series Novel

DEVNEY PERRY

**THE BITTERROOT INN**



ISBN: 978-1-950692-42-2



Editor: Elizabeth Nover, Razor Sharp Editing

www.razorsharpediting.com

Cover Artwork © Sarah Hansen, Okay Creations

www.okaycreations.com

Proofreader: Julie Deaton

www.facebook.com/jdproofs

# OTHER TITLES

## Jamison Valley Series

The Coppersmith Farmhouse

The Clover Chapel

The Lucky Heart

The Outpost

The Bitterroot Inn

The Candle Palace

## Maysen Jar Series

The Birthday List

Letters to Molly

## Lark Cove Series

Tattered

Timid

Tragic

Tinsel

## Tin Gypsy Series

Gypsy King

Riven Knight

Stone Princess

Noble Prince

Fallen Jester

## Runaway Series

Runaway Road

Wild Highway

Quarter Miles

Forsaken Trail

Dotted Lines

## Calamity Montana Series

*Writing as Willa Nash*

The Bribe

The Bluff

## CONTENTS

*To Bill, Will and Nash*

# PROLOGUE

## HUNTER

"Is this seat taken, ma'am?"

The elderly woman abandoned the book she'd been reading and looked up. The wrinkles around her eyes deepened with her warm smile. "Not at all, dear. Please sit."

"Thanks." I stopped spinning my car keys around my index finger and tucked them into my jeans pocket before sinking into the leather couch and surveying the room.

For a hospital waiting room, the space was especially nice. The chairs across from the leather couch were oversized and upholstered in a high-end woven fabric. The oil paintings on the walls were framed with a mahogany that matched the end tables. The magazines on the center table were current editions and wrinkle-free. This was the nicest waiting room I'd ever seen, which was saying something, because I'd spent my fair share of time in hospitals—though not in maternity wards. Expectant grandparents, aunts and uncles could be trusted with leather and glass-top coffee tables. Unlike the emergency room I'd been in three days ago, waiting rooms in this Bozeman maternity ward probably didn't see gushing wounds or projectile vomiting.

"What brings you here?" the elderly woman asked.

An innocent question. Would she take back her seat invitation if I told her the truth?

*Probably.*

I smiled and went with a vague response. "Oh, just waiting around for good news like everyone else. What about you?"

"My granddaughter is having her first baby. My first great-grandbaby." Her eyes sparkled as she turned them down the hall, where her granddaughter was likely knees up with a doctor perched between her legs.

"Congratulations. Is she having a girl or a boy?"

"A girl." She smiled but shook her head. "You young people these days leave nothing up to chance with your ultrasounds. I had four babies and each one was a surprise."

"Well, I don't have children but I happen to agree with you. I'd want it to be a surprise."

She patted my forearm. "Good for you."

At the elevator's ding, our conversation stopped and we both looked to the silver doors, waiting for them to split open. I tensed and held my breath, hoping that the reason for my hospital visit wasn't about to walk right in and let me ruin her special day.

My fists dug into my thighs as the elevator doors started to part. What the fuck was I even doing here? How had I let myself get dragged into doing this? I hated my goddamn life right now.

A man came out of the elevator first, ducking his head as he stepped onto the floor. His baseball cap and dark beard did little to hide his furrowed eyebrows and the worry around his mouth.

For a second I relaxed my hands, thinking he was alone, until one of his arms swung back to help a woman out of the elevator. His wide mass had hidden her from me.

Was that her?

No. It couldn't be her. Not her. *Please don't let that be her.*

Because this woman was a dream. An angel standing in the hallway of a hospital.

Her bright-blond hair framed her delicate and flawless face like a halo. Her smile was full of straight white teeth underneath soft pink lips. Her eyes would be too big on most faces, but because they were so perfectly placed atop her high cheekbones, they were her best feature.

"Beau," the woman said, pulling back on the man's arm. "Will you relax and slow down?"

He didn't stop moving toward the nurses' desk, tugging her along. "This is not the time to slow down, Maisy."

*Fuck me.* It was her. The breath I'd been holding rushed out so fast my chest caved.

"Look." Maisy wriggled her fingers out of Beau's meaty grip and stopped by the doorway to the waiting room. "This is where we part ways. This is your room." She pointed to an open chair across from my couch. "And I'll go get checked into mine. I'll text you in a bit."

He frowned. "You're having a baby. I'm not staying in the waiting room."

"Well, you're not coming into *my* room. I love you, but there are things you are not going to see. That includes me in a hospital gown with my feet in stirrups."

"You're not doing this alone, Maze."

"Mom will be here soon and—ooh. Owie!" She bent over her pregnant belly and hissed out a long breath through clamped teeth.

My legs started to push off the floor but I stopped before I could rise from my seat. It wasn't my job to comfort her through a contraction. She had her brother and her family for that. I was just a stranger.

Still, I wanted the job. I wanted to be the man rubbing her back and kissing her hair. I wanted to hold her hand and let her squeeze it with all her might. I wanted to tell her how beautiful she was as her baby made its way into the world.

How fucked up was that?

I'd seen her for the first time just a minute ago, but one look and all I could think about was making her mine. Two minutes ago, I would have told you that shit didn't happen in real life. Men like me didn't believe in love at first sight.

Two minutes ago, I was a chump.

"Are you okay?" Beau asked when Maisy stood straight.

She looked down at her belly, rubbing the sides as a smile lit up her entire face. "I'm okay. It doesn't feel great but it just means he'll be here soon."

"Let me come with you to get checked in. Please?" Beau asked, and when she nodded, he led her toward the nurses' desk and out of my sight.

My jaw tightened as realization set in.

I was here on a fool's errand.

That woman loved her unborn child and would never give him up.

The elderly woman at my side said something I didn't catch. So caught up with Maisy, I'd forgotten I wasn't alone on this couch.

"What was that?" I asked.

"I said I don't envy her," she repeated. "If that baby takes after its father at all, she's in for a rough delivery. He's as big as a mountain. For her sake, I hope she gets the drugs."

I shook my head and mumbled, "He's not the father."

"Pardon?"

I didn't repeat myself. Instead, I stood and walked out of the waiting room as quickly as I could, going straight for the stairs so I wouldn't have to wait for the elevator. The second the stairwell door slammed tight behind me, I pulled out my phone from my pocket. I pressed the most recent name in the call log and held the phone tight to my ear as I bounded down the steps two at a time.

"She's keeping the baby. Leave her be."

# CHAPTER ONE

MAISY

*Three and a half years later . . .*

"Do you think they're ever going to get over it?" Milo asked.

"Over me renaming the motel?"

"Yeah."

I smiled and shrugged. "Probably not."

Milo and I were sitting in a booth at the Prescott Café, eavesdropping on the Coffee Club as they debated whether the decision to rename my motel from The Fan Mountain Inn to The Bitterroot Inn was going to land me in bankruptcy. They'd been having the same discussion for over a year now and still hadn't come to any conclusions.

"I swear, these guys are running out of gossip," Milo said. "I remember their meetings being much more informative. Now they're just recycling old topics."

I giggled. "It's just because Seth Balan is on vacation.

Once he gets back, I'm sure he'll infuse the group with fresh material. He's their ringleader, you know that."

He nodded. "True."

The Coffee Club was the foundation of Prescott, Montana's gossip mill. For as long as I could remember, the group of local men had been meeting here at the café every morning for coffee. Since the club was mostly made up of retired farmers and ranchers, they spent their first cup discussing the cattle market and grain prices while cussing the weather. But after those topics were hashed out, everything else was fair game. How they got their information I had no clue. Not even my mom's quilting club could get the inside scoop as quickly as these men could.

"So, did you decide what to get Sara for her birthday?" I asked, changing subjects. He'd been stressing for weeks about what to gift his wife.

"No." He leaned back into the vinyl booth, turning to stare out the window beside us. "She's impossible to shop for," he told the glass. "If she wants something, she buys it for herself, which leaves me with spa gift cards and jewelry she rarely wears. I want to get her something special this year. Do something big. Any ideas?"

I shook my head. Sara was a good friend, but Milo was right; she was very difficult to shop for and I was struggling to come up with a birthday gift for her myself. "Why don't you talk to Nick?" I suggested. "He's always going over the top for Emmeline. I bet he could think of something big."

Milo turned back to the booth and frowned. "He's going to laugh at me if I walk into the garage and ask for gift ideas for my wife."

"No, he won't. He'll totally help." I knew for a fact that Nick Slater loved nothing more than going all out to make

Emmeline's special days even better, and he'd be all over helping Milo. I had the sneaking suspicion that Nick was the mastermind behind many of the birthday and anniversary gifts my friends had gotten from their husbands.

"I'll think about it." Milo reached for his pocket and pulled out a handful of cash. "I've got coffee today."

I smiled. "Thanks."

He dropped a few bills on the table, then slid from our booth and walked to the counter to pay the three dollars for our coffee carafe.

Milo Phillips and I had been meeting for coffee once a week since we'd been in our early twenties. Because our mothers were close friends, we'd grown up together. As young adults, we'd lost touch for a few years. He'd left Prescott for the police academy and I'd gone away to college, but when we'd both made our way back home, we'd started this weekly ritual at the café.

Back then, both of our mothers had been beside themselves that we were spending time together, taking every opportunity to not-so-subtly hint at their dream for us to marry one another. Unfortunately for our moms, Milo had always been more of a brother than a love interest.

Besides, the minute he brought Sara to Prescott, everyone saw he'd found the right woman. She was his other half. Kind and sweet, she loved Milo with all her heart. All she wanted was for him to be happy, and gossiping with me for an hour made him happy.

It made me happy too.

We teased the Coffee Club relentlessly, but the fact was, Milo and I weren't much better. Not much happened in our small town that neither of us knew about. Though, unlike the Club, we did our best not to spread rumors. When we'd been younger, both of us had been more loose-lipped. But now, for the most part, our gossip stayed between the two of us and the regular booth we sat in each week.

When Milo turned from the counter, I plucked my purse off the bench seat and started toward the door, waving goodbye to our waitress, who stood behind the counter at the back of the restaurant.

"Gentlemen." I greeted the Coffee Club at the row of square tables they'd pushed together in the center of the restaurant.

A chorus of "Mornings" and "Hi, Maisy" filled the room.

"What's the news today?" I smirked, knowing no one would answer and fess up to the fact they'd been gossiping about me.

As I'd expected, all eyes suddenly found the menus, paper place mats and salt shakers fascinating. These guys never seemed to realize just how loud they were or that Milo and I were chronic eavesdroppers.

"Maybe one of these days you'll invite me and Milo to your table." I did my best to sound hopeful even though I was kidding.

A couple of the men mumbled but Dean Taylor spoke up for the group. "You know how it goes, Maisy. We sit here for hours. You've got to be retired to have the time to join this old group."

"Well, when the motel goes bankrupt because of its new name, maybe then I'll qualify." A couple of faces flushed and Dean's mouth fell open. I giggled and waved as I walked to the door, calling, "Have a nice day!" over my shoulder.

The little bell on the door dinged as Milo pushed it open for me. "You shouldn't provoke them."

I shrugged and stepped out onto the sidewalk. "It's not

like they're going to say anything about me that hasn't already been said or printed in the weekly paper."

"Good point." He slipped on a pair of sunglasses and walked toward his cruiser.

Sometimes I had to remind myself that Milo was a cop, not just the lanky boy with a buzz cut who used to chase me around the playground. He still had the buzz cut and was as lanky as ever—his tan deputy shirt never did seem to fit his lean frame—but standing by his police car, he looked much more official and grown up.

"What are you doing today?" I asked. Milo had always been forthcoming with me about his work, so much so that it had gotten him into trouble a few years back. I still asked and he still told me, but I was more careful about keeping my mouth shut around others, especially his boss, the sheriff, who happened to be my best friend's husband.

"I'm on patrol today so I'll go check in at the station, then head out."

"Then I'll say good luck. May your day be filled with a plethora of speeding tickets."

"Thank you." He smiled but it fell as he looked in the seat of the car. "Shit. I've gotta run home. I forgot my sunscreen and Sara gets pissed when I don't have it on patrol days."

My eyes immediately found the wrinkled scar on Milo's forehead and the one underneath his jaw. His arms were covered with long sleeves, but underneath the starched cotton was a pattern of burn scars from an explosion he'd been caught in years ago. A sunburn would be the worst thing for his scars and Sara was smart to push the sunscreen.

"Okay, bye." I waved. "Think about talking to Nick about her birthday."

"Will do. Bye." He waved back before sliding into his car, backing out onto Main Street and zooming toward his house.

I smiled at his urgency. Not many men would put their wife's skin-care directives above getting to work on time, but Milo would do anything to make Sara happy. If wearing sunscreen at all times made her smile, he'd be the first to slather it on.

Seeing their relationship made me long for one of my own. I wanted a strong and honest man to come crashing into my life. I wanted to be swept me off my feet in a whirlwind romance. But more than anything, I wanted to find a man who I could trust completely. A man who wouldn't hide things from me.

Unfortunately, pickings were slim in small-town Montana and I wasn't about to settle for anything less than perfect. It wasn't just my heart on the line. I had a little boy to consider first. My three-year-old son, Coby, deserved the best, and since I'd made enough mistakes with his biological father, I'd vowed not to bring an unworthy stepfather into the mix.

Even if that meant I stayed single for the rest of my life.

If nothing else, I had my daydreams. I was currently holding out hope that a Chris clone—Chris Evans, Chris Hemsworth or Chris Pine—would wander into town and fall madly in love with me and my son. If I happened to be out of open motel rooms at the time he breezed into town, I'd gladly offer him my own bedroom for free.

"Good morning, Maisy!"

I turned away from the street and smiled at Mrs. Connelly as she opened the door to her pottery and kitchenware shop. "Good morning!"

The stores downtown wouldn't survive in most small towns, but thanks to the heavy influx of summer tourists, businesses like hers were flourishing in Prescott.

"Would you do me a favor?" she asked. "Next time you talk to your mom, let her know I just got in that Himalayan salt block she's been wanting to try."

"No problem." I smiled, then set off for the motel.

The early April air was cool but the sun was shining bright, keeping me warm in my jeans, sneakers and light-gray zip-up. I loved mornings like this when I could drop off Coby at his daycare, Quail Hollow, and then walk downtown. These mornings gave me a chance to appreciate my little town.

Not much changed in Prescott, and any changes that did come took time. Predictability was what made this home. Soon, the old-fashioned lampposts would be hung with flower baskets. Spring items in window displays would be swapped out for summer. Tourists would flood the quaint area and crowd the narrow sidewalks.

With them would come my busy schedule and I wouldn't have time for these little morning walks. I'd be too busy at the motel, frantically trying to keep up with check-ins and check-outs. I'd need the extra ten minutes to update a reservation or fold a load of linens.

Tourism wasn't just good for the downtown shops, it was my bread and butter too. Three weeks from now, tourist season would be well underway as out-of-towners flocked to Prescott on their way to Yellowstone National Park. I was already booked solid through the summer, and by the time winter rolled around, I'd trade my morning walks for morning naps in an attempt to catch up on months of missed sleep.

But for now, I was enjoying the spring air and my lighter morning routine.

"Morning, Maple," I said as I passed her setting up a sandwich board outside her coffee shop.

She popped up from behind the sign, curly gray hair flying everywhere, and smiled. "Hello, sweetie."

"Have a great day!" I called, not stopping to chat. I loved my walks but if I wasn't careful, I could spend hours visiting with everyone along Main.

Main Street was the hub of the town, its heart. The street itself started at one end with a community fishing pond and ended at the other with a pair of gas stations whose owners were locked in a never-ending battle to post the lowest gas price or beer special. Past the gas stations and up a rounded incline was the highway that led out of town. My motel was the closest business to Main Street from the highway, so I proudly considered it to be an integral part of the charm that was Prescott's downtown area.

As I approached the highway, I checked for traffic, then jogged across the near-deserted road, taking a moment to appreciate my most prized material possession.

The Bitterroot Inn.

Every extra cent I could scrape together went into improving my motel. I cleaned rooms, washed bedding and scrubbed toilets instead of paying for a full-time housekeeper. I took reservations and did all of the bookkeeping myself so I didn't have to hire an office manager. And rather than pay for professional contractors, I bummed help from my brothers and guy friends.

If I could do it with my own two hands, I did. I painted. I replaced light fixtures. I'd even taught myself how to lay bathroom tile.

I'd worked my ass off for almost three years and my efforts were finally starting to pay off.

Reservations were higher than they'd ever been, I'd built a solid reputation for my business, and my list of improvements left to make was nearly complete.

Walking past the staircase that led to the upstairs loft where Coby and I lived, I rounded the side of the building and unlocked the glass-paned lobby door. Flipping over the lobby sign to read *Come On Inn*, I crossed the small room, dropped my purse behind the tall counter and scanned the reservation list I'd printed out last night.

I only had four guests at the moment, with two others coming in tomorrow for the weekend. The light occupancy meant I wouldn't spend my nights doing laundry and instead could make more progress on renovating another guest room. I was making a to-do list for the day when the lobby door opened and my brother Beau ducked inside.

"Hey!" I abandoned my list to give him a hug. "What are you doing here? Aren't you supposed to be going to Bozeman today for your tux fitting?"

He scowled but nodded. "Yeah, but I don't have to leave for fifteen minutes. I thought I'd check and see how the tile turned out in room seven."

"It's amazing!" I did a little happy clap. "My best work yet. Let me grab the key." I went back behind the counter and pulled the key from the pegboard. While it wasn't fancy or common these days, my motel had actual metal keys. When they got lost, it was a total pain to change the locks, but the charm of real keys made all the hassle worth it.

"I talked to Sabrina last night," I said as I followed Beau outside. "She said you gave in on the live band."

He sighed and rubbed a hand over his thick, dark beard. "It will make her happy."

"You realize she's going to make you dance, right?" At six foot six, he was a mountain of a man, and just like our dad, Beau didn't have the physique for graceful dancing. The best he could do was a lumbering two-step and slow jitterbug.

"We're currently in negotiations about the dancing."

I pulled my lips together to hide my smile, knowing exactly how those negotiations would end. "Right."

Beau and Sabrina's wedding was in a month and it promised to be an extravagant affair, something rare around these parts. While Sabrina was loving every minute of the wedding planning, my brother—who was far from extravagant—was counting down the milliseconds until the honeymoon.

Beau threw an arm around my shoulders in a sideways hug as we strolled across the rectangular parking lot toward room seven. "This whole place is looking great."

"I was just thinking that earlier. It's really coming together." I smiled as I looked around at the front of the two-story, L-shaped building.

It was hardly recognizable from the motel I'd purchased. The once-faded yellow brick was now a crisp white. The posts that held up the second level's balcony had all been stripped, sanded and stained a natural tan. Their bases had been faced with a beautiful gray-and-brown rock.

I'd even spent the money to replace the hollow-core white doors with solid wooden ones stained to match the posts. With the black shutters around all of the rooms' windows, the iron railings running along the balcony and the fancy number plates I'd hung outside the fourteen rooms, my motel was far from the sterile and plain building it had once been.

"So what's on your list for the weekend?" Beau asked, knowing that my task list was never short.

"I was thinking about getting a head start on summer prep. The flower bed around the sign needs fresh potting soil, and I'm going to drag the flowerpots out from the storage shed. I'm hoping to bust out room cleaning and laundry so I can get started on painting in here." I slid the key into room seven and pushed open the door. The dingy smell that filled my nose would soon be a thing of the past.

I had three weeks to get this room finished before I needed it for customer reservations. With Beau's help, I had already remodeled the bathroom, but there was still a lot of work to finish the bedroom. Paint. Carpet. Trim. Furniture. Décor. It was going to be a push to finish it all, but I had come to rely upon my aggressive to-do lists.

Idle time wasn't good for my mental health.

Beau stepped past me and went straight for the bathroom at the back of the room, standing in the doorway to gaze at my latest masterpiece.

"Most amazing bathroom floor ever?"

He chuckled. "Damn straight."

I had found this gorgeous artisan tile with an intricate pattern of charcoal geometric arcs on a white background. Eight tiles put together created two different patterns that gave the bathroom floors character and class. As I took it in, I stood a little taller.

"I'm proud of you, Maze."

"Me too. But I wouldn't have gotten this far without all your help."

Even though I'd done this bathroom floor myself, Beau

had spent countless hours helping to remodel other parts of the building. All the work he'd done had saved me thousands of dollars. I used to pay him with free dinners, but now that he had Sabrina cooking for him, I was going to have to think of another way to thank him for his work.

"I'm always happy to pitch in," he said. "Especially if you keep the cookie plate in the lobby full."

"I can do that." Cookies for construction. I'd bake a dozen of his favorite tonight.

I wound my arms around his waist for another hug. I loved both my brothers, but Beau had always been more than just an older sibling. He was my hero, and I was beyond happy he had found Sabrina. She was a wonderful friend, aunt and new member of our family, but more importantly, she made Beau happier than he'd ever been.

The ding of his smart watch interrupted our moment and I tipped my head back to give him a grin. "Tux time."

He groaned and let me go, running a hand through his dark hair. "I probably shouldn't miss this appointment."

"Probably not." I stepped behind him and planted both hands on his back, then just like I'd done as a kid, I tried to push him around. Using all of my might, I pushed hard, digging my feet into the ground. As per usual, he started laughing but didn't budge.

"Come. On." I grunted and pushed even harder but barely rocked him forward on his feet.

"Give up yet?" he teased.

"Never!" I repositioned my feet and gave him all my weight, holding my breath as I pushed, but still he didn't move.

"Give up now?"

One last push with no success and I dropped my hands, panting as I straightened. "It's like you're made of rock."

He grinned. "No, it's because I'm a giant."

I laughed as I walked past him out the door. Coby and Beau had a long-standing game of playing giants. If they were together, Coby was always riding on Beau's shoulders, pretending to be a giant as they stomped Lego houses to smithereens or crashed cars off pretend roads.

After locking up the room, I walked Beau to his massive green truck. "Well, drive safe."

"Will do. Call us if you want help this weekend."

"Okay." I waved as he got into his truck, then went back to the lobby.

My Thursdays were reserved for bookkeeping and I had a stack of bills to pay before lunch. Settling into my office off the lobby, I wasted no time diving into my work. Two hours later, my bank account was lighter and I abandoned my desk in search of more caffeine from the mini fridge.

Opening a Dr. Pepper, I hopped onto one of the barstools behind the lobby counter and stared out the window toward the motel sign.

*It is so cute!* How could people not love it?

A little over a year ago, I'd surprised the entire town by having the old sign taken down. It had been too ostentatious, nearly as tall as a streetlight, and its words had long since faded from years of sun exposure. The sign I'd picked to replace it was understated, yet perfect.

Sitting in the center of a raised flower bed were two, short white posts. Between them swung a classic white sign from an iron bar. It wasn't just the new sign that had caused the uproar, it was what had been written on its face in clean black letters.

*The Bitterroot Inn.*

That sign, displaying the inn's new name, had been featured on the front page of the weekly Tuesday newspaper two weeks in a row.

To this day, not many people understood why I'd wanted to rename the motel, especially since I'd kept the previous name for so long. But I had spent so much time making this place my own that I wanted a name I'd picked too.

The bitterroot was Montana's state flower and a personal favorite. The moment I'd jotted down the words on a napkin at the café, I had known instantly it was right.

The next day, I'd ordered the new sign.

And the gossip had commenced.

The inn wasn't the only thing that had changed these last three years. I had changed too. With every stroke of my paintbrush, every swing of my hammer, every turn of my screwdriver, I had changed.

Gone were the immaturities of a girl in her early twenties—being a single mother and business owner had chased those away. Gone was the naïve woman who had let a monster into her life—though not before I'd gotten the one good thing he had to offer. Gone was the young nurse brimming with spirit who had talked incessantly—I had learned to listen more and be mindful of the people I brought into our lives.

I had learned the hard way just how deceptive people could be when you were too busy talking to pay attention to the red flags.

Taking a breath, I pulled myself out of my thoughts before they could spiral to a bad place. I reached for a sketch pad on the counter and flipped to an empty page. I had spent all my time and money renovating the motel but hadn't done much to my own loft. Now that I was finally on my last guest room, I was brainstorming all of the things I wanted to do for Coby's room and our home.

I was so lost in my sketching I flinched when the lobby door opened, and my pencil skidded off the page, leaving a deep mark even the eraser wouldn't undo. I frowned for a split second before looking up, ready to greet my visitor with a megawatt smile.

The smile fell, along with my chin.

My visitor was straight out of a magazine. His light brown hair was tied back in a neat man bun. His strong jaw was covered in an expertly manicured beard. His caramel-brown eyes, framed with long, dark lashes, were aimed at me with such intensity they nearly knocked me off my stool.

When he turned to close the door, I was suddenly very aware of the fact I was wearing no makeup and my clothes were about as dull as an economics lecture. *But hey! At least you washed your hair today.* Thank god I wasn't in my normal blue baseball cap.

I wouldn't look like a complete slouch in front of this man.

This man was all the good things about my Chrises rolled into one. This man should be in the middle of a photo shoot for a fifty-foot billboard, not standing inside my motel lobby.

This man was about to get the mumbling, fumbling version of Maisy Holt the likes of which no one had never seen.

*Super.*

# CHAPTER TWO

HUNTER

What the fuck was I doing?

I needed to leave. Being this close to Maisy was too much of a risk. I was supposed to be invisible. Hidden. I was supposed to be the man in the shadows, doing whatever I could to protect her without her knowing I was even here.

Walking into her motel in broad daylight was as far from hidden as I could get.

The last time I had been in Prescott, I'd been able to avoid Maisy completely. I'd resisted the lure of seeing her and had lived like a recluse, going to work every morning and then immediately retreating home each evening. I'd grocery shopped thirty minutes before Jamison Foods closed at midnight so I wouldn't accidentally bump into her in the aisles. I'd steered clear of all the restaurants, living off of my shitty cooking for a year, just so I wouldn't risk being in the same room. I'd spent next to no time exploring Prescott just to avoid meeting her on the street.

Last time, I'd been strong.

This time, temptation had won out.

This morning, I'd been desperate for a real meal and had braved the café. For the two-day drive from Illinois to Montana, I'd been living off protein bars, sour gummy worms and jerky. Rolling into Prescott at two in the morning, I'd parked at a campground and slept in my truck. Waking up to a crick in my neck and hunger pains, I'd hurried to the café, figuring the chances of Maisy coming into the restaurant while I scarfed down some food were next to null.

I needed to brush up on chaos theory.

Because while I had been shoveling scrambled eggs and fried potatoes into my mouth, Maisy had slid into the café booth three down from mine.

And that's when my whole plan to stay away had turned to shit.

All because that cop had made her laugh.

Hiding behind an open newspaper, I had stolen glances of her talking and smiling with him. Then he'd told a joke and her melodic ring had drowned out all other café noises. My hands had crumpled the sides of the newspaper beyond repair and I had lost control of any rational thought.

Fucking jealousy.

This entire morning of insanity was all jealousy's fault.

Because rather than getting back in my truck and putting a couple dozen miles between us after she'd left the café, I had followed her as she'd walked up Main Street.

I had watched peoples' faces light up when she smiled and waved good morning. I'd watched as she moved with an easy grace along the sidewalk. And I'd watched as the sunlight traveled with her.

By the time she'd reached the inn, I was under her spell.

After that, I had gone back downtown to retrieve my truck and drive around a bit, hoping some space would get me back on track, but my tires seemed to steer themselves right back to The Bitterroot Inn.

Right back to Maisy.

Now, here I was. Not hiding. Not invisible. Instead, I was staring at her and not wanting to blink. I was doing my best to ignore the voice of reason in the back of my mind.

*Hunter, turn your ass around.*

I took one step further into the motel's lobby.

*Do not speak. Leave.*

"Hi." I crossed the remaining distance to the counter.

"Um, hi," she squeaked, then cleared her throat. "Hello. Hi. Uh, good morning." The flush of her cheeks was so fucking beautiful, my heart pumped double time.

*Whatever you do, shit-for-brains, do not ask for a room. You have a plan, remember?*

"I was wondering if you have a vacancy?"

*Fuckwad.*

"Um, okay. I mean, yes!" she blurted. "I have a vacancy. For how long?" She started fumbling around with a stack of papers, scattering them across the counter and knocking some onto the floor.

"Three weeks?"

"Okay." Her hands frantically shoved the scattered papers aside and then grabbed for an appointment book. "Sure." She took a steadying breath and reached to pluck a pen out of a mason jar. "Three nights," she said, writing the words in her book.

"No, three *weeks*."

Her eyes snapped to mine and she blushed again at her mistake. "Weeks. Sorry."

"It's okay." My smile made her gasp and drop her pen. I was flustering her—an effect I had on a lot of women—but this was the first time I'd ever enjoyed it. I didn't want Maisy to be uneasy, but I really fucking liked that she found me attractive.

Because I found her incredible.

"Three weeks," Maisy repeated, looking back to the book to avoid my face. "I've got a long-term-stay unit open for the month. It has a kitchenette so you can cook, plus it has its own washer and dryer. The price is five hundred a week plus tax. The standard rooms are ninety-nine per night so it would save you some money as long as you don't mind that I only clean it every other day."

Five hundred dollars was three times the amount I had planned to pay for a rented RV, but Maisy could have every last cent I had to my name. "That's fine. I'll take it."

"Sweet," she whispered to the counter. "I'll just need to see an ID and your credit card."

She finally looked up again, giving me the briefest glimpse of her smile, before she walked to a slotted shelf on the wall to grab some paperwork. When she came back, her gray-blue eyes locked with mine. I'd never been close enough to appreciate their unique color before, having only seen her from a distance.

I memorized the color so I could keep them for my dreams when she was gone.

We stared at each other for a moment too long, the air getting thicker as we breathed. Fuck me. She had all my nerve endings firing. My hands itched to reach out, to touch her smooth skin, but this counter was keeping me away.

I didn't move. I just kept studying her eyes until she blinked and broke away. "I, uh, just need you to fill this out."

She set the paperwork and a pen on the counter and pushed them toward me.

I snapped out of her spell. "Sorry for staring. You just have beautiful eyes." The words came flying out of my mouth before I could lock them down.

She reached up to tuck a lock of hair behind her ear, using the gesture to try and hide her wide smile, but I still saw it and it hit me right in the heart. Damn, this woman was going to wreck me. Five minutes with her and I wanted a lifetime. But since I'd never get it, I had to get out of this lobby. Fast. For my own sanity.

Reaching for my wallet, I dug out my driver's license and credit card. "Here you go." I set them on the counter purposefully, not wanting to risk my fingers brushing with hers. Then I grabbed the pen, focusing on the paperwork instead of Maisy. I scribbled down my name, phone number and vehicle description while she photocopied my license and credit card.

"Hunter Faraday," she read my name from my ID as she brought it back from the copier.

"That's right." I studied her face, expecting a flash of recognition, but there was none. She just smiled and set the cards back on the counter.

*Good.* The less she knew about me, the better. If she didn't recognize my name, it meant I had done a good job of staying under the radar the last time I'd been in Prescott.

Too bad I couldn't say the same this time around.

"I'm, uh . . . Maisy. I own the Bitterroot, so just let me know if you need anything. If I'm not in the office, I leave my phone number on the door."

"Okay." I stuffed my cards back in my wallet and shoved it into my jeans.

"Here you go." She handed me a key attached to a small tooled-leather strap. "You're in room eight. It's the last room along the long side of the building. First floor."

"Thanks." I took one last long breath of her sweet lilac scent, then nodded and left the room. When the lobby door closed behind me, I wasted no time dragging my suitcases from my truck and into my new room. Sitting down on the white down comforter, I dropped my elbows to my knees and let my head fall.

*Way to stick to the plan, Faraday.*

I guess I'd be staying at The Bitterroot Inn after all, living three hundred feet from the one temptation I stood no chance at resisting.

"What a clusterfuck," I muttered just as my phone rang. I pulled it out of my pocket and frowned at the name on the screen. "Hello."

"Where are you?" she asked.

"You know where."

"Hunter, is this really necessary?"

I scoffed. "You tell me. Is it?"

Silence.

"That's what I thought. Listen, now isn't a good time. I'll talk to you later." I didn't wait for a response or a good-bye before hanging up.

Staying at Maisy's motel wasn't going to be easy, but if it kept her safe, I'd stay here forever.

---

MAISY

I banged my head on the counter.

"Worst. Impression. Ever," I told my shoes. "Ever!"

That had to be a record for the number of "ums" and "uhs" I'd ever said in a five-minute span. I hadn't stammered that much since being asked to participate in an impromptu high-school debate.

Hunter must think I'm a complete dork. Just another desperate woman fawning over his handsome face. No wonder his paperwork was full of chicken scratch. He'd been in such a hurry to escape the drooling, bumbling motel owner that he'd barely made his script legible. If not for having his driver's license and credit card, I wouldn't have known his name.

But what a name.

Hunter Faraday.

I stood up straight and tapped my chin. "Hunter Faraday," I whispered to the empty room. Where had I heard that name before? Had I met him?

I shook my head. No. His name was vaguely familiar but there was no way I'd forget that face. Or his body.

For the first time ever, I was jealous of a plain tan sweater. I wanted to be wrapped around those Olympic-swimmer-sized shoulders. I wanted to brush against his flat stomach. I wanted to hug his narrow hips. Those dark-wash jeans didn't know how lucky they were to cover those sexy long legs and skim down his flawless ass.

And his smell? I had dated men that wore Armani cologne before, but it had never smelled that good. When it'd wafted across the counter, I'd nearly fainted and he'd still been two feet away. Who knew what kind of a blathering fool I'd become if he ever came closer than that?

"Don't go there, Maisy Ann," I reminded myself.

Hunter was my guest and a paying customer. I needed to keep a professional distance. Three weeks of him staying in room eight would pay for Coby's new bedroom in the loft and I couldn't afford to creep Hunter out and drive him away.

"Work. There is always work to be done." Determined to move past our encounter, I shoved thoughts of the gorgeous Hunter Faraday aside and got back to work.

While I picked up the papers I had knocked on the floor, I tried not to think of his perfect smile. While I updated my appointment book with his reservation, I refused to picture his soft, full lips. When I jogged upstairs to the loft and ate a quick lunch, I did my best to ignore the sound of his deep voice ringing in my ears, saying he thought my eyes were beautiful.

By the time I walked back down the interior stairs that led from my loft to the lobby, I had shaken off the jitters from meeting Hunter. Well . . . mostly. He wasn't the type of man you forgot easily. Hunter was a benchmark type of man, a ruler I'd use to measure the physical appearance of any man in my future.

Even with his man bun.

I'd never found man buns particularly attractive before. Sure, some of Hollywood's A-listers could pull them off—my Chrises certainly could—but any time I'd seen one in person, they'd always looked so thin and greasy. Yet Hunter's hair was a thing of sheer beauty. It was thick and soft—not an oily strand in sight. The natural blond highlights around his face were more noticeable because of its length, and the way he'd pulled it back—into a clean, tight knot—highlighted the angles of his face.

*He's a guest. He's a guest. Stop daydreaming about his hair.*

I had only met a few men with a magnetic presence like Hunter's. All had left scars, especially Coby's father. And as a twenty-nine-year-old single mother with a business to run, the last thing I needed was another wound.

Another reason to steer clear of my new guest.

So I used work to busy my mind, spending the afternoon at my computer returning some overdue emails. Hours later, I stood from my desk, proud that I'd been so productive despite the handful of times thoughts of Hunter had threatened to distract. I grabbed my keys and purse from the lobby, about to walk to Quail Hollow to pick up Coby, when my phone rang.

"Hey," I said, greeting my younger brother, Michael. "What's up?"

"Would you care if I got Coby from daycare today?"

He had never picked up Coby before. "Uh, no. I guess not."

When Coby had been a baby, Michael had always been nervous around him, always worried about dropping him and unsure how to play with him. But now that Coby was running and talking, Michael had been working hard to build a new bond with my son. I loved that they were playmates. Coby might not have a father, but between my dad and brothers, he was not short on male role models.

"Do you want to come and get his car seat?" I asked. "Or were you going to walk?"

"I'm driving but I stopped by Mom and Dad's and borrowed the Yukon with his seat."

"Okay. Then I'll see you in few?"

"Yep. I'm going to take him for a quick stop and then we'll be there."

"Sweet! Have fun." Michael must have something special planned and I couldn't wait to hear all about it when Coby got home.

I hung up and glanced at the clock on the wall. With an extra thirty or forty minutes, I could clean the laundry room and cross it off my to-do list for tomorrow.

Owning and managing a small-town inn wasn't all that glamorous. The work could be disgusting and I'd gone through more rubber gloves than I could count, but the work was honest. It was real. It was something I'd come to appreciate and rely on.

Stepping outside and around the vending machines outside the lobby, I propped open the door to the laundry room and wheeled out my cleaning cart so I'd have room to clean the tiny space.

The laundry room and my office shared a wall, and one day, if I had my wish, I was going to eliminate my office completely and expand my laundry room. I'd gladly trade desk space for an actual table to fold sheets and some extra shelf space to stockpile toilet paper and laundry detergent.

But on the bright side, the laundry room was a breeze to keep clean because it was so small. By the time I had wiped down the appliances and mopped the cement floor, I heard a car door slam and a sweet little voice yell, "Mommy!"

I dumped out my bucket of bleach water and rushed outside. "Coby!" Seeing his adorable face was the highlight of my day, giving me a fresh infusion of energy for the remainder of the evening.

"Mommy! We got Pickle!" He tugged on Michael's

hand, trying to pull his large uncle faster across the parking lot.

Michael held up his free hand and waved. When he waved like that, it always reminded me of Beau. Michael looked more and more like our big brother every day, minus the beard.

Coby, on the other hand, was the spitting image of his father. I wished he looked more like me or my brothers, but we didn't share many features except for our smile.

"Hey, buddy!" I waited for him to run right into my legs before bending down to give him a hug and brush the brown hair off his forehead. "How's my little man? Did you have a fun day at school?"

He nodded wildly. "Mommy! We got Pickle!"

"Oh, really? I love pickles." I smiled and looked up at Michael. "Did you guys go to the grocery store?"

"Um, not exactly." Michael's eyes darted away from mine and back to Mom's SUV.

"Puppy! Puppy! Puppy!" Coby said, jumping up and down in my arms.

"A puppy? Cool!" Michael already had a dog but he loved animals so another pet would fit right into his house. "What did you get? I want to see." I stood and grabbed Coby's hand, racing with him toward the Yukon.

"Maisy, wait!" Michael called behind us, catching us quickly with his long strides.

"Boy or girl?" I asked at the same time Coby shouted, "Mommy, Pickle gets to live wif us!"

My feet skidded to a stop on the pavement.

Michael bumped into my back. Coby's body went lurching forward, and if not for his hand still attached to mine, his knees would have landed on the asphalt. I steadied him on his feet and dropped to a knee. "What did you say? Pickle gets to live with us?"

"Yes!" He started bouncing up and down again, his brown eyes full of pure joy. "Uncle Michael said Pickle can be my doggie!"

"Really." I stood and aimed a glare at Michael. "You bought him a dog?" I asked through clamped teeth.

How could he have not checked with me about this? I wanted Michael to be close with Coby, but a puppy? Coby was too young to care for an animal himself and I had plenty to do without adding puppy training to the mix.

"I can explain." He held his hands up, backing away before I could punch him in the gut.

I dug a fist into my hip. "I'm listening."

"Um . . ." Michael took another step back as Coby started pulling on my arm.

"One second, buddy," I told my son without breaking eye contact with my brother.

"Okay. Don't be mad at me," Michael said. "This was all Dad's idea."

"Mommy. Come. On." Coby jerked my arm with each word.

"Chill out, dude. Just one more minute." I squeezed his hand but kept focused on my brother. "Michael?"

"Can we go inside?"

"Nope." If Michael had already promised Coby the dog, taking it away would be brutal. I stood a chance at not breaking my boy's heart if the dog never entered our home. The second that animal was inside? I'd never get it out. "You'd better talk fast."

Michael sighed and raked a hand through his dark hair. "Did you hear that Dr. Kelly is retiring?"

I nodded. Everyone in town knew Jamison County's only veterinarian was retiring. "What does that have to do with me getting a puppy?"

"He's selling his practice to his granddaughter. She just moved back to Prescott last month."

"Alana?" I remembered her from school but she was a couple years younger than Michael, who was two years younger than me. I hadn't seen her since before I'd graduated and gone off to college.

"Yeah, Alana. She's back in Prescott. Anyway, she was getting lunch at the deli today, and Dad and I happened to be in line behind her and overheard that she had these puppies dropped off at the clinic. Some breeder was looking to sell a few in town."

"Mommy!" Coby yelled, still yanking on my arm.

"One more second." I hoisted him up on my hip, hoping that holding him would buy Michael and I a few more minutes to talk. "Keep going," I ordered Michael.

"I had a big crush on her in high school but she had a boyfriend. I was telling Dad about her at lunch and he said I should stop by the clinic. Welcome her back to town and ask her out. Dad thought that if I took Coby and told her I was buying my nephew a puppy, she'd definitely say yes to a date."

"So you bought me a dog because you were trying to impress a girl?"

He looked at me like my question was ridiculous. "Well, yeah. She's not just a girl. She's *the* girl."

I stared at him for a moment, unsure how to respond. Michael had never, ever expressed that strong of an interest in a woman before. He must really be crushing on Alana Kelly if he was desperate enough to take Dad's dating advice.

I sighed and turned to Coby. "Pickle is the doggie's name?"

"I picked it!"

He was so proud of himself that it made staying mad at Michael difficult. "That's a great name, buddy. Good job."

Leaning in, I kissed Coby's chubby cheek. His tiny hands came up to my face and squeezed my lips together, something he thought was hilarious. He started giggling and I tickled his side, sending him into a fit of flailing laughter. He was getting so big, I couldn't carry him for long and definitely not when he was squirming, so I set him back on his feet.

"All right." I let him pull me forward again. "Let's go see this dog."

"Yay! Pickle!" His shout sounded more like "Picko" than "Pickle." Coby had excellent enunciation for an almost-four-year-old, but we were still working on our *l* and *th* sounds.

Michael stepped around us and led the way to the back of the SUV. Then he opened the hatch, lifted out a metal dog crate and set it on the ground. Coby's arms were flapping everywhere as he waited for Michael to open the crate.

Inside was the most adorable beagle puppy I'd ever seen. All four of his feet had white socks. The white tip of his tail wagged with abandon as he bounced around the newspaper-lined crate. His coat was glossy and clean, black on his back and brown around his face. But it was Pickle's sweet brown eyes and floppy ears that were my undoing.

*Damn it.* I had a puppy.

"He's licking me!" Coby giggled, sticking his little fingers through the metal grid so Pickle could attack them.

"I bought a collar and leash," Michael said as he pulled out big plastic sacks from the Yukon. "There's food, chew toys in here and some rawhide sticks. I already prepaid for his next five vet visits, plus one for him to get neutered when it's time. When he's out of dog food, just let me know and I'll buy more."

"I can afford a dog," I told him, watching Coby, who was completely entranced by the puppy. "I just wasn't planning on getting one until Coby was older."

Michael's shoulders fell. "I'm sorry. I know I should have told you, but I got caught up in seeing Alana again."

"And you knew I wouldn't say no."

"Yeah," he muttered. "I can take Pickle if it's too much."

"No, look how happy Coby is. That dog isn't going anywhere." My son was now jabbering to his new pet. I tore my eyes away from Coby and looked up at my brother. "You really like this girl, huh?"

He nodded, his eyes softening with adoration. "A lot."

Alana was one lucky woman to have caught my brother's eye. He'd treat her like royalty if she let him.

"Did you at least get your date?"

His smile lit up his entire face. "Saturday night. I'm going to take her to The Black Bull."

"Ooooh. Fancy. Well, I can't compete with their steaks, we're just having kid food tonight, but you're welcome to stay for dinner."

"Are you making chicken nuggets?" he asked hopefully.

"And macaroni and cheese."

"From the blue box?"

"Duh."

"I'm in." He threw an arm around my shoulders and pulled me in for a hug. "You're sure you're not mad about Pickle?"

"Not really. He's adorable and we'll make it work. But

don't tell Dad, okay? I'm going to pretend I'm still mad at you both and guilt him into doing puppy training."

"Good idea. Remember how fast he trained Aunt Regina's dog?"

"Yeah, like a month." Dad had a magic touch with dogs, and if I could convince him to train Pickle, it would save me a world of hassle. "Come on. Let's go inside. Can you carry in the crate?"

"Sure." He let me go and looped the plastic bags on his arm, then bent to pick up the crate.

"Mommy, can Pickle sleep in my room?" Coby asked as he took my hand.

"No, sorry, buddy. We're going to find Pickle his own special spot." Our loft was so small his room barely had enough space for his bed and dresser. With the money I was making from Hunter's reservation, I was going to build a bunk bed in Coby's room to give him more space to play in.

We followed Michael from behind the SUV, toward the lobby. I was so focused on swinging Coby's hand back and forth, thinking about where I was going to keep Pickle's crate, I didn't notice the man standing at the vending machines until I was just five feet away.

Hunter turned at the exact moment I looked up, and our eyes locked. My feet stuttered to a stop and my breath hitched, but by some miracle I managed an airy, "Hi."

"Hey." His eyes swept down until they landed on my arm. The arm attached to my son.

"Mommy! Why'd you stop?"

*Because of a hot guy.* "Sorry, bud."

I looked back up to Hunter as my feet moved again. But he wasn't looking at me. His eyes had dropped to Coby.

Hunter's face had changed as he assessed my son, but

before I could make sense of his expression, he spun around on his brown Frye boots and walked back toward his room.

*Shit.* Was Hunter freaked because I had a kid? Or was he rushing away because of the impression I'd made earlier in the lobby? An anxious knot formed in my stomach and I took a long breath, willing it to disappear.

It didn't.

Because even though he was a stranger and just another guest in my motel, I wanted Hunter Faraday to be as interested in me as I was in him.

# CHAPTER THREE

MAISY

"Knock, knock! We're here!" I called as I walked into the farmhouse.

"Kitchen!" Gigi called back.

I let go of Coby's hand and closed the door behind us. "Okay, buddy. Take your shoes off and then you can go play."

He toed off his shoes, then bolted toward the kids' room, yelling, "Ben, I got a Pickle!" as he disappeared.

We were at the farmhouse for a spur-of-the-moment Saturday barbeque because the one thing Gigi Cleary loved more than her family, friends and Halloween was hosting parties. It was still early, only four in the afternoon, and Coby and I were the first to arrive. I was here to play sous chef while he ran around with Gigi's son, Ben, who was just a few months younger.

I hung my purse on a hook in the entryway and walked toward the kitchen at the back of the house. "Hey," I said, giving my best friend a one-arm hug, then depositing my grocery bag on the island. "I brought tortilla chips and fixings for my guacamole."

"Perfect! I think I've got all of the burgers, brats and hot dogs prepped. I made a fruit salad, a pasta salad, a green salad, baked beans and spinach dip. Oh, and some brownies."

There were only going to be eleven adults and six kids here tonight. "Yikes. We're probably going to run out of food," I deadpanned.

She smiled. "Probably."

"Hey, Maze," a deep voice said from behind me.

Gigi's husband, Jess, walked into the kitchen with their almost-two-year-old daughter, Adeline, perched on his arm. "Hi, Jess. Hey, Miss Adeline." I stepped up close and tickled her side.

She giggled and ducked her head into her dad's neck.

"What's new?" Jess asked, grabbing a handful of the trail mix Gigi had set out on the island.

"Not much. Just gearing up for tourist season. What about you? Arrest anyone lately, Sheriff?"

He smiled. "Nope. Things have been slow."

"Just the way we like it." Gigi slid into Jess's free side and wrapped her arms around his waist.

I smiled. "Good."

Blissfully happy and carefree was a great look for them. I gave myself a mental pat on the back for getting these two hooked up. I'd played matchmaker with them years ago, and though they'd gotten off to a bumpy start, they'd found peace and love in this farmhouse.

"Maisy!"

I spun away from the island and braced, ready to receive

a crashing hug from Jess and Gigi's oldest daughter. "Rowen!" Ever since she was a little girl, Rowen's hugs had been wild and crazy. So I made sure mine were just as wild and crazy back.

"Guess what?" she shouted with her skinny arms wrapped around my waist. "Daddy finally agreed to let me get my ears pierced! Mom and Aunt Lissy are taking me to Bozeman next weekend to get it done. Can you come too?"

"Totally! I'd love to." Roe didn't know it but Gigi had already invited me to join her and her sister-in-law, Felicity, while Jess watched Coby. All I needed to do was convince my mom, dad or one of my brothers to be on call at the Bitterroot in case something happened with a guest.

"I'm so excited!" She let me go and flipped her long brown hair over her shoulders so she could prance around the kitchen, holding out her naked earlobes. "I'm getting diamond studs because Aunt Lissy says they're timeless."

I swallowed a laugh. This girl was as diva as you could get for a nine-year-old. "Well, she's right about that."

"Roe, sweetie, can you run and check on your brother and Coby?" Gigi asked, letting go of Jess to start setting out plates and silverware.

"Sure, Mommy." She smiled and skipped out of the kitchen in her pink-glitter ballet flats.

I let go of the laugh I'd been holding in. "Do you think she's going to be crushed when she realizes the 'diamonds' at Claire's in the mall are fake?"

Gigi scoffed, shoving the silverware drawer closed. "Oh, didn't I tell you?" She flicked her wrist toward her handsome husband, who was shaking his head. "Jess came home with diamond earrings for her last night. He's going to surprise her tomorrow."

My jaw fell. "You're kidding." *I* didn't even own diamond earrings.

Gigi shook her head. "Nope. Tell her your reasoning," she ordered Jess.

He just shrugged and grabbed another handful of trail mix. "Figured if I set the bar high enough, she won't ever find a boyfriend that can live up to it. Probably won't want to date until she's thirty."

I burst out laughing. Now how could I argue with that? Gigi was trying to hide her smile behind her wineglass.

"When Adeline gets old enough, she'll have diamonds too." Jess pressed a kiss to the soft curls of her brown hair. "All my girls get diamonds."

"Honey." Gigi set down her wine and went back to Jess's side, tipping up her chin so her long brunette hair fell down her back. When Jess pressed a kiss to her freckled nose, I felt a twinge of jealously. It wouldn't be the last time that happened tonight.

It wasn't an evil kind of jealousy, just one that stemmed from loneliness. I'd be the only single adult at dinner tonight. My friends had all found amazing men to share their lives with and I'd be surrounded by happy couples all evening.

Beautiful women, adored by tall, strong and handsome men.

Though none of the men were as gorgeous as Hunter.

It had been two days since I'd seen him by the vending machine. Two days and I still couldn't get his image out of my head. It was crystal clear. I was actually grateful for the two-day reprieve. I'd been using that time to get over my embarrassment for turning into a blubbering teenager when we'd met. The next time I saw him, I was determined to come across like a normal woman.

Which would be a lot easier as of next week. My part-time summer housekeeper was starting next week and I was assigning her to Hunter's room. It would be much easier to keep my cool the next time I saw him if I wasn't changing his bed sheets every other day, wondering if he slept naked.

"Hey, are you feeling all right?" Gigi asked. "You look flushed."

I looked up from the counter and smiled. "Just stressed about my to-do list," I lied. Normally, Gigi would be the first I'd tell about sexy motel guests, but something about Hunter felt different. I wanted to keep him to myself, just for a while.

"Anything we can do to help?"

"No, I'll get it all done. Thanks, though."

"Coby should have a sleepover with Ben tonight," she said. "You can drink some wine, let loose for a change. If you get tipsy, Jess can drive you home. Then tomorrow you could sleep in."

Coby was an early riser and I couldn't remember the last time I'd slept past six. Mornings had become our special time together since the evenings were always so packed with activity. But a lazy morning? Total freaking heaven. "You really wouldn't mind?"

"Of course not. We'd love to have him."

"We still owe you for watching all the kids for our anniversary," Jess said.

I did a happy clap. "Thanks, you guys! I could use a recharge before busy season."

"Any time." Gigi slid a full wineglass across the counter. "Cheers!"

"Woo-hoo! Cheers!" I took a healthy sip and then got started on my guacamole.

Two hours later, the kitchen was full of women drinking wine, the kids were chasing each other all over the farmhouse, and the men were congregated around the barbeque outside, drinking beer and grilling meat.

"What are you two whispering about?" Emmeline asked Sara and Gigi.

When their eyes landed on me, I knew I was in trouble.

"Oh, just an idea," Sara said, brushing her strawberry-blond bangs to the side.

"Oh, no." I'd seen this look before. These two were going to try and set me up on a blind date.

Again.

"Will you give her more wine?" Gigi asked Felicity.

I held out my glass, knowing I'd need every drop she poured to resist this assault. My friends had set me up with every eligible bachelor in the Jamison Valley. I'd learned that they were all eligible because they were all duds.

Emmeline was a kindergarten teacher at the school and had once arranged for me to have dinner with the music teacher. That guy picked his nose at dinner and ate his score as an appetizer.

Felicity was a real estate agent so any single man moving to Prescott not only had her help in purchasing a home, they also had her help in getting a date. The guy from Boise talked about his two cats during our entire meal, the guy from Casper stared at my breasts all night, and the guy from North Dakota only fucked brunettes—his exact words—but he'd promised to make an exception for me.

The only reason Sabrina hadn't tried to set me up yet was because she was new to Prescott and was currently consumed with planning her and Beau's wedding.

"So there's this new doctor at the hospital," Gigi started.

A doctor? "No. Absolutely not."

"He's really nice," Sara pleaded. "He worked here before, a couple of years ago, but left to go back to the city. He's so ho—"

"No flipping way! Never happening."

"But—"

"No." I interrupted Gigi, shaking my head and setting down my wineglass. "No doctors." I hated being so firm, but there were some things I would never do. Dating another doctor was one of them.

Been there. Tried that. Had his baby.

Thankfully, Gigi didn't press. "Okay."

"Are you talking about Doctor Calvin Klein?" Felicity asked. "He's back?"

Gigi and Sara both nodded. "I guess going back to his city life wasn't as exciting as he'd thought."

"Does he need a house?" Felicity asked. Her bright blue eyes lit up with the possibility of finding a new client.

Gigi shrugged. "I'm not sure. I'll ask him on Monday."

Felicity turned to me. "You should make an exception to your no-doctor rule. Dr. Calvin Klein is hot."

"Wait." Sabrina spoke up before I could refuse. "Can we take a moment to appreciate the fact that my best friend of many, many years just referred to someone by a nickname?" She lifted up her wineglass for a toast. "To Felicity Grant. I'm so proud of you. Getting married to Silas. Having baby Victoria. Those moments were all well and good. But this? I'm just so happy. For years, you've teased me for nicknaming people, refusing to acknowledge how awesome some of them have been. I'm glad to see you've realized the error of your ways and come over to the dark side."

"Hilarious," Felicity muttered, taking a long sip of her wine as the rest of us laughed.

I looked over at Sabrina and mouthed, "Thank you." She tucked a lock of her blond hair behind an ear and winked. *Best future sister-in-law ever.*

Luckily for me, the conversation didn't return to my love life. We all broke into smaller huddles and I was saved from more dating discussions.

"How are you feeling?" I asked Emmeline, who was standing at my side. She looked beautiful, her skin was glowing, and her long auburn hair was as shiny as I'd ever seen. But I knew from experience that those pregnancy symptoms often belied others, like back pain, heartburn and—my personal favorite—urinary incontinence.

She looked down to her round belly and smiled. "Good right now. I'm grateful that it's almost summer break and I can spend these last three months at home relaxing and enjoying my pregnancy. Nick and I decided she's going to be our last so I want to savor this time."

I was happy for Nick and Emmeline, but back came the pang of jealousy. Being pregnant with Coby had been anything but relaxing. The first two months had been spent in constant worry because his father had wanted me to have an abortion. The seven months after that, I'd been dealing with the aftermath of killing the man.

Pushing those memories down deep, I focused on Emmeline and baby questions. "Did you guys pick a name?"

She leaned in and whispered, "Nora."

"Cute! Oh my god, I love that," I whispered back.

"Thanks. We actually let Draven pick. Nick came up with his top two names and then I came up with mine. We decided that the one Draven could pronounce the best would be the winner."

As if he knew she was talking about him, Draven, Nick and Emmeline's two-year-old son, came running into the room, hiding behind his mother's legs as Ben and Coby chased after him. As quickly as the boys had come into the kitchen, they scampered out, giggling and laughing as they disappeared.

"More wine?" Felicity asked me.

"Please." I held out my glass and decided it would need to be my last before dinner. If I didn't eat something soon, I'd be blitzed by the time Jess drove me back to the motel.

I wanted to enjoy my lazy morning without a wicked hangover.

"Okay," Felicity said as she poured, "so I think we've established you won't be dating any doctors. But how about a wealthy investor who happens to be recently divorced and now living in Prescott?"

I looked to the heavens and pleaded, "Save me."

"This guy is great," she insisted. "I met him a while back when he moved up from Denver. He's sophisticated and a real gentleman. Anyway, I ran into him earlier this week and thought you two might hit it off."

"What's his name?" Gigi asked.

"Warren Adams."

"I know him," Emmeline said. "That's the guy that bought my old house."

"Yep." Felicity nodded. "Help me convince her that he's a good pick."

"He really does seem nice," Emmeline said.

"I can't trust either of you." I took a gulp of wine and set down my glass. "You may have found wonderful husbands for yourselves, but you're on strike three with this girl. I can only take so many bad dates."

"Please," Felicity begged. "Please, just one dinner."

Everyone joined in the pleading until I crumbled under their good intentions.

"Fine!" I threw my hands in the air.

The entire kitchen erupted with cheers. When I looked over at Gigi, her mouth was set in a grin. I couldn't help but smile back. She was coming from a good place; all my friends were. They wanted me to find a love like they had found, and maybe Warren was my shot. At the very least, I'd get a free meal.

The men started filing in from outside with Jess bringing up the rear, holding a tray stacked full from the grill. "Dinner's ready."

Moms dispersed, chasing after kids to get hands washed and plates loaded. With Rowen in charge of the kids' table in the living room, the adults crowded around the dining room table.

Dinner was followed by more laughing and more wine. By the time the sun had set, my cheeks hurt from smiling and I was drunk. Not so much that I was slurring or unbalanced, but the happy drunk where everything was funny, I was talking a mile a minute and driving myself home was definitely not an option.

As people started to shuffle out of the farmhouse, exhausted children in tow, I said good night to Coby. He was so excited to spend the night with Ben I was barely able to corral him for a kiss and hug good-bye.

Then Jess drove me home, waiting in his truck while I rushed up to the loft to pack an overnight bag for Coby. As he pulled away from the motel, I went to collect Pickle from his crate for his nighttime potty trip outside.

"Aww. Did you miss me, boy?" As I carried him down the stairs, he licked my chin like a typical overexcited puppy. "I missed you too. Here you go." When I hit the bottom step, I set him down and clipped on the red leash that matched his collar.

At the base of the staircase that led to my loft was a small gravel area where I parked my black Toyota 4Runner. Behind the stairs was a narrow swath of grass that bordered the entire backside of the motel. Stepping off the gravel and onto the grass, I let Pickle pull me around by his leash, his black nose pressed to the ground as he searched for the perfect place to do his business.

"Come on, Pickle. Come." I tugged on his leash after he'd peed. "Let's get inside."

We had already walked nearly the entire length of the motel and rather than turn and go back the way we came, I led Pickle along the grass so we could cut across the parking lot. The evening air was chilly and I hadn't thought to bring out a coat. I was only wearing jeans, tan flats and an off-the-shoulder drapey white shirt that was too thin for more than five minutes outside.

I was just rounding the corner behind the building when a dark figure stepped right into my path, grabbing the sides of my arms as we collided. I gasped, too stunned and terrified to scream, so I reacted purely on instinct. Bringing my knee up as hard and as high as I could, I crushed it into the dark figure's groin.

Direct hit.

The man let go of my arms as he doubled in half, holding

his crotch while he groaned and fell backward onto the ground. "Oh, fuck," he panted, trying to suck in a full breath.

Oh, fuck?

*Oh, fuck.*

I knew that voice and I knew that dimly lit man bun.

Reality dawned and my hand flew up to my mouth as I gasped. "Hunter?"

He didn't respond. He just rolled over and faced the ground, rocking his body back and forth as sounds of pain and agony filled the air.

"Oh, no." Fear turned to guilt. "I'm sorry! I'm so sorry. I didn't know it was you. I got scared and just reacted. My brother, he taught me some self-defense, and we've been practicing lately and I didn't think. It just happened automatically. I thought you were a bad guy. Oh my god! I'm so sorry."

My mouth would not stop moving. The words came pouring out faster than water over Niagara Falls.

*Shut up, Maisy!*

My mouth didn't listen. The rambling apologies kept on coming.

"I'm so sorry. So, so, so sorry. What can I do? Can I get you something? An ice pack? Ooh! I think I have a bag of peas in the freezer. I'll go get them. You stay right there, I'll be back in a jiffy." I carefully sidestepped Hunter, ready to sprint to the loft for my peas, when he spoke.

"Maisy, stop," he grunted. "Just give me a sec."

"Okay." My feet immediately stopped.

I stood over Hunter, nervously swaying back and forth, as he stayed in the fetal position on the ground. When Pickle lunged for a chance to lick Hunter's face, I yanked back on his leash and held him close.

*What a disaster!* How was I ever going to recover from this? My second impression was worse than my first.

I desperately wanted to keep apologizing but I managed to seal my lips together. The wine buzz I'd had minutes ago was fading fast and the heat from my embarrassment had chased away the cold. So much for remodeling Coby's room. So much for getting Hunter Faraday to like me. I expected to see his room key in the drop box when I woke up tomorrow.

Pushing up off the ground, Hunter slowly stood up and faced me.

"I'm sorry." My hand came up to my mouth again, holding back another fit of word vomit.

"Don't worry about it," he panted. "I'll live, but I think I'll take those peas."

I nodded and burst into action, scooping up Pickle and running across the parking lot, then leaping up the stairs to my loft. With the puppy back in his crate and a bag of frozen corn in my hand, I slammed the door behind me and rushed back toward Hunter. I rounded the corner of the lobby and jogged across the parking lot toward his open door, light from his room spilling out into the walkway.

I burst right into his room. Hunter was slouched in the leather club chair by the door. His head was tipped back and his eyes were closed.

"Here you go." I was out of breath and the words came out too loud.

Hunter's eyes opened and he held out a hand so I could drop the corn into his large palm. "Thanks."

"It's corn. Peas are Coby's favorite and I never seem to buy enough. He hates corn but it should work for your . . . um, well, you know."

*Shit!* I was rambling again. Like he cared about my son's vegetable of choice.

Hunter pressed the frozen corn to his groin, sighing with relief.

And I just stood there, bouncing from one foot to the other as the reality of this nightmare sank in. I'd just kneed the man I'd been crushing on in the balls. Mortification wasn't a strong enough word for how I felt right now. I didn't know what else to do, so I apologized. Again.

"Like I said before, I'll live." He tipped his head back again and shut his eyes. "Is your kid okay by himself? I'll be fine if you need to get back."

"Oh, he's spending the night at a friend's house tonight."

"Hmm." His Adam's apple bobbed gently as he swallowed.

I really wanted to run my tongue up and down Hunter's throat.

*Really? You just assaulted the man!*

Clearly, I was still drunk because that was not an appropriate impulse at this moment. I shook my head, pushing all licking thoughts aside and remembering why I was in his hotel room.

"Can I get you anything else? I have Advil or Tylenol. If you need something specific, I could walk to the grocery store and—"

"Maisy."

"Yeah?" I braced, ready for him to tell me to get the hell out of his room.

"Sit down."

"Right." His request surprised me and I immediately obeyed, sitting stiffly on the edge of his bed. We both stayed quiet—a personal miracle—and I did my best to relax. Once my heart rate finally moved out of the red zone, the nervous sweating began. My forehead was damp and a drop of sweat slid down my side.

I really needed to get out of here. Why Hunter had asked me to sit was a mystery, one I didn't really care to solve. All I wanted was to scurry back home and hide. This was worse than the time in eighth grade when I'd accidentally touched Joey Marcus's crotch in the lunch line.

"Self-defense, huh?"

Hunter's question caught me off guard and I jerked, making the bed bounce. "Um, yes. Beau, that's my brother, he's been into karate since college. He's been teaching me some basics for a few years now." I clamped my lips together before I could blurt my life's story and the reason why I'd asked Beau to teach me self-defense in the first place.

"Well," Hunter said, "the next time you see him, tell him he's one hell of a teacher."

I winced, my shoulders lifting to my ears. "Sorry."

"You've apologized enough." He removed the corn from between his legs. "I'm sorry I scared you."

"It's fine. I just didn't expect to see anyone out this late. What were you doing out there anyway?"

"I was going for a run and thought I'd go out back to stretch in the grass."

Now his clothing made sense. He wore a tight green T-shirt that fit his chiseled arms like a second skin. The charcoal compression pants did the same to his muscled calves. The black shorts he wore over the pants covered his bulky thighs. He wore it all well, too well, and I bet it looked even better when he was sticky with sweat.

I swallowed hard, ignoring another onslaught of sexy-

Hunter thoughts and went for simple conversation. "It's pretty late for running."

He nodded. "I haven't been sleeping well. I thought a run might wipe me out so I could get some rest."

"Is it the bed? Is it uncomfortable?" My voice was laced with panic.

I had spent a fortune on new beds for each room. I'd slept in one, just to try it out, but when it came to mattresses, I wasn't all that picky. I was usually so tired I could sleep standing up. But an uncomfortable bed was not feedback I wanted from one of my guests.

"It's not the bed," Hunter said.

My shoulders sagged. "Oh, thank god. I was point five seconds from a full-on freak-out."

He grinned, sending a shiver down my spine, and stood from his chair.

I took it as my cue to leave and stood too. "I'll get out of your room. Are you sure there isn't anything I can do to make this up to you? Added cleaning? Extra towels? I know my way around an iron if you need a shirt starched."

His eyes softened as he shook his head. "I'm good. I feel better already."

I really hoped that was true and he'd still be here tomorrow. More than I wanted his reservation, I wanted the chance to show him I wasn't a crazy person. Maybe my third impression would be the winner. I hadn't really cared what a man thought of me since Coby's father. But Hunter? I really wanted him to like me. My desire for his affection was slightly unsettling.

"One last time," I said. "I'm so sorry."

He walked to the open door and leaned against its frame. "You're forgiven."

"Thank you." I crossed the room and stepped past him through the door. We were so close to touching, but I didn't dare brush against him. With the way I was feeling—drunk on wine, adrenaline and Hunter's presence—I wouldn't put it past myself to do something foolish. What I needed was to get home and pretend the last thirty minutes hadn't happened.

"Maisy?" he called before I could walk too far into the parking lot.

I stopped and turned. "Yeah?"

He stepped into the middle of the doorway, his large body filling its open space. "Actually, I do have one request."

"Okay."

"The next time you make peas for your son, maybe you could bring me some. I'm not much of a cook and they're my favorite too." He tossed me the frozen bag of corn.

"Peas. You want peas?"

He nodded. "I want peas."

I had a hard time believing he couldn't reheat frozen vegetables, but if that's what he wanted, then I'd make him peas. "Okay. Good night, Hunter."

"Good night, Maisy."

I crossed the parking lot with a smile on my face, not because I'd had a nice dinner with friends or because I had an upcoming date with Warren Adams, but because I needed to start a new grocery list.

A list with *Frozen peas x 10* at the top.

## CHAPTER FOUR

MAISY

"I hope you've enjoyed your stay." I smiled at the midforties couple checking out of the inn.

"We just love your inn and this little town," the woman said. "We're already planning to come back next year."

"Wonderful! I'd love to have you back, but I'll warn you, I fill up quickly in the summers. So as soon as your travel dates are finalized, give me a call so I can block a room for you."

"Thank you." The man nodded. "We'll call you next week."

As I handed them their receipt, the lobby door opened and Hunter stepped inside. He held the door open for my departing guests, smiling as they brushed by, then closed the door behind them.

I took a deep breath and pushed it out slowly when he wasn't looking, willing myself to act normally. *Be cool. Just be yourself.*

It had been four days since the knee-to-the-balls incident and I hadn't spoken to Hunter. By the time I'd shuffled Coby out the door each morning, Hunter's expensive white truck had already been gone to—where I assumed—was work. In the evenings, he wouldn't return until well after Coby's bedtime. Spying from my loft like a ridiculous teenage girl, I had been living for the moments when I'd catch a glimpse of him walking from his vehicle to room eight.

But now he was here, at six thirty on a Wednesday evening, holding two empty Tupperware containers.

"Hey." He waved the plastic boxes in the air.

That sexy voice was flustering me already. *Maisy. Be. Cool.* I took another breath and smiled. "Hi."

"I saw you in here and wanted to drop these off and say thanks."

"You're welcome. I know you only asked for peas the other night, but the mom in me didn't feel right leaving you dinner without properly representing all of the food groups."

He chuckled and stepped closer. "I appreciate it."

Two nights ago, I had made a chicken and rice casserole for dinner, then set some leftovers aside with Hunter's peas. I had abandoned my previous plan to have my housekeeper attend to his room and instead gave it my personal attention. After I'd cleaned yesterday morning, I'd left behind some leftovers in his fridge.

"Your food was great." Hunter set the containers on the lobby counter. "I haven't had a home-cooked meal in longer than I can remember. It hit the spot."

"Thanks. I'm glad you enjoyed it. If you're ever in search of a meal, my door is always open and I always have plenty of food. I'm not very good at making meals for one. All of my recipes come from my mom and she cooks for my dad and brothers, three of the biggest humans on the planet. So, um, you're welcome anytime."

Out came the words before I could really think them through and I immediately started to panic. Was a dinner invitation too weird? I had just assaulted the man, then used my key to leave a casserole in his room. Now I was asking him into my home? Did that sound desperate?

*Dope!*

I tensed, waiting for him to sprint out the door.

He surprised me by smiling and leaning closer. "I'd really like that. Thanks."

As he spoke, my eyes drifted to his soft lips and I got lost in their movement. Their color was a pale blend of peach and pink, the bottom one fuller than the top. They looked like the perfect lips for a hot, wet kiss. A rush of heat pooled between my legs and I yanked my eyes away from Hunter's mouth when I realized I'd been staring.

His eyes weren't waiting for mine as I'd expected. They were locked on my mouth, doing some lip inspection of their own.

Did he want to kiss me too? At the thought, my tongue darted out automatically and wet my bottom lip. Hunter's eyes flared and snapped to mine. He held my gaze for a moment, then another, before finally clearing his throat and leaning back.

Grateful that he'd broken the tension, I sucked in some heavy air and searched for a safe topic of conversation. One that had nothing to do with his lips. Or kissing. Or me still wondering if he slept naked.

"That's a nice camera." Slung across his broad chest was a nylon strap carrying an expensive Canon camera.

"Thanks." He patted the lens. "I got it a couple of weeks

ago and haven't had a chance to use it yet. I was going to head up into the mountains tonight and see if I could get a couple good shots of the sunset."

"Is that what you do? Are you a photographer?"

He shook his head. "No, this is just a hobby. I got into it a few years back but rarely have time to practice."

I nodded in agreement. "I know how that goes. I used to have hobbies, but with this place, I barely have time to think these days. Not that I'm complaining. I love my job." I caught the beginnings of a ramble and stopped myself before I got on a roll. "So if you're not a photographer, what do you do here in town?"

I was being nosy but couldn't help it. Normally when someone new moved to Prescott, I'd get the scoop about them from the gossip mill. I hadn't heard a lick of news about Hunter's background but I wanted it to stay that way. I wanted to hear all about him firsthand, starting with what he did for a living.

"I work at the—"

"Maze!" Michael burst into the lobby with a loud and exuberant shout. I'd been so caught up in listening to Hunter's deep voice I hadn't even heard Michael's truck pull up. But my brother's timing couldn't have been worse. I was finally getting over my Hunter jitters and proving that I could carry on a normal conversation, but now I'd just have to hope for the chance to try again another day.

*Damn it.*

"Hi, Michael," I sighed. "What's up?"

"I'm getting married!"

My jaw dropped. "What? What are you talking about?"

"I'm getting married." He came behind the counter and picked me up for a swirly hug. "I'm going to marry Alana

Kelly." He set me down and started shaking my shoulders as he smiled.

I stepped out of his grip and took a step back before he accidentally hurt me in his excitement. "You asked her to marry you? You just started dating! You're going to scare her right out of Jamison County!"

Michael had called me after his and Alana's dinner at The Black Bull and told me how great it had gone, but that had been just days ago.

He rolled his eyes. "No, of course I didn't ask her to marry me, but I'm going to. Maybe in a year or something. Or six months. Or four. I don't know, but she's the one."

"Thank goodness." I relaxed and smiled up at my younger brother, happy he'd found someone special. "I'm happy for you."

"I'm happy for me too." Michael finally looked around the lobby and noticed Hunter staring at us. "Oh, hey." He held out a hand. "Sorry to interrupt. Michael Holt. I'm Maisy's brother."

"No problem," Hunter said, shaking his hand. "We were just visiting."

"Cool." Michael nodded and helped himself to a seat at the counter. "Welcome to Prescott. How long are you visiting?"

"I'm actually moving here," Hunter said. "I'm having a place built but the construction crew isn't done yet, so I'm staying here for a few weeks while they finish it up."

"Nice," Michael said. "Where are you moving from?"

"Chicago."

"Great city." Michael started in on a story about his vacation to Chicago a few years ago while I racked my brain, mentally touring through all of the new construction in the area. I really wanted to ask Hunter about his house but I was trying to tone down the stalker-ish questions. So instead of prodding for an address, I sat quietly, half listening to the conversation, half thinking about where he could be living.

There was a new house being built down by the river but I knew the owners. Other than that, all of the new construction was outside of town in the mountain foothills. Those lots were huge and predominantly bought by outsiders wanting a "cabin" in Montana—cabins that were, at a minimum, twenty times the size of my loft.

As far as I knew, there were only three homes in the foothills currently in progress with Jamison Valley Construction. If Hunter's was the place I was thinking about, he had money. A lot of money, something I'd already suspected. It had been pretty hard not to notice the Rolex he'd forgotten by the bathroom sink or the cashmere sweaters in his closet when I'd been cleaning his room.

The money didn't bother me, though, especially since Hunter seemed so down-to-earth and modest. He seemed like the type of man who would downplay his wealth just to make sure he didn't make anyone feel uncomfortable. Most of the well-off men I'd met had always made a point to flaunt their wealth. Coby's father had been a doctor and he'd always made sure to drop hints about his fortune.

*Don't go there.*

I shook off thoughts of Coby's father and focused on Hunter and Michael's discussion.

"Are you a photographer?" Michael asked.

Hunter smiled at me, then looked back to Michael and said, "No, I'm a—"

"Mommy!"

Coby was shoving open the lobby door with Mom trailing close behind.

"Hey!" I stepped around the corner and bent low to give him a hug. "How was your date with Nana?" Every Wednesday night, Mom had a special dinner date with Coby at the café, just the two of them.

"I got ice cream!"

"Yummy. Did you bring me some too?"

His eyes got wide with worry as he turned back to Mom. "Nana, we forgot Mommy's ice cream." His words got jumbled in his panic and "forgot" came out more like "fwor-got" and "Mommy's" was a rushed "Mi's."

"It's okay, buddy." I stood up and ruffled his hair. "I have to eat some dinner first anyway. What did you guys have?"

"Cheeseburgers!" he and Mom shouted together. They always had cheeseburgers.

Coby's smile turned shy as he looked around and noticed a stranger in the room. Mom noticed Hunter too, but instead of getting shy, she gave his backside a full head-to-toe assess-ment, then turned her eyes to me and mouthed, "Wow."

I rolled my eyes and started introductions, hoping that Mom would stop fanning herself soon. "Mom, this is Hunter. He's a guest here. Hunter, this is my mother, Marissa. You might see her from time to time because she helps in the office when I'm busy."

He turned and held out a hand. "Nice to meet you."

"You too." Mom said without letting go of his hand. "Oh, you're a photographer!"

"Actually, I'm—"

"You should take pictures for the rooms!" she inter-rupted, still holding onto his hand.

"Mom, let him go."

"Whoopsie." She pretended to be embarrassed but she was still holding his hand.

"Mom, his hand?"

Reluctantly, she released him. "Sorry. Anyway, like I was saying. You should take pictures for the rooms. Maisy, tell him your idea."

I pursed my lips and gave her my best "butt out" look but she ignored me completely.

"Tell him your idea."

Hunter's eyes were waiting when I turned back his way. "Idea for what?"

"The artwork in the rooms. Right now, I have standard, cheap hotel art—obviously, you know that since you have a room. Anyway, I've been remodeling all the rooms for the last few years but haven't invested in art yet because I want to commission something special. I was thinking of doing a collection of photographs from places in town and the surrounding area and then having each room be different."

"Tell him the postcard part," Michael said before Hunter could comment.

I gave my brother the same "butt out" look—which also went ignored—and looked back to Hunter. "I thought I'd make postcards that correspond to each room's art, and guests would get one when they checked in. They could send them to family members or collect them from various stays. Whatever they want. I just thought it would be something unique."

Explaining the idea out loud always bothered me. Everyone loved my postcard idea, but I'd always wavered. Some days I thought it was a stroke of genius. Other days I thought it was lame and dorky. Since I *really* didn't want

Hunter to think I was a dork, I bit my bottom lip as I waited for his response.

"I like it," Hunter said. "The whole thing sounds like a nice touch. The pictures and the postcards. I think people would really like it and it's different from what you'd see in any commercial hotel."

My lip dropped out of my teeth. "You really think so?"

His face broke into a breathtaking, wide smile, showcasing his perfectly straight white teeth. "Really."

I was *so* doing those postcards.

"Excellent!" Mom clapped. "Then you'll take the pictures?"

"Mom!" I scolded at the same time Hunter shook his head.

"Oh, I'm not a professional. This is just an amateur hobby." He looked to me. "You probably want someone with talent."

"Oh, pish posh," Mom said. "This could be a chance for you to refine your craft. How about this? You take some pictures and show them to Maisy. If she likes them, she'll buy them. If she doesn't, you'll have had a chance to practice."

"Mom, you're being pushy." I looked to Hunter. "I'm so sorry."

He chuckled. "It's fine."

"Then you'll do it?" Mom said, completely misinterpreting him.

"I, uh, don't really know the area. I wouldn't have a clue where to start."

"That's okay. Maisy can show you around. Please, say yes? We've all been so anxious to see her rooms finally finished and she's worked so hard. To see that old artwork in those rooms, it just breaks my heart. She deserves to have them finished just right."

"Mother," I muttered at the same time Michael said, "A little too thick there, Mom."

Hunter looked to me and I shrugged. There was no arguing with my mother in the room, not when she was set on railroading Hunter and I together. Was this how Gigi had felt when I'd played matchmaker with her and Jess? If so, I was calling her the minute I got to the loft and apologizing.

"Come on, what do you say? Please?" Mom begged.

"I can't promise they'll be any good," Hunter warned.

"Yay!" Mom cheered. "This will be wonderful."

Before I could tell Hunter we could discuss the details later—and give him a chance to back out—Coby tugged on my leg. "Mommy, can I go play with Pickle now?"

My eyes dropped to Coby who was talking to me but looking at Hunter. Coby was normally a loud and energetic little boy, but with strangers around, he was shy. He must have been warming up to Hunter if he felt comfortable enough to speak up.

"Sure, buddy. One more minute." I looked back up to Hunter. "This is Coby, my son."

"Hey, Coby." Hunter crouched down in front of us. "Nice to meet you."

I watched Hunter's face carefully as he spoke to Coby. The last time Hunter had seen my son was when we'd passed him by the vending machines. At the time, he'd given Coby an odd look, but now, Hunter's face was nothing but gentle and kind. Maybe he wasn't intimidated by my single-mother status after all.

"Can you tell me where you got that shirt?" Hunter

asked. "Batman is my favorite too. Maybe the store has one in my size."

Coby let go of my leg and puffed out his Batman-covered chest. "The package man gave this to me."

The mailman was getting credit? No way! "Coby, *I* bought you that shirt. The mailman delivered it, but that was a gift from me." Coby was convinced that the mailman was his biggest fan and the person behind every delivered present from Amazon.

Coby frowned up at me, then turned back to Hunter. "You could ask the package man to bring you one too. He's really nice and good at giving presents."

"I can't win," I mumbled.

Hunter chuckled and stood. "Sounds like a good idea. I'd better hit the road. Thanks again for dinner." He said good-bye to Michael and Mom and walked to the door.

"Wait," Mom called before he could escape. "When are you guys going to start on the pictures?"

"She's nothing if not persistent," Michael mumbled at my side.

He had that right. Mom wasn't going to let Hunter out of her sight until this agreement was locked down tight and we had a firm date set.

"I'm free Sunday, if that works," Hunter said.

I nodded, more excited for a Sunday afternoon than I had been in years. "Works for me."

"Perfect!" Mom said. "I'll come over right after church and watch Coby. You two can get a late lunch, then head out."

"Okay. See you Sunday." He grinned at me before pulling the lobby door closed behind him.

I kept the smile on my face until I knew he was out of earshot and then I glared at Mom. "Thanks for that."

"You are so welcome, sweetheart." She started fanning herself again, oblivious to my sarcasm. "He is dreamy."

She had that right. As over the top as she'd been, I couldn't help but smile at the prospect of seeing Hunter on Sunday.

Maybe he'd even take me up on my dinner invitation before then. I had an upcoming date with Warren Adams at a fancy restaurant and I couldn't conjure an ounce of excitement, but the idea that Hunter might come up to the loft for a humble supper at my tiny table had me practically giddy.

Coby tugged on my hand. "Mommy, let's go."

"You got it, bud. Let me get locked up." I shut down my computer and locked the lobby door, hanging up my sign. "You guys are coming up, right?" I asked Mom and Michael. They both nodded and we all followed Coby up the stairs.

The second we walked into the loft, I cringed. I'd forgotten that I hadn't cleaned before inviting Mom upstairs.

I worked tirelessly to keep the motel spotless but sometimes ran out of steam before I could clean the loft. Mom didn't care if it was messy, but she also couldn't stop herself from picking up. She did so much for me already, between watching Coby and helping at the motel, I hated for her to clean my home too.

Just as I'd predicted, she walked in and got right to work as Coby sprinted past us to go to Pickle's crate by the back door.

"Mom, you don't need to do that," I said as she tidied the pile of shoes by the door.

"I don't mind." With the shoes arranged, she went right into the living room to fluff the pillows on my charcoal corduroy sectional, which divided the living room from the kitchen on the left. When she started putting toys back into their tan baskets underneath my entertainment center, I hustled to tidy the kitchen before she could beat me to it.

Thankfully, my kitchen was about the size of a thimble so it took me just a few minutes to wipe crumbs off the Formica countertops and load the dirty dishes into the dishwasher.

"I'll take that washcloth," Mom said and swiped it from the sink. Then she went to my small, four-seater, circular table off the living room and commenced wiping.

"Mom, I will clean up later. Just leave it."

She kept wiping. "This will take just a minute. You've got so much on your plate, let your mother clean. It's important to me."

I sighed. "All right."

Mom had told me once that helping her kids was her purpose in life. She had forgone a career to stay at home when we were younger, and now that Beau, Michael and I were grown, I think she felt a bit lost at times. We still needed her, me and Coby especially, but it was different than the chaos and constant buzz of having three kids in her home.

"I'll be right back," I told Michael, who was poking around my fridge.

Despite my protest, Mom wouldn't stop cleaning and I couldn't let her do all the work herself. I walked past the living room and down the hallway to the only bathroom in the loft. Picking up a towel from the linoleum floor, I used it to wipe Coby's blue toothpaste off the sink. Then I went to my room and swiped clothes from the floor, shoving them in the stackable washer in my bedroom closet. With my room presentable, I walked across the hall to Coby's room to quickly make his bed and put away the toys he'd pulled out this morning before daycare.

It wasn't *clean* clean, but it was an improvement and enough to get Mom to relax and just visit for a while.

On my way back to the living room, my eyes drifted out the window that overlooked the parking lot. They drifted to that window a lot these days, looking for any sign of Hunter. As expected, his truck was gone but that didn't keep me from checking anyway. I was becoming addicted to the rush in my heart and the flutter in my stomach any time I caught a glance of the man who had intrigued me so.

It had been a long time since I'd felt this way about a man. Not since Everett. Maybe it was a sign that I was finally ready to move on, to commit to a real relationship, not just date casually when forced by my friends. Maybe it was a sign that I was ready to let go of the fears Everett had instilled.

I just hoped that for my next relationship, I wouldn't pick such a bad apple. That I wouldn't pick someone so full of poison.

---

HUNTER

Pulling back into the motel, I glanced up at Maisy's loft, hoping to see her in the window. Her lights were out, no surprise since it was past eleven, but I checked that window every night regardless of the time.

Most men would steer clear of a woman who had kneed them in the balls. Normally, a man would send that woman as far away from him as she could get. Instead, I had become desperate for any chance to be near her, even if that meant just looking at her home and knowing she was inside.

Which meant I was fucked.

I'd had the perfect excuse to cut my stay at The Bitterroot Inn short. Having the owner assault your manhood was a justifiable excuse to cancel a reservation, but I hadn't been able to bring myself to pack my bags.

Maisy Holt was under my skin.

Hell, I'd almost kissed her today.

I'd been in Prescott for less than a week and she was all I could think about. I'd stare at her loft window each night, wondering what she was doing and praying that she wasn't with another man. Luckily, she didn't seem like the type to bring random men around her son.

Coby Holt didn't know how lucky he was to have Maisy as his mother.

Or Marissa as his grandmother.

Grinning as I walked from my truck to my room, I replayed Marissa's blatant setup. Her insistence had been unnecessary. The second she'd mentioned me taking those pictures, I'd wanted that job so badly it had been nearly impossible to pretend to resist.

I wasn't doing the job for the photographs. I wanted it for the time spent with Maisy.

This was the perfect opportunity to get to know her before I left. The chance for me to do something special, just for her. This would give me time to memorize her smiling face before she learned the truth and never smiled at me again.

# CHAPTER FIVE

MAISY

"Are you sure this is how you want to be spending your Friday off?" I asked Gigi.

She was on the other side of the bed I was making, tucking the white sheet under the mattress's corner.

"I'm sure." She smoothed out the cotton. "We haven't had much time with just the two of us lately."

Between the kids, friends and work, I couldn't remember the last time Gigi and I had done something alone. "True story. But we could plan something special instead, like a lunch date or afternoon pedicures. Do you really want to spend the day helping me clean and do laundry?"

"Yep. I miss working with you, so today, we'll work together."

I smiled and whipped the comforter onto the bed. "I miss working with you too."

Years ago, I'd been a nurse at Jamison Valley Hospital with Gigi. We'd met on her first day of work and instantly hit it off. But after everything that had happened that year, after that horrific night, I'd quit my job and given up my nursing career.

"Can I tell you something?" she asked.

"Yeah. Always."

Gigi stopped straightening the comforter and shook her head. "I had a nightmare about it the other night. About . . . you know."

Yeah, I knew.

"I haven't had a dream like that in years," she continued. "It kind of messed with me. Does that ever happen to you?"

I nodded. "Sometimes."

"Do you want to talk about it?" There was a hesitation in her voice.

Gigi and I hadn't spoken about that time much. Instead of hashing it out together, she'd confided in Jess and I'd seen a therapist for a while. It had been traumatic, for both of us, and instead of dwelling on the bad memories, we'd chosen to make the best of it and move on. We even held a party each year to mark the anniversary of our kidnapping. But after all this time, the pain from that night was still fresh. The bad memories I tried to trap in a bottle kept leaking out.

Maybe it was time to open the lid and empty the bottle dry.

I walked around to the foot of the bed and sank down on the mattress. "I don't have nightmares but I have these weird flashes sometimes. Like déjà vu, but worse. They're more real. I don't know how to describe them without sounding like a crazy person."

Gigi sat by my side. "You're not a crazy person."

I shrugged. "I try not to think about it at all. It's too easy to go back to the dark place, but lately it seems to be popping into my head more. I don't like to talk about it, but maybe we should."

Gigi reached out to hold my hand. "We don't have to."

"No, maybe it will help. But will you go first? Tell me what your dream was about."

She squeezed my hand and took a deep breath. "It was just like reliving it all over again. I was at the farmhouse and Everett showed up and took me. Then I woke up in the hospital basement and he brought you in. From there, everything went in slow motion. The fight. The scalpel. The blood." She shuddered. "I can still hear the rattle of that pill bottle."

"Me too," I whispered as chills traveled down my spine. I hated that sound.

"What are your flashes about?"

"Mostly the same except they don't always stay true to what really happened. Sometimes he gets me to take the pills. Sometimes he stabs me. No matter what, they are as real as if we were still in that basement. I can still smell it. Hear the sounds. Feel the chill in the air. They're so real."

Gigi's hand squeezed mine tighter. "Oh, Maisy, I'm so sorry."

"No, I'm sorry." I shook my head. "He was my boyfriend. I should have noticed the signs and seen how evil he was, then none of that would have happened to us."

"It is not your fault. None of us saw who he really was. He was a master at keeping his true self hidden."

I'd told myself that same thing for years, but I'd always wonder if I could have done more had I not been so blinded by his handsome façade.

The day Everett Carlson had set foot in Prescott was the day my life had changed. He'd been a new doctor at the hospital, gorgeous and charming, and I'd been completely infatuated with him from the beginning. I had looked at him with stars in my eyes and not seen the deceit hidden beneath his perfect smile.

Lies. Everything he'd done, everything he'd pretended to be during our relationship, had all been lies.

In truth, he'd been a drug dealer, smuggling pills from the hospital and then selling them around town. He'd kidnapped Gigi because he'd thought she was onto his operation. He'd kidnapped me because I'd gotten pregnant and refused to have the abortion he had wanted. That night in the hospital basement, he'd planned on killing her and shoving enough pills down my throat to kill my baby.

To kill Coby.

Everett hadn't gotten the chance. Gigi had fought back and created an opening for me to attack. To kill my child's father.

I hadn't stepped foot inside the hospital since that horrible night. There were too many memories there. Too many reminders of how naïve I'd been. Too many reminders that I had taken a life.

Too many reminders that I could have lost my son.

"I'm dreading the day Coby asks about his dad," I whispered. It was my biggest fear. "What do I tell him?"

Gigi shook her head. "I don't know, but whenever that time comes, I know you'll tell him the right thing."

"I hope you're right."

We sat together, holding hands, until a guest talking on his phone passed the room and broke the silence.

"Well, that got all kinds of serious." Gigi laughed. "Change of subject?"

I took a deep breath and nodded. "Yes, please."

"Are you excited for your date tomorrow?"

"Ugh," I groaned, standing to resume making the bed. "I guess."

"Felicity swears this guy is a catch. You never know, it could be fun."

"You're right. I shouldn't be so cynical." Once upon a time, I'd gotten excited for dates. I'd plan a special outfit. I'd put in effort to exfoliate, do my nails, spend extra time on my hair and makeup. But now, I just couldn't find the motivation.

"You're not cynical." She fitted a pillow in its case. "You've just been burned by one really bad relationship and some crappy first dates. You've got good reason to be guarded, but Maisy, not every guy is a drug-dealing killer. You just have to keep an open mind and remember some guys need a second chance. I recall you telling me that once when I wrote Jess off as a jackass."

I smiled. When Jess and Gigi had met, Jess had been a grade-A asshole, but I'd promised Gigi that he wasn't a jerk and encouraged—begged—her to give him a shot. And in time, he'd won her over. "Okay. I'll keep that in mind."

"Do you want to borrow anything to wear? We could finish up here, go grab some lunch, then head out to the farmhouse and you could raid my closet."

"I was actually thinking about just wearing a black blouse and some jeans."

She tossed me a pillow. "Black? It's spring."

"What? Black is a classic no matter the season."

"Fine. Are you at least going to wear heels?"

I scrunched up my nose at the thought of my toes pinched all evening in my black pumps. "How about flats?" I was a tennis-shoe-and-sneaker kind of girl these days, but I had one pair of patent flats that weren't too bad.

Gigi gave me her mom look and I knew there would be no winning an argument about my footwear.

"Okay, I'll wear heels."

"Good," she said smugly.

I smiled and went back to cleaning, glad Gigi was here and we could spend some overdue time together. I'd grown up in Prescott, and I had friends in town that I'd known since childhood. But my relationship with Gigi was special. Not only had we survived something traumatic together, but we connected on a deeper level than I ever had with another girlfriend. If I was struggling, she was always there with a comforting hug. When I'd found out I was pregnant, I'd gone right to her for advice. Besides my mom, she was my best friend and confidant.

And yet for some reason, as the day went on, I didn't once mention Hunter.

Normally, she'd be the first I'd tell about hot motel guests, but something about Hunter was different. I wanted to keep him all to myself right now. So I stayed tight-lipped about him all through the morning, even as we cleaned his room.

But by the time we made it back to the utility room to start the laundry before lunch, I'd decided to at least tell her about getting my photograph project started. "So, I think I've got a photographer to start taking pictures for new art in all the rooms."

"Really?" She handed me a pile of sheets for a washing machine. "That's awesome! Who is it?"

"He's a guest." I started one washer and then moved to the next. "He came into the lobby the other day with his camera and we got to talking. He's pretty inexperienced so we're just going to see how it goes, but I'm taking him around Sunday to show him some places I thought would be good for room photos."

"I hope he turns out better than the last photographer you approached."

I scoffed and dumped some detergent into the machine. "It can't be much worse."

When I'd originally had the idea to do local photos with matching postcards, I'd approached the one and only photographer in town. Unfortunately, she hadn't been interested in my project, preferring her weddings and senior portraits, and on top of that, I had a small budget. So I'd gone out of town and hired a cheap photographer to come to Prescott.

The guy had been my age and good looking with a hippy vibe. Basically, he'd been the anti-Everett. He had also been the first and only man I'd slept with since Everett.

The morning after I'd hooked up with the photographer, he'd left a note backing out of the photography job. Gigi and I had speculated that he hadn't wanted to get involved with a single mom. Maybe he'd thought I'd be clingy or ask for a discount on his photos. Whatever. To this day, I hadn't a clue.

Regardless, he'd left and I had decided to postpone the art replacement. Now I was getting excited about the project again and hoped things with Hunter would turn out better.

"I've been meaning to apologize," Gigi said, pulling me from those memories. "I shouldn't have brought up that new doctor the other night. Not in front of everyone else."

I shrugged and started folding a basket of towels. "It's okay. Sorry I got snappy about it. I'm sure your doctor is nice but I just can't go there."

"I understand." She took a towel too. "I should have known better than to bring it up but Sara was so excited, I couldn't tell her no."

"It's okay. I know everyone is coming from a good place."

"We just want you to be happy."

I set down the folded towel. "I am happy. Even if it's only ever me and Coby, I'm happy."

She gave me a sad smile, like she didn't believe me. "Okay."

We folded quietly for a few moments until Gigi asked, "Where are you thinking about taking the photographer on Sunday?"

Anywhere. I'd take Hunter Faraday anywhere, just for the chance to get to know him.

The butterflies in my stomach fluttered like crazy as I told Gigi about the places I'd brainstormed for Sunday. By the time we took a break for lunch, I could barely contain my excitement.

And it wasn't just for the pictures. I was beaming at the prospect of spending an afternoon with Hunter.

Warren Adams was going to have to bring his A game to our date tomorrow if he wanted to stand any chance at getting a second, because right now, I was all about Hunter Faraday.

---

I GLANCED at my phone for the twentieth time in the last forty-five minutes and still didn't see a message.

Warren Adams was nearly an hour late for our date. No text. No call. No email.

No nothing.

I had been stood up.

And if that didn't bruise a girl's ego, I didn't know what did.

*Oh, well.* It was for the best. Last night, I'd actually considered canceling with Warren because I hadn't thought it fair to date him when I was completely infatuated with another man. But I'd kept the date, feeling that a last-minute cancelation would be rude. Then I'd promised myself I'd give Warren a real chance.

I totally should have canceled.

I'd wasted precious hair and makeup product for nothing.

Grabbing my phone, I was in the middle of sending Felicity a text, telling her that she was never allowed to set me up again, when my waitress stopped by.

"No-show?" she asked.

I looked up and shook my head. "No. I guess I'll take my check for the wine."

"You bet."

Her sympathetic smile made me feel ridiculous. I didn't need a date to eat at a nice restaurant. I didn't need a man sitting across from me to order an expensive steak. Screw that and screw Warren Adams.

"Actually," I called her back before she could go too far, "will you bring me a menu and another glass of the house red?"

"Absolutely." She smiled and gave me an "atta girl" nod. "Be right back."

I grinned and sat a little taller in my high-backed booth. Dinner tonight would be a gift to myself for all the hard work I'd been doing to get ready for this year's tourist season.

Taking a sip of my wine, I relaxed in the thickly padded

maroon bench seat and inspected my table. Each table at The Black Bull was unique, made of the same wood but charred with different cattle brands. Together with the dark paneled walls made from reclaimed barnwood and the chandeliers made of animal antlers, the restaurant struck the perfect balance of rustic and refined.

Table inspection complete, I went back to my phone and finished the text message to Felicity. I'd just hit send when a figure appeared by the end of my booth. I looked up, expecting to see my waitress, but instead it was Hunter.

"Oh." I blinked twice. "Hi!" My greeting came out overly excited and a touch too loud.

"Hey."

Dressed in jeans and a soft gray sweater, his eyes were sparkling in the dim light. His hair was pulled back in his signature man bun, but the strands that were usually loose at his ears had been trapped tight.

It was official. Every time I saw Hunter, he got sexier.

"Are you eating alone?" he asked.

Realizing I'd been staring, I dropped my eyes to the table. When I looked back up, I forced an easy smile so he'd think I ate dinner by myself all the time. I really didn't want Hunter to know that I'd been stood up for a date. "Yep. Just me tonight."

"He showed!" The waitress's timing was lousy.

My smile fell as my cheeks burst into flames.

She set my second glass of wine on the table. "Better late than never."

"Were you meeting someone?" Hunter asked as she hustled away.

I shrugged. "I was, but he didn't show."

He pointed to the booth's open space. "May I?"

"Um, sure." I scrambled to pull my napkin to my side of the table and scoot my wine out of his space. As he slid into the booth, I wiped my sweaty hands on my pants underneath the table, then took a sip from my water.

His feet were inches away from mine. I could smell his cologne from across the table. Was Hunter going to eat with me? Or just keep me company for a bit? *Oh, god.* What if he was just biding his time with me until his own date arrived?

He was probably just sitting here out of pity, waiting for his supermodel date to come and claim him. "Is your date running late?"

He shook his head. "No, I'm here alone."

*Yes!* I fist pumped under the table.

"I was craving a steak," Hunter said. "Would you mind if I joined you tonight since we're both alone?"

*Woo-hoo!* "Not at all." I gave myself a mental pat on the back for not blurting out my immediate response.

Our waitress returned and handed Hunter a menu. "Here you go," she said, glancing at him but then doing a double take. I smiled as she blushed, completely understanding her need to gawk.

Hunter was the type of man women looked at more than once.

After ordering himself a beer, we spent a few moments studying our menus. No matter how many times my eyes focused on the letters, I'd lost the ability to read. I'd never felt this kind of dumbing attraction to a man before, not even with Everett.

"You look beautiful," Hunter said.

My eyes ran up the menu and landed on his. The intensity of his stare was so breathtaking all I could manage in response was a breathy thank-you.

He grinned just as our waitress returned to take our orders and deliver Hunter's beer. I used the brief reprieve to cross my legs and shift in the bench, hoping to quench some of the throbbing between my thighs.

"Where's Coby tonight?" Hunter asked after taking a swig from his beer.

"He's with my brother Beau and his fiancée, Sabrina. They're having a campout."

"Isn't it a little cold? There was frost on the ground this morning."

I smiled. "Their campouts are in Beau's basement. He's got a special tent for Coby and everything."

"Sounds like fun."

"Yeah, they'll have a good time. Beau and Sabrina are getting married next month and Beau is really close with Coby. Sabrina loves the campouts because they give her a chance to bond with Coby as an aunt."

"And then you get a date night."

I huffed and took another sip of my wine. "I am done with date nights."

"Why is that?"

"I just haven't had a lot of good dates lately."

He nodded. "I know how that goes."

"You do?" Hunter was gorgeous and could have any single woman he desired as a dinner companion. There should be no such thing as a bad date in his world. "Have you had a lot of bad dates lately?"

"Kind of."

*Kind of.* I grimaced at the words. The one response I hated above all others was "kind of."

It hadn't used to be that way, but Everett had said "kind of" more times than I could count and he'd ruined me on the phrase. It wasn't a yes. It wasn't a no. It was the perfect answer to dodge any question.

Kind of. *Blech.*

I swallowed the bitter taste in my mouth with more wine. Hunter didn't know my aversion to that phrase and I certainly wasn't going to explain tonight, just like I didn't expect him to explain his dating history. If he didn't want to talk about past relationships, I wouldn't pry. For all I knew, he could have just had a breakup or gotten a divorce.

Since that topic was a nonstarter, I decided to pick another. This dinner was the perfect opportunity to get to know Hunter before we set off to take pictures on Sunday. "So you said the other day you're from Chicago?"

He nodded. "Born and raised."

"Why'd you choose Prescott? It's about as different from Chicago as you could get. Did you not like the city?"

"No. I like Chicago. Moving to Prescott was . . . necessary."

Necessary? What did that mean? I waited a few moments for him to elaborate but he didn't. The silence at the table turned awkward so I went for a different topic.

"Have you been here before or did you move here blind?"

"I was here once."

Again, I waited. And waited. And waited some more.

What was happening? Was Hunter shy? He sure hadn't seemed like that during our other encounters. Why was he clamming up now?

When I didn't get any further explanation, I decided to try another subject, one that was safe and sure to spark a natural conversation. "When did you take up photography?"

"A while back."

*A while back.* Another vague answer that I hated just about as much as "kind of." Ignoring the tension creeping up my spine, I kept talking, hoping he'd open up. "I've always wanted to have a cool hobby like photography. I love taking pictures but there isn't really anywhere to learn around here. Did you learn from someone or are you self-taught?"

"I had a mentor." Hunter smiled but it was distant, not full of the warmth it usually held. When his eyes broke away from mine, I sagged.

*I give up.*

Hunter was shutting me out. I knew that body language. That tone in his voice. It was entirely too familiar. Familiar and unwelcome.

Hunter Faraday was sending me Everett Carlson vibes and I really didn't like the reminder.

When I'd first started dating Everett, we'd gotten along perfectly. Our conversations had always been light and impersonal, mostly centered around the hospital and our coworkers, but as time went on, I'd started asking the normal questions a girlfriend would ask. When is your birthday? Where are you from? Do you have family?

He'd never answered me. Never. Not even to tell me his middle name.

Everett had only wanted me to be the pretty face that warmed his bed. Nothing else. He'd shut me out whenever I'd tried to get close.

As much as I liked Hunter, I didn't need to go through all that again.

So I gave up my questions and sat quietly, alternating sips of water and wine while Hunter studied the brands on the table. He opened his mouth once only to shut it again before speaking.

*Dates suck.* Of all the awkward dinners I'd had lately, this was by far the worst. I so badly wanted to know Hunter, to see if there was more between us than just a physical attraction. But it didn't look like I was going to get the chance.

He just kept staring at the table, unspeaking.

I wasn't shy. He could at least ask questions about me.

Thankfully, our meals arrived a few minutes later and I dove into my steak, chewing each juicy bite longer than I normally would just to keep my mouth occupied. Though the food was delicious, the knot in my stomach kept me from enjoying the meal.

By the time I'd finished my dinner, I'd decided to go for it again, to give Hunter one last chance to share just a little about himself. "Is your family going to come out and visit once you get moved into your new house?"

He looked up from his steak and met my eyes. "No."

A one-word answer.

I waited with my fingers crossed, hoping he'd keep talking, but he took his last bite and stayed quiet.

Well, I guess that was that.

As much as I wanted to spend time with Hunter, I wouldn't be ignored. I wouldn't be kept at arm's length. Not ever again.

My eyes searched the restaurant for our waitress. When she glanced my way, I held up a hand and signaled for the check. "Well, I'd better be going. I've got some work to do tonight. Thanks for joining me so I didn't have to sit alone." I didn't wait for the check before diving into my purse for my wallet, yanking out five twenty-dollar bills.

"You don't have to rush off. Did you want to stay for another drink or dessert?"

"No." *See that, Hunter? I can give one-word answers too.*

He nodded. "All right, but I've got dinner."

"This wasn't a date so I'll pay for my own. Thanks though." I tossed my money on the table and slid out of the booth, but before I could make my escape, his hand gently wrapped around my elbow.

I gasped at the electricity zapping up my arm and my feet stopped. I turned and stared down at Hunter as my eyes followed his every move.

He grabbed my money, slid out of the booth and stood right in my space. My chin tipped back so I could keep his eyes. How had I never noticed just how tall he was? When his hand fell away from my elbow, I immediately wanted it back. How was it possible to be annoyed with a man but still want to wrap my arms around him at the same time?

"Maisy." His voice was back to the warm, rich timbre I'd been hearing in my good dreams this past week. "I'm buying dinner."

I swallowed hard. "Okay."

"Thank you for letting me eat with you. I'm sorry for not being very talkative tonight. I guess it was just a long day."

How would I know if he'd had a long day? He hadn't told me anything. In the hour that we'd been sitting together, I knew no more about him than I had two days ago.

"Sure, I understand. It's fine." It wasn't, but I didn't tell him the truth. I wanted some space, some time to mourn another bad date. Some time to come to grips with the fact that this chemistry between us was all we'd ever share. "I'm just going to head out. Good night, Hunter."

"Wait." He touched my elbow, and again, my body's response overruled my brain's decision. "I'll meet you in the lobby tomorrow at one o'clock."

*Shit.* The pictures. "Don't worry about it. You're off the hook. I appreciate you appeasing my mom the other day but you don't need to—"

"Tomorrow. One o'clock. I'd really like the opportunity to do this project."

I was tempted to argue, to tell him I wanted a photographer with more experience, but the hopefulness in his eyes melted my resolve. "Okay. Tomorrow."

Our waitress came over with the bill and I used her arrival as my chance to leave, not wasting any time rushing out the doors and getting in my 4Runner. *What a bummer.* By the time I got home, I was ready for my dessert. I sat on my couch with a pint of Häagen-Dazs and told myself I was glad.

I was glad I hadn't told Gigi about Hunter. I was glad I didn't have to call her and explain that he and I hadn't hit it off after all. I was glad I'd learned all this before my heart could get attached.

I was glad things between us would be simple.

I'd let Hunter take pictures for the motel. I'd let him rent out room eight for a couple more weeks. Then I'd say goodbye to Hunter Faraday and hope my feelings for him disappeared as soon as he checked out of my inn.

# CHAPTER SIX

HUNTER

Ten feet from the motel's lobby door, my phone rang. Digging it out of my pocket, I cursed at the name on the screen. *Nell.*

If I didn't answer, she'd keep calling all afternoon and I didn't want her distracting me from my time with Maisy. I hit accept and pressed the phone to my ear. "Yes?"

"I was just calling to check on you. See if you're doing okay. You sounded so down last night."

"I'm fine. I told you the same last night."

"Oh, Hunter. I miss you so much."

What a damn liar. Her gentle and sweet voice was as fake as her nose. "Is there a reason for your call? I've got somewhere to be."

"Are you sure you don't want to come back to Chicago?"

"I'm sure." Something else I'd told her last night. "My house will be done soon. Work is going great. I think Prescott is the right place for me to settle down and plant some roots."

I knew that last part would get her all riled up, but I didn't care. She'd been calling nonstop from the moment I'd left Chicago and my patience had worn thin.

"You can't mean that."

"I do. I'll stay here for as long as it takes for you to drop this ridiculous idea."

"It's not ridiculous," she spat.

Now the real Nell was coming out. Her teeth were bared and her sharp claws out. I bet that as soon as I hung up, she'd have an epic tantrum. I felt bad for the housekeeper on days like today because Nell would rant and rave, taking her anger at me out on anyone in the vicinity.

"I'm going to hang up now. Enjoy your Sunday."

"Hunter, don't you dare hang up on—"

I ended the call and not two seconds later it rang again.

"Enough," I answered. "Stop calling me. I've told you how I feel and I won't change my mind. Back off before I'm forced to do something drastic."

"Are you threatening me?"

"Yes. Stop this, Nell. Last warning."

"Don't you threaten me, Hunter. Remember who you're talking to, *dear*," she hissed.

I remembered. My loyalty to Nell was weak, but I remembered why I took her shit. We had too much history to overlook, and as much as I'd like to say good-bye forever, I couldn't find the guts to just cut her out of my life.

But that didn't mean I'd stand idly by and let her do something so wrong.

"Back off." My heart was racing but I managed to keep my voice low. "Back off now or everything I've been keeping quiet for years will come out so fast you'll get whiplash."

"You won't," she dared.

"I will. I'm done pandering to you. Don't push me on this and don't call me again. Not unless it's to tell me you've fired your slime-bag attorney. Good-bye."

I ended the call and waited, expecting it to ring again, but it stayed silent. I tucked it away in my jeans and took a couple of deep breaths, settling my heartbeat before continuing down to the lobby.

I'd either made a mistake by threatening Nell and she'd go off the deep end, or I'd done something I should have done years ago. Only time would tell. But I couldn't worry about Nell right now. Today, I had to fix a different mistake.

I had to reverse the damage I'd done last night at dinner with Maisy.

How had she managed to only ask me questions I really couldn't answer? My past wasn't something I could talk about yet. Certainly not my family. I'd felt her pull away after a couple of my brush-off answers and from there, dinner had gone downhill fast.

Which meant today I needed to do some explaining.

Somehow, I had to figure out how to open up without revealing too much.

---

MAISY

"Hey," Hunter said, pushing open the lobby door.

He'd trimmed his beard since last night. The image of his shortened whiskers rubbing against my jaw popped into my mind and I shook my head, trying to get it out. That was not the road I wanted to go down today. I was still disappointed in how things had gone at dinner but I was resigned to acting professionally during our outing today. This was official business for the motel, after all. Thinking about his beard on my skin was a no-no.

"Hey back. Ready to go?" I grabbed my purse from the counter and slung it over a shoulder. Mom was upstairs with Coby and I wanted to leave before she came down and harassed us about our plans for the afternoon. I wouldn't put it past her to force some sort of dinner date and I didn't want to drag this out.

"Ready," Hunter said. "Have you had lunch?"

I shook my head. "Just a snack when Coby ate around noon. I thought maybe we could get something to-go from downtown."

"Sounds great."

I nodded for him to go out first so I could hang up my sign and lock up the lobby door. He stood close, and when the breeze picked up, his cologne filled my nose. Mindlessly, I took in an extra-long breath, then huffed it out when I realized what I'd done.

Enjoying his smell was another no-no.

"All set." I stepped away from the secured door and followed him to his white truck. He went to my door first, opening it for me to hop inside, then closing it when I was set. While he walked around the hood of the truck, I glanced around his truck.

The front seat was clean, the leather new and recently conditioned, but the back was a mess. There were empty jerky bags on the bench seat and the floor was scattered with protein bar wrappers. In between all of that were a few crumpled white takeout bags from the café.

"Sorry for the mess," Hunter said as he slid behind the wheel.

"No problem."

"I'm not great at cooking for myself so I've just been grabbing food from the café or sandwiches from the gas station. I eat in here a lot and haven't gotten around to taking out the trash."

None of this surprised me. I was due to clean his room tomorrow but I already knew what I'd find: empty kitchenette cupboards, unused dishes and a refrigerator with various bottles of Vitaminwater.

I bet Hunter regretted sliding into my booth last night at The Black Bull. He'd come looking for a nice meal, an escape from takeout and gas-station food, and instead we'd had an awkward non-date.

I slumped in my seat. Had I gone too far with all of my questions? I probably shouldn't have gotten so annoyed that he hadn't spilled his entire life story. I'd let a few vague similarities between him and Everett's demeanor ruin the night.

Before Hunter put the truck in drive, he looked at me. "I need to apologize for dinner. I'm not used to sharing much about myself, and I didn't mean for things to get uncomfortable."

I could respect that. There were things I didn't like to share either. So swallowing my pride, I sighed. "No, dinner was my fault. I was being intrusive. Forgive me for being nosy?"

"There's nothing to forgive." He smiled, looking as relieved as I felt. "Ask all the questions you want, just know I might not answer. It's not easy for me to open up and I'll apologize in advance because it's probably going to happen again. Can you live with that?"

"Sure." I didn't really like it, but I could live with it. At least Hunter was honest—something Everett had never been.

And like Gigi had said, not every guy was a drug-dealing killer. I just needed to give Hunter some time to open up. "Any chance we can forget about dinner and just enjoy the day?" Starting over with Hunter seemed like the best idea I'd had in years.

"I'd really like that." He smiled at me again and my heart melted to goo. "What do you feel like for lunch, Blondie? The café or the deli?"

"Uh, Blondie?"

He grinned. "That cannot be the first time someone has called you Blondie."

"No, not by a long shot." I giggled. "And I'd prefer the café if you don't mind."

"I don't mind."

For the rest of our short drive downtown, my smile was firmly fixed in place. How was it that a pet name could make me feel so special? Blondie wasn't particularly unique or creative, but it *really* worked for me in Hunter's sexy voice.

By the time we parked and walked into the café, all of the distress I'd felt earlier had vanished. The rock that had taken up residence in my stomach last night turned to dust and my crush on Hunter came raging back to life.

"So what's your master plan for today?" Hunter asked as we sat at a couple of empty stools by the counter in the café, watching our sandwiches being made in the kitchen.

"I thought we could start here on Main Street. I'd like to do a mixture of iconic places in town and landscape pictures from around the county. We could start down here today since it's relatively quiet. I was thinking the movie theater for sure. Maybe the café too?"

He nodded. "Good idea. An inside or an outside shot?"

"Either one is fine. I'd also really love to get a shot that looks down Main Street. Maybe something from an elevated point of view if you could manage it?" It was the photo I wanted maybe the most, but I knew it wasn't going to be easy short of renting an airplane.

He thought about it for a moment. "I wonder if one of the gas stations would let me up on their roof."

"Would that be high enough?"

"I think so."

"Sweet! I will call the owners tonight and see if either one would allow it. I'm sure the Gas 'N' Go will let you. The owner's son went to school with me and put gum in my hair once. That family owes me."

He grinned down at me before he started chuckling. "Do you know everyone in this town?"

"Pretty much everyone." Everyone except him. Hunter was the most mysterious person to move to Prescott in years.

He chuckled. "I'll have to keep that in mind. Where else are we taking pictures?"

"I'd like to do one of the community fishing pond. It's where my grandpa and dad taught me and my brothers to fish. I was thinking maybe we could do something with Coby there. I'd like it to be a candid, maybe just his silhouette from behind or something?"

"Wait. You fish?"

"I fish. Worms and all," I declared proudly. I had my girly girl moments but I embraced my inner tomboy too. "Why do you look so surprised?"

He just smiled wider. "I've never met a woman that looks like you but admits she'd willfully touch a worm."

"Is that a compliment?"

His eyes softened. "A big one."

With the slightest touch, he plucked a stray hair off my

shoulder. Tingles ran down my arm, leaving goose bumps in their wake. How could such large hands be so delicate at the same time? I wanted to know what they could do to my skin in softer places.

*God, I am crushing hard on this guy.* Harder than ever before.

And judging by the heated look in his eyes, he was crushing on me too.

"Here you go." Our waitress plopped a white sack on the counter, breaking our moment. "That will be eighteen fifty."

I peeled my eyes away from Hunter's and dove into my purse for my wallet.

"I've got it." Before I could fish out my wallet, Hunter had left a hundred-dollar bill on the bar and tucked the bag under his arm.

"I can pay for these. Really. I should. This is a business expense—"

"Maisy." He cut me off. "I'll always pay for meals. It's just one of those things I was raised to do."

Dad had taught my brothers the same thing. Mom had taught me to let them. "Okay. Thank you."

I'd pay Hunter back with a home-cooked meal every day for the next two weeks. Hunter's room would be fully stocked with Tupperware by the time he checked out of my motel.

Waving good-bye to the small late-lunch crowd in the café, I followed Hunter outside to the sidewalk where he handed me my turkey sub, then dug out his ham. Each of us unwrapped and rewrapped the deli paper around our sandwiches so we could walk and eat at the same time.

"All right, so we've got the theater, the café, the Main

Street shot and the fishing pond," he said after chewing. "What else?"

I swallowed my bite and rattled off the rest of my wish list. "I'd like one of the Jamison River but I'm not picky on the spot. I'd like to do one of the inn but not until I get flowers planted. Oh, and there's an old homestead barn on my friend's ranch that is really cool. I thought we could go check it out. And then I was hoping to do one up at Wade Lake."

"That's only eight. You've got, what, fourteen rooms total?"

"Yeah, but I can just double up." It was a lot to ask that I get fourteen unique photographs at fourteen locations, and since he was doing this in his free time, I didn't want to impose. I'd just make do with eight.

"No." Hunter stopped on the sidewalk. "You're not doubling up. You need to think of another six spots."

"Since we never discussed price for your time, let's just go with eight. I don't want you to feel obl—"

With his free hand, Hunter touched my arm. "Six more spots, Maisy. We'll hit those up next weekend." His voice was gentle but firm. "However long this takes, it doesn't matter. I'll give you all the time in the world until you get this exactly the way you want."

"Are you sure?"

He nodded. "I'm sure. I want to do this. Please let me?"

"Thank you. Thank you *so* much." How had I gotten this lucky? How was it that this man, a photographer, had walked into my motel? I'd be thanking my fairy godmother for years to come if this all worked out right.

We ate a few more bites of our sandwiches as we strolled downtown. With Hunter's food demolished, he tossed the wrapper in a trash bin and wiped his hands free of crumbs. "I think I'm set down here unless you had something specific to show me."

"Nope," I shook my head, "nothing specific here."

"Okay, then how about you take me up to Wade Lake and show me around?"

"Sounds good."

We turned around and walked back to his truck, me eating quickly and disposing of my own trash. As we pulled onto the highway and out of town, I decided to brave asking Hunter a question. I didn't want to pry into his personal life but I did want to get to know him more. Ever since we'd left the motel, our conversation had been so genuine and natural.

I didn't want it to stop.

Crossing my fingers on my lap, I took a deep breath. "Is talking about your new house a safe topic? Or should I stick to the weather?"

He chuckled. "The house is safe."

I smiled at my small victory. "How's it coming along?"

"It's going to be great, but I went by this morning and there's still a lot to do. I called my contractor and he said they're behind."

"Yikes. How long?"

"He thinks two weeks, which probably means four. I don't suppose you've got an open room for another month."

"Sorry. Two more weeks and I'm in full-blown tourist season. The only empty space I have is an old housekeeper's room, and it's more like a closet than an actual living space." There wasn't even a window. It had come as no surprise when the previous owners had told me that no housekeeper had ever chosen to live in that room.

"I'll take it."

My head whipped around. "What?"

"The housekeeper's room. I'll take it."

"Oh, Hunter, no. I was kidding. That room is awful."

"Hey, I'm desperate here. I don't want to rent out a house and I can't stay in mine until it's finished. How bad can it be? It's only for a month."

"How bad can it be?" I repeated. "I've only ever used it for storage. It's smaller than my college dorm room. And the finishes are . . . gross." Hunter exuded class and stature. He would clash in every possible way with the seventies floral linoleum, carrot-orange bathroom counter and twin-size bed.

"I don't care. Does it at least have a bathroom?"

"Yes, but there's no kitchen."

He laughed. "Considering that I don't know how to use nine out of ten kitchen appliances, I think I'll be fine."

"Nine out of ten? Really?"

"Really."

I opened my mouth to explore that further but didn't let myself go down that bunny trail. "Anyway. I'll tell you what. Tomorrow, I'll go clean up that room a bit and you can check it out. If you still want to stay, you're more than welcome. But if you don't, I get to say 'I told you so.' "

He looked over at me and grinned. "You've got a deal, Blondie."

"I can't wait to say 'I told you so.' " I caught a look at my unbridled smile in the side-view mirror.

How crazy was this? I had expected today to be awkward after our dinner last night, but this was, hands down, the best possible outcome for today. And the afternoon wasn't even over yet.

"So how'd you come to own the motel?" Hunter asked as he drove. "Was a career in hospitality always the plan?"

"Actually, I went to college for nursing. I did the four-year program, came home and started working at the hospital, but it wasn't for me." That was a bit of an understatement, but I kept going. "The previous owners of the motel were looking for a manager so I said, 'What the heck?' and gave it a shot. We got along really well, and when they decided to retire, they made me an offer to buy it from them."

"How long ago was that?"

"Three years in June. The previous owners are now traveling the country in their RV, sending me postcards along the way, and I've spent those three years updating the inn."

"Oh, yeah? What kind of updates?"

I smiled and shifted in my seat so I could face him better, then I launched into stories about remodeling projects, spending the rest of our drive to Wade Lake talking about the Bitterroot.

The gravel road got bumpier the closer we got to the lake, and the trees that bordered the road were so thick you couldn't see more than fifty feet into the forest. But as we coasted over one last rise, the trees opened and the lake appeared.

Hunter parked the truck in the wide gravel lot that met the lake's shore. "I can see why you'd pick this place."

"It's hard to beat." I kept my eyes locked on the scenery as I pushed open my door and stepped outside.

The water's surface was covered with small ripples today. The breeze swished in the trees that sloped down steep hills to meet the water's edge. With the sun shining brightly, the wavelets' tips glittered as they rolled.

Picking up a flat rock, I flicked it toward the water,

counting three skips before it sank. Hunter did the same, his rock going twice as far as mine.

"What kind of a photograph are you looking for up here?" he asked.

"How about a sunset? Or a sunrise?" I stepped over to a thick piece of driftwood and sat down.

"Sure." He nodded and followed, taking a seat next to me as we both looked out over the water.

We sat quietly for a while, enjoying the view and the cool, clean air. It was just us today, the weather still too cold for much lake activity, but soon that would change. People would flock to the lake to enjoy camping vacations as my free time evaporated with the summer sun.

"Did you ever find out what happened to that guy you were supposed to meet last night?"

"Yeah." I frowned. "I guess he showed but took one look at me and left. Apparently, I reminded him too much of his ex-wife."

"Ouch."

"That's not even the worst of the dates I've had lately." I smiled and told him my worst blind-date tales from the last few years. "How about you? Have you had any booger-eating first dates lately?"

He shook his head. "No. My ex-girlfriends were better about hiding their crazy. My most recent ex didn't let hers show until we'd been dating for six months. She started stealing money from my wallet and telling people we were engaged. After I broke it off with her, she snuck into my house at night and crawled into my bed. I had to change my locks and get a restraining order."

"Yikes."

He shrugged. "It's over now. Anyway, sorry about the guy who ditched you. He's an asshole."

I sighed. "I've been on an asshole streak lately." A five-year streak, to be exact.

"I hope I'm not included in that streak."

"Well . . ." I leaned over and playfully bumped him with my shoulder. "Since last night wasn't a date, I guess you don't count."

He chuckled. "This is true. Maybe one of these nights you'll let me take you on an actual date and I can try and break that asshole streak."

My smile fell. *Did he just ask me out?*

*Hell yes, he did!*

I swallowed the urge to jump for joy—and by some miracle from above—managed to play it cool. "I'd, um, really like that."

"Me too."

Smiling again, I turned back to the lake, still unable to believe how incredible this day had turned out. Last night was all but forgotten, Hunter was nearly as excited about my art project as I was, and he'd asked me out on a date.

"Thanks for bringing me up here today," he said.

"You're welcome."

"I wish my dad was still here. He'd love to see a place like this."

His statement caught me so off guard I didn't know what to say, so I just stared up at his profile, hoping and waiting for him to keep opening up.

"Dad loved to fish," he said. "Living in the city, he didn't get to go much, but whenever he had the chance, he'd bring me to lakes like this one. Something quiet and secluded. We spent a lot of time fishing in Michigan but this would have been right up his alley too. He passed almost six years ago but sometimes it feels like just yesterday."

"I'm sorry." I hadn't lost a parent but could imagine that it was extremely painful, especially if Hunter and his father had been close. "If you don't mind me asking, how did he pass?"

"Cancer. He had pancreatic cancer. By the time he told me, it had progressed to stage four and he'd only had a few weeks left."

"I'm sorry."

Hunter looked down at me with a sad smile. "It's okay. He was actually the one that got me hooked on photography. He always brought a camera with him whenever we went fishing."

Now it made sense why he hadn't wanted to talk about his photography mentor last night. And rather than respecting his boundaries, I'd gotten frustrated when he hadn't wanted to share something painful. Guilt—a feeling I hated second only to fear—settled in my gut as words started pouring out of my mouth.

"I'm so, *so* sorry. I shouldn't have brought up your family last night. No wonder you didn't want to talk about them. How inconsiderate!" My hand slapped against my forehead. "I'm so sorry, Hunter."

I was the worst date. Ever.

Even worse than the nose-picker.

"Hey." Hunter chuckled and lifted my hand off my forehead. "You didn't know."

"Still. I'm sorry." Mentally comparing Hunter to Everett was exceptionally unfair. "And I'm sorry about your dad."

"Thanks. We were close, me and dad. My mom died in a

car crash when I was seven, and we only had each other for a few years until he remarried."

Two parents. Hunter had lost two parents.

"I keep saying it, but I don't know what else to say. I'm so sorry."

"No need to be sorry. It's just that seeing places like this makes me think of him. And I guess . . . I just wanted you to know."

"I'm always glad to listen." Anytime he wanted to talk, I'd make sure I was there to lend an ear.

Staring out at the water, we resumed our silent appreciation of the scenery. Then and there, I made a decision. I wasn't going to push for information or interrogate Hunter with personal questions. Gigi had given Jess time to come around from his jackass ways and now they were one of the happiest couples I knew. Maybe all Hunter needed was time too. I would fight my natural instinct to pry, and I would respect his privacy. I'd give him some trust that he'd tell me about himself on his own timetable.

*And stop being such a total flipping hypocrite.*

My closet was full of skeletons, skeletons I had no intention of letting out this early in a potential relationship. I couldn't expect him to reveal his secrets when I was keeping my own.

It was time for me to chill out and just let things develop.

We sat quietly until a cluster of clouds blew in and took away the water's sparkle. I was just about to suggest we head back to town when Hunter surprised me with a random question.

"How old are you?"

"I turned twenty-nine in March. Why?"

He shrugged. "Just curious. I'm thirty-four. My birthday was yesterday."

My mouth fell open and then snapped shut with a click. With a full arm swing, I back-handed him in the chest. "What the ever-loving hell, Hunter Faraday?"

"What?" He shied away, clutching his chest to keep me from hitting him again.

His guard didn't work. I wound up again, this time smacking his rock-hard bicep. "Your birthday was yesterday? And I'm just now learning this?"

"You had my driver's license."

I smacked him again. "I don't study those. Do you know how many driver's licenses I have copied? Hundreds. Now don't make excuses. Why didn't you tell me it was your birthday at dinner?"

He shrugged. "I don't know."

"Well," I huffed. "You're in trouble. As soon as we get back to the motel, I'm going to tell Mom it was your birthday yesterday. That's your punishment for not telling me last night."

"How is that a punishment?"

My grin was evil. "You'll see. Come on." I stood up from the log and held out a hand to help him up. When he slipped his large grip over mine, consuming my slender fingers, an electric current shot up my elbow.

Hunter felt it too, because he stuttered a bit as he stood. "Um, uh, where to now?"

I slipped my hand out of his so I could form coherent sentences. "Back to the motel. How would you feel about a redo birthday dinner?"

"You want to brave another night at The Black Bull?"

I shook my head. "How about a home-cooked meal instead?"

He smiled. "Sounds even better. Got any peas?" With a quick wink, he started back toward the truck.

*Heavens above.* That wink had just ruined me for all other men.

## CHAPTER SEVEN

MAISY

"I'm back!" I called into the loft.

Hunter closed the door behind us as he followed me inside.

Little footsteps pounded as Coby came racing down the hallway with Pickle hot on his heels. "Mommy!"

"Hey, buddy!" I bent to give him a hug. "How was your afternoon with Nana?"

"Good! We played with Play-Doh."

My eyes snapped to the dining room table to see evidence of the cursed dough. *Super.* Tiny specs of blue, green and yellow were scattered across the table, the chairs and the surrounding floor space. I loved my son so I indulged his affection for Play-Doh, but it was my worst enemy. No matter how much I cleaned, I always missed a piece. Inevitably, I'd find it days later after stepping on the dry, pointy shard with bare feet.

"Darn." Mom came walking down the hall with a towel

in her hand. "I was hoping to have this all cleaned up by—" Her steps faltered when she noticed Hunter. I held back a laugh as she blushed. Like mother, like daughter. "Hunter!" She regained her composure and smoothed out her shirt as she walked to the table. "How are you? Did you enjoy your afternoon exploring?"

"Nice to see you again, Mrs. Holt. And yes, we had a great time. Your daughter is an excellent tour guide."

"Mrs. Holt, pish." Mom giggled as she cleaned. "Call me Marissa."

"Marissa." He looked down at Coby and smiled. "Hey, Coby."

Coby stared at Hunter for a long moment with discerning eyes.

"Coby, do you remember Hunter?" I asked.

He nodded but didn't break his study of our guest. Finally, he blinked and cocked his head to the side. "You have long hair. Isn't long hair just for girls?"

"Buddy."

I fought a laugh at the same time Mom gasped, "Coby Lawrence Holt!"

Hunter chuckled and knelt down to Coby's level. "It is kind of long, isn't it? Do you think I should cut it?"

*No!* This time it was my turn to gasp.

Thankfully, Coby just shrugged. "No, it's okay."

I was sure Hunter wouldn't style his hair according to my three-year-old's opinion, but the thought of him cutting those light-brown locks was unnerving. Hunter's man bun was a thing of beauty but I really wanted the chance to see his hair down one day. I never thought I'd be attracted to a man whose hair was longer than mine, but boy was I ever.

Pickle yapped and caught Coby's attention and the pair ran over to the living room to pull out more toys.

"What are you two up to now?" Mom asked.

"Dinner. Guess what I learned today?" I shot Hunter a smug look as he stood back up. "Yesterday was Hunter's birthday."

"Oh!" Mom straightened and abandoned her cleaning. "And you're new in town. Wouldn't it be wonderful to have a barbeque to celebrate your belated birthday and welcome you to the community?"

"Oh, that's not necessary," Hunter said. "I don't want you to go to any trouble."

"Trouble? It would be my pleasure! I'll invite my quilting club, of course, and probably Brock's skeet club. A few folks from church. Hunter, are you religious?" She didn't wait for his answer before rattling off more potential invitees.

"Really. I'm not one for big parties." Hunter's protest fell on deaf ears. Mom was now audibly brainstorming the menu.

I looked back to Hunter who was staring wide-eyed at Mom as she yammered. I nudged his arm and leaned in to whisper, "Don't worry. It will take her months to plan it. By that point, the whole town will have been invited and the party won't even be about you anymore."

"You weren't kidding about this as a punishment."

"Remember that." I tapped my temple. "This isn't even the worst I can do."

"So noted."

"Make yourself at home and I'll get started on dinner." I wanted to pat his arm, to touch him in just some small way, but I resisted.

Walking to the kitchen, I dropped my purse on the

counter, then took a quick inventory of my food supply. Peas —lots of peas—and the fixings for chicken bacon ranch wraps with sweet potato fries. It wasn't fancy but it was something Coby would inhale without constant reminders to take a bite.

I pulled out supplies and got the bacon going in a frying pan. Back in the living room, Hunter had settled on the floor with Coby as Pickle bounced on them both. Coby had brought out his Hot Wheels collection and was going through each car, showing them to Hunter one by one.

"So? How'd it go?" Mom whispered, joining me in the kitchen.

"Good." I smiled. "He asked me out."

Her face broke into a huge smile and she shot her hands in the air. I laughed as she danced around the kitchen, her hair bobbing around her shoulders. When she settled down, she came right into my space for a hug. "I'm so happy for you. He's a dreamboat."

"A dreamboat?" I mocked. "Please don't start calling him that, especially to his face."

"I can't make promises like that, sweetheart."

I laughed. "Try. Please."

She rolled her blue eyes and made a sour face. I giggled, knowing that was exactly how I looked when I did the same gesture. I was a younger version of my mom, our only difference being eye color. Hers were bluer than the gray-blue irises I'd inherited from Dad.

"I'll get out of here so you can have some time alone." She picked up her keys and phone from the kitchen counter. "Call me tomorrow and let me know how dinner went."

"Definitely."

She looked past me into the living room. "He seems to be great with Coby."

I looked past her and saw what she meant. Hunter was now rolling cars along the floor next to Coby. Both were smiling and making pretend engine noises.

*Phew*. My heart swelled at the same time a nervous wave rolled in my stomach.

This was the first time I'd ever brought a potential love interest home to meet Coby and I'd done it without much thought. Should I have waited to get to know Hunter more before bringing him home? What if behind that handsome and sweet exterior was an evil soul? What if—

I stopped my mental flip-out. Coby and Hunter playing in my living room wasn't something I needed to overcomplicate. As far as my son needed to know, Hunter was just another male presence, like his uncles. In time, if things became more serious, I could introduce Hunter to Coby as something more.

"I hope he's as good as he seems," Mom whispered so quietly that I doubted she'd meant to say it out loud.

"Me too," I whispered back.

Mom gave me another hug, then went into the living room to say good-bye to Coby and Hunter. Waving, she let herself out and I finished making dinner.

"Okay. We're ready!" I called after setting the table.

"Let's go wash your hands." Hunter stood from the floor and held out a hand for Coby. "Can you show me to the bathroom?"

A smiling Coby tugged Hunter down the hall. "It's this way!"

The sight of them disappearing into the bathroom, hand-in-hand, conjured a familiar rush of worry. Coby was missing out, not having a father. My son deserved to have a playmate every day, not just when my brothers or dad were over for a visit. He deserved to have a good man tuck him into bed every night. To have a dad he could brag about.

I had that with my dad. I wanted that for my son.

"This looks great," Hunter said as he and Coby came back from the bathroom and took their seats.

"Thanks. Okay, guys, dig in."

"Hunter—" Coby started but his mouth was full of fries so I cut him off.

"Chew first, bud. Don't talk with your mouth full."

He scrunched up his nose and chewed as fast as his jaw would work. With one big swallow and a swig of chocolate milk, he looked back at Hunter. "Hunter, do you know what sticky boots are?"

"No. What are they?"

"They're special boots to climb walls. Mickey Mouse has 'em."

Hunter shook his head. "They sound pretty awesome. Do you have some?"

Coby gave him an exaggerated pout. "No. Mommy says they're dangerous."

Hunter grinned at me, then looked back at Coby. "She's probably right about that. Moms are always worried about dangerous stuff, aren't they?"

"Yeah." Coby shoved another fry in his mouth and kept on talking. "Have you driven in a monster truck before?"

"No. Have you?"

Coby shook his head. "No. Do you think ants cough?"

"Hmm." Hunter swallowed his bite. "I don't know that much about ants. What do you think?"

"I think they cough."

"You're probably right."

Coby's questions continued on from there. We learned that Hunter thought Coby's dream job of super spy was spot on, that he agreed the T. rex was the coolest dinosaur and that he'd never seen Coby's favorite movie, *Cars*.

I stayed happily quiet throughout dinner, enjoying the questions Coby would ask and the answers Hunter gave.

"I see he's inherited your curiosity," Hunter teased when we were done eating.

I smiled. "That he has."

Hunter stood from the table and picked up his plate. "Coby, do you want to help me do the dishes?"

"Okay!" Coby nodded and scrambled off his chair, taking his plastic green plate carefully to the kitchen.

I stood and picked up my plate too. "You don't need to worry about these. I can do the dishes."

Hunter shook his head, taking the plate from my hand and nodding toward the living room. "Take a break. We've got this."

I retreated to the living room, sinking onto my gray couch and turning sideways so I could spy on the kitchen activities. While Hunter rinsed, Coby stood over the dishwasher and pointed to the spot for Hunter to deposit the dish.

All I could do was smile.

Coby was enamored with Hunter. His smile and bright eyes were full of joy only a child's face could show. I loved seeing my son so happy, but on top of that, I really liked the look on Hunter's face too. He seemed just as fascinated with Coby as my son was with him.

"What's next?" Hunter asked Coby as he dried his hands.

"Now we have to take Pickle for a walk," Coby declared.

"All right. Lead the way."

Coby hustled over to Pickle's crate and got out the leash. I walked over too and grabbed a doggie poop bag. Then we all set out for the puppy's evening walk, slowly descending the stairs at the back of the motel as Coby led us to the grass path.

"He's a great kid," Hunter said as Coby ran ahead. "Smart too. I couldn't believe all of the stuff he was telling me when we were playing with his cars. Like all the colors? He was so specific. Maroon. Copper. Cobalt. Most kids would have just said red, orange and blue."

"Thank you. We spend a lot of time coloring and he always likes me to tell him the names on the crayons. I guess they stuck."

Pride swelled as I watched Coby petting Pickle. I wasn't a dummy by any means, but I knew most of Coby's brainpower had come from Everett's gene pool. It was a good reminder that not everything about Everett had been bad. He hadn't wanted to be a parent—hence the homicidal push for an abortion—but he had given me my greatest treasure. For Coby, I'd always be grateful to Everett.

Coby ran back to us after a few minutes, dragging Pickle along. "Can we watch *Cars*, Mommy?"

Glancing down at my watch, I saw it was nearly seven. "Sorry, not tonight." By the time we finished with Pickle and got Coby in the bath, we'd only have thirty minutes before bed to read a few stories. If it was a Friday night, not a Sunday, I'd make an exception for the movie, but as it was, we had a busy week ahead of us and I didn't want to start off Monday morning with a tired kid.

"But Mommy, Hunter has never seen it. He doesn't know about Lightning McQueen and Tow Mater."

"Sorry. Not tonight." I hated seeing Coby's face fall.

Hunter bent to eye level with my son. "If it's okay with your mom, maybe I could come back another night and watch it with you?"

Coby's face lit up. He bounced up and down, begging me silently as he waited for my approval. "Yes," I said, "that's fine with me. Now let's go inside and get ready for bath."

"Yay!" Off Coby ran with Pickle trying to keep up.

The minute we were inside, Coby dropped the puppy's leash and ran off toward his room, stripping clothes as he went. "Little boys and their nudity." I shook my head. "He's not even kind of shy."

Hunter laughed. "I'll leave and let you get him to bed. Let me know when you deem that housekeeper's room acceptable enough to show me."

I rolled my eyes. "I'm doing this preemptive clean for your own good. Trust me."

"Sure you are," he said dryly. "I think you have this idea that I need fancy things. I don't. Fancy is overrated. Trust *me*."

"Well, then I'm doing it for me. I don't want you to see my mess."

"Maisy, do you think a mess is going to scare me away?" He took one step closer, breaking the barrier on my intimate space. The heat from his broad chest warmed my face and I held my breath, waiting for his next move. "If you haven't figured it out by now, I'm staying until you make me leave."

I shivered when his hand came up and framed my jaw. The tingles on my cheek spread down my neck as his thumb drew a small circle by the corner of my mouth. With a racing heart, my lips parted, inviting him in for a kiss. I hadn't been kissed in so, *so* long. I wanted Hunter to break that streak. I wanted his soft lips, his tongue—

"Mommy! I'm naked!"

Hunter and I both jerked, stepping apart as the moment vanished.

"Sorry." I shook my head to clear the haze. "I'd better get to him."

"It's no problem. I'll see you soon." He leaned forward and softly kissed my cheek before letting himself out.

I stared at the door with my hand pressed to my cheek. Then I closed my eyes and memorized the feel of his lips on my skin.

"Mommy!"

My eyes snapped open and I stuttered into action. "Coming!"

I hustled to the bathroom and ran Coby's bath. While he splashed and blew bubbles, I replayed Hunter's words.

*I'm staying until you make me leave.*

Until I made him leave? I doubted that would ever happen.

---

"THIS IS RIDICULOUS," I told my pillow. Craning my neck, I looked at my alarm clock. 3:24 a.m.

Three hours.

I'd been lying in bed, awake, for three hours.

After bath and bedtime, Coby had zonked right out. I'd had a glass of wine, picked up toys, then headed to bed early. Mistake. I'd woken up after midnight and my brain had been busy ever since. Nothing I'd tried could shut it down for sleep.

First, I'd run the gamut on my standard worries. Was I making the right choices for Coby? Was I spending enough time with him? Was I doing enough to make sure he wasn't just surviving, but thriving?

Once those questions had been exhausted—without conclusion, just like every other time I'd hashed out my mommy worries—I'd moved on to my concerns about the inn. I'd recounted my to-do list for the next two weeks and all the things that needed to be done. Reservations were already starting to pick up and I was running out of free time.

*I need to be sleeping!* I had things to do tomorrow. Important things. Things that needed me to be rested, not walking around like a zombie.

Tossing and turning for another fifteen minutes, I finally gave up.

"Screw it." I kicked my white down comforter off my legs and got up, reaching to turn on my bedside lamp.

If I couldn't sleep, I'd make a new list to reduce some stress. My tasks lists were my sanity. Typically, I had three or four versions of the same to-do list going at once because the physical act of writing down my tasks helped me tackle them.

And because of nights like this, I'd learned to always keep pens and paper in my nightstand. Opening my drawer, I pulled out a notepad and then reached back in, patting around for a pen. My fingers hit a cold, metal pen, heavier than the standard plastic ballpoint, and I instantly froze.

My vision blurred as an Everett flash consumed my mind.

There was a scalpel in my hand, not a pen, and I was in the cold basement of the hospital. Everett was looming over Gigi on her knees because he'd just hit her in the face. And I was standing behind him ready to strike. My movements from that night replayed in slow motion. The windup of my shoulder, the plunge of the scalpel into Everett's neck and the heat of his sticky blood as it coated my fist.

That night, Everett had dropped to the floor and Gigi and I had run away. But tonight in my flashback, he yanked out the scalpel from his neck. His brown eyes—my son's brown eyes—were locked on mine as he lunged.

I gasped, standing from my bed and scrambling backward. When my butt hit the floor, the flashback broke.

*Damn it to hell.*

A tear dripped down my cheek as I worked to breathe and calm my racing heart. I was losing my mind. When would these flashes end? How many years would it take for me to forget that horrible night? To forget that horrible man?

Pushing up off the floor, I bent down and picked up the pen that had fallen to the carpet. Marching it straight to the bathroom, I tossed it in the trash before going to the sink to splash some cold water on my face. I dabbed it dry with a towel and looked at myself in the mirror.

*You're losing it.*

Was it time to go back to therapy? After I'd killed Everett, my parents had insisted I talk to a therapist to help deal with the aftermath of that traumatic night. Therapy had really helped but I'd stopped going after Coby had been born and I'd bought the inn.

My therapist lived in Bozeman, and between the two-hour round-trip plus the session time itself, therapy had taken too much time. I'd had a newborn to feed and a business to build so therapy had been an easy item to fall off the priority list. But with these flashes as vivid as ever, maybe I needed to make the time and try again.

But in the absence of anyone to talk to tonight, I opted for my distraction of choice: work. Work would once again be my savior.

I brushed my teeth, then went back to my room for clothes, tossing on some gray joggers and a black zip-up. Then I pulled a black cap over my head, slipped on my fuchsia sneakers and headed to the kitchen with my phone in hand.

Opening up my video monitor app, I checked Coby's room on the screen. Sure enough, he was sprawled on his bed and completely zonked out. Unfortunately, nights like this weren't uncommon so I'd invested in a top-of-the-line monitor so I could work downstairs while Coby slept. Nine out of ten emails I returned were sent after midnight and I'd lost track of how many loads of laundry I'd done before sunrise.

Carefully shutting the door, I slipped downstairs through the interior stairwell to the lobby. The loft had two sets of stairs. The staircase outside we used the most but the interior was handy for after hours. Since I didn't like to wander far from the loft on nights like this—just in case Coby woke up—I always stayed within a thirty-second sprint back to this stairwell. That limited my radius to the lobby, my office, the utility room and—conveniently for tonight—the housekeeper's room.

With my master keys in hand, I went outside and straight to the utility room, collecting a garbage can and two bags. Then I headed next door to the housekeeper's room to start my cleaning.

Opening the door, I was assaulted by a wave of musty air. I leaned into the room and grabbed a can of paint to prop the door open before flipping on the light, revealing piles of leftover remodeling supplies.

The room was long and narrow, with a cramped bathroom and a narrow closet taking up the entire width at the back. The twin bed was pushed tight against one wall opposite a small dresser loaded with paint supplies. Next to the dresser were stacks of unused tile and rolls of carpet remnants. On the small TV stand at the foot of the bed was a box filled with random tools.

I started with the stuff on the bed first, hauling the toolbox Beau had bought me into the utility room. Then I used a laundry basket to load up my extra sink fixtures and doorknobs. When I came back in again, I decided to relocate the tile to my office. Picking up one of the cement pieces, I brushed my fingers against its smooth white and gray surface. I was lost in my inspection of the beautiful scrolled design when a hand landed on my shoulder.

"Ahh!" I screamed and jumped, spinning around with my tile leading the way. It connected first, hitting before my eyes could take in the person behind me. When they did, I dropped the tile and gasped as it cracked on the floor.

"Fucking shit, Maisy." Hunter stepped back and clutched his temple.

This wasn't happening. Not again. "Hunter?"

"Yes, Hunter. I called your name. Didn't you hear me?"

"No!" I yelled, flailing my hands in the air. For the second time, I'd physically assaulted Hunter, and just like the last time, out came the words. "Oh my god! Why did you sneak up on me? You know I react first! Are you okay? Tell me you're okay. Shit. I'm so sorry! So, so sorry. Do you think you have a concussion? Are you dizzy? Oh my god, you're bleeding!"

Hunter pulled his fingers away, red on his fingertips. "Damn."

I rushed closer, my hands going to his face and twisting it so I could get a better look. The tile had gashed him right in the forehead about two inches above his temple.

"Come on." I grabbed his hand and pulled him outside. I didn't stop to lock up the housekeeper's room or even close the door. I just dragged him behind me, through the lobby and up the interior stairs to the loft.

"Maisy, it's not a big deal. Will you slow down? I'm fine."

"No, it's not. Come on." I kept pulling. Every time he tugged for me to slow, I just pulled harder.

"Maisy, I'm fine," he repeated when we reached the loft.

"You're bleeding. That is not fine, Hunter." I pulled him through the entryway and down the hall toward the bathroom. "I can't believe I made you bleed. Oh my god, I'm so sorry. I really hurt you this time. This is bad. Really bad."

"Maisy—"

"It's not fine!" I clapped my free hand over my mouth and froze. I'd just shouted right outside of Coby's bedroom.

We both stood still, staring at Coby's closed door and listening for the sound of him rustling from his bed. When all remained quiet, I resumed my pulling on Hunter's hand to the bathroom.

"Sit." I pointed at the toilet while I closed the door and turned on the faucet to warm up the water. "I've got a first-aid kit in here."

I crouched down and started digging through my cabinet under the sink. In my haste, out came the tampons and pantyliners, both spilling out of their respective containers right onto the floor by Hunter's feet. "Shit!" Could this get worse?

The last thing I wanted was for Hunter to be front and center with my feminine products. I wanted him to think of me as sexy and alluring, not bleeding and bitchy.

"Here." Hunter bent to pick them up.

"No! Don't touch those!" I swatted his hands away as I scrambled to shove everything back in the blue tampon box. "Sorry. It's just . . . I'll get them."

Hunter's deep chuckle filled the room.

"No laughing," I hissed as I stuffed the tampon box back under the sink and pulled out the first-aid kit.

He just kept on laughing. "Come on, admit it. It's kind of funny."

"Absolutely not! I hit you. Again! That's twice now that you've scared the bejesus out of me and I attacked you. This is bad. This is so, so bad."

"Maisy, I'm fine," he said as his laughter drifted off. "I just need a washcloth and a Band-Aid."

"I'll be the judge of that. I was a nurse, remember?" I grabbed a washcloth from a drawer and held it under the warm water.

"Yeah? Well, I'm a—"

"Hold still and no talking." I stepped into his space and pulled his hand away from his gash. "If you need stitches or have a concussion, we need to figure that out right away. This could be serious."

"For the last time, woman, I'm f—"

"Shush!"

Hunter frowned and glared up at me but stopped talking.

"Okay. Here goes." I pulled in a deep breath and readied

the washcloth. Gently, I pressed it to his wound, cleaning the cut and giving it a good look. It wasn't deep and wouldn't need stitches, and since he didn't wince or move, it must not have hurt much. All he'd need was a butterfly bandage and some antibiotic ointment.

"You're fine," I breathed as my shoulders fell.

"I recall telling you that once or twice."

I ignored his sarcasm and continued with my examination. "Are you dizzy? Light-headed? Seeing white spots at all?"

"I'm. Fine." He took the washcloth from my hand and stood, pushing past me to stand in front of the mirror over the sink. He rifled through the first-aid kit, found a bandage and closed up his cut. "See? All better."

As my panic faded, a level of embarrassment the likes of which I'd never felt before took its place. I sank down onto the toilet seat and hung my head, burying my face in my palms. "I'm so sorry. For the cut. For going a little, um . . . crazy. God, I'm sorry."

I waited for the sound of the opening door and his retreating footsteps as he ran far, far away from this crazy lady, but instead he crouched in front of me.

"Hey." He pulled my hands away from my face. "It's fine. I'm sorry I scared you."

"This is not your fault."

"Yeah, it is. What are you doing up cleaning at this hour, anyway? Is everything okay?"

"I couldn't sleep so I decided to just get up and do some work. What about you?"

"Couldn't sleep either. I was actually just leaving for Wade Lake. I thought I'd head up and see if I could catch the sunrise for your picture."

"You were?" I whispered.

His gentle eyes answered my question.

Was this guy for real? How was he still here?

Maybe I'd paid my dues with the jerks of the world and Hunter Faraday was my reward.

"Do you want to wake up Coby and come with me?" he asked.

Rousing my three-year-old from his bed before dawn would be the absolute worst decision as a parent. Sleep for kids was so critical and a few extra hours would put me ahead on my list for the week.

But none of those facts stopped me from whispering, "Yes."

Hunter smiled and stood, holding out a hand to help me up. I gave myself two heartbeats to savor the feel of his skin on mine, then I went into Coby's room and scooped him up, grabbing his favorite blanket for the trip to my car. Coby didn't wake up once, not as I walked down the stairs or as I was buckling him into his car seat and covering up his bare feet.

Meanwhile, Hunter jogged around to the parking lot and grabbed his camera from his truck, and when he came back, he took the keys to my car and drove us all to Wade Lake.

Sitting on the hood of my 4Runner with Coby asleep in the back, I watched as Hunter took his first photo for my inn. The sunrise over the lake was gorgeous, but mostly I sat and stared at Hunter.

I had forgotten how good it felt to fall for a man.

Too good.

I just hoped it wasn't too good to be true.

# CHAPTER EIGHT

MAISY

The week after Hunter had taken us on our early morning trip to Wade Lake went by in a frantic, frazzled, freaking mess.

I'd gotten an influx of spur-of-the-moment reservations on top of my previously scheduled bookings. On top of that, my part-time housekeeper had come down with the flu. So instead of ticking off items from my renovation list, I'd spent my days cleaning and doing laundry to turn over guest rooms.

By Sunday, my bookkeeping was overdue, my loft was a disaster, and Hunter's housekeeping room looked exactly the same as it had the night I'd clobbered him with the tile. I had given up on anything I'd deemed noncritical including doing my makeup, eating lunch, and, unfortunately, spying on Hunter from my loft window.

Since Hunter had gone back to his normal early morning, late-evening routine, I hadn't seen him all week. Our only communication had been through sticky notes. I'd leave him a smiley face or a *Hi!* on the Tupperware meals I delivered to his refrigerator each day. He'd respond with emptied containers and a scribbled *Thank you.*

Except on Friday. Friday, he'd left me a note with his phone number, asking me to text.

My fingers had never typed a text so fast.

For the last day and a half, any time my phone dinged, I would stop whatever I was doing and race to my phone, smiling whenever I saw Hunter's name on the screen.

"Mommy!" Coby called from his room. "Is he here yet?"

"Not yet, buddy. Pretty soon," I yelled back from the kitchen.

Hunter wouldn't be here for another twenty minutes. He was coming over to spend another Sunday afternoon with us and we'd planned on getting lunch at the café and then going to the pond to take some photos of Coby fishing.

My son was bouncing-off-the-walls excited.

So was I.

It had only been a week but I *missed* Hunter. Last Sunday, he had made a lasting impression. I missed his smile. I missed hearing his voice. I missed the smell of his cologne, which had faded from my car.

*Twenty minutes.* I only had to wait twenty minutes and I'd have it all back.

I went back to my massive pile of dishes in the sink, hoping I'd have them done before Hunter got here, when my phone rang on the counter. I rushed over, wet hands and all, hoping it was him wanting to come over early.

"Darn," I muttered seeing the unknown number. It wasn't uncommon to get calls from blocked numbers for the inn, and since I'd forwarded the lobby phone to my cell, I cleared my throat to answer. "Thank you for calling The Bitterroot Inn. How can I help you today?"

The line was silent so I waited a few seconds. "Hello?"

Still no sound. I lifted the phone away from my ear just as a woman's voice finally came over the line. "Hello. Is this The Bitterroot Inn located in Prescott, Montana?"

*Double darn.* Not a potential guest, a telemarketer. As much as I wanted to just hang up, I couldn't do it. So I'd listen, multitasking as I waited for the sales pitch I'd politely decline.

"Yes, this is The Bitterroot Inn." I sandwiched the phone between my shoulder and cheek and went back to my dishes.

"May I speak with Maisy Holt, please?"

"This is Maisy."

"The same Maisy Holt who murdered Everett Carlson four years ago?"

The plate in my wet grip slipped right out, crashing into the bottom rack of the dishwasher. "Who is this?"

The woman didn't answer.

"Who is this?" I demanded through gritted teeth.

When she didn't answer, I hung up. Tossing my phone aside, I braced my arms on the counter and closed my eyes, taking a few long breaths to calm down. This wasn't the first time I'd received a phone call like that and they always made me angry.

The first year after Everett's kidnapping, I'd been hounded relentlessly by the press. Everyone wanted to sell my story—or their version of my story—hoping it would make them a few dollars. The fact that I'd declined comment without exception just made me that much more interesting. That much more of a challenge.

Some reporters had been ruthless in their attempts to get

me to comment, saying anything and everything to make me mad so I'd slip. Some reporters were nicer, offering me money or a TV exclusive, but I'd always declined those too.

My story was my business and didn't belong in the headlines. The only person who would get an explanation was Coby, when the time was right.

Why was I even considered news after all this time? Weren't there other topics far more interesting than my simple little life? With phone calls like that to bring it back up, how was I ever going to move past that horrific night with Everett?

*Work.* I'd get back to work and busy myself until my anger was buried deep.

Doing just that, I finished the dishes and cleaned my kitchen. Then I dusted the living room until a knock sounded at the door.

Coby flew out of his room, sprinting past me with Pickle trying to keep up.

"Wait up, bud." I jogged over to the door as he was attempting to yank it open. "It's locked."

I checked the peephole first, making sure it was Hunter, and smiled when I saw his man bun. Flipping the deadbolt, I swung open the door to see his handsome face. He grinned and my world was better. Gone was the stress from the past week and the annoyance from that reporter's phone call.

"Hunter!" Coby yelled as Pickle yapped.

"Hey, Coby! What's happening?" Hunter asked, ruffling my son's hair as he came inside.

"We're all going fishing!"

"I'm pretty excited," Hunter told him. "Do you think I'll catch the biggest fish?"

Coby shook his head. "No way."

"Maybe I will." My statement earned me two misbelieving looks.

Hunter leaned in to kiss my cheek. "Hey, stranger."

"Hey, back."

"Are you guys ready to go?"

I nodded. "Yes. I just need to grab our stuff." I was about to order Coby to get his shoes and hat but he had already plopped down on the floor to pull on his Crocs.

I hustled to the refrigerator to get the white Styrofoam cup of worms I'd dug up from my flower bed yesterday, and with it in hand, I grabbed Coby's fishing pole from the corner. I slid on my shades and locked the loft's door, following Hunter to the 4Runner, where he was already buckling in Coby to his seat.

My stomach was full of jitters, but the good kind. The kind that only came with a crush.

"Do you still want to grab lunch?" Hunter asked as he drove.

"Yes, please. I'm starving."

He took us straight to the café where the Sunday after-church crowd was starting to thin so we were lucky enough to get a booth by the window.

"Want to play tic-tac-toe?" Coby asked Hunter, flipping his paper place mat over and digging for a pen in my purse.

Hunter's shocked face came to mine. "He can play tic-tac-toe?"

My mouth spread in a proud-mom grin. "I taught him a couple of months ago. He's getting the hang of it." I leaned in closer to whisper. "But he always needs the middle square."

"Middle square. Got it."

Hunter and Coby played a few games, Coby always the victor, until our waitress brought over a kids' menu and crayons. With our orders placed and Coby contentedly coloring a dinosaur picture, Hunter and I caught up on the crazy that had been my last seven days.

"I thought you said tourist season normally didn't start until the middle of May."

I sighed. "So did I. But I'll get caught up. I always do." I might not sleep much this week, but I'd get through my list. "How about you? How was your week?"

"Good."

I smiled on the outside though his one-word answer made me cringe on the inside. If our friendship developed into an actual relationship, I'd have to tell Hunter how much I hated one-word answers. But as it was, my mouth was staying shut. If he wanted to say "good" and leave it at that, I'd suck it up.

The decision I'd made last week at Wade Lake was still holding strong. I would not be nosy. I didn't know what Hunter did for a living. I didn't know if he'd gone to college. I didn't know if he preferred grape jelly over strawberry. The questions were right on the tip of my tongue but I swallowed them down. When Hunter wanted to share, I'd be all ears.

For now, I'd let conversation about my life monopolize our time.

"Is your housekeeper feeling better?" he asked.

I nodded. "She is, thank god. She'll be back tomorrow and is going to pick up some extra hours this week. I need it too. I'm still one room short because I'm trying to get the remodel finished."

"Which room?"

"Seven. Right next door to you. I'm painting it tonight after Coby goes to bed." Michael had already volunteered to come over and sleep on the couch so I didn't have to worry about Coby.

"You're painting it tonight?" Hunter asked. "Why not wait for tomorrow?"

"My fault. I put it off for too long. I have to paint it tonight because the carpet gets installed tomorrow with the trim. Then once that's all done, I still need to get it furnished, decorated and cleaned." It would be hectic but if I could punch out that room, it would take a huge weight off my shoulders.

"Can I help with anything? I've got good furniture-moving muscles."

That was no joke. I could see the contours between his biceps and triceps underneath the fitted quarter-zip he was wearing.

I smiled to myself, noticing that we nearly matched today. Jeans. Gray quarter-zip. Tennis shoes. At least my shirt was light while his was nearly black and his shoes weren't lime green like mine.

"Maisy?"

"Huh? Oh, sorry." I blushed and smiled at my water glass. "I was just noticing that our clothes kind of match today. Anyway, I've already recruited my brothers to help with the furniture. Thank you, though."

Hunter was still a paying guest, and although he was doing my photos, I couldn't bring myself to ask for more help and risk taking advantage.

"How did your meeting with your contractor go yesterday?" I asked.

He'd texted and said they were doing a walk-through of the remaining construction items. I was secretly hoping it would take longer than he'd guessed just so he would be at the motel a little longer. Even if I didn't get to see him much, it was comforting just to know he was there, sleeping right underneath my loft.

"The meeting was okay. Just like I'd guessed, it's going to be another month at least."

"Bummer." I sipped my water to hide my grin.

"It'll be worth the wait. Did I tell you my property is right in the foothills going up the road to Fan Mountain?"

I shook my head. "No, but I'd kind of guessed. There isn't a lot of new construction in Prescott. There are some pretty big houses up that way." I had narrowed his house down to one of two that were currently being built in that area. One was massive and the other was big but tasteful. I really hoped his was the latter.

He nodded. "Yeah, some are huge. I think mine will be the smallest for miles."

*Yes!* I fist pumped under the table, glad that Hunter wasn't the type to go for gaudy extravagance just because he had money.

The waitress arrived with our food, ending our adult conversation. Instead of grown-up talk, we spent the rest of the meal fielding kid questions from Coby. Thanks to my son's interrogation, I learned that Hunter was not afraid of sharks, he had never been to the moon, and his favorite color was blue.

After Hunter paid the lunch bill, we took the short drive down Main Street to the community pond.

"Stay back from the water!" I called to Coby as he ran across the grass toward his favorite fishing rock.

"Okay, Mommy!" he shouted over his shoulder.

"Cool spot," Hunter said as we walked. "Does all of this water come from the river?"

"Yeah. It was built back in the fifties. The town dug the pond and then a channel to feed the water from the Jamison. They stock it with fish—"

"Come on, you guys!" Coby yelled.

Hunter and I both laughed and picked up our pace. I hurried to get Coby set up with his fishing pole while Hunter got out his camera. Casting out the line for Coby, I stepped back so Hunter could capture a few pictures without me in the shot.

Once he was done with the photos, Hunter took over casting for Coby. Cast after cast, we didn't say much until Coby caught a fish and our trio broke out into cheers. I used my phone to take a video of Coby reeling it in with Hunter standing proudly at his side.

"Smile for a picture." I did a photo burst of Coby and Hunter before they unhooked the fish and set it free.

"That was fun!" Coby cheered.

"It sure was. Do you want to stay longer or are you all done?"

"Um." His eyebrows came together as he considered his answer. "All done fishing. When we get home, can Hunter watch *Cars* wif me?"

Hunter smiled. "I don't have any other plans."

I smiled back. "Then let's go watch *Cars*."

Coby squealed and raced back to the car.

"I can hang with him if you want to get ahead on your painting," Hunter offered as we walked to catch up.

"Thank you, but that's okay. I'll just do it tonight when he's asleep. I haven't gotten to spend much quality time with him this week and a movie with some popcorn is more important."

Hunter's steps slowed, a strange look on his face. It was

the same look he'd given Coby the first time he'd seen my son by the vending machines. Puzzled wasn't the right word to describe it, though his eyebrows were knitted in the middle. Awestruck, maybe?

"What?"

"Nothing." His face relaxed into a grin. "It's just, he's a lucky kid. You're a good mom."

I'd been keeping track of Hunter's compliments.

That one just hit the top of the chart.

"Thank you."

Hunter jogged ahead to load Coby in the car, and with his back to me, I hop-skipped my next three steps. I worried daily that I was being a good mom to Coby—I probably always would—but Hunter's compliment was enough to banish those insecurities for today.

Reaching the car just as Hunter was closing Coby's door, I tossed the fishing pole in the back. By the time I closed the hatch, Hunter was just getting into the driver's seat. "You know, I can drive. This is my car."

"Blondie, don't pretend to protest when we both know you like to ride shotgun with me at the wheel. I saw that smile when you handed over your keys for me to drive up to the lake last week."

He had me there.

So I just smiled and got in the passenger seat. I was buckling my seat belt when my phone rang in my lap.

My face scrunched up at another unknown number. Chances were this was probably a legitimate call for the inn, but since I was still on edge from the reporter's call earlier, I ignored it and let it go to voicemail.

The missed-call banner popped up on the screen at the

same time Hunter's phone started ringing. He pulled it out of his jeans pocket and frowned.

"Do you need to get that?" I asked. "We can wait in the car while you take it outside."

"It's no one important." He declined the call and dropped his phone in his lap. With a quick smile to Coby in the back, he turned the key in the ignition.

We were almost back at the motel when my phone rang again. Another unknown number. If this was the reporter, I'd give her kudos for her persistence. With a grunt, I declined this call too.

"Everything okay?" Hunter asked.

"Probably just a telemarketer."

I hated lying but today wasn't the day to get into the reason why I was being hounded by a reporter. That story would come some other time. Hunter hadn't asked about Coby's father yet and I was glad for it, because when he did ask, I wanted to give him the full story. I wanted him to know what he was getting into with us.

I just hoped that once he learned about my past, he wouldn't run away to his house in the foothills and stay away for good.

---

HUNTER

I was about one phone call away from blocking Nell's number.

She'd called eleven times during *Cars*. Eleven. If I hadn't been on call, I would have shut off the damn phone, but as it was, I had to decline it every time and tell Maisy it was no big deal when she'd repeatedly offered to pause the movie.

But finally, the calls stopped as we sat down for the homemade cheeseburger pizza Maisy had made for dinner.

Three pieces demolished, I went back for a fourth. "This is the best pizza I've ever had." Considering how much pizza I'd consumed during undergrad and med school, that was saying something.

"I'm glad you like it." Maisy smiled proudly and dug into her own slice. "Eat as much as you like."

I patted my stomach. "I will, but I'll be running an extra mile tomorrow. Pizza has always been one of my weaknesses."

"Mine too. That and cookies."

I smiled. I loved that Maisy wasn't afraid to eat. She had an awesome body, probably from working her ass off every day, but she didn't stress about calories. Every meal we'd shared, she had never ordered a salad or picked at her plate.

"Cookies rank up there on my list, but probably not as much as other temptations."

"What's a tem-pation?" Coby asked.

"A temp-ta-tion. It's something you have a hard time resisting. An indulgence." He was still confused so I kept going. "Something you go crazy over. Like pizza or cookies."

He bounced in his seat. "I know. Like cheeseburgers!"

I laughed. Damn this kid was smart. "Like cheeseburgers. Or gummy worms."

"Gummy worms?" Maisy and Coby asked at the same time.

I nodded. "I can't resist. I'm a sucker for gummy worms. Especially sour ones. And Lay's potato chips. I used to survive on those alone in college."

"Any other temptations I should know about?" Maisy asked.

I locked my gaze with hers. "You."

She smiled but didn't look away, even as her cheeks flushed.

"Do you like brownies?" Coby asked, forcing me to break away from Maisy.

"Yeah, bud. I like brownies. Especially ones with chocolate chips."

"Me too."

*Damn, this was nice.* It was all I could think about as we finished our meal. Coby, Maisy and I were so comfortable around each other. Everything was easy here. If only I could ignore the world outside her door and stay in this loft for the rest of my life.

Maisy stood and started clearing plates to the kitchen before I could offer to clean up. "I've got dishes tonight."

"Coby, bud, why don't you go get Pickle's leash and we'll take him for his walk?"

"Okay!" He scrambled off the seat.

I grabbed his yellow plate and took it into the kitchen, setting it on the counter. "Thanks for dinner tonight and all of the other nights this week."

"It was my pleasure."

I leaned a hip against the counter, studying her perfect profile as she faced the sink. "You don't have to cook for me, you know? You've got a lot going on and making me food isn't necessary. I can just eat downtown."

"I want to," she said as she rinsed a fork. "I cook plenty for me and Coby, so setting aside some for you is no big deal. Besides, I hate the idea of you always eating out or only eating junk. I've got too much of my mom in me to let you survive on processed foods alone."

I opened my mouth to thank her again but nothing came out.

She'd rendered me speechless.

Other than my mother, no one had ever really cared about what I had to eat. I'd never gone hungry, our house chef had made sure to always have something prepared, but he'd done it out of obligation, not love. Maisy was feeding me simply because she cared.

All those years ago, when I'd first seen Maisy in the maternity ward of the hospital, I had made an assumption about her. Spending time with her these last two weeks, I now knew I'd been right.

Maisy Holt was pure joy. She was goodness personified. She was a beam of sunshine breaking through the clouds in my life.

I'd walked away from her back then.

I'd avoided her the last time I'd lived in Prescott.

I wouldn't do either ever again. I wasn't giving her up without a fight.

I'd come to Prescott with a plan: to look out for this beautiful soul. My plan had just changed. Now I was here to win her heart.

Maybe—if she could fall in love with me—she wouldn't push me away when she learned the truth. Maybe she'd love me enough to forgive all the omissions and the half-truths.

Maisy deserved the full story. The entire truth.

Just not yet.

Until the time was right, my secrets were my burdens to bear. Then, when the time was right, she'd get it all. Every miserable detail. She could ask me any question her heart desired and I'd give all the answers.

But not yet.

Not until I won her over completely and stood a chance at keeping her—forever.

As I stared at her profile, determination coursed through my veins. I had never faced a bigger challenge but I'd never had this much to gain. Three hearts were on the line here: Maisy's, Coby's and mine, and I'd do whatever it took not to break them all.

"Ready!" Coby bounced into the kitchen with Pickle's leash.

I tore my eyes away from Maisy and stood tall, smiling down at the overexcited puppy and his boy. "I'll take these two out for a walk."

Maisy stopped washing and worried her bottom lip. "Oh, um . . . that's okay. We can all go when I'm done with this."

*Shit.* Did she not trust me alone with Coby? She'd declined my offer to watch him earlier so she could paint, and now this. Winning her over was going to be fucking hard if she didn't trust me with her son.

But, not wanting her to be uncomfortable, I backpedaled. "I get it. It's too soon for a strange man to be alone with your son. No pressure at all, I just wanted to help."

"Oh, no. It's not that." She giggled. "I trust you with Coby."

One sentence and my shoulders sagged. *I trust you with Coby.* "Then what?"

She scrunched up her nose. "Pickle has had, um . . . diarrhea. Coby gave him too much people food last night and I didn't want you to have to deal with that mess."

"I've got the dog." I snagged the leash from Coby and

picked up Pickle. "You do the dishes and take a five-minute break." I winked at her, loving how it always made her smile, then walked outside with my own wide grin.

"You know what's special, Coby?"

"What?" he asked, hopping down the steps.

"Your mom's smile."

He looked over his shoulder. "Why?"

"Because it never stops."

"Huh?"

I shook my head and chuckled. "Never mind, bud. Here." I set down the puppy at the base of the stairs and hooked on his leash. "You can lead Pickle but I'll take care of his poop. Okay?"

"Okay." And off they went into the grass.

One day when he was a little older, I'd explain why Maisy's smile was special. And then when he was a lot older, I'd explain how lucky he was to have inherited his smile from her and not his father.

Coby was the spitting image of Everett. His hair. His eyes. The shape of his face. Everything except for that smile. Everett's smile had always been too cold. Too calculating. A genuine smile on his mirror image's face suited it much better.

Physical traits aside, Coby was otherwise one-hundred-percent Maisy. He had her curious nature. He had her energy and spirit. And his presence brought peace to my heart, just like his mother's.

Maisy and Coby Holt were remarkable people, proving something I'd always known.

Everett Carlson had been one stupid motherfucker.

---

FOUR HOURS LATER, I was lying on the bed in my room, listening for sounds next door. The second I heard a faint rustling through the wall, I flew off the bed and walked outside in my old jeans and white T-shirt.

"Maisy, it's me, Hunter." I smiled as I called out from the walkway outside the room. "I'm coming over there." I took a few steps. "Here I come." One more step. "I'm not going to attack you so please don't throw a paintbrush at my head."

I stepped into the doorway and held up my hands to ward off a potential attack.

"Ha ha," she muttered. I dropped my hands to catch her rolling her eyes but smiling. "You're freaking hilarious, Faraday."

Entering the empty room, my eyes immediately feasted on Maisy's bare, toned legs. She was wearing cutoff denim shorts and a white tank top, exposing her smooth and lightly tanned skin. Her electric-blue sports bra was peeking out underneath her tank top and she was barefoot, her toes painted the same blue as the bra.

When she bent to set down the paint tray she'd been holding, I quickly adjusted my dick so she wouldn't see the tent in my jeans.

"What are you doing?" she asked.

I crossed the room and took a paintbrush from the box in the middle of the floor. "I'm helping you paint."

"Have you ever painted before?"

"Walls? No. The last time I remember painting was with Crayola watercolors in middle-school art. But I'm kind of a smart guy so you can teach me."

She sighed. "Hunter, you don't have to do this. I really appreciate the offer but you're already doing so much with the photographs and—"

"Hey." I stopped her and stepped into her space. "Let me help. Please."

Her breath hitched as I leaned just a bit closer. She smelled so good. So sweet. *Fuck, I want to kiss her.* I wanted to wrap her in my arms and take her mouth. To hold her all night long after I'd exhausted her completely.

But tonight, she needed to get this room painted, and if I kissed her, it was going to take a while.

Our first kiss was going to be the lasting kind. The kind she'd never forget. The kiss that erased all others from her past.

Tonight, we didn't have that kind of time, so instead, I leaned down and whispered in her ear. "Are you going to teach me to paint?"

She shivered as she whispered back, "Yes."

I grinned and forced my feet to take a backward step. Then we got to work.

Three hours later, the ceiling was white, the walls were "dove gray," and I had paint specks all over my clothes, hair and skin.

"Thank you," Maisy said as she surveyed our work. "This would have taken me a lot longer by myself. Now Michael might actually be able to go home and not sleep on my couch."

"Anytime."

I meant that too. I'd help her anytime. The smile on my face would last all week just because I got to spend my Sunday night working side by side with Maisy.

# CHAPTER NINE

MAISY

When I was twelve, I planned my dream wedding. My cousin had just gotten married and I'd spent an entire day of summer vacation filling the better portion of my diary with ideas and drawings for my own wedding. I'd wanted pink. Everything pink. The cake. The flowers. The dresses. Lots and lots of pink.

Had I seen the majesty of Beau and Sabrina's wedding back then, that diary would have been a whole lot different.

Sabrina and Beau were married at six o'clock in an open meadow not too far up into the mountains. With the smell of pine in the spring air and the sun's bright rays slowly fading to a glow, the two of them stood together and exchanged their vows. There were no chairs, no aisles and no fancy decorations. Just Beau and Sabrina standing with the minister as close friends and family stood by to watch.

Beau and Sabrina were so in love, I don't think they even knew the rest of us were there.

After their kiss and some pictures, we all came back into town for the reception. While the ceremony had been simple and intimate, the reception was another story. Sabrina had gone all out to plan an extravagant party for hundreds of guests.

There weren't a lot of large event venues in small-town Montana, so Sabrina had been limited to the school cafeteria. She'd magically transformed the space. Now it looked more like a fancy ballroom in a city hotel than the room where I'd eaten my lunches as a child.

"This is something else," Dad said for the third time as he looked around the room. We were dancing on the large wooden floor in front of the stage where the live band was playing.

"It sure is. It's beautiful."

The entire ceiling had been strung with lights that gave the room a soft glow. Round tables and chairs, all covered with fancy linens, filled the floor space behind and around the dance floor. The plain walls had been hidden with black curtains lining the entire room. Stunning floral arrangements of green and ivory adorned every table.

"Wasn't that some dinner?" Dad asked.

"I ate *way* too much. Coby was too busy playing so I ate my plate and most of his. But it was totally worth it." Prime rib, Copper River salmon, roasted potatoes, fresh dinner rolls and about a half dozen salads. I'd tried it all.

"Do you think it was okay that I hit the carving station a couple extra times?" Dad asked.

I giggled and reached up high, smoothing the worry lines on his forehead. "I think the father of the groom can eat as much as he wants. I wouldn't worry about it."

Brock Holt was no small human. He was Beau's size

except for the huge beer belly he'd been growing over the last ten years, and wow, Dad could eat.

"Thanks." He smiled and twirled me around. "Your brother seems happy."

"He sure does."

We both looked over to Beau slow dancing with Sabrina. Beau was wearing a simple suit instead of a tux, something Sabrina had surprised him with at his fitting, and Sabrina was in a gorgeous white dress, the top half all lace with half sleeves and an open cutout at the back.

"Are you having fun?" Dad asked.

"Yeah. This has been a great night."

"You look beautiful, honey. That dress suits you."

I leaned further into his chest. "Thanks, Dad."

I loved my bridesmaid dress. True to everything else about this wedding, it was classy. A simple black chiffon V-neck dress with an A-line skirt cut at tea length. I didn't have to wear Spanx, I could wear a normal bra, and the skirt had pockets for my phone and lip gloss.

Bonus, it made me feel pretty.

"Coby sure did look grown-up today in his suit," Dad said.

"Isn't that the truth? Can you believe he'll be four this summer? It feels like just yesterday I was bringing him home."

Dad gazed adoringly over my shoulder. I craned my neck to see Coby and a slew of other boys racing around the tables. Coby had shed his jacket for dinner but had refused to take off the bow tie his aunt Sabrina had bought special, just for him.

"It's hard for your old man to believe you're all grown-up," Dad said, pulling me a bit closer. "Beau's married.

Michael's barely looked away from Alana all night. You've got Coby and the inn. I'm getting old. I miss the days when you kids needed me around."

"We still need you, Dad."

"You do?"

I nodded. "Especially me. You have to train my dog."

HE SMILED at my joke and twirled me again. "You're not still mad about that, are you?"

"No. Of course not. You know I can't hold a grudge for long." The minute someone apologized to me, anger and resentment just flittered away.

"That's because my Maisy-girl's heart is too sweet for grudges."

"Some might call me a doormat."

He scoffed. "Absolutely not. You're forgiving, not a doormat. And I think that's a damn strong trait. When someone hurts you, the easy thing to do is cut them out, but you don't. You give second chances when people probably don't deserve them. You keep your heart open instead of becoming bitter and jaded. There's nothing *doormat* about you."

"Okay, Dad." I patted his chest, trying to stop him before he got all worked up, but he kept on ranting, drawing attention from a couple of dancers close by.

"Remember that time Jessica Cummings wrote that mean note about you in sixth grade and got caught passing it in class? Not a lot of kids would have let that go. Not to mention the fact that you then volunteered to be her debate partner because no one else could stand the little brat."

"Dad," I scolded. "Jessica wasn't so bad." She'd called me a bug-eyed goody two-shoes in the note, but she'd apologized the next day. We'd partnered for debate and had actually become friends until we'd lost touch after high school. *I wonder what she's doing these days.* Tomorrow I'd send her a Facebook message and say hello.

"My point is, you're one of the most loving—one of the strongest—people I know."

I smiled. "You're just biased."

"I am. But I'm damn right too."

"Thanks." I hugged him tighter as we finished our dance.

When the song ended, I looped my arm through his and let him escort me back to our table, where Mom was into another glass of champagne with Sabrina's mom. Both were laughing and talking too loudly.

"Uh-oh," Dad muttered.

"You can say that again. You'd better cut Mom off soon or she's never going to be able to host brunch in the morning."

"I think you're right." He let me go and walked to the back of Mom's chair, gently rubbing her shoulders. Dad wouldn't be cutting her off. He'd let Mom indulge as much as she wanted and take her home. Then tomorrow morning, he'd wake her up with coffee, orange juice and painkillers.

And I would be setting my alarm two hours earlier than planned so I could get to their house first and help Mom with brunch.

Grabbing my chair, I spun it around from the table so I could watch people on the dance floor. About two seconds later, Gigi came up from behind and slid a chair next to mine.

"Champagne?" she asked me, reaching behind us for the bottle.

"No, thanks. If I have any more I'll have a miserable headache in the morning."

She filled the glass she'd brought over and then got out her phone from her dress's pocket. "How effing cute is that?" She started snapping pictures of the dance floor where Jess was dancing with his daughters, spinning and twirling them around so they would giggle.

"Totally effing cute. He's so good with them."

She smiled. "Yes, he is."

A pang of envy hit hard. It wasn't the first tonight.

I wanted a fancy wedding to a man who looked at me like I'd hung the moon. I wanted more kids. Maybe a little girl who I could dress up with frilly dresses and precious slippers. Or another boy who would idolize his big brother. I wanted a man like my dad who would move mountains to make his family happy.

It scared me a bit that when I pictured all of that in my daydreams, the man at my side was Hunter. We were so new, so many things could go wrong, but I was keeping my fingers crossed. I was holding out hope that he was the good man I'd been waiting for.

"How was the rest of your week?" Gigi asked.

I tore my eyes away from the crowded dance floor and smiled at my friend. "Good actually. Very productive."

I'd busted my butt to get through my to-do list early in the week so I could help with all the wedding stuff over the past two days. Sleep had been sparse but it had been worth it to check all the boxes on a couple of lists.

The room I'd painted with Hunter was now done and ready for the reservations scheduled next week. The housekeeper's room was all set up so he had a place to stay. I'd even managed to fit in a quick trip to Bozeman to buy him a new mattress, bedding and a flat-screen to mount on the wall.

"I worry about how hard you work." Gigi leaned, our shoulders touching.

I leaned back. "I like to work hard. It gives me a lot of satisfaction to know that I'm the reason for the inn's success."

"I know and I'm so proud of you. But I just . . ." She trailed off and sat back in her chair. "Never mind."

"Just what?"

She sighed. "I just don't want the motel to be the significant other in your life. I want you to find a piece of that." She swung her hand out to the dance floor where more of our friends had joined Jess and her daughters.

Silas and Felicity were dancing with Victoria between them. Nick was carefully twirling Emmeline and her pregnant belly around. Sara was laughing hysterically at Milo, who was trying to impress her with his goofy dance moves.

It was fitting that the band was rocking a love song.

"Sorry," Gigi said before I could respond. "Forget I said anything. These weddings always make me feel sappy."

I turned my head and smiled. "Don't be sorry."

"No, I shouldn't have said anything. I told you that I'd stop pushing. So this is me officially no longer pushing."

I reached behind us and grabbed the bottle to top off her champagne.

"Thanks," she said. "So what's happening with Michael and the new vet?"

"Oh, he's in lurv," I swooned.

"Any fool can see that. I'd say that lurv goes both ways."

Michael and Alana were sitting alone at a table in the back of the room. They were pressed so closely together she was practically on his lap. "You're right about that. I'm betting we'll be at their wedding next."

"Hmm. Interesting." She tapped her chin. "I don't know. I've got a feeling we'll have another one before them.

"Really, who?" I looked around, inspecting all the couples. Everyone here was married or single and a long ways off from finding "the one."

"I don't know. It's just a feeling." Gigi held out her hand for a shake. "I'll take your bet. Winner buys pedicures for us both?"

My hand fitted with hers. "Done."

I glanced back at Michael and Alana again. They were sneaking out the door hand in hand. Gigi saw it too—that and my smug grin.

I was totally getting a free spa treatment.

Gigi and I visited for a while until Jess came over and claimed her for a dance. I spent the rest of the evening laughing with friends and family. When midnight rolled around, the party was getting rowdy and the free bar was running low on whiskey.

I moved to a quieter table at the back of the room and I held a sleeping Coby as I watched the party with a wide grin.

"How are you doing, sweetheart?" Mom appeared at my side, her words slurring.

"I think you'd better sit down, Mom." Her swaying was making me nervous.

"Good idea." She plopped into the chair next to mine.

"Did you have fun?"

She hummed and rested her head on my shoulder. "So much fun. I'm so happy for Beau."

"Me too."

"I hope they have a baby soon. Coby's so big now, I want another grandbaby for my rocking chair."

I smiled down at my son and stroked his soft brown hair. No matter how big he got, he'd always be my baby boy.

Mom yawned. "When you and Hunter get married, will you promise to give me more grandbabies? I want a lot."

My fingers stilled in Coby's hair. "Mom, we're not even dating." The last thing I needed was Mom thinking we were a serious couple and spreading that around town. "Please don't tell people about him. Okay? Not until I actually know if this thing is going to go anywhere." I waited for an answer. "Mom?"

She had passed out on my shoulder. Smiling, I shook my head and went back to people watching. Bridesmaid by day, human pillow by night.

"Who needs a date when I have you two?"

Earlier this week, Mom had begged me to ask Hunter to the wedding but I'd repeatedly told her no. Hunter and I needed some definition before I brought him around my family and friends. I wanted some time for things between us to develop.

The last time I'd brought a man home to my family, things hadn't worked out so well.

Stupid Everett.

I'd invited Everett to my family's home for Christmas. At the time, things between us had been rocky and I'd been on the verge of dumping him. I'd actually marched over to his house one night, ready to break it off, but he'd been apologetic and sweet. I'd thought we'd turned a corner in our relationship so I'd invited him for Christmas. Mistake. He'd broken up with me in my parents' living room thirty minutes before Christmas dinner.

So, no. I wasn't ready to parade Hunter in front of my family.

Hunter wasn't Everett, but I was still being cautious.

"There she is." Dad was standing behind my shoulder, shaking his head at my snoring mother. "I came back from the bathroom and couldn't find her anywhere."

I smiled up at him. "I think she's ready for bed."

He scoffed. "I think so too."

Dad came to her chair and gently swept her up in his arms. "Come on, baby," he whispered to Mom, then looked to me. "Night, honey. We'll see you at brunch."

"We'll be there. Good night, Dad."

I watched them go, happy that after all their years together he still called her "baby."

Sliding my phone out of my dress's pocket, I checked the time. It was well past midnight now and time for me to get my kiddo home. I shifted Coby in my arms to get a better hold, then stood. Carefully, I made my way over to the coat rack to grab our jackets and my purse. Balancing him and our stuff with practiced ease, I slipped out the doors and made a silent exit into the night.

With Coby buckled in his car seat, I climbed in the driver's seat just as my phone dinged with a text.

*Hunter: How was the wedding?*

My heart picked up a beat as I typed my reply.

*Me: It was really fun. We're actually just leaving now.*

*Hunter: Drive safe.*

The drive from the school to the motel was maybe a minute, but he still told me to drive safe.

I really, *really* liked that.

Hunter and I hadn't spent any time together this week but we'd been texting. He'd sent me a message each morning, thanking me for whatever meal I'd left him the day before. I'd texted him funny things Coby had said and weird stuff people had left behind in their rooms after checking out.

Our messages weren't serious, but there was an intimacy there. We checked in with one another. We were thinking about each other. And I liked that he was thinking about me tonight.

I pulled into my parking space behind the motel and reached over to the passenger seat to collect my stuff. When I looked up, I yelped and jerked in my seat. A man was standing outside the window of my car. I only relaxed when the figure bent low to knuckle tap on the glass.

Hunter.

My breathing was still labored when I pushed my door open and stepped out. "You scared me again."

He winced. "Sorry, I didn't mean to. I just thought you might want help carrying Coby inside."

That was sweet. So sweet it chased the adrenaline away. "Well, at least this time I couldn't physically retaliate."

He grinned. "My balls are grateful."

I giggled and clicked the locks so he could open the back door and collect Coby. Leading the way up the stairs, I opened the door to the loft and immediately kicked off my heels as Hunter strode past me with Coby in his arms.

I followed them to Coby's room and stood in the doorway, watching Hunter lay my son down gently in his bed.

He stepped back and I moved in, tugging off Coby's shoes, socks and bowtie.

With his sound machine on, his starry nightlight shining and him tucked under his blanket, I closed the door to Coby's room and followed Hunter to the living room.

"How was your night?" I asked.

"Quiet. I packed up my stuff so I can check out of that room tomorrow."

"Do you want the key to the housekeeper's room? I was going to drop it off in the morning, but since you're here, I can give it to you now."

"Sure."

I got my keys from my purse and pulled my phone from my pocket, turning on Coby's monitor app. With bare feet, I led Hunter down the interior stairs to the lobby. Grabbing the room key off its peg, we went outside and down two doors to his new space.

Before I unlocked the door, I turned and met his gaze. "If you hate it, if it's too small, please don't feel obligated to stay. I won't be hurt or upset at all if you don't want—"

"Maisy." He placed a hand on my shoulder. "It will be fine."

"Okay." I took a deep breath, turned the key and opened the door to step inside. Though the room was clean, it was outdated and cramped. Too small for someone of Hunter's size. "I'm going to bring over my mini fridge from the lobby so you can have that in the corner. The cable company is scheduled to come over on Tuesday to get the TV hooked up. But I know it isn't much."

He walked past me, inspecting the bed on his way toward the bathroom.

I stood nervously by the wall as he assessed the space.

This room was not anywhere near the type of room I wanted to give Hunter, but it was all I had.

"I like it," he said after coming out of the bathroom. "It reminds me of my college dorm except with its own shower and no farting roommate bunking above me."

"That is awful." I laughed. "You're sure this will work?"

He nodded. "I'm very sure."

The tension I'd held in my shoulders floated away. "Then it's all yours for as long as you need it."

"Thank you. I appreciate you letting me rent this out."

"Oh, I'm not letting you pay."

Hunter frowned and crossed his arms over his chest. "Maisy—"

I held up a hand to stop his protest. "No arguments on this one, Hunter. Please? I cannot charge for this room. It's far below the standard I want to set here, so please, don't try and pay me. Please? Please, please, please? I'm begging here. Paying for meals is important to you. This is important to me."

He stared at me for a long moment but then dropped his arms and frowned. "All right."

*Phew*. I had been practicing that speech all week.

"Thank you." I was exhausted and really should go to bed, but I didn't say good night and go home. Instead, I crossed my fingers behind my back. "I'm going to have one glass of wine before I go to bed. Would you like to join me?"

"I'd like that."

*Yes!*

When I turned, his hand found the small of my back. It stayed there all the way outside, back through the lobby and up the stairs to my loft.

"Beer or wine?" I asked.

"Beer."

"Okay. Make yourself at home."

He went to the couch as I hurried into the kitchen. The prospect of time with Hunter had given me a fresh burst of energy. I joined him in the living room, handing him his beer before settling into the corner of the couch with my legs stretched out in the space between us.

"So you had fun tonight?" he asked.

I nodded. "Yes, it was awesome. It was, like, the most beautiful wedding I've ever seen." The minute the sentence was out of my mouth, I automatically pinched my leg.

The sting in my skin was still sharp when Hunter touched my ankle. "What was that?"

"Huh?"

"Maisy, you just pinched yourself so hard your whole body flinched."

"Oh." My cheeks flushed but I waved him off. "It's nothing. Just an old habit."

His eyes softened. "Listen, I know I'm new in your life but I'd like to stick around until I'm not so new anymore. Part of that is getting to know each other. I appreciate that you haven't minded that I don't talk much about my family and life in Chicago. I know I haven't been forthcoming these last three weeks, but please believe me when I say, that's temporary. I want to give you that same concession, but you sitting here hurting yourself, that's not okay with me. You've got to tell me what's going on. Is it me? Did I say something?"

"What? No!" I sat up straighter. "No, it's not you." I closed my eyes and admitted the truth. "I pinched myself because I said 'like.' "

"Like?"

I nodded. "Like. I said, 'It was, *like*, the most beautiful wedding I've ever seen.' Like. A valley-girl like."

"Oh," he said, now understanding. "And how does that lead to you pinching yourself?"

I took a deep breath. I didn't want to get into the reason tonight but I could tell he wouldn't let this go.

"I used to say 'like' all the time. I never really noticed, I guess. No one had ever told me it was annoying, until Coby's father. The night he broke up with me, he said I said 'like' too much. He also said I was too young and he wasn't interested in putting in the time while I matured. All of this said right in front of my parents and brothers on Christmas Day. Anyway, I took his words to heart and I started pinching myself so I'd stop saying 'like.' "

It sounded crazy when I said it out loud.

For the first year after Everett's death, my thighs had been covered in tiny bruises, but the training had been effective. Slowly, I'd broken my habit.

"I still say 'like' every now and then. I don't care as much as I used to, but unfortunately the pinching habit is more engrained than saying 'like' ever was."

I studied my wineglass, embarrassed that I'd had to admit all of that to Hunter.

"I sound crazy."

"No. Not at all." His hand was still gentle on my ankle. "Maisy?"

I forced my eyes up.

"Say whatever the fuck you want, especially around me. But don't ever pinch yourself like that again. Understood?"

I nodded.

"Say it," he ordered. "Say 'I promise not to pinch myself again, Hunter.' "

I fought a smile. "I promise not to pinch myself again, Hunter."

"Good." He set down his beer, then slid closer. "It's late and I know you've had a long day, but I'd really like to know more about what that asshole did to you."

*That asshole.* Well, he had that right.

"It's not a fun story."

"I've got nothing but time for you. If you want to tell me tonight, I'd like to know. If you want some time, I'll wait for as long as you need."

I examined my wineglass as I considered my options. I could wait and tell Hunter about Everett when we knew each other better. Or I could tell him now. He'd been in Prescott nearly a month, and the more we were seen together at the café or around town, the more people would talk, the more risk I'd face that someone would feel the need to inform him of my past.

And I didn't want him to hear this story from anyone but me.

"All right. I'll give you the abbreviated version." I sat up straight, tucking my legs underneath me and making room so Hunter could sit even closer.

"Coby's father's name was Everett Carlson. He and I worked together at the hospital when I was a nurse. We started dating, and at first, everything was great. Then it wasn't. We broke up, and then I found out I was pregnant. He asked me to get an abortion because he had no interest in being a father, but I refused."

Hunter's jaw ticked as he clenched his teeth.

"He decided to kidnap me because I wouldn't get an abortion. He broke into my house and came after me in a rage. I tried to fight back, but he knocked me out."

Terrifying as it had been to have a crazed lunatic bust through my door and chase me around my living room, it hadn't done near the emotional damage as what had happened in the hospital. Still, when I'd had the chance to move out of that place and into the inn's loft, I'd jumped at the chance.

"He kidnapped my friend Gigi too and took us both to the hospital. We learned that night he was a drug dealer and all-around psychopath."

Hunter's hands were fisted on his thighs and his teeth were grinding.

"Easy there. You're going to chip a tooth." My attempt to lighten the mood worked.

Hunter's jaw relaxed a bit as he sighed. "Okay, keep going."

"When I woke up, he tried to force-feed me a bunch of pills. Gigi fought him off, and since he'd forgotten to tie me up when I was unconscious, I was able to find a scalpel on one of the storage racks. It was still in its sterile wrapper but those things are really sharp. I rammed it into his neck and then we ran away. When the cops got there, Everett had already bled out." I'd hit him right in the carotid.

The silence of the next few moments was unbearable. Hunter was fuming, I could feel the heat waves radiating off his panting chest, but he didn't speak. I wanted so badly for him to stay but I wouldn't blame him if he left. My baggage could fill an aircraft carrier. I wouldn't hold it against him if he wanted to find a woman who only traveled light.

"Maisy." My name was full of pain and pity. "I'm so sorry."

"You don't have to be sorry. I've replayed that night a

million times. I don't think there was anything else I could have done, but still, I wish it had ended differently."

Hunter placed his hand on my knee. "You did what you had to do."

"That's what I keep telling myself, but it doesn't make it easier. It doesn't make the fears go away."

His eyebrows furrowed. "What fears?"

"I fear the day Coby asks me about his father," I whispered. "What am I going to tell him? The truth? That I killed his father because the alternative was a forced overdose that would probably have killed us both?" I shook my head. "I can't tell him the truth, but I'll have to. This town is too small to keep secrets."

"When the time comes, you'll know what to say," Hunter said gently.

"I hope you're right." Since I was on a roll with my confession, I kept going. "Do you want to know what scares me even more? That people will talk about Everett and somehow Coby will bear the burdens of a man he never knew. And I won't be enough to shield him from everything. I won't be a good enough mother."

My throat closed and tears pricked my eyes. No one—not Gigi, not my brothers, not my mom—knew how terrified I was of making huge mistakes in Coby's life. No one knew how scared I was that Coby would suffer because I'd chosen a criminal for his biological father.

But Hunter got it all.

Now he knew exactly what he was getting if he chose to stay.

Taking the wine from my hand, Hunter set it aside and scooted closer. With one arm around my shoulders, he pulled me into his side. "You can't think like that, baby. If you can't see how wonderful of a mother you are to that little boy, I'll tell you every day. You are enough."

I leaned back, blinking the threat of tears away. "You called me 'baby,' " I blurted.

In the whole string of shining sentences that Hunter had just delivered, that one word stuck out as the brightest.

He grinned and pulled me tighter into his side. "Yes, I did."

"I liked it," I whispered.

He leaned down to smell my hair. "Good to know."

I untucked my legs and settled my head into his shoulder. With his hand gently tracing circles on my arm, his smell and warmth surrounding me completely, I drifted off to sleep.

The next morning, I woke up alone. Still in my dress, I sat up and found a sticky note on my nightstand.

*You are enough.*

# CHAPTER TEN

MAISY

I *will take him from you.*

My eyes popped open, but otherwise, I didn't move. I lay stiffly, staring at the nightstand as my heart pounded and Everett's threat echoed in my mind. The clarity of his voice terrified me more than his words. It was like he'd been standing right above me, bending to speak in my ear, instead of just an imaginary figment of a dream.

I stayed still for minutes trying to block out his voice, and when the shock of the nightmare slowly passed, I flipped off my covers and sat up on the edge of my bed. Closing my eyes, I took a few deep breaths and listened to the silence in the room.

*Everett is dead.*

*I killed him and he will never, ever take my son.*

*It was just a dream.*

When my heart rate was back to normal, I stood up and rubbed my hands over my face. "Well . . . that was new," I muttered to my dark room. Between my flashes when I was awake and Everett's voice now visiting my sleep, I really was losing my mind.

Reaching for my phone, I unplugged it and checked the time: 1:46 a.m.

There was no way I'd get back to sleep, not after that dream, which meant I was going to be exhausted tomorrow.

I opened the locked screen and saw that I had two new Facebook notifications and one missed call alert three hours ago from Unknown. I frowned and cleared the red dot on my phone app.

I'd been getting Unknown's phone calls at least once a day ever since the first call, and I'd become an expert at declining calls before they rang more than once.

Whatever. This flipping reporter could call all she wanted because I wasn't giving in.

Plugging my phone back in, I went to my closet for a sweater to pull over my tank top and sleep shorts. Then I went to the kitchen, flicking on lights as I went to make a pot of coffee. With a steaming mug in hand, I stood in the living room and assessed my loft.

Sleepless nights meant remodeling, but with my motel projects done, I could finally start on my own home. The ideas I'd been sketching and dreaming about for years were going to come to life.

And Coby's room was up first.

Mom and Dad had requested a grandson sleepover after Mom's Wednesday-night dinner so Coby was at their house tonight. It had been two weeks since Beau and Sabrina's wedding and now that the craziness was over, they wanted some quality time with Coby. Pickle was there too so he could start his puppy training with Dad first thing in the morning.

With the loft to myself and some hustle, I could have Coby's room tarped and the ceiling painted before I needed to get to work. Then tomorrow, I could juggle my schedule a bit to paint the walls while he was at daycare.

He was going to be so excited. I couldn't wait to see Coby's face when he came home to blue walls, and just thinking about his smile gave me one.

Coby's room was going to have an antique car theme. Because Dad loved antique cars, he'd turned Coby on to them too. My son wanted nothing more than to be like his gramps and the two of them had been collecting old license plates lately. I'd been stashing them in my closet to hang on the walls as decorations. Those, along with the bunk bed Beau was going to build Coby, would make this place my son's little sanctuary. He'd have steps in lieu of a ladder to his bed and a play space underneath the bed with shelves for his books and toys.

It was going to be awesome, and the prospect of diving in gave me a second wind. Who needed sleep? *Not this girl.* She was going to paint.

Slugging back more coffee, I set down my cup and went downstairs to my office for supplies. Since Hunter was staying in the housekeeper's room, my office had now become my renovation supply closet.

With drop cloths, rollers and ceiling paint in hand, I carted it all upstairs. Then I came back down for my ladder. Coby's bed and dresser got pushed to the middle of the room. His toy baskets and beanbag chair got tossed on top of the pile. Then I covered the heap in plastic.

I went back to the kitchen and swallowed a few big gulps

of my cold coffee before propping open the outside door and opening all the windows. Stripping off my sweater, I went back to Coby's room and filled my paint tray. I set the ladder up as close to the middle of the room as I could manage and climbed up. Balancing the paint tray in one hand and my coated roller in the other, I let the back and forth motion soothe my stresses away.

Painting had become my favorite coping mechanism.

I'd thrown myself so completely into fixing up this building it had allowed me to bury my troubles. How was I going to deal with the flashes, strange dreams and sleepless nights when my renovation projects were done? Once the loft was remodeled, I'd be out of wall space to recolor.

I needed to find a new distraction.

Maybe I'd take up reading. All my friends were avid readers—Sabrina was even an author—but I'd never had a passion for the pastime. The idea was appealing though. I could escape Everett by disappearing into a book.

I'd be willing to give it a shot, but thankfully right now, I still had my painting.

I coated my roller again and stepped up another rung on the ladder so I could stretch and hit the space above Coby's tarped bed. I was extended to the near-tipping point when a deep voice filled the room.

"What are you doing?" Hunter boomed.

"Ahh!" I screamed as my muscles jerked violently. The sudden movement caused my ladder to rock onto two legs and tip to the side, sending me flailing backward with my paint tray and roller still in hand. But before I could crash onto the floor, Hunter caught me at the waist.

He also caught my paint.

My tray flew up, tilting in slow motion as it turned over and coated us both in sticky white.

"Fuck," Hunter cursed as he steadied me.

My heart still racing, I spun around and pointed the roller toward his face, sending paint splatters everywhere. "You scared me! Again! What are you even doing here?"

His eyes narrowed. "I'm up here making sure you're okay. I heard a bunch of noise from my room. Remember? The one right down there?" He pointed to the floor. "Then I came up here and found your door wide open. What the hell? Anyone could have come in here. You keep that shit locked at night, Maisy. I don't give a fuck if you're painting. The door stays closed!"

"Oh, no you don't! You don't get to be mad at me. This is all on you." I used my roller to wildly showcase the disaster that was our mess. "Quit. Scaring. Me!"

We glared at each other while our chests puffed up and down. Slowly, the scowl on Hunter's handsome face turned up into a grin. The white of his teeth matched the paint all over his chest. I was still glaring up at him when he looked down at his ruined shirt, shook his head, then roared with laughter.

Hunter's unfettered laugh in his smooth tenor voice sent tingles rippling across my skin. His Adam's apple was more pronounced when he laughed. And sexy. Damn sexy. I was just as obsessed with getting my tongue on that bump as ever.

I couldn't hold my glare with his gorgeous smile so close. Giggles bubbled in my chest, and within seconds, I was laughing hysterically too. The sound of our combined laughter filled my loft, echoing off the walls in Coby's tiny room.

I was laughing so hard, the roller slipped out of my hand and crashed onto my bare toes, only making me laugh harder. For the first time in months, I laughed like I didn't have a worry in the world, just like Coby did when I tickled him.

I laughed like a happy woman.

A happy woman covered in paint.

Finally getting myself under control, I wiped the tears from the corners of my eyes. "Is it your life's goal to scare me to death?"

"No." He used his thumb to wipe a paint drop off my cheek. "My life's goal is to keep that smile on your face."

I opened my mouth but closed it before speaking.

*Heavens above.*

He hadn't even kissed me yet but I was totally falling for this man. I was falling for the way he made me feel precious. For how he saw the best in me, especially when I didn't see it myself. For how beautiful I felt when he was around, even in bed hair and wrinkled old pajamas and paint.

"You're blushing, Blondie," he whispered and stepped closer.

My breath hitched and the flush in my cheeks got hotter. My chin tipped up so I could keep a hold of his eyes. The brown was darker tonight, not their normal caramel, but more like milk chocolate. Even in the dim light, I could see the flecks of cinnamon near their centers.

"How determined are you to finish this painting tonight?" he asked.

"I don't, um . . . huh?"

His hand came up and tucked a piece of hair behind my ear. "I really want to kiss you but it's going to take a while. If you're set on painting, then we'll do that instead."

I swallowed hard. "Kiss."

The second the word left my mouth, his came crashing down. The soft heat from his lips melted mine open so his tongue could sweep inside. Hunter's arms wrapped around my back, pulling me tight and the paint on our clothes glued us together. Fisting the material of his T-shirt on his back, I held on as he plundered my mouth.

His tongue worked so smoothly against mine, stroking and exploring, that when he nipped my bottom lip, I gasped. Hunter grinned against my lips, then did it again, this time sending a pulse right to my center. We kissed for what felt like hours, standing locked together, until the paint on my fingers started to crack. When we finally broke apart, my lips were wonderfully swollen and I was desperate to fill my lungs with air.

"Hunter," I moaned on an inhale as his kisses trailed across my cheek and over to my ear.

"What do you want, Maisy?" His question was hoarse and rough, the vibration just making the ache in my core even stronger.

"You. I want you." I dropped his shirt in my hands and trailed my palms down to his firm ass, giving it a hard squeeze.

He growled in my ear, pressing his erection against my hip, then bit the sensitive spot behind the hinge of my jaw. The sting made the throbbing between my legs nearly unbearable.

My hands left his ass and came to the hem of my sticky tank. I leaned back to yank it up my torso but Hunter's hands came down on mine. "Let me."

I dropped the sticky cotton and let him take the hem. With one fast tug, I was naked from the waist up. My nipples were already pebbled from our kiss, but the cool air drifting in from the windows made them prickle. Hunter's large hands cupped both of my breasts, squeezing the soft, small curves as he dragged his thumbs across my nipples.

"Close your eyes," he ordered.

I obeyed, shuddering as he kept at my breasts. With every squeeze, every tug, every roll, the throbbing at my core intensified until I was dizzy. When one of his hands ran down my stomach and into the waistband of my shorts, I knew he'd find me wet.

His fingers slipped between my folds, circling my entrance and bringing the wetness up to my clit. When he gave my bud two flicks, I nearly collapsed. Hunter's other arm abandoned my breast and banded around my back, holding me up as his long and talented middle finger continued dipping in and out.

My head fell back, my neck limp, when his mouth closed over my nipple. "Hunter," I gasped. His teeth nipped, then sucked hard and my pussy clenched once around his finger. I felt his smile on my skin before he slid two fingers inside and hooked them to hit the right spot.

"Oh my god." My legs gave out completely and his mouth broke away from my nipple so he could stand tall and keep me from falling into the paint-covered plastic.

"I've got you, baby."

I forced my eyes open and found my feet. "Bed. Let's go to my bed."

He nodded, and when his fingers slipped out of me, I squeaked. A grin spread over Hunter's face before he took a step back. Reaching behind his neck, he yanked his shirt over his head and dropped it on the floor.

At the sight of his bare chest, my mouth fell open.

Clothes did not do his body justice. Not even close. His broad shoulders were wrapped in sinewy muscle. His abs and narrow hipbones formed that perfect V. His washboard stomach was so defined I could run my paint roller over the top and miss all the grooves that separated the squares.

"Your feet are soaked," he said.

"What?" I blinked, breaking eye contact with Hunter's chest to look down. White paint was pooling between my toes from the roller I'd dropped on them earlier.

Before I could bend down to wipe them off, Hunter dropped to his knees. Using his own gray T-shirt, he carefully cleaned my feet. When they were no longer coated, just lightly smeared with white, he looked up.

I was a goner.

Those eyes. That soft and loving look behind his dark lashes. I was totally flipping gone for this man.

My palms took his face. My fingertips combed through his short beard. My hands traveled up his cheeks into his hair. With one tender pull, I took out the elastic tie and smiled as his wavy locks fell to just past his shoulders. Threading my fingers close to his scalp, I combed his soft tresses, tugging hard enough for his eyes to flare.

I only got that one pass through his hair before Hunter stood, planting his shoulder in my belly and picking me up in a fireman's hold.

"Hunter!" I giggled as he carried me across the hall to my bedroom. With one toss, I was on my back in the center of my strewn sheets. I pushed up on my elbows as Hunter stripped off his jeans, then the white boxer briefs beneath.

Entering the bed on his knees, he planted a hand on my sternum and pushed me back. His hands came right to my shorts, roughly dragging them down my legs and tossing them to the floor. Tracing the skin on my calves, he trailed his gentle hands up to my inner thighs.

He was torturing me. Rubbing up and down, back and forth on the inside of my legs but never getting close to my throbbing core. By the fifth pass, I started writhing on the bed.

"Hunter. More."

His hands froze, his eyes locked on mine as he roughly grabbed my knees and thrust them apart. I nearly came undone. He spread me wide, making room for his hips, and slowly came down on top.

"Eyes on me, baby."

I nodded as my breath came in labored gulps.

"Watch us together." His hips pressed into mine and he ground his erection right into my clit, making my hips buck.

"Condom?" he asked.

My heart sank as the air rushed from my lungs. I didn't have condoms.

*Wait. Yes, I did!*

I'd found an unopened box of condoms in a guest room last year and I'd stashed them in my nightstand. I'd kept them, wishfully thinking that one of my blind dates would pan out and I'd need them.

*Thank god.* If that guest ever came back, he'd get his room at a discount.

"There's a box in my drawer," I breathed, grinning at Hunter's handsome face.

He grinned back before leaning over and rifling through the nightstand, ripping open the box. Using his teeth, he tore open the foil packet and rolled on the condom before coming back down on top of me.

Hunter's grin got bigger as he reached between us. With

his thick cock fisted in his hand, he worked it up and down my slit. A shudder rolled down my spine with every stroke. My eyelids were heavy but I fought to keep them open so I could watch us together, like he'd instructed.

"I'm going to fuck you now, baby. I'm going to fuck you and you're going to say my name when you come." Hunter's dirty words made my pussy clench again. "Ready?"

I nodded and tensed, waiting for him to push inside. I never enjoyed this part—a man's first thrust. It would always get better but not until the painful stretch at the beginning had burned away.

Our eyes were locked and his hand was still working his cock between us, but he wasn't coming inside. What was taking him so long? I lifted my hips, hoping it would move him along, but he pulled back his hips from mine.

"Take a breath, Maisy."

I did, in and out with a quick puff.

His eyes narrowed. "Take a deep breath this time."

I obeyed again, filling my lungs so completely my chest rose and brushed against his.

"What's wrong?" he asked as I exhaled. "Do you want to stop?"

I shook my head. "No. It just, um, hurts at the beginning."

His eyes softened as his lips dropped to mine. "Not this time."

Then he kissed me, slow and wet. His tongue worked so smoothly against mine, I closed my eyes and just let him take over. So lost in his kiss, I didn't have the chance to tense or brace before his cock slid slowly inside, filling me completely. The stretch was still there but it didn't hurt. It was . . . incredible.

"Fuck, you feel good," Hunter groaned, breaking apart from my lips to hover above me.

I hummed my agreement and kept my eyes locked with his as he moved. He pulled out his cock, leaving just the tip inside, then pushed back in with a measured stroke. He did it three more times before he did exactly what he'd promised. He fucked me until every one of my muscles was trembling and his name was the only thing on my mind.

My orgasm built fast and right before I came, Hunter's thrusts got harder. "I'm—" I couldn't finish my sentence, the buildup was too powerful.

"My name. You say my name, baby."

He didn't even need to ask. When my climax broke, I cried out his name as my neck arched into the pillow. Fisting the bedsheet, I rode out my pulsing orgasm as it hit me with wave after wave of heat.

"You are so fucking beautiful," he grit out as his strokes got even faster.

After the longest and most intense orgasm of my life, I opened my eyes and found Hunter's, wanting to see what he looked like when he came. When his legs started shaking and the cords in his neck bunched tight, I refused to blink. My hands slid up his arms braced at my sides, dipping into the contours as they traveled, and then into his hair. I pinned it back with a tight fist so it wouldn't get in the way of my view.

And what a view.

When I tugged his hair, Hunter's jaw clamped shut and he came with a rich moan from deep within his chest. It was magnificent. Planting himself deep, Hunter collapsed onto my chest. Then he slid his hands under my back and held me tight. My hands untangled from his hair and traced patterns on his back.

*Heavens above. Did that just happen?* I stared up at my ceiling, replaying everything until it all sank in. Hunter and I had just had totally freaking awesome sex.

How had I gotten so lucky that this man had walked into my motel?

I didn't have an answer but I was grateful regardless.

With Hunter's hair free from my grasp, it draped around our faces as we relaxed. The smell was so clean and familiar that I took a few deep breaths trying to place it. It wasn't the complimentary shampoo and conditioner I left in the rooms. I knew from cleaning that he'd been using those when he was in room eight. No, this was different. It was a smell I remembered from my high-school days.

"Herbal Essences?"

Hunter chuckled and lifted up. "I give you an incredible orgasm and the first thing you ask is my brand of shampoo?"

I smiled. "I'm right, aren't I?"

He answered with a wink.

Then he kissed me softly and sweetly with light brushes of his lips. Sliding out, he stood to his full naked glory and held out a hand to help me off the bed.

"Come on." Pulling me behind him with our fingers threaded, we went to my bathroom to shower off the sex and paint. When we were clean, we came back to my bedroom for clothes.

"Do you need to paint or do you want to try and get some sleep?" Hunter asked, pulling on his briefs.

Sleep. Except I couldn't leave Coby's room like it was. "I need to paint."

Standing at my closet with my back to him, I stepped into clean panties and tugged on an old tank top. Then, nervous to face him, I spoke to my hanging clothes. "Don't, um, feel like you have to stay. It's late and I'm sure you're tired. I can handle painting on my own and I'm sure you want to sleep in your own bed."

I held my breath, waiting for his response. I desperately wanted him to stay, to prove that he wasn't like the photographer that had screwed me, then run away, but if Hunter wanted to leave, I wouldn't be upset. It was late, after all.

*I will not be upset.*

His footsteps came my way and then he wrapped me in his arms. "I know we just started but I'm all in, Maisy. I'm serious about you. And serious means I'm helping you paint your son's ceiling. It means, when we're done, we're going to sleep together in your bed. And serious also means that, at some point, I want you to feel comfortable introducing me to Coby as the man that sleeps in your bed every night."

Lucky. I was a lucky girl.

"I'm all in too."

"Good." He hugged me tighter and pressed his lips to my neck.

Then he let me go and we painted Coby's ceiling in our underwear.

# CHAPTER ELEVEN

MAISY

"Stop!" I shouted, struggling to get free from Hunter's grip.

I was thirty seconds away from peeing my pants.

He was sitting on top of my hips and his hands had my wrists pinned above my head while Coby was relentlessly tickling my ribs.

"Get her, Coby!" Hunter yelled over my laughing cries.

My son's fingers dug in harder, then traveled up to my armpits.

"No!" I squealed and twisted, trying to escape, but my struggle was pointless. Hunter was too big and I was laughing so hard I could barely breathe. Tears were running down my temples and into my hair. The corners of my jaw were aching and every muscle in my core was flexed tight.

"Okay! Okay. Stop! Oh my god, stop." My bladder was about to give way.

Coby took pity on me and stopped his tickling but

Hunter didn't let me up. "Who gets to eat the last two cookies?"

"You do," I panted. "You guys get the last two cookies. I give up."

Hunter was off me in a flash, standing up and raising his arms triumphantly in the air. "We won!" Then he bent down to give Coby a high five. "Good job, bud."

Coby smacked his hand into Hunter's, then started singing, "Mommy is the loser. Mommy is the loser," and danced around me still lying on the floor.

"Yeah, yeah," I muttered, wiping my eyes dry. "You guys won. Again."

It had been two weeks since Hunter and I had started sleeping together, and in that time, he and Coby had bonded even closer. Their new favorite thing was to gang up on me. Everything was a vote these days. Games. Movies. Even the dinner menu. I'd become a perpetual loser, outvoted two to one every single time. Whenever I'd try and put up a fight, I would get tickle-tortured until I'd cave.

"This is so not fair," I told Hunter, faking a pout.

He shrugged and smiled down at me still on the floor. "Boys rule, girls drool."

"Oh my god." I rolled my eyes as Coby started singing that instead.

I smiled, not really minding that I was constantly outvoted if it brought Hunter and Coby closer together. Besides, I was having fun too. I'd laughed to tears more times in two weeks than I had in all my twenty-nine years combined.

With his victory smirk in place, Hunter stretched out a hand to help me off the living room floor.

"Thanks." I smoothed out my hair, getting rid of the

static from the carpet, and then straightened my chambray shirt. When Hunter wasn't looking, I quickly tugged my panties and khaki shorts out of my butt crack.

"Okay," I said. "That was fun and all but I've got to get going. Coby, you're going to be a good boy for Hunter, right?"

"Yep!"

"He always is." Hunter ruffled Coby's hair. "We'll be fine."

"You're sure you don't mind bringing him to the rodeo? I can always bring him with me now. He can just hang out in Mom's booth and—"

Hunter swooped down and cut me off, brushing his lips against mine for a chaste kiss. "Go. We'll see you in a couple of hours."

I sighed. "All right."

Dashing to my room, I slipped on my light-blue tennis shoes and donned some silver hoop earrings. After clasping on my favorite necklace, a simple silver chain with Coby's initials etched into a silver disk, I walked back toward the living room.

I stopped in the hallway at the sight on the couch.

Hunter was in the middle of the sectional, the TV remote in one hand as he scrolled through cartoon channels. His other arm was wrapped around Coby, keeping him tucked right into his side. My son was smiling and bouncing his bare feet as they rested on Hunter's jean-covered thigh.

*Where is my phone?* That was a picture worth saving.

I smiled and pushed onward, rounding the couch to sit down next to Coby. "Hey, buddy." I patted Coby's leg so he'd take his eyes off the TV as Hunter hit mute. "We need to have a quick talk before I go. Do you remember a couple weeks ago when I told you Hunter was going to be my boyfriend?"

Coby nodded. "'Cause he gives you hugs and kisses and Eskimos."

"That's right." I bent forward to rub our noses together. "I was thinking that it might be fun for Hunter to start having special sleepovers. That way he could eat breakfast with us. What do you think?"

My eyes darted up to Hunter's surprised face as Coby started shouting.

"Yay! He can sleep in my room!" Coby bounced into Hunter's lap. "You can sleep wif me!"

"Your bed is kind of small, bud," Hunter said. "Maybe your mom would let me sleep in hers? It's a lot bigger."

Coby stared at him for a second, considering his suggestion, and then looked back to me. "Can he stay in your bed, Mommy?"

"My bed? Hmm. I guess that would be okay. Good idea." I tickled Coby's side, causing him to fall into Hunter's chest as he laughed.

"Are you sure?" Hunter mouthed over his head.

I nodded. "I'm sure."

We'd spent almost every night together these past two weeks but I was sick of shuffling him out the door at dawn. He'd been patient, understanding I wasn't ready to introduce sleepovers to Coby yet, but the time had come.

We'd have a sleepover tonight after we made our relationship public.

Hunter and I had been enjoying the intimacy and privacy of our new relationship. We'd been getting to know one another in the comfort of my home, avoiding the café and other restaurants in favor of home-cooked meals at my small table. Rather than seek entertainment downtown, we had been content to spend evenings inside, playing games with Coby and watching kids' shows. And after Coby was fast asleep, Hunter and I would spend our nighttime hours making each other come until we'd both pass out, utterly exhausted.

No one knew I was seeing Hunter except Mom—who I'd begged to keep quiet—and these past two weeks, she'd proven that miracles do happen. Marissa Holt had kept a tight-lipped secret for the first time ever. As far as I knew, the only other family member who knew about Hunter was Dad.

The secrecy had worked for us, but now it was time to move forward.

Hunter and I were making our first "official" public outing as a couple at the annual June county rodeo.

I was nervous. Really nervous.

Knowing we'd get to come back for a sleepover would give me something to look forward to if the evening went to crap.

"Should we have pancakes in the morning?" I asked Coby.

"With chocolate chips?"

"Duh. And Mickey Mouse ears." He smiled and I leaned in to kiss his cheek. Then I stood from the couch and glanced at the wall clock by the dining room table. "I've still got a few minutes before I need to leave. I'm going to take Pickle out for a potty break."

"We can do it," Hunter said.

"It's fine. It won't take me more than a few minutes. You guys can go back to your cartoons."

He smiled at me before settling Coby back into his side and unmuting the TV.

I scooped up Pickle from his spot in the kitchen where he was gnawing on a rawhide bone. "Come on, puppy."

Taking him downstairs, I plopped him in the grass without his leash. His training with Dad was going so well he was now obeying "sit," "stay" and "come," so I didn't have to keep him leashed at all times to avoid him running away.

I followed him slowly as he let his nose lead him to the perfect pee spot. When he selected the place, he lifted his leg and did his business, then trotted up ahead to mark more grass. "Come, Pickle," I called when he was done. He bounded over and I scooped him up again to go back inside.

"Hello!" a woman's voice called out right as I started up my stairs.

I turned and saw one of my guests and her husband walking down the sidewalk, ready to cross the highway and head for Main Street.

"Hi!" I waved. "How are you? How is everything with your room?"

"We're great and the room is just so lovely. We're heading downtown to do some exploring."

"Sweet! Enjoy the sunny afternoon. If you're up for some fun later, you should check out the county rodeo. It's out at the fairgrounds." I pointed down the highway in the opposite direction from town and rattled off directions.

They both nodded eagerly, excited to check out something "Western" and then continued toward Main Street.

And I went back upstairs with a smile.

This time of year was hectic. Reservations were packed as closely together as I could fit them, and on any given day I had at least seven rooms to turn over. But the interactions with my happy guests made it all worth it. I loved being a part of family vacations, part of bucket-list trips. I loved helping people get acquainted with my hometown.

Settling Pickle back down with his bone, I collected my things from the kitchen. With my purse slung over my shoulder and an enormous box of triple-chocolate-chip brownies in hand, I came back to the living room. "All right. I'd better get going."

Hunter tipped his head backward. "Bye, baby. I'll text you when we get there."

"Okay." I brushed my lips to his. "My car keys are on the counter."

"Got it."

"Bye, buddy. Be good." I touched Coby's hair and got an absentminded, "Bye, Mommy."

I walked to the door and swiped Hunter's truck keys from the dining room table. The moment my hand touched the metal cluster, his phone, also in the jumble, lit up with a text notification. A text my eyes read without permission.

NELL: *What happens next is your fault.*

I BLINKED, unsure what I was reading. Then the screen went black.

Nell? Who was Nell? And why was she threatening Hunter?

I turned around to the couch to ask, but I closed my mouth before the words came out. I'd just invaded Hunter's privacy by looking at his phone, and as much as I wanted to know about Nell, I couldn't bring myself to ask.

Hunter was as private as ever about his past. During this last month, I'd been patient, waiting for him to open up about his family and life in Chicago, but I hadn't learned much because we spent so little time talking.

We spent our nights entertaining Coby and my son didn't care about Hunter's upbringing, career or family tree. And after Coby would fall asleep, I hadn't cared either. I'd been much more concerned about getting Hunter naked than deep, heartfelt conversations about his job or childhood upbringing.

Who was Nell and why was she threatening Hunter?

I was his girlfriend but I hadn't the first clue.

"Maisy, you're going to be late."

"Huh?" I jerked out of my stupor and focused on Hunter. "Oh, right. Bye."

I walked out the door and around the office to the parking lot in a daze. Climbing into Hunter's truck and adjusting the seat, I pulled onto the highway and headed toward the fairgrounds, still in a fog.

My mind was stuck on that text.

Was Nell an old girlfriend? Maybe a coworker from Chicago? God, could Nell be an ex-wife? The idea of another woman saying vows to Hunter made my stomach roll.

The text and the mysterious Nell were bothersome, but not as much as the fact that I'd put myself in this odd position. I was going to introduce Hunter to my friends and family tonight, I was going to bring him fully into my life, and I barely knew him.

*Shit.* I didn't even know what he did for a living.

I'd ask, "How was your day?"

He'd say, "Good. How was yours?"

I'd ask, "Did anything exciting happen at work today?"

He'd say, "Nope. It was slow. What happened here?"

And that was it.

We talked about me, the motel and Coby. He'd always put a priority on my life and my activities.

Was that weird? That I didn't know what he did for work? *Yes.* But it hadn't bothered me until today. I'd been learning other things about Hunter that had just seemed . . . more important. I'd learned that he did the voices when he read stories to Coby. I'd learned that he was allergic to shellfish. I'd learned that he never went a day without telling me I was special.

But tonight, things were changing.

Hunter had promised he was all in. He'd promised we were serious. So it was *seriously* time for him to start sharing more.

My time limit on the nosy questions had just run out.

I was so distracted thinking of all the things I wanted to ask that when my phone rang I didn't even acknowledge the name before hitting accept and pressing it to my ear. "Thank you for calling The Bitterroot Inn. This is Maisy, how can I help you today?"

"You can start by telling me how you murdered Everett Carlson."

My hand fisted the steering wheel with white knuckles.

*The reporter.*

"No comment," I said through gritted teeth, then pressed end.

Anger replaced anxiety and I shoved my phone back in my purse before ramming my foot down on the accelerator. Breaking the speed limit didn't help and I was still upset by the time I parked in the lot at the fairgrounds.

I stomped across the gravel parking lot to the arena. It was still early, the rodeo wouldn't start for another two hours, but all of the contestants were here tending to their horses and milling around. Passing the participant lot filled with trailers and large trucks, I crossed through the arched entrance of the fairgrounds.

Metal stands rose high above me and I could see snippets of the wide dirt arena on the other side. Underneath the stands were rows of boxed concession stands and one beer garden at the end of the row.

I wasted no time going right to my mother.

"What's wrong?" she asked as I tossed down my purse and brownies on the counter of her concession stand. Today, her quilting club was selling baked goods to raise money for the senior center and she'd asked me to help her get set up before the rodeo started.

I looked past her at the cash register to see a whole slew of her club members stacking baked goods on trays. "Nothing. I'm fine," I lied.

"Maisy Ann," she warned.

I sighed and opened my box of brownies. Taking out the biggest one I could find, I peeled back the cellophane and shoved a corner in my mouth. I needed chocolate before telling Mom about that reporter's phone call.

Mom frowned as I chewed, then turned around and walked to an ice chest. She took out a Coke and brought it back to me at the counter as I chomped bite number two.

I swallowed that bite, then popped the top on my soda, chasing my brownie with a fizzing gulp. "Thanks."

"Sure." She glanced over her shoulder to confirm we were alone. "Now, what's wrong? Did something happen with Hunter?"

I shrugged but didn't answer. Before I complained to her about my issues with Hunter's secrecy, I wanted to address them with him first. So she'd just get my rant about that snooping reporter. "This reporter has been calling me."

Mom gasped. "No. Not again."

"Yep." I nodded. "She's persistent. It's been over a month and she hasn't stopped."

"Who is she?"

"Heck if I know. I keep hanging up on her."

"Good for you," she said. "Just give it a bit more time. I'm sure she'll get bored and stop soon. And if it doesn't, you might have to stop by the sheriff's office."

"Yeah. I hope you're right and it doesn't come to that, but if it keeps up, I'll tell Milo or Jess."

"Good." She patted my hand. "Is Hunter still bringing Coby tonight?"

I nodded and went back to my brownie, this time taking a normal-sized bite. Then I walked around the side of the stand and through the narrow door, smiling and greeting all of the ladies who were unloading cookies, pies and more brownies.

Without delay, I got to work. Because work was good. Work meant I couldn't dwell on Hunter's text, his secret career or why this stupid reporter was so set on how I'd killed Everett.

An hour and a half later, I felt better. Every inch of the counter was covered in sweets and Mom's club had descended into full-fledged gossip mode.

"Did you hear they're getting a divorce?" one of the women whispered.

"After thirty-four years?" another gasped.

"I heard she's been cheating."

"Nooooo." That shocked the whole club.

I just shook my head and kept loading the register with cash. They were gossiping about my retired high-school math teacher whose wife had been having a secret affair with my retired high-school science teacher for the past six months. This I knew because they'd rented a room at the motel for one of their torrid rendezvous. Personally, I was glad Mr. Palermo was kicking his wife to the curb. He was a nice guy and deserved better.

I sighed as I loaded the cash register with bills.

The Palermo divorce wouldn't be the only topic of gossip tonight. The annual rodeo ranked second behind high-school football games for local attendance. Nearly the entire county would be here. Everyone would come to enjoy the event and talk about their neighbors.

The brownie I'd scarfed earlier wasn't sitting so well in my anxious stomach. What were they going to say about me and Hunter? How were my friends going to react to my secret boyfriend?

I'd find out soon enough.

Taking my phone from my purse, I checked the time. With less than thirty minutes to go, the arena was starting to fill with people. Hunter hadn't texted yet but I was expecting him and Coby any minute.

"Mom?" I patted her shoulder, stealing her attention from the huddle. "The register is loaded. I'm going to head out."

"Okay, sweetie. Thanks for your help and the brownies. Are you going to bring Hunter and Coby by later?"

"Sure." I smiled when she turned away and told her club mates that I was dating a "dreamboat." The women erupted into questions and excited clapping, but I ignored them all, waving good-bye and ducking out of the booth.

I made my way to the stands, smiling and chatting with people as I shuffled in line and up the ramp to the bleachers. Turning the corner, I stood at the base of the steps and looked for an open space.

Gigi spotted me at the same time I saw her above an empty metal row.

I waved and climbed the stairs. "Hello, Cleary family!" I gave my best friend a hug before doing the same with her kids.

"Maze," Jess said as he hugged me too. "Where's Coby?"

"He's coming. He's, um . . ." I looked to Gigi as I trailed off.

Gigi's beautiful face smiled down at me from the row above. "He's what?"

"Uh . . ."

Where did I start? I totally should have told Gigi earlier about Hunter. My announcement was going to come out of the blue and hurt her feelings, especially because it wasn't like I hadn't had the opportunity to share. Gigi visited me for lunch breaks all the time and we talked at least twice a week on the phone. But I'd stayed quiet this whole time. I'd even backed out of our girls-only pedicure night because I hadn't had the energy to deflect love-life questions.

But there'd be no more avoidance. Surrounded by a sea of people, I had chosen the worst possible time to spill the beans on my relationship.

How could I have thought this was a good idea a few hours ago? *Stupid, Maisy Ann. Stu-pid.*

It was too late to back out now, so with one deep breath, I blurted, "He's coming with a guy I've been seeing."

Gigi's smile fell at the same time Felicity and Silas shuffled into my row.

"Hi!" Felicity said, interrupting my explanation with a hug. "I was hoping you'd be here. It seems like it's been forever. We missed you at pedicure night."

"More like wine night," Silas muttered. "Hi, Maze." Felicity stepped past me so Silas could give me a hug, then handed over Victoria so I could give her a fast kiss before she squirmed for her mama. Handing her over to Felicity, I reluctantly turned my eyes back to Gigi.

Her arms were crossed on her chest and her eyes were locked on me.

"What's wrong with you?" Felicity asked Gigi, standing by my side.

"Oh, nothing." Gigi flicked out her wrist. "I'm just waiting to hear about this guy that Maisy's been dating. The same guy who she trusts enough to bring Coby to the rodeo."

"What!" Felicity spun on me and I cringed. "Who?"

"I—"

"Hey, guys!" I looked past Silas to see Beau and Sabrina join our group.

*Gah!*

We all shuffled, taking the time to exchange greetings and scoot down the row so our whole crew could fit together. The entire time Gigi stood stoically staring at me, making everyone else move around her.

While the kids crawled around parents' legs, the adults converged. Jess was glued to Gigi's hip, also waiting for my explanation. Felicity refused to budge from the seat next to mine as Silas peered on from over her shoulder. That left Beau and Sabrina unsure why Gigi was wearing her unhappy face.

"Okay, what's going on?" Sabrina asked.

"Spill," Gigi demanded.

I took another deep breath. "I've been seeing a guy for a couple of weeks."

"What?" Beau roared.

I flinched.

"Take it easy, Goliath," Sabrina said, patting her husband's puffing chest. "Let's get the story first. Who is he?"

"He's, um, new to town. He's been staying at the motel while his house is being built. We hit it off and have been getting to know each other."

"And why are we just hearing about this?" Beau clipped.

I ignored him and looked up at Gigi. "I just wanted to be sure. Before I brought him around, I wanted to be sure."

I wasn't ashamed of Hunter, not at all, and we really had been having fun just the two of us. But part of my reluctance to bring him around was because of more Everett baggage.

Everett had started getting weird right after I'd introduced him to Jess and Gigi. I knew now that his behavior had been because of Jess's job as sheriff and Everett's job as drug dealer, but old fears still lingered. I was scared that once I told my friends about Hunter, things between him and me would change.

Pain flashed on Gigi's face but she didn't speak.

"He's great," I said. "Really sweet and kind. He adores Coby."

"You've never kept a secret from me." Gigi's whisper broke my heart.

"I know. I'm sorry."

My phone dinged in my shorts pocket but I didn't

answer. It was probably a text from Hunter, saying they had arrived.

That ding meant I had minutes to apologize again and work things out with Gigi. All of our friends would give him the third degree tonight, especially my big brother, and before Hunter was fed to the sharks, I needed Gigi's forgiveness.

I needed her on my side.

"I'm sorry," I told her. "I know this is an awful time to tell you and I should have done it sooner. I'm stupid for waiting. Forgive me? Please?"

The group stayed quiet as my pleading eyes looked up to Gigi in silent apology. When her arms fell from her chest, I let go of the breath I'd been holding.

"What's his name?" she asked.

I opened my mouth but Milo and Sara interrupted. "Hey, guys!"

The seat shuffle started again, and when we were settled in our new arrangement—sitting this time—Sara leaned down from her seat.

"Maisy, why is Coby with Dr. Faraday?"

# CHAPTER TWELVE

MAISY

D*r. Faraday?*

"What did you say?" I asked Sara.

"Dr. Faraday," she repeated. "I was just wondering why he had Coby."

My eyes followed her pointing finger down the bleachers to Hunter and Coby standing at the base of the stairs. Coby had a huge smile on his face as he clutched Hunter's hand.

*Dr. Faraday* was scanning the crowd, looking for me.

"Do you know him?" she asked.

*Do you know him?*

Easy enough question. Did I know him?

No. No, I really didn't.

My palms felt clammy and the blood drained from my face as I stared down at Hunter.

He was still scanning the crowd with an easy smile. It grew wider when he spotted me but fell fast as he studied my face. Urging Coby up the stairs, he made the slow climb with his eyebrows worried in the middle.

"Maisy?" Gigi bent down to talk into my ear. "Are you okay? You got all quiet."

I shook my head but kept my gaze on Hunter.

"What?" she whispered. "What's the matter?"

"He's a doctor," I whispered.

"Uh, yeah. I assume since he's with Coby, he's your secret boyfriend?"

I nodded.

"Well, now I'm really confused why you didn't tell me about him. He's the guy we wanted to set you up with."

"But he's a doctor."

"Yes. We've established that."

"I didn't know," I hissed.

"What?" She was getting louder as she spoke right into my ear. "How could you not know?"

I spun around and motioned her close so I could whisper in her ear. "He doesn't talk about himself. Like, ever. And I've been trying to respect his privacy. Remember? You told me to keep an open mind?"

"Yes, but don't you guys talk? I don't understand. How did his job never come up?"

"I never asked, okay? And he never offered it. He comes over and we play with Coby. You know how it is with kids around. They dominate the conversation."

"True, but what about after Coby is in bed? Don't you guys talk then?"

"No." I leaned back to check that no one else was listening. "We don't talk because we're busy doing other things. You know, adult things? Then we fall asleep and he leaves first thing in the morning."

Hunter and I were in that stage of our relationship where we couldn't keep our hands off each other. Two weeks and I'd lost count of the orgasms he'd given me. In bed, I knew Hunter Faraday extremely well. Too bad I couldn't say the same for when we were fully clothed.

"So," Gigi whispered, "you've been too busy having sex with the hot doctor to learn that he was a hot doctor?"

I nodded.

She leaned away and muttered, "Eff," just as Hunter reached our aisle.

Coby pushed past Beau and Sabrina at the end of the aisle and climbed on my lap. He was only there for a second, simply using me as a platform to get up to the next row up. "Hi, Ben!" he cheered, joining the other kids as they played with some toys Gigi had brought.

Everyone else's eyes were on me, waiting for introductions.

I ignored them and simply stared at Hunter. What else didn't I know about this man who'd been sharing my bed?

Thankfully, Gigi came to my rescue. "Dr. Faraday! Glad you could join us."

His eyes left mine and he smiled at my friend. "Hi, Gigi. Please, it's just Hunter, remember?"

"Yes, of course. Hunter. Welcome."

"Thanks." His eyes came back to me and the lines in his forehead furrowed deeper.

Before Hunter could slide down the row, Beau stood and blocked his path. "Hi, I'm Beau Holt, Maisy's brother."

Hunter held out a hand. "Hunter Faraday. Nice to meet more of Maisy's family."

"More?" Beau shook Hunter's hand but turned his head to aim his question at me.

"He's met Michael and Mom."

Beau's lips pursed before he turned back to Hunter and released their shake. "Nice to meet you. I wish I could say I've heard a lot about you, but since my sister has been keeping secrets lately, I haven't heard a thing about you yet."

"Beau," Sabrina scolded, standing from her seat. "Let's not overreact. I'm sure she had her reasons." Sticking out her hand, she introduced herself to Hunter. "Hi. I'm Sabrina, Beau's wife."

Hunter smiled and took her hand. "Congratulations on your wedding. Maisy said it was beautiful."

"Thank you," Sabrina said. "We'd better let you sit."

Hunter was still stuck on the stairway, forcing people to squeeze by, but he couldn't get out of the way because Beau was still blocking the entrance to our row.

"Beau." Sabrina grabbed Beau's jeans pocket and tugged hard. "Move it, Goliath."

Beau slumped down into his seat so Hunter could shuffle between me and Felicity. "Hi." He wrapped an arm around my shoulders. "Everything okay?"

I shook my head and looked to my feet. If I looked in his eyes—those beautiful eyes that I saw each night before drifting off to sleep—I'd flip out.

Why wouldn't he just open up to me? Why did he have to keep secrets? After everything I'd confessed to him, why wasn't he willing to trust me with his past?

I hated how this was bringing back feelings from when I'd dated Everett.

Oblivious to my frustration, Hunter touched the back of his hand to my cheek. A doctor inspecting his patient. "What's wrong? Are you sick? You look pale."

I shook my head.

"Too much sugar at the bake sale." Gigi rescued me again. "So, Hunter, I know it's been a few years, but do you remember Jess, my husband?"

Hunter turned sideways and shook hands with Jess. "Hi. Good to see you again."

Before Jess could respond, Gigi kept at the introductions. "And do you remember my sister-in-law, Felicity Grant, and her husband, Silas?"

"Hi." Hunter waved at Felicity and Silas sitting on his other side. "Good to see you both again. The last time I was here you weren't married yet. Congratulations. And I see you're expanding the Grant crew."

"Yes, this is Victoria." Felicity bounced her daughter on her knees.

They all chitchatted for a few minutes, but all I could think about was that Hunter knew my friends. My stomach bunched tighter and I closed my eyes.

*Hunter knew my friends.*

And they knew him, probably better than I did. Hunter had said once that he'd been to Prescott before. That had been an understatement. He'd actually lived here. All this time, I'd been thinking he was new to town, that he'd only ever been here to visit once before, but all of my assumptions had been wrong. He was a part of the community. My best friend was his coworker. Jess and Felicity's mom had been his patient.

He was the "new doctor" I'd heard mentioned a year ago. He was the "new doctor" that had decided to move back to Prescott. And I hadn't been avoiding "new doctor" like I'd thought.

I'd been sleeping with him.

No wonder his name had sounded familiar the first day

we'd met. I'd heard it in passing around town.

*Damn it.* Of all the professions in the world, why did he have to be a doctor? And why hadn't he told me? That was a detail I'd needed to know.

"Hunter!" Coby launched himself into our backs, jolting us forward. "Is it time for hot dogs yet?"

"Not quite, bud. Let's wait until the rodeo starts and then we'll go get dinner. Is that okay with you?" Hunter asked me.

"Fine," I mumbled.

*Fine.* Things were far from fine.

Hunter was the doctor that had been hired into Everett's vacant position. He was the doctor my friends called Dr. Calvin Klein.

And I had been clueless.

I'd been dutifully respecting his privacy.

He'd been dutifully keeping me in the dark.

Snippets of conversations ran through my mind. I replayed discussions at the dinner table. All perfect times for him to tell me about his job or that he'd lived in Prescott before. Hell, I'd asked him point-blank at The Black Bull.

*"Have you been here before or did you move here blind?"*

His answer? *"I was here once."*

An understatement from a man committed to keeping me at arm's length.

Just like Everett.

And who was I? I was the stupid woman who hadn't learned her lesson from the first doctor she'd dated.

"Ladies and gentlemen," the announcer blared over the speakers. "Please rise and remove your hats for our national anthem."

We all obeyed and stood, crossing our right hands on our

hearts as we watched the rodeo queen ride her horse around the arena with the American flag.

"Coby, be quiet please." I twisted to give my order at the same time Jess shushed Ben.

As *The Star-Spangled Banner* filled the air, I took a few deep breaths, relieved for the inch separating me from Hunter.

The surprise of learning Hunter's job was fading. Now I was just mad and there wasn't a damn thing I could do about it.

I was going to have to suffer through tonight. As much as I wanted answers from Hunter, the rodeo—with all of Jamison County watching—was not the place to get into a fight.

So when the anthem stopped, I sat down, clamped my mouth shut and let Hunter wrap his arm around me again. Then I watched as the rodeo got into full swing and listened as my friends laughed and talked.

"How are you liking Prescott this time around?" Silas asked Hunter.

"It's been great," he answered, rubbing my arm. "I missed the slower pace when I was in Chicago. The year I was here before got me hooked."

"You've been gone for what, a year?" Felicity asked.

"Year and a half."

I closed my eyes and took a long, slow breath trying to calm my temper. What an informative conversation. Maybe I'd know more about Hunter if I had brought him around my friends sooner. The privacy he seemed to covet with me had vanished in good company.

"Do you have a house?" Felicity asked.

"Yeah, I'm building one up in the foothills."

"Up Fan Mountain Road?" Silas asked.

Hunter nodded. "The crew is actually finishing this week. I've been staying at the motel while they wrap up construction."

*Hey! Something I actually know about my boyfriend.* Apparently, the only thing he felt like talking to me about was his house.

"How are you liking the hospital?" Sabrina asked.

"It's great. One of the best I've worked at. It's small, but they've got a great setup." Hunter looked behind him and smiled at Sara and Gigi. "That and I've got amazing coworkers."

The conversation continued and, with it, my frustration. Thirty minutes into the rodeo, the event crew was switching out the barrel racing to bare-bronc riding and I was in desperate need of a break.

I stood and bent for my purse. "I'm going down to get some dinner."

Hunter rose from his seat. "Do you want help?"

"I'll get it for you," Beau said. "Coby, want to come with me to get hot dogs?"

"No, I'll g—"

"And chips!" Coby abandoned his playmates in favor of his uncle.

"Do you guys want anything?" Beau asked me and Hunter.

"I can go down, really," I insisted but Beau just shook his head.

"If you're not feeling well, you should stay. I'm hungry anyway. Be back in a flash." He hoisted Coby up on his shoulders and they descended the stairs, stealing my reprieve.

I dropped back to the bench and kicked my purse under my seat. Hunter's arm found my shoulders again and I aimed my eyes at the rodeo. A rider was settling on top of a horse in a chute at the far side of the arena.

A few minutes later, the buzzer rang and the chute's gate flew open as the horse came bucking out, its back hooves at least six feet off the dirt. The rider's free arm shot behind him for balance as he fought to keep his seat, but the horse was too much. With one hard buck, the rider went flying sideways, losing his hold on the rigging.

But before he could clear the horse, the animal turned and bucked again, slamming its hooves into the rider's side. The horse moved again, but the rider didn't. He lay unmoving with his face in the dirt.

An immediate hush fell over the crowd as people sat on the edges of their seats. All eyes were locked on the motionless body. The only movement was from the rodeo team who were corralling the bucking horse into the opposite side of the arena to release its flank strap.

At the same time the horse ran out of the arena, the county ambulance rushed in.

Hunter stood and dug my car keys out of his pocket, tossing them into my lap. "I'm going down."

"Okay." I nodded, grateful for that rider's sake that Hunter was a doctor. As I swung my knees out of the way, Hunter slid by. "I'll just leave your truck keys in the gas cap."

He acknowledged me with a wave right before he bounded down the steps two at a time. When he hit the railing, he planted his hands on the top bar and vaulted over the edge and down six feet into the dirt. Then he ran over to join the EMTs and assess the rider.

The stands were deathly quiet; even the kids had

stopped making noise. We all just sat perfectly still and stared as the emergency crew and Hunter strapped the rider onto a backboard and loaded him into the ambulance destined for the hospital.

The only relief came right before the ambulance's doors closed and the rider lifted up a hand and waved.

Hundreds of relieved sighs joined the early evening breeze.

"I hope he's okay," Sabrina said.

I nodded. "Me too."

We sat, leaning together, as the emcee asked for a moment of silence before the rodeo resumed.

The rider's accident dulled the crowd's mood and gave me an even stronger desire to flee. Gigi would want the full story about my relationship with Hunter, but I didn't have answers. Not anymore.

"I think I'm going to go." I grabbed my purse.

"Are you sure?" Sabrina asked.

"What? Not yet," Gigi said. "We need to talk."

I ignored their protests and waved good-bye. "I'll call you later. Promise."

Jogging down the stairs, I met Beau and Coby as they were coming up the ramp into the stands.

"Where are you going?" Beau asked.

"Home. Coby, bud, come on." I steered his shoulder in the other direction.

"But Mommy!" he whined. "I don't want to go yet."

I grabbed his hot dog. "I know, but it's time."

"Maze—"

I cut Beau off and kept walking. "I'll call you later."

He frowned but let me go.

"I wanted to play, Mommy," Coby protested as he trudged by my side.

"I know, but we're all done playing for today."

His mouth turned down and he started to cry.

*Shit.* Could I cry too? Now I felt guilty for ruining my son's night.

I stopped walking to kneel at his side. "I'm sorry, Coby. I really am, but we need to leave. I'll make it up to you. How about we get a cookie at Nana's before we go?"

He nodded and fell into my chest.

I wrapped him up for a tight hug before standing and taking his hand as we walked to Mom's concession stand.

"Hi!" Mom's smile fell when she saw my face and Coby's tears. "What's the matter?"

"We're leaving. Can I get a couple of cookies to go?"

"Sure." She went right for Coby's favorite M&M monster cookies. "Where's Hunter?"

"At the hospital with that rider."

She froze and looked back to me with guilty eyes.

"You knew," I guessed. "You knew he was a doctor."

She nodded and her face paled.

"Mom, why didn't you tell me?"

"I knew you wouldn't give him a chance."

I scoffed. "Yeah. You were right about that."

"I'm sorry, sweetheart. I didn't tell you at first because I wanted him to have a shot at winning you over. Then it went on so long, I thought maybe you knew and were okay with it."

"No, I didn't know." I took the cookies from her hand and shoved them in my purse. "How could you not tell me? You of all people? You saw how hard it was for me to deal with everything after you-know-who. I would have expected you to understand if no one else did."

She hung her head. "You're right. I should have told you."

I opened my mouth to keep on scolding but chose to shut up instead. Fighting with Mom always gave me a stomachache and I had enough to deal with already.

I was confused and angry.

I was scared.

Present emotions were mixing with those from the past and I didn't know how to sort them through.

"We can talk later," I muttered. "Come on, bud."

I led Coby to the parking lot, and by some miracle, I didn't have to walk up and down every aisle to find where Hunter had parked my car. I hit my key fob and its taillights flashed at the end of a row. We loaded up, and with Coby buckled and inhaling his hot dog, I pulled through the fairground gates and drove.

I drove home.

"Dad?" I called as I pushed inside my parents' house.

"In here!"

Coby ran past me to the living room. "Gramps!"

I found Dad in his recliner, wearing plaid pajamas and a threadbare T-shirt. A bottle of Budweiser was on his side table. It sat next to the TV remote and the empty plate of dinner Mom had likely made before she'd left for the fairgrounds.

Coby climbed up on Dad's lap, immediately thrusting him the remote. "Can we watch my shows?"

"Sure, Grandson." Dad pulled up one of Coby's recorded Disney movies.

"Cars!" Coby cheered and squirmed down off the chair,

stretching out on the floor with his chin propped on his hands, completely consumed by his favorite movie.

"What are you guys doing here?" Dad asked. "I thought you'd be at the rodeo."

I shook my head and sank into Mom's recliner next to his. "I don't want to talk about it."

"Okay. Is everything all right?"

I shrugged. "I'm just . . ." I searched for the right word. "Sad."

"What's wrong, honey?"

My eyes filled with tears at the same time the words came pouring out. I told Dad all about Hunter, leaving out the R-rated details and using a code name for Everett. But otherwise, I unburdened it all—from the moment Hunter had walked into my motel to him rushing to the rescue at the rodeo.

When I was done, Dad did what Dad did best. He didn't comment or offer advice. He didn't bad-mouth Hunter for keeping secrets. He just waved me into his chair for a cuddle.

And just like I'd done countless times before—as a sick kid, a girl with scraped knees or a pregnant woman dealing with a very heavy heart—I got up from my chair and snuggled into his side.

Because even at twenty-nine years old, I still needed my dad.

"It will be okay," he said to the top of my head.

I believed him. "You're right. Can we stay here tonight?"

"Like I've always told you, honey, this is your home. Come and go as you please."

I smiled and snuggled deeper into his chest, letting Dad's embrace settle my nerves.

Tonight, I was pushing my worries aside.

And when my phone rang with Hunter's call, I pushed it aside too.

---

*PINK. White. Red. Yellow. Orange.*

Pink was up next. I grabbed a pink petunia from the box and shoved it into the hole I'd just dug.

It was the morning after the rodeo and I was filling the flower bed underneath the sign at the inn. Coby was with my parents at Sunday school and I'd come back to the inn to immerse myself in work.

Stabbing the dirt with my trowel, I scored another hole in the earth and shoved in a white pansy. The midmorning sun had chased off the cool night air and sweat was beading on my forehead.

I'd woken up at my parents' house mad.

Fuming mad.

Mad at Hunter and mad at myself.

I'd let another doctor's handsome looks and charm fool me. I'd been so worried about driving him away with my natural curiosity I'd become complacent. I'd let a stranger into my home, my bed and my son's life.

Shame on me.

And shame on Hunter for feeding me so much bullshit over the past two months.

All morning long I'd been thinking about all the things I wanted to say. When a shadow fell over my face, I knew now was my chance.

Hunter was standing above me with his legs planted wide and his arms crossed over his chest. "Where have you been?"

I looked up, then back to my dirt, shoving in a red petunia. "Working."

"And last night? I was fucking worried, Maisy."

"How is that rider? Is he okay?"

"He's going to be fine. Now answer my question. Where have you been?" His shadow changed and I looked up again. His arms were hanging by his sides and his face was etched with worry.

I ignored the pang of guilt and dug another hole. "I was at Mom and Dad's."

"And they don't have cell service? Why didn't you answer when I called?"

"I needed some time alone to think."

"To think? About what?"

I stuck my trowel into the dirt and stood and pulled off my green garden gloves. "You're a doctor."

"Yeah. So what?"

"So what?" I mimicked. "In all this time, you didn't think to tell me about your work?"

"You were a nurse, Blondie. I *can't* talk about work. Patient confidentiality? The Hippocratic oath? Doctors kind of have to abide by that."

"You should have told me. I had to learn about it from my friends."

"I thought you knew. You know everything else about the people of this town. I assumed you knew I was the new doctor too. I mean, you talk to Gigi all the time. How did I never come up?"

Because I'd kept him a secret. "Well . . . it just didn't." My arms flailed as my voice got louder. "And you never brought it up. You never bring anything up! And since I promised not to be nosy, I don't know anything about you."

He frowned. "Yes, you do. You know a lot about me. Maybe not every detail from my childhood but you know the important things. Me being a doctor doesn't change that."

"It does." I planted my hands on my hips. "Hunter, I can't be with a doctor."

"What?" He was looking at me like I was crazy. "You're fucking kidding, right? This is a joke?"

"I'm not dating a doctor. Not again."

His jaw clenched. "I am not Everett."

"Well, you sure have a lot in common." My arms were flailing again. "He was the master of secrecy and you're just as bad."

"Don't hold his shit over my head." Hunter pointed at my chest. "I promised that I'd tell you everything and I will. I just need time."

My heart was racing as the words came pouring out. "Time. More time. Time to what? Time to use me for sex, then cut me out when you've had your fill? Time to work your way into my son's heart, then break it when you decide to leave? No, that won't work for me. We need to be done. I want to be done. We need to end this now before Coby gets hurt."

"Where the fuck is this coming from, Maisy? This is all because I'm a doctor? Because I have the same profession as the fucking asshole from your past? That's bullshit and you know it. This is you running scared and comparing me to Everett."

I shook my head. "This isn't about me. This is about you."

"The fuck it is. I am not Everett!" he roared.

"Then who are you!" I yelled back.

Hunter's anger vanished. "I'm the man falling in love with you, Maisy. I'm the man falling in love with your son."

Tears pooled as I whispered, "It's too familiar. I can't be with another doctor who keeps secrets."

"I get that, but I'm asking you to take a leap of faith with me. Trust me with your heart."

"So you can crush it?" That was unfair. I knew it the second it came out. The second before pain slashed across Hunter's face.

"If you really think I'd crush your heart, then you're right. You don't know me at all."

# CHAPTER THIRTEEN

MAISY

I double-checked the drop box, hoping I'd missed a note or something the first time I'd checked. It was empty. The only thing in there had been the key now resting in my hand.

Hunter had moved out of my motel.

I hadn't heard from him since I'd watched him drive away from the motel yesterday after our fight by the flower bed.

I shouldn't be surprised that he'd dropped off his key. His house was done and I'd known he'd always planned on leaving this week, but that didn't make this easier.

"Mommy, are you sad?"

I sniffled and swiped the tears away. "A little bit, buddy. But I'll be okay."

Forcing a smile, I bent down and kissed his forehead and then I put away the key on my pegboard.

"Come on, buddy. Let's go make dinner and play with Pickle." I guided Coby toward the stairs.

"Is Hunter coming?"

I shook my head. "No, he isn't."

"Why?"

"Just because. Do you think Pickle might want to go for an extra-long walk tonight? Maybe down to the ice cream shop?"

"Yeah!"

I followed Coby upstairs, glad I'd been able to dodge his questions about Hunter for one more evening. Answering them would just bring back the tears I'd been fighting all day.

---

"COME ON, Coby. Help me put these away, please." I was on my hands and knees, picking up Hot Wheels strewn around the living room.

He picked up a car and drove it across the carpet to the storage tub. "Can Hunter have a sleepover tonight?"

Another day had passed and I had spent all evening answering Hunter questions from Coby.

"No, buddy. Remember what I told you?"

"He's at his own house now," he moped.

"But we can still do fun stuff. After we get these put away, should we do a special bath? Maybe use a color bomb?"

"Yeah! A blue one!" He dropped the car and stripped off his clothes as he raced to the bathroom.

I closed my eyes and sighed. Two days since our fight and I hadn't spoken to Hunter. He'd called and left me a voicemail. He'd pleaded with me to call him back so we could talk.

But I'd stayed silent.

I'd thrown myself into work these past two days, hoping my normal pre-Hunter routine would help me make sense of everything. I'd hoped that after a couple of days, I would know what I wanted to say.

But for the first time in years, work hadn't helped.

No matter how hard I'd tried, all I could think about was Hunter.

He was on my mind while I scrubbed bathrooms and while I made beds. He was on my mind while I lay awake at night, unable to sleep.

All I'd thought about for two days was if I had the guts to take him back.

---

DAY three after my fight with Hunter and I was a mess.

My entire body ached, my eyes were rimmed with dark circles, and my stomach was so knotted I hadn't been able to eat.

But I was putting on a good front for Coby's sake. At least I was trying.

"Mommy, is Hunter still going to come to my T-ball game tomorrow?"

Tucking his blanket around Coby's shoulders, I sighed. "Maybe, buddy. But Hunter has a really important job and he might not be able to make it. Do you want to know what he does?"

He nodded and snuggled further into his pillow.

"Hunter is a doctor. He works at the hospital helping sick people. Sometimes that means he might not be able to hang out with us or go to T-ball games because he's working. But isn't that awesome? That he can help other people feel better? He's a superhero, helping other people kind of like police officers do."

"And Captain America."

I nodded. "And Captain America."

Coby's forehead furrowed. "But if all the people are better, Hunter can come to my game, right?"

I caressed his hair. "Maybe." It broke my heart that I'd put a wedge between Hunter and Coby, but before I could tear up, I changed the subject. "Now, tell me what you want to dream about tonight. Monster trucks? Dinosaurs?"

"Snakes!"

"Snakes! Blech." I cringed. "No snakes." I made a hissing sound and slithered my fingers along his neck until he giggled. "Good night, buddy. I love you."

"Love you too."

Kissing his forehead, I tucked him in tighter and then walked out of his room. As soon as the latch caught, my shoulders slumped. Every cell in my body was tired. The only thing three days of wearing myself to the bone had done was make me realize just how much I had overreacted.

Hunter wasn't Everett.

I'd been holding things against Hunter that weren't his fault. I'd been afraid of being hurt so I'd driven him away. But in these last three days, I'd learned I had something bigger to fear.

Losing Hunter.

Which meant the voicemail I was about to return was days overdue.

I went to the bathroom and brushed my teeth, then I put on some pajama pants and an old T-shirt to climb into bed. Cuddled deep underneath my covers, I opened my phone and touched Hunter's number. When the ringing started, my feet started tapping beneath my sheets.

*Please answer.*

By the third ring, the bouncing in my feet had spread up to my legs and the entire bed was shaking.

"Hey."

My legs stopped moving and tears flooded my eyes at the sound of his voice. "Hi," I choked out.

We both stayed quiet for a moment until Hunter spoke first. "I'm sorry, Blondie."

I inhaled a shaky breath and whispered, "I'm sorry too."

He sighed. "I miss you."

"I miss you too." Three days of stress and anxiety erased with just one simple call.

"I shouldn't have gotten so pissed on Sunday, and I really am sorry I didn't tell you I was a doctor. Please believe me when I say I honestly thought you knew. I mean, you're Gigi's best friend. You talk to her all the time. I've always got my phone in case I'm on call. I just assumed you knew and understood why I couldn't talk much about work."

I'd just assumed he was as attached to his phone as me and most other people in the world. "It's okay. I'm sorry too. It wasn't fair of me to compare you to Everett. I just . . . I hate secrets, Hunter. Everett was so secretive. I'm not trying to compare you. I'm just telling you why it scares me."

"I understand, and I know it's hard. There's a lot you don't know about me, but I'm begging here, stick with me. Please? Give us some time. Give *me* some time and I promise you'll know me better than anyone else."

I nodded into my pillow. "Okay."

Giving Hunter time wouldn't be a problem. These last

few days had been so miserable I'd do just about anything not to go through a separation again.

"Thank you," he breathed.

"Can you do something for me though?"

"Name it."

"Just tell me more about your day. I don't need patient specifics but just a little more about what your day is like."

"Done."

I grinned. "And no more one-word answers. They make me cringe."

He chuckled. "I'll do my best to use wordy sentences from now on."

It wasn't everything. But it was something. "Thank you."

"Are you in bed already?"

"Yeah. I've had a hard time sleeping."

"Me too, baby. This fight? I'm wrecked. I haven't slept since before the rodeo. Apparently, I need you in my arms in order to sleep now."

I smiled. *He needs me to sleep.*

"Can I come and see you tomorrow over lunch?"

I yawned. "Yes, please."

"How's Coby?"

"Good, but he misses you. He's been asking about you nonstop."

"I miss him too. I was planning on sneaking over to watch his T-ball game tomorrow."

"No sneaking allowed. Let's just go together." I yawned again but didn't want to hang up yet. "How's your house?"

He chuckled. "Empty. Really empty. I was giving you one more day to cool off and then I was going to come to the motel on Friday. My plan was to beg for your forgiveness and then bribe you with interior decorating to win you back."

"I like the sounds of this bribe. Maybe I'm still mad at you then," I teased.

"Well, I guess I'll have to give you my credit card and free rein to do anything you want in my house."

My smile got bigger. "Keep talking."

"I need furniture. All I have is a bed."

"What else?"

"All the walls are white. You can paint them any color you want."

I giggled. This man had me pegged. "Sold."

We talked for a while about nothing. I told him about my guests the past few days and Coby. Hunter told me how much he liked working at the hospital with Gigi.

When I yawned for the third time, Hunter deemed it time for bed. "You'd better get some sleep."

"Yeah. See you tomorrow?"

"Yes. Sleep well, baby."

"Hunter?" I asked before he could hang up.

"Yeah?"

"I'm falling in love with you too."

He sighed. "There. Now I'll be able to sleep."

I disconnected and set the phone aside, then I snuggled into my pillow with a smile.

It was still on my face when I woke up after a long night's rest.

---

HUNTER

"Hunter," Maisy gasped as her back bowed off the bed.

The second her orgasm hit, I grabbed her hips and

pinned her to the mattress as my tongue stroked her clit even faster. She bucked and twisted as her moans filled the room. The louder she got, the more I sucked as my fingers curled inside and stroked her pulsing walls. When she collapsed onto the bed, I abandoned her clit and started lapping up her juices while her body twitched with aftershocks.

"I missed your taste on my tongue." I kissed the inside of her thighs, then I lifted up to use the sheet to dry off my beard.

"Wow." Her eyes were still closed and her chest heaving.

I chuckled and got off the bed. "That was the best lunch I've had in days."

"Hunter!" She laughed and sat up, reaching for a pillow to toss at my head. "I can't believe you said that!"

"What?" I caught the pillow and tossed it back. "I'm just saying. Your pussy is a lot better than frozen meals in the hospital break room."

"Oh my god." She blushed and rolled out of bed, reaching for the panties and jeans that I'd stripped off the second we'd hit her bedroom.

"I have to get back," I said, "but I've got a light afternoon so I'll meet you here before Coby's game."

"Wait. What about you?" She stepped closer and dug her hands into the front pocket of my jeans. When her fingertips found my hard cock through the cotton, she rubbed the tip.

I hissed, my hips jerking back as my hands came to hers and stopped them before she could go any further. "Any more of that and I'll never go back to the hospital." I leaned down and brushed my lips to hers, knowing she'd get her own taste. "Don't worry. I'll let you make it up to me tonight."

She grinned against my lips. "I'll spend the afternoon thinking of something creative."

My dick got harder. After days without her, I'd be getting creative too. I just hoped she'd gotten enough sleep last night because she wouldn't be getting much tonight.

With her fingers laced in mine, she walked me down to the lobby. After one long kiss, she stood by the sign and waved as I pulled out of the parking lot.

Fuck she was beautiful.

She was the big fish.

That's what Dad had always said about my mom. He'd used fishing analogies to teach me about women.

*Catch the big fish, Son. And when you do, don't let her go, no matter how hard she fights.*

Maisy was going to put up a hell of a fight when she learned about my past. I just hoped she'd find forgiveness for me too. I wasn't just falling in love with Maisy Holt. I was head over heels.

If I fucked this up, if I lost her? My heart would never recover. So my timing had to be just right. I couldn't tell her everything too soon. Not until I knew she loved me and might be willing to move forward. I couldn't tell her everything too late. If I waited longer than absolutely necessary, she'd never get over the secrets.

Really, I should have fessed up years ago. But it was too late now so here I was, hoping that Maisy wouldn't ask me to leave once she learned the truth. When she learned about Nell.

Fucking Nell.

I dug my phone out of my pocket and hit her number. She'd called me all morning but I'd ignored her. She didn't have anything original to say, just more threatening texts and voicemail messages.

*What happens next is your fault.*

These conversations were always some variation of the same. Idle threats.

But this time around, I was calling her bluff. If she hadn't retaliated by now, I doubted that she would. I just hoped one day soon she'd get bored and move on to torturing someone else.

"It's about time you returned my call," she snapped after the first ring.

"What do you want, Nell? Your message said something about my stuff?"

"Yes. I found some of your old things today. I need to know where I should ship them."

"Donate them to charity. Throw them in the trash. I don't give a fuck. I told you already, I don't want any of it."

"Nothing? You want nothing?"

"That's right. Nothing." I had everything I already needed. I had clothes. I had my camera. I had my parents' wedding picture. I had the one picture of my dad and me fishing two summers before he died. I wish I had found Mom's wedding ring, but since it was lost, whatever else Nell had found in my old stuff, she could have.

"I can't believe this. I can't believe you!" she shouted.

"Believe it." I ended the call and kept driving.

She was pissing me off, but I wouldn't let it wreck my day. By the time I pulled into the hospital, I'd brushed off Nell's call and was ready to get my day over with so I could go to Coby's game.

"Someone had a nice lunch." Gigi greeted me as I walked by the counter in the emergency room.

I smiled. "Not too bad." *Pretty fucking delicious, actually.*

"Considering she just texted me and said you two have worked things out, I'm guessing that smug grin has to do with my best friend."

"It does."

She smiled. "Good. She needs a good guy like you."

Gigi and I had seen one another in passing this week but hadn't had a chance to discuss my relationship with Maisy. I'd been waiting for Gigi to comment, so I watched her for a moment, waiting, but she just stood there smiling.

"That's it?" I asked. "No interrogation? No threats about making her happy?"

She shook her head. "Not from me, but don't you worry. You'll get plenty of that from her brothers. If you hurt her, Beau and Michael will skin you alive. And I know for a fact that Beau could hide your dead body in a place no one would ever find it."

"Right." Message received. "I can't promise I won't screw up, but what I feel for Maisy is real. I'm doing everything with her feelings in mind and whatever I can to make her happy."

"See that you do." She slid an iPad over the counter. "I've input a few new patient notes for your afternoon rounds."

"Thank you." I took the iPad and walked toward the stairs, but before my feet hit the first step, I paused and turned back to Gigi. "She hasn't healed."

Gigi shook her head. "No, she's buried it all. She lets that motel run her life, and she focuses all of her energy on the Bitterroot and Coby. She puts on a smile. She tells everyone she's happy. But no, she hasn't healed. She doesn't even know what she's missing."

"I'll help her heal," I promised.

She studied my face. "See that door right there?"

I looked over my shoulder to the metal door that led to the basement—the basement where Everett had tried to kill the woman I loved.

"If you can get her past that door," Gigi said, "you might just have a chance. She's got to face what happened. She thinks she's a killer. She doesn't see that she's a savior. Make her see that, Hunter."

I nodded.

If it was the last thing I did, I'd make her see.

---

"HUNTER!" Coby sprinted toward my legs. "Are you coming to my game?"

I bent and caught him before he could crash into my knees. Then I picked him up and tossed him high. "You bet I am! I've got to be there to cheer when you hit a home run."

Coby's smile was infectious. As much as I loved Maisy, I was in just as deep with this boy.

I settled him on my hip and let him wrap his arms around my neck. "I missed you these past few days, buddy."

"I missed you too." He hugged me tighter. "Mommy said you were taking care of other people because you're a doctor. She said you're like Captain America."

Maisy was bragging me up? Now that felt amazing.

I looked over to her at the door and winked. "Thanks, Blondie."

She smiled and made my world a little brighter.

I squeezed Coby again, then set him down, smoothing out his Prescott Café T-Ball shirt. "Where's your glove?"

"My room."

"Go get it."

As Coby ran off, I bent down to pick up Pickle, who was attacking my feet. This was a good day. Even the dog had missed me. I set Pickle back down and I stepped over to Maisy, pulling her into my side.

"No more nights apart. Even if we fight, we've got to work it out. I can't be gone from you guys for this long."

Her head fell into my chest and her hand slipped into my back jeans pocket. "No more nights apart."

I kissed her temple and let her go just as Coby came barreling back down the hall. "Ready!"

After depositing Pickle in his crate, I took the keys to Maisy's car and loaded up my girl and my boy to drive them to the T-ball game.

"Uncle Beau!" Coby shouted the minute I lifted him out of his car seat.

"Coby, remember you have to call him Coach Holt tonight," Maisy said, stepping out of the 4Runner.

"Oops." He giggled. "Coach Holt!"

"Wait, wait, wait." Maisy grabbed Coby's hand before he could go running off. "You're in a parking lot."

He smacked his palm to his forehead. "Whoops. I forgot."

"Goofball," Maisy teased. "Come on. Look both ways, then we can go."

She slipped her hand in mine and we crossed the gravel parking lot.

I scanned the people standing in huddles on the green grass and recognized a few faces. I spotted Beau and Jess, the team's co-coaches, talking to a group of guys leaning against the chain-link fence that bordered the field. Gigi and her girls were sitting on a wooden bench while Ben was lapping the bases with a couple of other kids.

"This is a nice complex," I told Maisy as we walked.

"I think so too. Prescott might not have a lot of kids, but the community is great about supporting the teams we have."

It was one of the things I loved about this town. It was one of the many things I loved about Maisy. The pride she had in her town. The pride she had in The Bitterroot Inn. She'd worked hard to create a place that the citizens of Prescott cherished.

And they didn't just love her motel. They loved her.

Over the last few days, word that Maisy and I were together had spread like wildfire. Oblivious to our fight, all of the patients I'd seen in the last four days had done nothing but sing her praises.

"You know, you're a part of that," I told her. "People take a lot of pride in what you've done at the motel."

"Oh, I don't know," she told her flip-flops. "I think people are still waiting for me to fail."

I shook my head, wishing she knew just how special she was. "They're proud of what you've built."

She shrugged and waved to her parents, who were setting up camp chairs in the grassy rise behind home plate.

I dropped the motel conversation but silently vowed to make her see just how remarkable she was. Just like I'd been telling her over the last month how lucky Coby was to have her as his mom.

In time, I'd make her see it all.

"Hi, guys!" Marissa said as we reached their spot. She finished laying out a huge denim blanket on the grass, then came over to Coby for a kiss on his cheek. She hugged Maisy, then turned to me. "I'm so glad you're here, Hunter."

"Me too."

Marissa gave me a hug, then looked over her shoulder to summon Maisy's dad. "Brock! Get over here and meet Hunter."

A large man, Beau's size but with an unhealthy belly, came walking over with Michael at his side.

I held out my hand as he did the same. "Mr. Holt. Nice to meet you. I'm Hunter Faraday."

He grabbed my hand and shook it back with two hard pumps. "Brock Holt. Glad you could make it."

He let me go and I held out my hand to Michael. "Good to see you again."

"You too. Glad you could make it."

Both of the Holt men gave Maisy a hug, then doted on Coby.

"Remember," Michael told his nephew, "you've got to hustle to first as soon as you hit the ball. Don't stop. Run *through* the bag."

Coby nodded. "I practiced with Un—Coach Holt."

"And don't forget, Grandson," Brock said. "They might not be keeping score, but I am."

"Dad," Maisy scolded at the same time my eyes snapped to Brock.

"What?" I asked. "They're not keeping score? Then who wins?"

"Exactly!" Brock boomed, throwing up his hands. "Who the hell knows? Why wouldn't you keep score? Teach these kids about winning and losing. Nope, everyone here is a winner."

"Now, Brock. Don't get all worked up," Marissa said.

"Too late," Michael muttered as Brock completely ignored his wife and started telling me all about the problems with children's sports in today's society.

"Shoot," Maisy muttered, standing as the teams on the field got ready to start the game. "I forgot the waters in the car. Keys?"

I dug them out of my pocket and dropped them in her outstretched hand.

"Be right back."

When she was out of earshot, Michael looked over his shoulder from his seat below me. "Beau will give you the full lecture, but I'll just say this: if you hurt my sister, I'll help him hide your body."

Gigi hadn't been far off on her warning today.

"I won't hurt your sister." I didn't care that her brother was threatening me. I was glad Maisy had such a loyal family. I looked to my right at Brock, expecting the same type of warning, but he just shook his head.

"You won't get a warning from me. My boys will take care of their sister, but I will say this." He leaned closer to speak softly. "My girl, she needs to know it's safe to fall in love. She needs to see that she can trust a man. Be that man for her, Hunter. Protect her from the shit in this world. God knows, she's seen enough. It's time for her to get some peace."

I nodded and turned back to the T-ball game, where Coby and his team were practicing on the field while the opposing team was huddled by their dugout.

When he looked over, Coby waved the ball and shouted, "Watch this, Hunter!" He wound up and threw from second plate to first with all his might. It made it about three-quarters of the way there before hitting the dirt and rolling to a stop.

I clapped and cheered, "Good job, buddy! Nice toss!"

He beamed and I waved again.

*That kid.* He was amazing.

When my eyes met Brock's, his thoughts were transparent.

He didn't just want a man for his daughter. He wanted a father for his grandson.

I nodded.

That man would be me.

# CHAPTER FOURTEEN

MAISY

Two days after the T-ball game, Coby and I were standing in the middle of Hunter's empty living room.

"What do you think?" Hunter's voice echoed in the open space.

I spun around and took it all in. Dark hardwood floors. Exposed beams in the vaulted ceiling. Rough-cut stone surrounding the fireplace.

"It's beautiful." The crew at Jamison Valley Construction had outdone themselves. "I know it took longer than you'd hoped, but I'd say if this is the end product, it was well worth the wait."

Hunter smiled. "I'm glad you like it."

"Hunter, watch this!" Coby shouted before whizzing one of his Hot Wheels across the bare floor. Because there was no furniture to block its path, the car zoomed all the way from the kitchen, through the space where a dining room table belonged and over to us in the living room.

"Nice!" Hunter knelt on the floor and caught the car, revved it up and sent it speeding back.

"Are you sure you want me to decorate?" I asked. "Furniture would ruin your racetrack."

Hunter grinned and stood. "Nah. We'll just race around it. Huh, bud?"

Coby nodded as he backed up to the farthest wall in the kitchen and sent the car flying again.

While Hunter raced the car a few more times, I explored the rest of the main room. I loved the open floor plan. I loved the enormous island that separated the kitchen space from the dining area and the light-gray cabinets. I loved how much natural light flooded in from the abundance of windows.

I loved this house.

Except for the plain white walls—something I'd happily fix—this was a dream house.

"Should we finish the walk-through?" Hunter asked.

"Yes, please." I ran my fingers across the cool granite countertops before following Hunter toward the stairs.

"Do you want to stay and play or come upstairs?" I asked Coby.

"Upstairs." He pushed off the floor and sprinted past me to catch up with Hunter, sticking close to his side while we toured the spacious second floor.

With each room Hunter showed us, I fell more and more in love with his empty house. The spare bedrooms were large and airy. The Jack and Jill bathroom that separated two of them was lit with a bright skylight. The bonus room above Hunter's four-car garage was enormous, perfect for a home theater and gaming room.

If I hadn't already been falling, the master suite would have won my love. "This is . . ." I didn't have the right word.

The far back wall was filled with windows overlooking the trees behind Hunter's house. The ceilings had been vaulted and an iron chandelier hung down from the center. Hunter's only piece of furniture, a California-king-sized bed, looked nearly too small for the expansive space.

"It's a big house," Hunter said, looking out a window. "Do you think it's ostentatious?"

I shook my head. "It's just right." While his neighbors had homes that screamed "money," Hunter's home was the perfect blend of lavish and comfort. All of the finishes were top-of-the-line—it was clear he had invested money here—but they were tasteful. And it wasn't *too* big.

"Bathroom?" I pointed to the door in the far corner of the room, then let my feet follow my finger. My jaw fell open as I took in the space. "This is nicer than a spa."

Hunter chuckled from the doorway behind me as I inspected the floor-to-ceiling marble tile. Then I opened the door to the adjoining walk-in closet.

"Okay. This is just not fair. Your closet is barely smaller than my entire bedroom."

"Let me see." Coby pushed his way past my hip and into the closet. He drove his car along the custom-built shelves, then came right back out. "Is it time for dinner yet? When can we get my cheeseburger?"

I shook my head and muttered, "No appreciation."

"Huh?" he asked.

"Nothing, little man. Let's go to dinner."

"Let's race! I'm gonna win!" he yelled as he raced out of the room and disappeared down the hall.

"Now that you've seen it all, are you going to help me make this livable?" Hunter asked as we slowly followed Coby.

"Totally." I smiled. "I'm super excited to spend all your money."

He chuckled and took hold of my hand. "What would you think about making one of these rooms up for Coby?" He pointed into a spare bedroom as we walked by its door.

My ankle rolled and I crashed into his side. Had he just asked us to move in here? Did he think we were ready for that big of a step? Because I wasn't. Not yet.

"For sleepovers," Hunter clarified as he helped me regain my balance.

"Oh, gotcha. Then yes." I nodded. "I'm sure he'd like to have his own spot."

"I don't want to rush things."

"Me neither."

"But . . . I'd like you to think about living here one day. When you're decorating, pick things you'd like in your own home. We need some time, but in the future, I want you and Coby with me."

I laced my fingers with his. "I can do that."

We did need time and I was glad Hunter recognized that too. While I had no intention of ending our relationship, living together would be rushing too fast. Yes, Hunter was practically living in the loft, but we still had separate homes. I wasn't quite ready to share an address.

Having sleepovers here, on the other hand? Those were starting as soon as the bare essential furnishings arrived. I couldn't wait to spend a night out here, then cook a big breakfast in his fancy kitchen.

"*Can* you live out here?" Hunter asked as I followed him down the stairs.

"What do you mean?"

"I guess I didn't think about the inn. Do you need to live in town?"

"Huh," I hummed. "I haven't really ever thought that far ahead. I figured I'd be in the loft until Coby was off to college and it was just me."

Hunter stopped on a step and turned. "It's not just you anymore, baby."

No. No, it wasn't.

Since he was at eye level, I leaned forward and set a soft kiss on his lips.

"Mommy! Hunter!" Coby yelled from downstairs. "Is it time for cheeseburgers?"

I kissed Hunter once more before he continued down the stairs.

"I don't think *I* have to be in town, but I do think it would be nice to have someone around the motel," I said. "Just in case. Someone I could trust in case of an emergency."

"As a manager?"

"I can't afford a manager," I sighed. "At least not until my mortgage is paid off. But maybe I could get someone to live in the loft and discount their rent if they kept an eye on things and called me if there was a problem."

*That could totally work.* How much could I charge for rent? Who could I ask to live there? As numbers and potential rental candidates started racing through my mind, I smiled wider.

Maybe I'd be ready to live at Hunter's sooner than I'd thought. The idea seemed less shocking than it had a minute ago. Now it just seemed like the right next step.

"Coby!" I called when we walked into the kitchen. He

didn't answer, just giggled from behind the island where he was hiding. "Coby! Oh, no, Hunter. We've lost Coby. I guess I'll have to drink his Oreo milkshake myself since he can't go to dinner."

"Here I am!" Coby shot out from behind the island and ran over to the front door.

I followed my son outside to get him into his car seat while Hunter locked the door behind us. As we slowly drove out of the long drive that met up with the main road, I watched through the side-view mirror as Hunter's house disappeared into the trees.

The cedar siding was stained brown, the perfect exterior for a home in the trees. The gables above the covered porch added a touch of soft elegance to the otherwise rustic exterior. The stone columns bracketing the entryway would look beautiful with barrels of flowers at their bases.

*Yeah, I want to live here someday.*

Not just for the house, but because with the house came the man.

I looked over at Hunter in the driver's seat and smiled as my phone rang in a center cupholder. Glad it wasn't Unknown—who had been as persistent as ever—I answered. "Hi, Mom."

"Maisy."

I sat up as straight as my seat belt would let me. "What? What's wrong?"

"You need to come to the hospital right now." Her voice was shaking. "Your dad . . ." She trailed off as she started crying.

"Mom?" My heart thundered. "What's wrong with Dad?"

"He . . . he had a heart attack," Mom whispered.

My hand flew to my mouth as I gasped.

"He's in with Dr. Peterson right now," Mom said. "They're doing some tests."

"But he's okay? He's alive?" I choked out the words as my eyes flooded.

"Yes," Mom whispered and started crying again.

*Thank god.* "Okay. We're on our way. I love you." I hung up and looked over at Hunter through blurry eyes. "We need to go to the hospital."

He nodded and hit the gas. "What happened?"

"Dad had a heart attack." Tears fell down my cheeks even though I was trying to hold them in for Coby's sake. But the idea of losing my dad was too much and my breath hitched with a loud sob.

My hand came back to my mouth to muffle my cries.

"Take a breath," Hunter said.

I nodded and sucked one in but it didn't help.

I couldn't imagine my life without Dad. I needed him. I needed him to help me raise Coby to be a good man. I needed him to walk me down the aisle if I ever got married. I needed his cuddles when I was feeling blue.

"Mommy?" Coby's panicked voice had me swiping furiously at my face as I took another slow breath.

"It's okay, buddy." I unbuckled my belt so I could turn around and rub my son's knee. "It's going to be okay."

He nodded but tears formed on his lower lashes.

"What did your mom say?" Hunter asked.

I turned back around and rebuckled. "Just that they're doing some tests."

"Peterson is on call. He's good." He reached for my hand and held it tight.

"Okay." Hunter was right. Dr. Peterson had worked at the hospital for as long as I could remember and he'd seen it all. Other than Hunter, I trusted him more than any other doctor.

"We can't take Coby," I whispered.

Hunter's answer was to reach for the phone in my lap and pull up a name. "Gigi, it's Hunter. We've got an emergency with Maisy's dad and need to go to the hospital. Can you watch Coby?" He listened to her for a second, then said, "Okay. We'll be there in a few." He hung up the phone and handed it back. "Where do I go?"

"Back to the highway, then toward town."

As Hunter drove faster, I said a silent prayer for my dad and pulled in another shaking breath before turning back around to Coby. "Buddy, we need to go to the hospital to check on Gramps because he's sick. Can you play with Ben for a while?"

He nodded as more tears fell. "Okay."

"Gramps is going to be okay," I told us both.

"Are you going to fix him?" Coby asked Hunter.

Hunter looked into the rearview mirror. "I'll do my very best."

*Please, let him be okay. Please. Please.*

My pleading prayer ran on loop.

We drove to the farmhouse in silence, other than me giving Hunter directions. When we pulled up, Jess and Gigi were waiting for us outside. Jess went right to the back to get Coby out and Gigi reached in through my open window for a hug.

"We've got him," Gigi said.

"Thank you." I looked over her shoulder to see Coby's head resting on Jess's strong shoulder. "We haven't had dinner yet."

She waved me off. "We'll take care of everything. Just go."

"Thanks." Hunter waved and then pulled out of the gravel driveway, pointing the car toward town. With one hand on the steering wheel, he let me clutch his other tightly on my lap. The closer we got to the hospital, the tighter my grip became. When we turned into the Jamison Valley Hospital parking lot, my entire body was shaking.

The last time I'd been in this parking lot, Jess had been driving me away from Everett's dead body.

My heart was racing and sweat was beading at my temples but a cold shiver crept under my skin. No matter how many breaths I sucked in, I couldn't seem to fill my lungs.

"You can do this." Hunter pried his hand out of my grip and opened his door.

*I can do this. I have to do this.*

Inside the hospital was my dad. I needed to be there for him. For my mom. For my brothers. I had to go inside a building that held all of my most feared memories.

My fingers fumbled with the car handle but I managed to get a grip and push the door open with my foot. The moment my tennis shoes hit the pavement, my knees weakened. Using the side of my car for balance, I shut the door and took one step. Then another.

*I can do this.*

Hunter came around the side of the car and held out his hand. "I'm with you the whole time."

I nodded and placed my hand in his. With every step across the asphalt, my feet got heavier. What little strength I had was used to just keep myself standing because the fear of crossing through the sliding-glass ER doors in front of me was dizzying.

"You can do this, baby."

I shook my head. "I can't."

"Yes, you can. One step at a time. Do this for your dad."

I could do this for Dad. "Okay," I whispered.

Crossing the parking lot was slow but we finally made it. When we hit the censor above the sliding doors and they slid open, the smell of the hospital hit me in the face and my stomach rolled. Five years since I'd been here, but I could still remember the smell. I could shut my eyes and pretend I was someplace else, but the smell wouldn't go away.

"Hunter," I pleaded. My feet were stuck again.

"One step," he said. "Just take one more step."

I clutched his hand tight and picked up my right foot.

"Good. One more."

My steps were barely a shuffle but he had managed to get me past the doors.

"Think about the good things you had here. Only the good things."

I nodded. *Good things.*

My eyes darted around the ER lobby. Ahead of me was the counter where I'd met Gigi on her first day of work. I'd been gossiping about Everett—about how handsome I'd thought he was and how I'd had such a crush on the new doctor. Young and stupid Maisy. I hadn't seen past his handsome to the crazy beneath.

My feet stopped again.

"Tell me a good thing."

I swallowed hard and looked up into Hunter's worried eyes. He knew I was about three seconds away from a full-fledged panic attack. All I wanted to do was close my eyes and run away, but as if he could sense me wanting to flee, he tugged his hand free of mine to wrap his arm around my shoulders.

"Tell me a good thing," he repeated.

I leaned into his side, using him as my anchor as we took another step. "I met Gigi right there." I pointed toward the ER counter.

"Good. Tell me something else."

"I opened my first real paycheck in this spot." I pointed to the floor.

I'd been standing in the middle of the ER lobby, giddy that I'd just finished my first two weeks of work as a nurse. Without my direct deposit set up yet, they'd given me an actual check. I'd never been more excited to open an envelope.

"You're doing great," Hunter said, taking care to shorten his stride so I wouldn't feel rushed. "Keep them coming. More good things."

"My cousin had a baby here when I was in high school and I got to come see them."

"Boy or girl?" he asked as he steered me toward the waiting room.

"Girl."

I was thinking of another good hospital experience when my family in the waiting room spotted us. Mom jumped up from her seat and rushed right over, followed by Beau, Sabrina and Michael.

"Can you take her?" Hunter asked Beau.

Beau nodded as Hunter gently transferred me into my brother's side. I loved Beau, but the minute Hunter's touch was gone, my panic escalated. But as much as I wanted him to stay with me, it was better that he checked on Dad.

"Sit tight," Hunter said. "I'll be back as soon as I can." He squeezed my mom's shoulder before jogging past the ER counter and disappearing toward the exam rooms.

"Come on, Maze," Beau said softly.

I closed my eyes—blacking out the visual reminders of time spent flirting with Everett in the waiting room—and blindly let my brother lead me to a chair.

"I'm proud of you," Mom said, sitting in the chair next to mine and grabbing my hand.

Proud of me? She had so much to worry about with Dad, she shouldn't need to be proud of me. I should be here comforting her, not the other way around. I didn't need people to be fussing over me when they should be focusing on Dad.

Shame replaced panic.

Everett had been dead for years but I had been letting him control my life. I'd let his memory taint this hospital. I'd avoided it at all costs, scared of what being inside these walls would do to my sanity.

I opened my eyes and looked around.

Instead of picturing Everett in this waiting room, I watched Beau and Sabrina comforting each other. I watched Michael tapping his foot as he checked his watch. Then watched Mom, who was pale and on the verge of more tears.

I blocked out Everett from the hospital and saw it just for what it was. A hospital. A building. A place with good memories and bad.

It was time to let go of some fears and focus on my family.

"What happened?" I asked Mom.

She sniffled and wiped her eyes. "We were just eating

dinner. He got up from his chair to take his plate to the kitchen. He hasn't cleared his own plate in years."

This I knew. Mom waited on Dad. She liked doing it and he liked to let her.

"He came back from the kitchen and started rubbing his chest. The next thing I know he's telling me to call 9-1-1 because he thinks he's having a heart attack. So I ran to the bathroom and got him some aspirin. Then we sat together on the couch and prayed until the ambulance got there a few minutes later."

"How long were you here before you called us?" Beau asked.

"Just a few minutes. They started Brock on some medicine in the ambulance and Dr. Peterson was only a minute behind us getting to the hospital. They started doing that EKG test thing and I stepped out to call you. When I got back, they told me I had to wait out here."

She started weeping again so I bent to dig a lace handkerchief out of her purse.

She dabbed her eyes. "Thank you."

Michael started rubbing her back. "It's going to be okay, Mom."

I prayed he was right.

We all sat quietly and stared down the hall where Hunter had disappeared, holding tight to one another. When Hunter emerged from the hall almost an hour later, we stood and grabbed for each other's hands.

Hunter walked right to Mom and laid his hand on her shoulder. "He's fine. He'll be fine."

We all sagged, then hugged closer to Mom.

"The heart attack wasn't severe, and since you came in right away, Dr. Peterson was able to get the blocked artery opened back up. The anticoagulant medicine wasn't working enough so Dr. Peterson put in a stent. We had to give Brock a mild sedative, so he's groggy, but as soon as we get him settled into a room upstairs, you can see him."

"How long does he have to stay?" Beau asked.

"At least overnight," Hunter said. "If things look good tomorrow, you can probably take him home."

"And then he's going on a diet," Mom declared.

"He's going to love that," Michael scoffed. "No more Fried-Foods Fridays."

"That's right." Mom nodded, then looked back at Hunter. "I think I'll stay tonight, if that's okay?"

"That's fine."

"Are you sure, Mom?" Beau asked. "Don't you think you'd be more comfortable at home?"

She shook her head. "I'll be fine."

Mom had slept next to Dad for decades. There was no way she'd be going home without him.

"Come on." Hunter swung out a hand. "I'll take you up."

"I know the way." Mom walked toward the staircase with Michael, Beau and Sabrina following behind. Hunter and I followed them all, hand in hand.

He bent down to kiss my hair. "How are you doing?"

"Better now that Dad's going to be okay."

Better now that I'd made my resolve.

While we'd been sitting in the waiting room, I'd made a decision. I wasn't leaving this hospital tonight until I could come back tomorrow and visit my dad without Hunter having to practically drag me through the doors.

Before I left tonight, I was going back to the place where my nightmares began. I was going to the basement.

But first, I wanted to hug my dad.

When we reached Dad's room on the second floor, the nurse was just walking out of the room and he waved us in.

"Oh, Brock," Mom gasped and put her hands on her cheeks.

Dad was blinking at us like he'd just woken up. "Hey, baby."

Dad's endearment brought a fresh wave of tears and I buried my face in Hunter's side to keep quiet. He just held me tight, whispering into my hair that it would be all right. When I'd regained my composure, I shuffled into Dad's room behind my family. Then one by one, we all hugged Dad.

"I love you, Dad," I said into his neck.

"Love you too."

"We'll let you get some rest."

"Marissa, can we get you anything?" Sabrina asked.

Mom shook her head and took Dad's hand. "I've got everything I need."

"We'll be back first thing in the morning." Sabrina bent to kiss Dad's cheek and then hug Mom good-bye.

Beau did the same before hugging me and shaking Hunter's hand. "Thanks."

Hunter nodded and then gave Sabrina a hug.

"I'm going to stay for a while," Michael said. That meant he was going to stay all night. There was no way he'd let Mom sleep here alone.

"Thank you," I mouthed.

He nodded and settled into one of two guest chairs.

Hunter and I said our good-byes to Michael, Mom and Dad, then left them alone.

"I need to do something before we go," I told Hunter as

we walked down the hall. "But I'll need your help. I don't think I can do it myself."

Somehow, Hunter knew what I meant without having to explain. "Are you sure you want to do this tonight? It's been a rough one already."

I nodded. "I want to do it while I'm brave enough."

"Okay, baby." His hand rested at the small of my back. "Then I'll be right here."

Descending the stairs, I gripped the railing tighter with every step. My free hand was shaking by the time I hit the first floor.

"Okay?" Hunter asked.

I nodded and took another step toward the basement door. When my fingers wrapped around the metal handle, they barely had the strength to twist the knob and turn.

Luckily, it wasn't locked and the heavy door squeaked as I pulled it open. The cool, stale air from the basement blew into my face. With Hunter propping the door open, I stepped through the frame and stood on the landing above the stairs.

*I can do this. I can do this.*

I would do this.

And then maybe I'd be free.

One step at a time—with Hunter's hand reminding me he was there—I descended the cement stairs into the basement of my terrors. Then slowly, I made my way to the deadly storage room at the end of the hall.

Looking over my shoulder, I got a reassuring nod from Hunter, then turned and stepped into the gray room.

Not much had changed in all these years. Some things had moved. Others hadn't. It was still cold and smelled like concrete. I didn't move any further into the space than just inside the doorway. I didn't need to move further. From this spot, I could survey the entire room.

Expecting one of my flashes, I braced as my eyes hit the spot where I'd stabbed Everett.

When it didn't come, I waited a few more heartbeats. Then some more.

Still, nothing happened.

My eyes swept the room twice more and then I turned around. I didn't need to stay longer. I'd done what I had needed to do. I'd taken a small piece of me back, a piece Everett had stolen years ago. He didn't get to keep the hospital anymore. It was mine again.

"I'm done here."

Hunter nodded and, without comment, held my hand to lead me out of the basement. When we reached the lobby, he shut the basement door and pulled me into his arms. "I'm proud of you. That couldn't have been easy."

"It wasn't." I pressed my cheek to his heart. "Thank you for coming with me and for helping me inside earlier. I wouldn't have been able to do it without you."

"You would have found a way, but I'm glad I could help. How are you feeling?"

Exhausted. Numb. Strange. "I thought it would feel different." It had been harder to cross through the ER doors than it had been to look upon the place where I'd taken a man's life.

"Different how?"

"I guess I thought it would be harder. More emotional maybe? More final?"

"Give it time." He let me go and took my hand. "Let's go get Coby."

"Okay." As we walked, I looked over my shoulder at the basement door.

I had expected to feel some sort of closure from going into that basement—some sort of ending—but I didn't.

Something was still looming. Something with Everett was still unsettled.

Unfinished.

I just didn't know what.

# CHAPTER FIFTEEN

MAISY

"Good night, buddy." I kissed Coby's hair and eased out of his room.

It had been a month since Dad's heart attack and life was getting back to a new normal.

Per Mom's promise, she had put Dad on a diet—something he hadn't protested one bit. He'd already lost twelve pounds and was committed to the healthier lifestyle we were all supporting.

Beau had started taking Dad on regular mountain hikes, Michael had swapped out all of Dad's heavy Budweiser with Michelob ULTRA, and I had replaced the weekly cookie plate I'd been taking Dad for years with bowls of fresh fruit.

It had taken nearly the entire month, but my fear of losing Dad was finally starting to go away. And whenever I'd start to worry, Hunter was right by my side. He'd pull me into his arms and reassure me that people recovered from heart attacks all the time and went on to live many, many more years.

Without Hunter, this whole ordeal would have been miserable. Without Hunter . . . well, I didn't like to think about that. I had him and wasn't letting go.

"What are you doing?" I plopped down on my couch next to Hunter.

He turned his laptop away so I couldn't see the screen. "It's a surprise. Is Coby out?"

"Like a light. What's your surprise?" I careened my neck to get a peek but Hunter tickled my ribs. I yelped and sat back as I swatted his hand away.

"Quiet." He laughed. "You're going to wake up Coby."

I made a "yeah, right" face. Coby had barely made it through two pages of his bedtime book before zonking out. He was deep in dreamland along with Pickle, who was sleeping on the floor by his side.

"Come on, show me your surprise. Is it for Coby? Because I'm great at keeping surprises secret." I zipped my lips shut, turned the lock, then opened my mouth to toss in the key.

Hunter chuckled and leaned over to brush his lips against mine. "You're impossible to deny."

I grinned as he handed over the laptop.

"The surprise is for you, but I'm not quite done with editing yet."

"Are these my pictures?" I nearly came off the couch I was so excited.

"Yeah. Just click through to the right."

I hunkered back down, hovering over the laptop, with a huge smile on my face. Taking up the entire screen was a picture of Coby from behind as he fished at the community pond.

"Hunter," I whispered, shaking my head in disbelief. "This is . . ."

It was exactly the shot I'd imagined in my mind but better. The light had been touched up and there was a sunbeam coming down on the water. The grasses had been blurred to give the photo a softened edge. And somehow Hunter had managed to capture enough of Coby's profile to see that my son was overjoyed.

"You don't have to use them," Hunter said. "It won't hurt my feelings if you decide they aren't good enough. We can get a professional photographer to come and try them again."

I tore my eyes away from the photograph. "No. This is amazing. Like, the best picture I've ever seen."

"Really?"

"Totally." I ran my fingers across his bearded jaw. "Hunter, this picture is unbelievable. It's just as good as any paid professional could have done. I'm just . . ." I dropped my hand and looked back to the laptop. "I'm just so proud that you did this. It makes this whole project so much more special."

A smile consumed Hunter's handsome face.

"Can I see the rest?" I asked.

He nodded and scooted closer to watch.

I clicked through the photo slides, my amazement growing with every picture. "Oh my god! This one is perfect!" I couldn't help but shout. The picture Hunter had taken from atop the gas station was incredible and deserved an extra couple of decibels. He'd captured all of Main Street with the bridge leading out of town in the background. It was everything I loved about my town, captured in one single shot.

"That one is my fourth favorite," he said.

"Fourth?" Besides the picture of Coby, this one was my number two.

He smiled. "Keep going."

I clicked again, then gasped. The next one was from our early morning trip to Wade Lake.

It stole my breath away.

Hunter had done the nearly impossible. He'd taken a photo that did the scenery justice. He'd captured the rich colors of early dawn. The sunshine barely cresting the mountain ridge. The glassy water reflecting the clouds above. He'd gotten it all perfectly.

"That one turned out great," he whispered.

"No, incredible." Great was an understatement.

I clicked through the next two pictures but froze when the last photo filled the screen. It was a picture of me and Coby in a booth at the café. Coby and I had our noses pressed together in an Eskimo kiss. We were both smiling and his small hand was on top of mine on the table. I hadn't even remembered Hunter taking it.

"That one isn't for the motel," he said. "That one is just for me." Hunter grinned at the screen. The adoration in his eyes melted my heart.

He loved us. Without a doubt, he loved us.

The way he was looking at that picture was the way my parents still looked at one another. It was the way Beau looked at Sabrina. It was how Jess looked at Gigi and their kids.

Hunter loved us.

And we loved him.

*I* loved him.

"I love you." Once again I'd proven that whatever came into my head more often than not came rushing out of my mouth.

Hunter's eyes snapped to mine and he stared at me for three torturous heartbeats. Then a smile tugged at the corners of his lips. "I love you too."

By some miracle, the laptop didn't get dropped as our bodies collided together. With his lips moving roughly against mine, I climbed into his lap as he slid his tongue inside. *I love kissing this man.* Everything about his mouth was delicious. He'd alternate stroking my tongue and sucking on my bottom lip. When I angled my head for deeper access, he rewarded me with a nip of his teeth.

His muscled arms banded across my back as he crushed me against his chest. I gave him all my weight, settling my rocking hips against the straining erection beneath his jeans. He thrust his hips up, sending a jolt of heat right to my core as his lips left mine to trail openmouthed kisses down my neck.

"Hunter," I moaned as his teeth grazed my collarbone.

"God, I love that sound." He kissed the hollow of my neck and my hips rocked harder, searching for some friction to relieve my aching clit. "Grind down hard, baby."

I obeyed, circling my hips hard into his lap. He groaned and thrust higher, sending another pulsing current to my core.

"Bed. I need you to take me to bed." My plea elicited a rumble from his throat.

"You want my cock, baby?" His rough voice, his dirty words, his hands kneading my ass sent a shiver through my body. "Yeah," he said against my neck. "You want my cock."

Hunter stood fast, his strong arms setting me on unsteady feet so he could drag me to the bedroom. The second the door clicked shut, I started whipping off my clothes. When my shaking fingers fumbled with the button on my jeans, I huffed in frustration, trying to clear the fog from Hunter's kiss so I could get naked. *But this damn button!*

Before I could yank the metal disk free from the buttonhole, I was flying through the air. My back bounced onto the bed from Hunter's toss. My weight was still unsettled when his hands came to my pants and he yanked the traitorous button free. Then with a hard tug at my ankles, he jerked my pants off my legs, releasing me from the denim. While he quickly dispensed of his own clothes, I wiggled out of my lace thong.

"Fuck, Maisy. Look how wet you are." Hunter's weight hit the bed as he knelt between my legs. His fingers trailed up my calves to my knees, the tips just barely ghosting my skin. When he reached my knees, he gripped hard, digging into my flesh as he shoved my knees apart.

A strangled noise came from my throat and my eyes rolled back into my head. My choppy breathing echoed in my ears as I lay there, completely spread and open for Hunter's inspection.

"You are beautiful. So beautiful." His fingers found my soaking-wet center and I gasped when he plunged two right inside.

He rubbed my tender spot and my hips bucked. If he kept at it, I was going to come but I wanted it to be around his cock. "Hunter, I need you. Please."

Without delay, the head of his thick, gorgeous cock pressed against my entrance. His chest came down to rest against mine as his elbows bracketed me beneath him. Then with one slow press, he sank deep, filling me completely.

"Yes," I moaned into his ear as he pulled out, then slammed in a hard thrust. We'd stopped using condoms a while ago and the feel of him bare against me inside me was nothing less than incredible.

Hunter worked his cock in an ever-changing rhythm—hard and fast, then deep and slow—exactly the way I liked it. He knew my body, my cues, everything. He knew how to bring me to the edge and then drag me away, again and again, until I was a shaking mess and completely at his mercy.

"Are you ready to come, baby?"

I nodded as he sank his hot, wet mouth onto mine for another kiss.

His cock thrust deep and he stayed rooted so he could grind the base into my throbbing clit. Then he leaned back, coming up on his knees. With his hands under my thighs, he lifted them up, the angle changing so he could fuck me deeper.

When he pulled out and rammed back inside, my head and shoulders jerked forward, coming off the bed, then flying back down. "I'm going to come," I gasped as pleasure swelled, spreading from my core in a wave of tingling heat.

Right before my orgasm hit, I reached up and drove my fingers into Hunter's hair, yanking out the elastic tie and gripping his locks by the scalp. Hard. White spots broke behind my eyelids as I let the explosion go. My whole body pulsed, squeezing him as he powered faster, drawing out my orgasm in the hardest he'd ever built.

"Fuck me," he hissed. "I love you." My walls milked his cock until his own release was spilling into me with hot spurts. I forced my eyes open to watch Hunter's orgasm, savoring the view of his eyes squeezed shut with pleasure and his Adam's apple bobbing as his throat rumbled.

I loved this man. I trusted this man. Whether it was to take tender care of my heart or to satisfy my body when we were having hot, carnal sex, I trusted him to love me like I loved him.

Selflessly.

Hunter's heaving chest collapsed on top of me as his arms snaked behind my back to hold tight. Boneless, I barely had the strength to wrap my arms around his back and stroke his sweaty skin.

"I love you, Maisy Holt," he said into my neck. "How did I get so lucky to win you?"

Overcome with love for this man, my breath hitched and tears leaked from the corners of my eyes. "I love you too, Hunter Faraday."

We were both lucky. From now until the end of my life, I'd count my luckiest day the one when he came into my motel. All the bad—all the crap Everett had put me through—I'd do it all over again if that meant this man was my reward.

"Don't cry." Hunter rolled to his side and pulled me tight against his chest. His cock was still buried deep inside me. "Don't cry, baby."

My heart had never felt so full. So complete. The happiness was so strong and overpowering, I didn't know how to process it other than to cry.

"I just . . . I love you. I'm too happy."

He kissed my forehead. "I know how you feel."

He held me tight, giving me a few minutes to let go of it all, before he slid out. Then he went to the bathroom and brought back a washcloth to gently clean between my legs.

When he slipped into bed, we tangled our naked bodies together. I was lying on his side, his arm behind my neck and my cheek pressed into his chest. My foot was trailing up and down his calf as his hand was threaded with mine on his washboard stomach.

"Thank you for taking my pictures," I said to his bare chest.

"You're welcome. I'll finish editing and get the canvases ordered."

I snuggled deeper and closed my eyes. "Thank you."

"Will you do me a favor when they get in?"

"Sure."

"I'd like to hang the picture of you and Coby in the office at my house."

I smiled and kissed the valley between his pecs. "I can do that."

"And I'm paying for all of them."

My smile turned down. "No way."

"Maisy," he warned.

"Hunter." I mimicked his tone. "This is my motel and those pictures are a business expense."

"Those pictures are a gift to the woman I love."

"Damn it," I muttered. I wouldn't turn down a gift and he knew it. "Well played, Dr. Faraday."

He chuckled.

"Your furniture should be getting here early next week," I said. "Maybe once we get it all set up we could start our sleepovers?"

"I'd like that. I'd like that a lot."

"Good, then it's settled." I smiled, excited about what

was about to be delivered.

Because there wasn't a huge selection of home goods in Prescott and I hadn't had time to drive to Bozeman to shop, I'd ordered most of Hunter's furnishings online. The living room couches and chairs would arrive first. Then the bed for Coby's room. And then the desk I'd had custom built for his office and the massive dining room table.

I couldn't wait to surprise him with everything. I'd already arranged for Beau and Michael to help me get it all set up so that next week I could take him up there under the ruse of unpacking shipments when really, it would be all done.

I'd even recruited Mom to help me furnish the kitchen since I'd been so busy at the inn. She'd had a blast buying dishes, pots and everything else a kitchen could need. I'd been stashing everything in her garage, which was filled with bags and boxes, so Hunter wouldn't get wind of my surprise.

"What time do we need to be downtown for the parade tomorrow?" Hunter asked, pulling my thoughts away from decorating.

"It starts at ten but if we want a good spot we'll need to be there at nine."

"Okay," he yawned. "Did you set an alarm?"

"No, I forgot." I rolled off of him and reached for my phone on the nightstand. I smiled at the blank screen when I opened it up.

It had been over a month since I'd gotten a call from Unknown. That reporter had finally given up. Now I was just hoping that she had been the last. That the reporters of the world had found better news, and in time, I'd get the closure I'd been searching for since killing Everett.

I'd conquered my fears of the hospital. Now if I could

just get over the random flashes, I'd feel like Hunter, Coby and I could truly move on. I hadn't had a flash in a while, the last happening when I'd been cleaning a couple of weeks ago, so I'd been keeping my fingers crossed that the times between them were getting longer. Maybe one day they'd vanish altogether.

"There." Setting my alarm for six, I curled back into Hunter's side and kissed his chest. "Good night."

He kissed my hair. "Good night, Blondie."

I smiled.

Good nights. All I wanted was a lifetime of good nights with Hunter by my side.

And if things kept going like they had been, I might just get my wish.

---

HUNTER

Time was up.

She loved me, which meant it was time to tell Maisy the truth. It was time to tell her about my past. About Nell.

About Everett.

It was time to tell her about everything and then cling to her feet when she tried to run away.

"Who is Nell?"

Maisy's question caused my hands to flinch on the steering wheel. The car jerked to the side before I righted us back on the road toward Nick and Emmeline Slater's garage for their annual Independence Day party.

"Whoa. Everything okay?" Maisy asked.

"Yeah. Sorry, I thought I saw an animal on the road," I

lied.

"Oh."

She stayed quiet for a minute and I hoped she'd let her earlier question go. Maybe she'd forgo asking about Nell again since we were just minutes away from our destination.

"Who is Nell?" she repeated.

*Fuck.*

Her question was another sign that it was time for me to tell her the truth.

My hands gripped the steering wheel tighter. I took a breath and opened my mouth, but before I could respond to her question, Maisy waved her hands in the air.

"Sorry. Forget it. I shouldn't pry. I, um, saw her name on your phone a while back and was just curious. I didn't mean to snoop but it popped up with a text right as I was walking by and the text wasn't very nice. I kind of forgot about the whole thing but then we ran into the Mitchells at the parade earlier and their daughter is named Nellie and I remembered the text and—"

"Hey." I took her hand to stop her nervous babbling. "It's okay. Nell is . . . well, she's not a fun topic."

"I figured."

I thought back through all of Nell's texts. The majority were *Call me* or *Stop ignoring me*. Except for one.

*What happens next is your fault.*

That had to be the text that Maisy had seen.

Fucking Nell.

She had stopped harassing me and I'd been holding out hope that we were done and she'd finally processed my choice to live here. I hoped that she'd realize I was never coming back and she'd move on with her own life and leave me to mine. Foolish hope.

It would make it a fuck of a lot easier to tell Maisy about Nell if that was true.

"I'll tell you about her but now isn't the time." I jerked my chin back to Coby, who was kicking his legs wildly, jittery from all the parade candy he'd consumed after his afternoon nap.

"But you're okay?" Maisy asked. "She's not threatening you or whatever?"

"No. She's not. And I'm great." I brought her hand to my mouth for a kiss.

"I shouldn't have looked. Sorry."

"Don't apologize. Don't ever apologize. Your curiosity is one of the things I love about you."

That and her patience. All this time and she'd kept her promise to not pry about my family or past relationships. She'd given me more leeway than any other woman would have in her position.

But she wouldn't need to for much longer.

I'd tell her the truth, then I'd get on my knees and beg her to forgive me for the lies and omissions. She loved me and it was my small sliver of hope that we might actually make it through all of this together.

"I hope the firework show goes well for Michael tonight," Maisy said, changing topics. "He's so nervous. He's done this before but I think he's worried that something will go wrong and Alana will see."

I chuckled. "He'll be fine."

In Alana's eyes, Michael could do no wrong. His firework show could consist of one sparkler and a flaming lotus flower and she'd say it was the most spectacular event in Prescott's history.

"We're here!" Coby shouted when I pulled into the parking lot in front of Slater's Station.

Maisy sat straighter in her seat and undid her seat belt. She was out the door before I'd even shoved the 4Runner in park.

Then she got mobbed by her crew.

After the women dispersed, Gigi went right to the backseat to unbuckle Coby so he could run off and find the other kids. Felicity and Sabrina popped open the back of the car to get the cookies Maisy had made for dessert. By the time Emmeline waddled over from the garage with her heavily pregnant belly, we were ready to turn back.

"Will you grab the cooler?" Maisy called to me as she walked with Emmeline.

"Got it." I waved and went to the backseat for the drinks.

With the cooler deposited by the fridge in the garage, I joined the guys huddled around a classic black Camaro Nick was restoring.

"Hey." I shook Nick's hand. "Thanks for having us."

"Welcome. Glad you could make it."

I shook hands with Jess, Silas and Beau. I'd met some of the other guys before, including Nick's dad and brother, who were in town for the weekend and staying at the Bitterroot.

"This is sweet," I told Jess, running my hand across the hood of the car.

"No shit. Makes me want one of my own."

I nodded. "It would be fun to get an old one and rebuild it. Maybe do it together with Coby."

Conversation stopped and all eyes came to me.

My spine went straight. "What?"

Across from me Beau was grinning. "Just glad you're stepping up."

I relaxed and grinned back. Fuck yes, I was stepping up. Beau's time as Coby's father figure was over.

That was my job.

"I—"

A woman's cry interrupted my sentence and all heads turned to the open garage doors at the front of the shop. Jess and I moved first, both of us trained over the years to recognize the sound of pain. Nick sprinted past us, knowing the sound of his wife's cry. When we got outside, all of the women were hovering over Emmeline, who was bent over and clutching her belly.

"What happened?" I asked when I reached Emmeline's side.

"Contraction," Emmeline hissed. "A big one."

"How far apart are they?"

"Ten minutes or so. I've been having them all day but nothing too close so I wasn't worried. But that one came right on top . . . uh-oh."

A trickle of water ran down her leg. "Okay. Time for the hospital. Are you ready to meet your baby girl?"

She looked over to Nick at her side and smiled.

Then chaos erupted as the party got shut down, the Slaters roared away to the hospital and I kissed Maisy on the cheek before following.

Nine hours later, I stepped out of Emmeline's hospital room, leaving her, Nick and baby Nora alone to rest.

Dr. Peterson was Emmeline's primary care physician but I'd stuck around, wanting to learn from a doctor with incredible experience. I hadn't delivered many babies outside my residency, and since I was staying in Prescott indefinitely, eventually I'd be the senior doctor at Jamison Valley Hospital. I couldn't have picked a better baby to welcome into this community. Nora Slater was as perfect as newborns could be.

Rushing to the locker room, I changed out of my scrubs and dug my phone out of my jeans pocket. Then I called Maisy. It was three in the morning but I didn't care that I was going to wake her up. She wouldn't either.

"Hey, baby," I said when she answered.

"Hi. Is everything okay?"

"Healthy baby girl. Seven pounds, three ounces. Ten fingers, ten toes."

She sighed. "Oh, good. Are you coming home?"

*Home.* I smiled. "I'm on my way."

"Okay," she yawned. "See you soon."

I hustled home and into bed, curling my Maisy into my arms.

Then I made myself a promise.

Tomorrow, I'd arrange for Coby to spend the night with Brock and Marissa one night this week so I could tell Maisy everything.

As soon as my confession was behind us, we could move forward. She'd be wearing my ring, Coby would be my son, and my baby would be growing in her stomach.

This was the last chalk mark on an otherwise clear slate and it was time to wipe it clean.

---

"HEY," I called into the lobby of the motel.

"Hi!" Maisy rushed from behind her computer at the counter to give me a kiss. "What are you doing here?"

"I came to see if you wanted lunch. I had a break."

"Okay, sure. Do you want to go somewhere or just eat

upstairs?"

I shrugged. "It doesn't matter."

"I'd like to finish those leftovers from dinner last night. Especially if Coby is spending the night with Mom and Dad tonight. That way we can go eat wherever."

"All right."

It had been two days since Nora Slater's birth and my resolve to tell Maisy the truth was as strong as ever. Tonight, she'd learn everything. Then I'd fight through the tears, the yelling and the hurt to get us to the other side.

The door behind me opened and I turned to see a man in a gray suit walk into the lobby.

"Hi," Maisy greeted. "How can I help you?"

"I'm looking for," he glanced at the manila envelope in his hand, "Maisy Holt."

"That's me."

"Can I see some ID, ma'am?" the man asked.

The hairs on the back of my neck prickled. Some ID? What the fuck did this guy want? He wouldn't make eye contact with me so I couldn't get a good read on him, but my gut was telling me something bad was coming.

Maisy went to her purse on the counter and dug out her wallet to get her driver's license. When the man looked it over, he handed it back along with the envelope.

"Maisy Holt, you've been served."

He wasted no time leaving the lobby as Maisy and I stared at the envelope. With shaking hands, she ripped open the seal and slid out papers. As her eyes scanned the white sheets, her face paled and her mouth fell open.

"What?" I moved to stand by her side and scan the pages myself, but they fluttered to the floor as Maisy whispered.

"Everett's mother is seeking custody of Coby."

# CHAPTER SIXTEEN

MAISY

"We need to talk, baby."

"No, we don't." I sidestepped Hunter in the living room of my parents' house.

Before I could make my escape to the back patio, his arms wrapped around my shoulders, trapping me against his chest. "Maisy—"

"No, Hunter. No." I shook my head. He'd been insisting on having "a talk" over the last month, but I'd denied him every time. "I told you. I don't want to know. If whatever you have to say is just going to hurt, then I don't want to know."

"Please," he begged. "I *have* to tell you some things about my past."

"No." I squirmed out of his embrace and turned, planting my hands on my hips. "I love you. I *need* you. I can't make it through this if you aren't by my side. And if you have to tell me something that's going to make me want to send you away, then I don't want to know."

His jaw clenched tight. "You don't know what you're asking."

"Yes, I do." I stepped closer and covered his bearded cheek with my palm. "I know that whatever you're going to tell me is going to ruin us. It's going to break us apart. I see it in your eyes every time you've asked to talk. But I'm barely hanging on by a thread here. Please, don't cut it."

He sighed and closed his eyes.

I fell into his chest and snaked my arms around his waist. "Do you love me?"

"You know I do." He wrapped his arms around my back.

"Then please do this for me. I trust you."

He kissed my hair. "You won't."

My heart fell. "And that's why I don't want to know."

It was foolish and naïve to stick my head in the sand about our relationship—I didn't care. I'd slid backward this month, every day losing more and more of the confidence I'd found these last few years. The progress I'd made to move past Everett's actions had disappeared, and the only thing keeping me from completely going off the rails was Hunter. Whatever secrets he had to confess about his past or family would have to wait until I knew the fate of my son.

Coby needed all of the strength I could summon. He needed all of my wits and my focus. I couldn't let Hunter break my heart when Coby needed it to stay intact.

So, like I'd been telling Hunter over and over, I needed him by my side. He was part of the glue keeping all my pieces together. After Monday, when the judge made his decision about the petition, then I'd let all the pieces fall apart.

"Dinner!" Mom called from the kitchen.

Hunter let out a deep breath. "I'll go get Coby." He

kissed my hair one last time, then let me go, walking out of the living room and toward the back patio where my brothers were watching Coby play in the yard with Pickle.

I turned and walked to the dining room, the mountain of stress on my shoulders making my footsteps heavy.

It had been thirty-six days since Everett's mother, Eleanor Carlson, had served me with a custody petition. Thirty-six days of spontaneous crying fits. Thirty-six days of skipping meals because food rarely sat well in my knotted stomach. Thirty-six days of greeting myself in the bathroom mirror each morning with dark circles under my eyes.

Thirty-six days of waiting for a judge to decide my fate.

If not for Hunter, I never would have survived this month. I'd lost count of the number of times he'd reassured me things would be okay. The number of times he'd pulled me into his arms because he'd known I'd been on the verge of tears. Other than when he'd go to work, he'd been constantly by my side. He'd even come to every appointment with Stuart Redhill, my attorney.

Including the one I'd had this afternoon.

I wasn't looking forward to telling my family about my meeting with Stuart, but that was why we were here. This special Friday-night dinner was to prep everyone before the custody hearing on Monday morning.

"Mommy!" Coby came racing inside, followed by Hunter and my brothers. "Uncle Michael said he's taking me wif him to the park!"

"That's awesome!" I pretended to be shocked even though we'd already arranged for Michael to distract Coby so that Hunter and I could talk to the others about the custody case. "You just have to eat a big dinner first so you've got lots of energy, okay?"

"Okay." Coby smiled wide, then ran off toward the bathroom.

I watched him until he disappeared, memorizing everything about the way his hair flopped when he ran. What would I do without him? I wouldn't make it. That little boy was my entire world. The idea of him spending even one night away from me and with *that woman* was too much to bear.

My nose started to sting and my eyes watered as I took a seat at the table. Pinching some skin under the hem of my shorts, I squeezed tight and twisted. I swallowed an "owie" and let the pain snap me out of my pity party.

The self-punishment I'd once used to stop saying "like" now stopped me from crying in front of Coby. When he was at daycare or asleep, all bets were off, but I'd worked diligently to keep it together in front of him. As far as my son knew, life was good. He didn't know a thing about this custody hearing and wouldn't unless the unthinkable happened and he was forced to meet his "grandmother."

A snarl formed on my lips.

Eleanor Carlson was the devil.

I didn't hate many people, but I *hated* that woman for trying to take my son.

"Uh-oh," Michael teased as he sat in the chair across the table. "I bet I know who that look is for."

"Yep," I muttered and dropped my snarl. "This looks great, Mom."

She set down my favorite potato salad. "Thank you. Eat as much as you'd like." She was worried about the five pounds I'd lost this month and had been going above and beyond to make my favorite foods and drop them by the loft.

"I will." Since I hadn't eaten anything all day, I was actually hungry for a change.

"I'm starving," Dad said, sitting at his regular seat at the head of the table. He reached for a huge scoop of potato salad but then paused, sighing as he dropped the scoop and went back for a smaller portion, plopping just a dollop onto his plate.

"I'm proud of you, Dad." He'd lost nearly twenty pounds since his heart attack two months ago.

"Me too," Sabrina said as she sat down.

He smiled at us both. "Thank you, girls."

Everyone else took their seats at the table, Hunter and Coby each taking a chair at my side, and after Coby said grace, we all dug in for a delicious meal. Conversation was quiet as we all scarfed until Beau broke the silence.

He cleared his throat and covered Sabrina's hand on the table. "We've got some news."

Forks and spoons clinked on plates and all eyes landed on my brother, whose face was split in a silly grin.

"You're pregnant!" Mom shrieked, standing from her seat next to Dad.

"Jeez." Dad winced and rubbed an ear. "Marissa, would you let them talk?"

She stayed on her feet and stared at Sabrina, waiting.

Finally, my sister-in-law put Mom out of her misery. "I'm pregnant."

"Yes!" Mom's hands flew toward the ceiling.

Cheers filled the dining room.

"Congratulations!" I clinked my Dr. Pepper can with Beau's beer and Sabrina's water.

When I turned to Hunter, he winked at me. If I hadn't already been smiling, I would have by reflex. That wink had been the catalyst for most of my smiles this past month, so he'd give it to me at least once a day. Besides offering me comfort, making me smile had become Hunter's mission in life.

"I love you," I mouthed.

His eyes softened. "Love you too."

We both turned back to our plates, and per Mom's request, I ate a second helping of potato salad while we all fussed over Sabrina and offered up baby names.

*What a lucky baby.* He or she would have devoted parents and adoring grandparents. I was glad that Beau and Sabrina would never be put through the mess that Everett's mother was dragging me through.

"Coby, you ready?" Michael asked as he popped one last bite into his mouth.

Coby nearly came off his chair. "Is it time to go to the park?"

Michael nodded and stood. "Let's do it."

"Have fun." I kissed Coby's hair before he climbed off his chair and rushed to the door to put on his shoes.

Mom and I cleared a few plates while Michael secured Pickle to his leash, but the moment the door clicked shut, we sat back down and wasted no time cutting to the chase.

"Okay. What did Stuart say?" Dad asked.

Hunter clasped my hand as I started the recap of my attorney's message.

"To start, we all need to be at the courthouse before eight thirty on Monday morning. Stuart wants us in our seats and ready so that when the judge starts the proceedings at nine, we're not rushing in or out."

Dad nodded. "We'll be there before eight."

The doors wouldn't even be open until eight, but since

I'd be there early too, they could keep me company on the sidewalk.

"What else?" Beau asked.

"You've all had your preliminary meetings with Stuart. He wanted me to remind you to stick to honesty. Don't try and memorize a speech, just speak from the heart. Tell them what kind of a mother I am and your honest opinion of how Coby would react if he was placed with Eleanor."

"He'd be miserable," Mom said, shaking her head. "His home is here. He has no business living in Michigan."

And he had no business living with Eleanor Carlson.

Eleanor had made quite an impression during our court-mandated interactions this past month. Basically, she'd proven she was a nasty bitch without a loving, nurturing, playful or grandmotherly bone in her body.

The week after I'd received the custody petition, Eleanor and I had appeared before the district judge so he could explain how our case would be handled. Given the small-town nature of Prescott's court system, it had been a fairly informal meeting. The judge had explained that because this custody petition wasn't due to parents divorcing, but instead a grandparent requesting custody—not just visitation—the process would be unique.

He'd ordered Coby to be evaluated by a child psychologist in Bozeman. He'd ordered Eleanor to present any evidence deeming me an "unfit" parent. And he'd ordered both of us into mediation to determine if we could come to an agreement outside the courtroom.

Eleanor had barely looked at me during that first court appearance. And the few times we had made eye contact, I had been met with an angry glare. Stuart had done all of the talking on my behalf and I'd just sat there for the thirty-minute meeting, trying my best not to cry.

The mediation had gone even worse.

Eleanor had refused to budge an inch on her petition. She was asking for Coby to live with her in Michigan for six months. *Six months.* She'd sat in silence as the mediator had tried to convince her to compromise on something more reasonable. But every time, Eleanor had just said no, then shot me her evil snarl.

Finally, after three hours, the mediator had given up.

"Did Stuart have the psychologist's final report?" Dad asked.

I nodded. "Yes, and it all came back fine. She called Coby a 'delightful and happy little boy.' Stuart thought that with the psychologist's report, plus the fact that Eleanor doesn't have any evidence proving I'm an unfit parent, she won't get the custody she's after. But . . ."

"Uh-oh," Mom muttered.

This was the part of the recap I didn't want to give. "Stuart was very honest with us today. There's a good chance the judge will grant her some time. Maybe a weekend a month. Maybe a month around the holidays. Judge Tubor is going to be fair, but at the end of the day, Eleanor is Coby's grandparent. If it's in his best interest to see her, then the judge will allow it."

"But it's not in his best interest!" Mom flew off her chair. "How can bringing in anyone related to that *monster* be in his best interest? I don't care if Eleanor is Coby's grandmother. She is Everett's mother. Period. The last thing my grandson needs is to be confused about his biological father. Coby knows nothing of Everett and it should stay that way until he's older. This is . . . this is *fucking* ridiculous!"

Mouths around the table fell open. I could count on three fingers the times Mom had ever said the *f* word in my presence and the curse didn't sound right in her sweet voice.

"Mom, really?" Beau said, stifling a laugh. "Please don't ever say that again."

She huffed and sat back down, crossing her arms.

I fought to keep my laugh inside but Mom's face was so hilariously red, I lost the battle. The minute I started giggling, the entire table broke out in laughter. Dad was the only one who tried to hide it with a cough.

The thing was, Mom wasn't wrong.

This was ridiculous. *Fucking* ridiculous.

So much so, that instead of screaming like I'd wanted to for thirty-six days, I let go of my frustration through hysterical laughter. Laughter that filled the room for a few minutes, easing some of the tension from earlier.

As my laughter slowly faded away, I wiped the corners of my eyes. "Thanks, Mom. I needed that."

She pouted. "Glad I could help."

"Oh, Marissa," Dad chided, pulling Mom into his side with a playful shake. She relaxed and let go of her frown.

"Anyway, what else did Stuart say?" she asked.

"Not much. Mostly just wanted all of us to be prepared."

"But he's confident?" Beau asked. "Stuart is confident that Eleanor isn't going to get the fifty-fifty split she petitioned for?"

I nodded. "He's confident."

Though there was still a slim chance that she could get her wish, Stuart had no doubt that Judge Tubor would deny that request.

"Do you think this is all part of her strategy?" Sabrina

asked. "She asks for six months; the judge feels bad and grants her more than she would have gotten otherwise?"

"Maybe." I shrugged. "All I know is that she's the devil."

"Did we ever find out why *now*? Why does Eleanor want custody after all this time?"

"The judge asked her that at our first appearance. She gave him a line about it being because of Coby's birthday. That she couldn't bear to miss any more of her grandson's birthdays."

"Absurd explanation." Mom's hands fisted her napkin into a tight paper ball. "If she'd wanted to be a part of Coby's life, she would have made an effort years ago. This is all lies."

"Total lies," I agreed.

As much as it would have pained me, I never would have denied Eleanor access to Coby. All she'd had to do was call and ask. She could have come out and visited on my terms. Instead, the papers from her attorney were the first I'd ever heard from her.

And what a first impression.

Hunter's thumb started stroking the back of my hand. "It will be okay."

I leaned into his side and rested my head on his shoulder.

It will be okay.

Hunter's ever-present reassurance.

"I can't wait for this to be over," Mom said.

I sighed. "Just a couple more days."

I wasn't sure if I should dread Monday or wish it would come faster. Until Monday, Coby would be mine and only mine, but I'd be living with the unknown. After Monday, I'd know our fate but Coby could be required to spend time with Eleanor.

"Speaking of things being over, I've been meaning to

ask." Mom looked to me. "Have those calls from the reporter stopped?"

"Reporter?" Hunter and Beau asked in unison.

I lifted my head off Hunter's shoulder to meet his gaze. "Some reporter was calling me a couple months ago, wanting details about Everett. It wasn't the first time a reporter has called so I just ignored them. But they've finally stopped. I guess they found someone who was actually newsworthy."

"Wait." Sabrina held up a hand. "That seems strange. Your story was dead years ago. Why is it of interest now?"

"I don't know. Any ideas?" Sabrina had once been an investigative journalist in Seattle. If any one of us knew why my story was still garnering interest from the press, it would be her.

Before Sabrina could answer, Hunter asked, "What did he say?"

"It was a she, actually, and I only talked to her twice. The first time, she asked if I was the Maisy Holt who had murdered Everett Carlson. The second time, she asked if I was ready to talk about it."

"Where did the calls come from? Which media outlet?" Hunter asked.

I shook my head. "I don't know. I never asked. Why?"

"Just curious." His eyes dropped to his plate and he got a faraway look. "Do you have her number?"

I shook my head again. "No, it always came up as Unknown."

His forehead furrowed. "Why didn't you tell me?"

"I don't know. I guess I just figured they'd stop."

"And now they have, thank goodness." Mom stood and started clearing more dishes. "Let's just hope that was the last reporter."

Sabrina still looked confused, like she wanted to keep discussing the reporter, but Dad came to my rescue and changed the subject. "Let's talk about the party before Coby gets back. Everything set for Thursday?"

I nodded. "Yes, I just need to get some balloons. Gigi is making the cupcakes. Mom has all the other food. I've got the decorations."

I refused to let this custody hearing impact Coby's birthday Thursday, and no matter what the judge said, he was getting a party. Just like the other three birthday parties he'd had, we were having a barbeque at Mom and Dad's. This year's theme was water. Michael was building a Slip'N Slide and we were giving all the kids water guns, then telling them to go crazy. And tomorrow, Beau, Michael and Hunter were building my present to my son.

His bunk bed.

"What did you guys get Coby this year?" Beau asked Mom as she came back from the kitchen.

"We got him those neon shirt-and-shorts sets he loves so much and some shoes that light up when he walks."

It was the perfect gift. Coby was obsessed with neon clothes, something his nana knew well—unlike Eleanor Carlson. Why? Because she'd never made an effort. She'd just filed her custody dispute like a coward.

"Hunter, what did you get?" Beau's question stopped my internal rant.

Hunter, who had been staring absently at his plate, jerked at the question. "Sorry. What was that?"

"What did you get Coby?" Beau repeated.

"A new fishing pole."

Sabrina smiled. "He'll love that."

Hunter smiled back. "He's going to love the new fishing boat I bought last week too."

"Hold up. What?" My mouth fell open. "You bought a boat? When? How did I not know about this?"

In addition to working my ass off at the motel, I'd nearly completed decorating Hunter's house. We'd had a sleepover there two nights ago. How had I missed a boat?

He chuckled. "You need to spend more time in the garage, Blondie." He stood from his seat and bent down to kiss my forehead. "I need to make a quick call. Be back."

"Why would I go in the garage?" I asked Sabrina. "Wait, do garages need decorating? Should I get some of those industrial shelves or something?"

Beau and Dad shared a look.

*I guess that means no on decorating the garage.*

Turning, I watched Hunter walk toward the living room. His shoulders were hunched forward, and as he pressed his phone to his ear, he pinched the bridge of his nose.

"I've got a headache," Sabrina muttered to Beau.

I turned back around to see him kiss her temple. "Sorry, Shortcake."

"Caffeine withdrawals. I wish I could take something."

"What about Tylenol?" I asked.

She nodded. "I can but I don't have any and I haven't made it to the store yet."

"I have Tylenol," Mom said, coming back to the table. "One second." Off she went in search of pregnancy-safe painkillers.

"Be back." I stood from my seat and started toward the living room to find Hunter.

Behind me, Mom said, "Found it!" in the kitchen and shook the pill bottle.

That noise . . .

A chill crept down my spine and my mind snapped to a different place.

*"Maisy, love." Everett walked across the cold floor toward me. The plastic covering on the hospital bed beneath me crinkled as I pushed onto my elbows. "I want you to understand that your actions have brought this upon you. You should have terminated this pregnancy. I told you I had no interest in fathering a child. But no matter. The fetus will not be alive much longer."*

*What was he saying? He was going to kill my baby? Our baby?*

*Everett reached into his pocket and pulled out an amber prescription bottle with a white lid.*

*"You're going to take these." The pills rattled as he shook the bottle. "You might survive them. That fetus won't."*

*"No!" I screamed but it was cut short when his hand whipped out and slammed into my cheek, stunning me silent.*

*"You will," he growled. "Or I'll slit Gigi's throat right in front of you."*

*I shook my head, frantically scrambling backward on the bed. I had to get away. I had to run. I had to protect my child.*

*But despite the panicked questions racing through my mind, I could still hear that rattling sound above all others. The bottle rattled as Everett leaned his body over mine, pinning me to the bed. It rattled as he fought to pry my mouth open. It rattled as I kicked and clawed and twisted, trying to get free.*

*It rattled—*

"Maisy?"

Everett's mouth formed my name but it was Hunter's voice that came out.

I blinked once. Then twice. *Poof*, the flash was gone. I was back in my parents' house, standing in the hallway outside the living room. My senior picture was on the wall next to Michael's and Beau's. Coby's baby picture was framed on the other side of the hall. And Hunter was standing right in front of me, his hands on my shoulders.

"Maisy? What's wrong?"

I didn't answer. I was still too busy inspecting the room. The beige walls. The white trim. The tan shag carpet.

"Maisy?"

"Huh?" I blinked, focusing my eyes on Hunter. "Oh, sorry."

He frowned and grabbed my elbow, gently steering me to the privacy of the living room. When we were out of earshot of the others, he fisted his hands on his hips. "What was that? You were white as a ghost and you looked at me like . . . like you were scared of me."

I closed my eyes and pushed out a deep breath.

This explanation wasn't going to be fun.

"That wasn't you. That was, um . . . Everett."

"Everett?"

"I kind of have these, um, flashes sometimes about that night. They just pop into my head, like déjà vu but more real." I looked to my feet, embarrassed that I'd had to tell Hunter about my craziness. Other than Gigi and my therapist from years ago, no one knew about my flashes.

His finger hooked under my chin and tipped it up. "Flashes? Like flashbacks?"

"Yeah. I guess."

"How long have you been having flashbacks? Did the custody hearing bring them up?"

I shook my head. "I've had them all along."

He dropped my chin. "Since that night?"

I nodded.

He closed his eyes. When they opened, his eyes were full of concern.

"I know it's crazy," I said, "but please don't ship me off to the loony bin. That was actually one of the shorter ones I've ever had. So, that's a good thing. Shorter is better. Well, sometimes. I'm glad you're not short. Anywhere."

The corner of his mouth turned up at my joke. With a fast tug, he pulled me into his arms. "This is all too much. You've got a lot going on up here." He kissed my forehead. "I think we need to get you somebody to talk to."

I nuzzled into his chest, soaking up his comfort. "I agree, but not until all of this stuff with Eleanor is over and tourist season comes to an end. I can't take anything else right now. I'm just . . . I'm maxed out."

"I know you're maxed out, baby, but I really need to tell—"

"No." I cut him off and hugged him tighter. "No. Just hold me close and tell me it will be okay."

His arms squeezed tight. "It will. I promise. I'll make this okay."

---

HUNTER

"Stuart." I shook his hand. "Thanks for meeting me on a Saturday. I apologize for interrupting your weekend."

Wearing jeans and a white polo, Stuart looked ready for a round of golf or an afternoon picnic.

"No problem at all," he said. "Your call yesterday sounded a bit urgent. Is everything okay?"

"I'll let you decide."

He nodded toward his office. "Then you'd better come on in."

While he walked behind his desk, I took one of the guest chairs I'd become all too familiar with this past month.

"Can I get you anything to drink?" he asked.

I shook my head. "No, thank you."

I didn't have much time to stick around. I was supposed to be at the hardware store buying another box of screws and then picking up lunch. Beau and Michael were currently at the loft, framing Coby's bunk. Maisy was cleaning a couple of rooms at the inn with Coby as her assistant.

That meant I didn't have time to chitchat with Stuart. I needed to get to the point and get the fuck out of here before they knew I'd been gone too long.

Stuart rested his dark forearms on the desk and leaned forward. "I'm ready when you are."

"I need you to get access to some phone records. Can you do that before Monday?"

"Um, I can request them. Before Monday, though? That's going to be tough. Why?"

I took a deep breath. If Maisy wouldn't hear of my past, I'd at least tell her attorney. So that's what I did. I spent the next thirty minutes confessing my secrets to Stuart Redhill.

Secrets that were going to destroy Maisy's trust in our relationship.

But secrets that would keep Coby out of Eleanor Carlson's grasp.

# CHAPTER SEVENTEEN

MAISY

"This chair is uncomfortable," Dad grumbled.

"Mine has a squeak. See?" Behind me, Mom wiggled her chair so hard the wooden legs clacked on the floor and the squeaking—which hadn't been all that noticeable earlier—echoed throughout the room.

I opened my mouth to scold my parents but Beau beat me to it. "You're not helping."

"Sorry," Dad muttered at the same time Mom stilled. "We're just nervous."

Nervous. Jittery. Edgy.

There wasn't a word strong enough to describe my level of anxiety. I was coming out of my skin.

Sitting in the small room at the county courthouse, I drummed my fingers on the wooden table in front of me. Stuart was on my right. Mom, Dad, Beau and Sabrina were in the row behind us. Jess, Gigi and Michael were behind them. There was only one empty seat on my half of the courtroom.

The seat where Hunter's perfect butt was supposed to be sitting.

I glanced over my shoulder, looking at the door for the hundredth time in the last half hour. Where was he? He was never late. Was he mad because of this morning?

Hunter had tried earlier to—once again—unload whatever was on his mind about his past. And—once again—I'd dutifully shut him out. I'd kissed his pleading lips good-bye and shut the door on his face. Whatever he had to tell me could wait until after the hearing. Whether it was about his family or an ex-girlfriend or our relationship, it could wait.

Coby's hearing came first.

But even if Hunter was mad, he could at least be here on time.

I sighed and turned back to the front, taking in the other half of the room. Eleanor Carlson's side was barren. The devil herself, her witnesses and her attorney had yet to arrive.

I glanced up at the white clock on wall behind the judge's bench: 8:50 a.m. The hearing would start in ten minutes and the key players had yet to arrive, including the judge. The only other person in the room was a stenographer setting up her machine at the front. Didn't the others believe in being prompt? Was there anything wrong with starting things a few minutes ahead of schedule? Because if this hearing didn't start on time, the chances of me flipping out completely were really, *really* high.

But at least I wouldn't be alone when I went berserk. I could feel Dad's tree trunk of a leg bouncing on the floor and Mom was squirming in her squeaky chair again.

"Where is Hunter?" Mom whispered.

I just shrugged. *Good question.* Where was Hunter?

"He'll be here," Stuart told Mom.

I turned to look at the wooden doors again, wishing for one to open with Hunter on the other side. He was my calming presence, my steady hand to hold, and I desperately needed some steady right now.

*Open. Open. Open.*

I stared at the doors for another second as I willed them to open, but the dark mahogany stayed shut.

Turning back to the front, I surveyed the décor for the twentieth time. Was it a requirement that all courtrooms be decorated in wood and only wood? Was it supposed to be comforting and calming? If so, it was having the opposite effect on me. I felt trapped in this wooden chair behind this wooden table in this wooden room.

Dark paneling covered the walls from floor to ceiling. The judge's oak bench towered above us. The wooden seat at his side was bracketed by wooden spindles. The only thing in the room that wasn't wooden was the freshly waxed linoleum floor, which shined under the florescent lights above.

I was smack in the middle of an episode of *Law & Order*.

"Deep breaths." Stuart covered my hand with his to stop my drumming fingers.

I obeyed, filling my lungs with air before pushing it out with a breathy, "I'm sorry."

"It will be fine. Trust me."

I nodded, and when he let go of my hand, I slipped it under my thigh.

The air shifted as the doors pushed open and my half of the room spun to see who was walking in. *Please be Hunter.*

My hopeful gaze turned to an annoyed glare when Eleanor Carlson stepped through the door, followed by her attorney. I looked past the short, balding man, expecting to see a witness or two, but the pair was alone.

No witnesses? I wouldn't complain. No witnesses for her was a good thing for me.

Because without witnesses and evidence showing I was unfit to parent Coby, it would be Eleanor's word against mine. Judge Tubor might be less likely to give her time with Coby if she came across as the bitch she clearly was.

Eleanor's high heels clicked sharply on the linoleum as she strutted to the front of the room. Her black blazer and pencil skirt silhouetted her rail-thin frame. The top button on the black blouse under the blazer had to be choking her. With dark hair tied in a fierce bun, the fine lines of her forehead had been stretched to near invisibility. I'd give Eleanor one thing; she was a beautiful woman. She looked well younger than her years and clearly had the money to maintain herself. Her nose had a stiffness that was far from natural.

With her chin held high, Eleanor walked to her table opposite ours. Only when she sat did she bother making eye contact. She aimed a nasty glare right at me before sitting in her own wooden chair.

That glare was all too telling.

I'd come to a conclusion after our initial court appearance and our awful mediation attempt. This custody battle wasn't about Coby, it was about me. Eleanor Carlson was punishing me for killing her son. I just hoped—for Coby's sake—that Judge Tubor saw it too. My son didn't deserve to be used as a pawn in this war between adults.

As Eleanor's attorney settled into his own chair, I looked back to the clock.

*Five minutes.*

Five minutes and this ordeal would be underway.

Five minutes for Hunter to get his ass to the courthouse.

Where was he? Had something happened at the hospital? Had he gotten called in for an emergency?

I bent to my purse under the table and felt around for my phone. The screen was blank. Firing off a *Where r u?* text to Hunter, I quadruple-checked that my device was on silent before putting it away.

Then I sat deathly still. The silence in the room was ominous. I was having trouble taking a full breath, and as much as I needed to suck in some oxygen, I didn't dare. Breathing would be too loud.

Two minutes passed like twenty until the judge's chamber door opened behind his bench and out he came.

This was it. The wait was over.

I swallowed down the bile that had risen in my throat and concentrated on the judge so I wouldn't puke.

Judge Tubor was an older man, likely in his late fifties, and had lived in Prescott my whole life. His hair was fully gray but his youthful face betrayed his age. The olive skin of his face was nearly wrinkle-free except for some laugh lines around his eyes.

He'd been the district judge for Jamison County for as long as I could remember. Our community loved him and no challenger had ever been able to beat him in an election. He'd always won my vote because of his fair but firm judgments, but if he took Coby away from me, I'd never vote for him again.

"Morning." Judge Tubor nodded to us all and then sat on

his bench, adjusting his black robe before shoving on reading glasses to review the papers at his desk.

With the judge not looking at us, I stole one last glance at the back doors just in time to see Hunter's broad frame slip in sideways.

*Finally.* My shoulders relaxed as I sighed.

"Sorry," he mouthed before taking the last empty seat at the back.

I nodded and swiveled toward the front. As I turned, I caught a glimpse of Eleanor glaring again. But this time, her snarl wasn't aimed at me, but at Hunter.

*Okay, weird.*

A twinge of unease pricked the back of my neck but I ignored it when the judge started speaking again.

"All right. Let's get started." He nodded down to the stenographer, whose fingers started flying as she dictated every word of Judge Tubor's legalese. He kicked off the proceedings with a summary of the custody petition and the activities he'd mandated during our first appearance.

"It is my understanding that no agreement between Ms. Carlson and Ms. Holt could be reached outside of court. Correct?"

"Yes, Your Honor," Eleanor's attorney and Stuart answered in unison.

"Okay." Judge Tubor looked up from his notes and took the reading glasses off his face. "Then I'll be rendering a custody decision this morning. Ms. Carlson, since you are presenting this petition, we'll start with you. I'll ask you some questions and then you'll have the opportunity to present witnesses on your behalf."

Eleanor and her attorney both nodded.

Then the judge looked to me and my posse. "Once Ms.

Carlson has presented her statement and witnesses, Ms. Holt, you'll have the chance to respond and present witnesses of your own."

Stuart and I both nodded.

The judge leaned forward. "Before we start, I'd like to remind you all that my concern is and will remain with the child. My decision will be made in order to provide the best possible environment to ensure the child is given every possible opportunity to thrive."

I did my best to keep my face impassive, but with every "the child," my jaw clamped tighter. Judge Tubor knew my family. He went to our church. His wife helped my mom organize potluck Sundays. And he knew Coby. Calling my son "the child" was impersonal and did nothing to ease the ball of tension in my gut.

"With that understood, let's begin," Judge Tubor declared. "Ms. Carlson, your petition is fairly uncommon for a grandparent. You're seeking six months of full custody with limited visitation during that time from the child's mother. You have no evidence suggesting Ms. Holt is an unfit parent. Can you explain why you feel you need to have the child for such an extended period of time away from his home?"

The child. *Seriously?*

"Your Honor, I feel that my grandson would do well living with me for a good portion of the year. It would give us a chance to bond and catch up on all of the years I've missed because he's only been with his mother."

I swallowed a growl. This missing "bond" was entirely Eleanor's doing. She could have reached out years ago. Shipping my son to Michigan was not the answer.

"Why do you feel that living with you in Michigan is the

only way for you to catch up?" the judge asked, as if reading my thoughts. "Couldn't you plan more visits here so as to not interrupt Coby's home life?"

"I think the separation is necessary," Eleanor answered. "I need him to be away from her so that I can be sure my grandson is getting a proper moral upbringing."

*Proper moral upbringing?* I nearly came out of my chair and would have if not for Stuart's hand landing on mine. Mom was getting worked up too because behind me, her chair started squeaking again.

I shook my head as I clamped my mouth shut.

Eleanor Carlson was nuts. She thought she could teach my son a proper moral upbringing? Her own son had become a drug dealer and had thought killing innocent women was acceptable.

Before I could mutter a sarcastic retort about her own parenting skills, Judge Tubor continued. "Ms. Carlson, you're suggesting that Ms. Holt is unfit to raise Coby yet you have no evidence proving she isn't providing him a proper home. The child psychologist has sent me her report, and by all accounts, Coby is a happy and well-adjusted child. The parenting plan you're proposing would cause an extreme disruption to his home life. Why should I grant your request when you haven't given me any reason to take Coby from his mother for six months out of the year?"

I leaned forward to stare at Eleanor's profile. She was floundering a bit, her brown eyes widening as she looked to her attorney for an answer.

I smirked at her lack of an answer. Had they given no thought to the questions the judge would ask? Had she not practiced answer after answer in her bathroom mirror like I had? Did she honestly think she'd just waltz in here and get custody of Coby without proving she deserved it?

Maybe I'd spent the past month worrying for nothing. Maybe Eleanor wasn't just crazy, but stupid too.

Eleanor's attorney final spoke up. "Your Honor, if I may—"

"You may not." The judge shut him down. "I'd like Ms. Carlson to answer the question."

Eleanor straightened and cleared her throat. "I don't have specific evidence that she is an unfit mother. What I do know is that woman knew nothing about my son. If I don't get the chance to get Coby away from her, he'll never have the opportunity to learn about his father. He'll be brainwashed into thinking my wonderful Everett was a monster."

"I have never, not once, said anything derogatory about Everett to Coby." The words were out of my mouth before I could think them through.

The judge's eyes sliced to mine and he frowned.

I shrank back into my chair. "Sorry."

"You'll get your chance, Ms. Holt." Judge Tubor dismissed me and went back to Eleanor.

"Keep it together," Stuart whispered, patting my hand.

I nodded and took a breath.

"Ms. Carlson," the judge continued, "this petition seems like an extreme solution to your concerns that he won't learn about his father. I'd like to know why you couldn't spend time teaching Coby about his father while he remained in his home."

"I can't be around that woman." Eleanor's snap surprised us all; the collected façade she'd brought into the courtroom was falling to pieces and fast. We'd only been here ten minutes and already she was crumbling?

"Why is that?" the judge asked, still pressing for more.

"Why do you think? She murdered my son!"

At Eleanor's outburst, Mom gasped and I jerked in my chair. Eleanor might as well have slapped me.

The worst part of it was, I didn't have a rebuttal.

I had killed Everett. I hadn't murdered him in cold blood, but I had taken her son's life. And even though I hated her, I could see how hard it would be for Eleanor to be in the same room with me.

"Let's all take a minute," the judge said calmly. "I understand this is an emotional situation, but remember, we're doing this for Coby. I agree with you, Ms. Carlson, that the best way for him to learn about his father is from someone who knew him well. As Coby's grandmother, your influence could be very beneficial in his life and help him make a connection to the memory of his father."

Over my dead body. The last thing Coby needed was to be introduced to Everett's memory.

"Thank you." Eleanor sniffled and dabbed the corner of her eye. Maybe she wasn't as frazzled as I'd thought a second ago. Maybe this was all part of her plan. Fake dramatics. Shed some tears. Get the judge to pity her.

He wasn't buying it, was he?

*No. Oh god, no.* My heart raced even faster as the blood drained from my face. Just the idea of Coby being around Eleanor sent my head spinning.

If Eleanor sank her claws into Coby, she'd do nothing but confuse him. She'd paint Everett as the brilliant yet misunderstood genius doctor and me the slut nurse that had gotten knocked up and then committed murder. Coby would never understand. My loving, caring, gentle little boy was about to be put in the middle of a situation most adults would have a hard time comprehending.

*Please, Judge Tubor. Please don't do this to him.*

He sat on his bench, ignorant to my silent pleas. "Do you have anything else you'd like to say before we start talking to witnesses?" he asked Eleanor.

She shook her head. "No, Your Honor."

"All right. You may proceed with calling your witnesses."

Her attorney cleared his throat. "We have no witnesses at this time, Your Honor."

The judge's eyebrows creased. "None?"

"No, Your Honor," her attorney answered.

*Yes!* I did a tiny fist pump for the Holts.

"All right." The judge looked over to me but before he could start his questioning, Hunter's voice filled the room.

"Your Honor?" I spun my head around. Hunter was on his feet, an arm raised. "I apologize for the interruption. My name is Dr. Hunter Faraday. I am Ms. Carlson's stepson and would like to say a few words, if you don't mind."

*Wait, what did he say?*

Hunter's eyes came to mine as I replayed his words.

*I am Ms. Carlson's stepson.*

Stepson? My heart plummeted into my stomach as my mouth fell open, the words looping through my mind over and over.

What the actual fuck was happening?

Hunter was Eleanor's stepson? Was that what he'd been trying to tell me? Because if it was true, that meant he had known Everett.

All this time.

And he'd tried to tell me, but I'd shut him out.

I couldn't breathe. I couldn't think. All I could do was sit and stare at the man in the back of the room who had just shocked me to the core.

"Dr. Faraday, please come forward."

My eyes tracked Hunter as he obeyed the judge's command. I couldn't look away. In my periphery, Beau was fuming, Mom had been stunned into silence, and Dad's wounded eyes were locked on me. But I just kept my gaze locked on Hunter.

The man I loved. The man who had been lying to me for months. The man who had tried to confess just this morning.

"Please, take a seat." The judge nodded to the chair at his side. "I think I'd like to hear what you have to say."

"That makes two of us," Dad muttered.

"Deep breath," Stuart whispered. "This is a good thing."

My eyes snapped to my attorney. Stuart knew. When Hunter couldn't tell me, he'd told Stuart instead.

I closed my eyes as a mix of emotions made me dizzy. I was hurt. I was angry. I was a fool. Never in a million years would I have expected this to be Hunter's big secret. Never. Now I really wished I'd let him explain.

When I opened my eyes, they went straight to Hunter. He sat, solemn, in the front of the room, his pleading eyes begging for a chance to explain.

*No.* I didn't want his explanation. He might have been trying to give me one recently, but he'd had months before this custody drama to come clean. Yet he'd stayed quiet. Anger beat out the other emotions and blood roared in my ears. I gave Hunter the tiniest headshake and ripped my gaze away, not daring to look at him, otherwise I'd scream.

I sat frozen in my wooden chair and listened, my eyes glued to the stenographer's flying fingers as my own gripped the armrests of my chair with as much force as I could muster.

"Okay," the judge said. "Whenever you're ready."

"Thank you." Hunter nodded. "As I said, Eleanor Carlson is my stepmother. And full disclosure, I am in a relationship with Maisy Holt. We've been dating for around three months, not long after I moved to Prescott."

And in all that time, he hadn't bothered to mention he knew exactly who Coby's father was.

My teeth gritted hard as Hunter's gaze raked over my face but I refused to tear my gaze from the stenographer. I was barely holding on to my emotions, and if I looked at Hunter, I'd lose it. Coby couldn't afford to have me lose it.

I swallowed a dry laugh. How ironic. I'd been thinking lately how wonderful it would be if Hunter might become Coby's father one day. I didn't need to worry about that though, because he was technically Coby's uncle.

My heart kept sinking as other questions swamped my mind. Had our relationship been a ruse? Was this all part of Eleanor's evil plan to take my son? Had Hunter been playing me all this time?

The pain was getting the best of me and my chin quivered. Doing the only thing I could think of to stop the angry tears from welling, I pinched my leg. Hard. Now was not the time to think about Hunter's betrayal. I could process that after I knew the fate of my child.

As the sting in my leg burned, Hunter's voice faltered, and I couldn't help but look up at him. His mouth was turned down in a sad frown.

He'd seen that pinch.

"Dr. Faraday, are you speaking on Ms. Carlson's behalf today or on behalf of Ms. Holt?" Judge Tubor asked.

"Actually, I'd like to speak on Coby's behalf today."

One sentence and all of my anger vanished in one hot tear rolling down my cheek.

Hunter loved Coby. The entire wooden room echoed with that love in his voice.

Which only made his lies hurt that much more. The fleeting thought that this could all be a ruse flittered right out of my mind. Hunter might have betrayed me, but he was staying true to Coby.

At least there was that.

"I met Coby about four months ago when I met Maisy," Hunter said. "In that time, I've had the honor of spending time with him. He's a remarkable child. He's got his father's intelligence. And his mother's heart."

My fortitude wavered. Hunter's eyes, full of regret and apology, were waiting for mine. His shoulders tensed before he glanced at Eleanor.

"Your Honor, if your concern is introducing Everett to Coby, I will ensure that happens. But I can't in good conscience keep quiet about Nell's character. Coby would not benefit from spending time in Michigan."

*Nell?*

The judge asked the same question.

"Nell, her preferred name," Hunter clarified.

Eleanor was Nell.

The blows kept coming and I sank, defeated, into my stiff chair. I had asked Hunter specifically about Nell and he'd shut me out. That would have been the perfect opportunity for him to come clean.

"Let's hear about these character issues," the judge said.

Hunter nodded. "Coby needs love and affection. He's no different than any other child. Nell doesn't have it in her to give him the love he needs. It's just not part of her makeup. Nell married my father when I was ten, and in the twenty-four years that I have known her, she has not once given me a hug. She's never made me a meal or told me that she cares. All of those things, those motherly things that Coby gets from Maisy, will be entirely absent in the time he spends with Nell."

As wrecked as I was that Hunter had kept his secrets, my heart still felt sad for his childhood. His mother had died too young. His father had had to cope with the loss of his wife. Hunter had gotten stuck with a cold stepmother and Everett as a stepbrother.

*But he'd lied.* I couldn't forget that.

"Coby is a happy child, Your Honor," Hunter continued. "Separating him from his mother would only cause stress in his young life. If Eleanor had been more loving in my youth, I'd agree that a grandmother's influence could be beneficial for Coby, but I don't think that is the case here."

The room went silent as Hunter's last words rang through the room. Everyone sat motionless, digesting his statement.

Moments later, Judge Tubor broke the air. "Would you like to respond, Ms. Carlson?"

Eleanor stared shocked at Hunter, blinking a few times as she formulated her response. "My chef makes delicious meals and the boy would have an excellent nanny for the other parts."

"Coby," Hunter said. "Not 'the boy.' His name is Coby."

Surprised turned to hate and her face twisted in a snarl. "I hate that name. If *she* hadn't murdered Everett, he'd have a decent name."

Every Holt in the room gasped.

"I apologize, Your Honor," Eleanor's attorney spoke up after shushing his client.

"It would be in your best interest, Ms. Carlson, to leave your opinions about your son's death out of these proceedings."

"Of course," her attorney answered.

"Do you have anything else you'd like to add, Dr. Faraday?" the judge asked.

Hunter shook his head and nodded to Stuart. "No. Thank you for the opportunity to speak."

"You're excused."

Hunter nodded and rose from his chair. As he walked past me, I studied the table until he'd returned to his seat. When I looked up, Judge Tubor was staring at Eleanor's attorney.

"Do you have other witnesses?"

The bald man shook his head.

"Okay." Judge Tubor looked to Stuart. "Mr. Redhill. You may proceed with your witness statements."

"Before we jump into witness statements, Your Honor, I'd like to bring something else to your attention."

*What? What else was there besides our witnesses? When were we going to run out of goddamn surprises?* I opened my mouth but clamped it shut when Stuart shot me a quelling look.

He pulled a small stack of papers out from underneath his legal pad and stood, taking them to the judge. "Your Honor, my client and I are very concerned about Ms. Carlson's history of harassment."

*Harassment?* What was he talking about?

"In the last few months, Ms. Carlson has made an extreme number of calls to Ms. Holt. As you can see in those records that Sheriff Cleary received last night, the number registered to Ms. Carlson has called Ms. Holt's number at least once a day for a period of nearly two months. She asked Ms. Holt about her son's death, to which Maisy did not respond."

My head was spinning again. Eleanor, not a reporter, had been calling me all spring? Eleanor averted her guilty eyes from her red-faced attorney.

"As she's demonstrated today," Stuart continued talking to the judge, "Ms. Carlson has little reverence for Ms. Holt. These obsessive phone calls are nothing but harassment. We believe that Ms. Carlson is seeking these extended, unsupervised periods with Coby to alienate him from his mother."

The judge frowned as he kept inspecting the phone records. When he set them down, he leaned his elbows on his desk.

"Ms. Holt, would you be opposed to allowing Ms. Carlson supervised visits with Coby once a month?"

I shook my head. "No, Your Honor."

"Very well. Ms. Carlson, I am denying your request for split custody. I will award you one weekend visit per month with Coby. Location, supervision and duration of those visits will be determined by Ms. Holt. Any questions?"

Eleanor started to speak but her attorney held out a hand. "No questions."

"Mr. Redhill?"

"No," Stuart said. "Thank you, Your Honor."

"Then this matter is closed and adjourned." He rapped his gavel on its block and stood, looking down at the stenographer. "Ended early. Let's hope the rest of the day stays on schedule too." Then he hastened back to his chamber.

The second his door closed, Eleanor, followed by her

attorney, stood from their table and stormed toward the door. She yanked it open but paused to sneer at Hunter. "Your father would be ashamed of you for betraying me."

"Good-bye, Nell" was his only response.

She left the courtroom, and if my lucky streak continued, she'd be gone from Montana before dark.

Stuart breathed a sigh of relief as the door swung shut. "Battle won."

As I stood from my seat, a wall of large bodies formed in the row behind us. Dad, Beau, Michael and Jess were all standing shoulder to shoulder. I couldn't see their faces with their backs to me, but I knew they weren't smiling.

And past them was Hunter. He was looking right through them to me.

Stuart had been right. We'd won one battle.

But there was about to be another.

# CHAPTER EIGHTEEN

MAISY

"Give him a chance to explain." Stuart leaned over to whisper.

My jaw ticked in response as I picked up my purse and slung it over my shoulder. "How long have you known about the calls?"

Stuart held up his hands. "I just learned it was a possibility on Saturday. Hunter had a hunch that they were from Eleanor so he had me pull the records. We didn't know for sure until late last night. You were so freaked this morning, I made a judgment call not to tell you. I didn't need you trying to claw Eleanor's eyes out in front of the judge."

My head fell. "That was probably a good call."

Annoyed as I was with the secrets, I couldn't be upset with the outcome of the case. Eleanor had been likely to get some time with Coby no matter what, but at least now that time was under my control.

"Please let me know if there is anything else I need to do to wrap this up," I told Stuart.

"I will. The ball is in Eleanor's court now. If she makes contact, you can set the terms for her to see Coby."

I nodded. "Thank you."

"Don't thank me." Stuart collected his papers and briefcase. "Thank Hunter."

I would.

For Coby.

Stuart shook my hand and left, nudging through the blockade of bodies. His vacant space at my side was immediately filled with Gigi.

"I'm guessing this was all news to you today?" she asked.

"Yep." Though in all fairness, it was only new because I'd refused to listen to Hunter's pleas. Major fail on my part for not hearing him out. Major fail on his part for hiding this secret way too long.

She looked toward the back and frowned. "What are you going to do?"

"I have no flipping clue. For now, I'm going to go to the inn and catch up on the weekend checkouts. Then I'm going to pick up Coby and take him out for a celebration tonight, just the two of us. He won't know that we're celebrating but I don't care."

"And Hunter? You can't avoid him forever, sweetie."

I sighed, the exhaustion of the last hour settling heavily on my shoulders. "I don't even know how to feel right now. I can't talk to him until I figure that out first."

She gave me a sad smile and squeezed my hand.

"Thanks for being here today. Even if you didn't have to say anything."

"I'm always here. Whenever you need."

"Maze?" Beau called from over his shoulder.

"Yeah?"

He nodded to the back of the room where Mom had walked up to Hunter.

"Uh-oh," Gigi muttered.

I braced, waiting for Mom to either slap Hunter or start scolding him, but she did neither. She just wrapped her arms around his tense body. "Thank you." As quickly as she'd hugged him, she let him go, immediately walking to the door. "Brock, time to go."

Dad didn't say a word as he followed. He nodded at Hunter, opened the door for Mom and escorted her out.

They both knew I'd catch them up later. And they both knew that their place was not in the middle of my relationship.

"Your parents are the best," Sabrina said, joining me and Gigi.

"Yes, they are," Gigi and I agreed in unison.

"Do you need anything?" Sabrina asked.

"No. Thank you for coming today."

"No problem." She smiled at me, then announced, "Beau, it's time to go." She walked up to his back and laced her hand with his. When he didn't budge, she jerked on his arm, but he still didn't budge. "Beau." Sabrina's tone had sharpened. "We need to leave. This is not your business."

He huffed. "Not my bus—"

She held up a hand and cut him off. Her movements were firm but her voice a gentle whisper. "This one isn't your fight. Maisy can do it on her own."

Beau's shoulders deflated as he stared at his wife, then looked to me. "Call me if you need anything?"

I nodded. "I will. Thanks for being here today."

"Okay. See you soon." He turned and slapped Michael on the back, then pushed him down the aisle after Sabrina. Without a word, they passed Hunter and left the room.

Gigi hugged me good-bye, then threaded her hand with Jess's. "Let's go, Sheriff."

When the door closed behind them, Hunter and I stayed in our places, separated by two rows of uncomfortable wooden chairs. After a few moments, the silence became too much and we both spoke at the same time.

"I need to go to work."

"I'm sorry."

I took a step toward the aisle and repeated, "I need to go to work."

"Can we talk?"

I shook my head and started walking toward the door.

"Maisy?" he whispered when my hand hit the door handle.

I stopped but didn't turn to look at him. "I need some time to think."

"Please let me explain."

My eyes teared as I stared at the wooden door. "Thank you for speaking for Coby today." Before I started to cry, I tugged on the handle and opened the door.

"Maisy, please. Let me explain."

"I should have listened to you, but Hunter, you had months before all this." I pushed the door shut but kept my hand tightly wrapped on the handle. "Months to explain. Why did you wait so long?" A tear fell and I swiped it away with my free hand.

"I didn't want to lose you. The second I told you who I was, you would have slammed the door in my face."

"That's not—"

"It is. You know it is."

"Then you should have *made* me listen."

"I fucked up," he whispered. "I should have tried harder, and I'm sorry."

I nodded. He *should* have tried harder. He should have pinned me to the bed, taped my mouth shut and forced an explanation on me. A courtroom was not the place for me and my family to learn he was related to Everett.

"I'm going to go." I cracked the door again.

"Maisy, I love you."

I loved him too. Despite my confused and frustrated head, my heart loved Hunter. Another tear fell and I knew more were about to follow. "I can't do this here. Just . . . give me some time."

"Okay." He surprised me by not arguing. "Go to work. Lose yourself in a to-do list, but can I come over tonight? Please?"

I nodded and yanked the door open all the way, making my escape.

And then, just like Hunter had known, I went to the inn and lost myself in work.

---

SITTING on the landing of the staircase to the loft, my back was to the wall and my legs were stretched across the top step. A wineglass rested on my thigh and my head was tipped back so I could study the sky. Even after nine o'clock and well past Coby's bedtime, it was still light this time of year. I rarely sat and appreciated the summer sunsets, usually too busy with motel chores, but tonight I had run out of steam so I'd retreated to the stairs.

"Hey."

I dropped my head from the fading sky. Hunter stood on the bottom step. "Hi."

He started up the stairs. "What are you doing out here?"

"I just wanted some air." And some peace. Gigi watched the sunsets almost every night because she said they gave her peace, and since work hadn't helped me today, I was willing to try just about anything.

"Do you want to go inside to talk?" Hunter asked when he was three steps away from the landing.

I shook my head.

"Okay." Hunter came up the last few steps, sitting down on the top step too. With my legs stretched out between us, my feet were at his hip and I had the perfect view of his handsome profile.

I took a sip from my glass. "Do you want some wine?"

"No, I need to drive home."

It was a relief that he had already planned to go home. After Hunter gave me his explanation, I would need space. My bed was officially a Hunter-free zone until further notice.

"Where do you want me to start?"

I took a deep breath and drained the last of my wine. "Why didn't you tell me earlier?"

"Remember the day you got Nell's papers? I had planned on telling you that night."

That was the night he'd arranged for Coby to spend the night with my parents. I'd been so excited that day, thinking Hunter had something special planned for just the two of us, but the moment I'd gotten Eleanor's petition, all of that had fallen to the wayside.

"Why not before then?" I asked. "Why not right after we met?"

"I didn't want to lose you. I was scared you'd tell me to leave. I knew I should have told you, but I didn't want you to shut me out. From the moment you started babbling to me in the motel lobby that first day, I just wanted to be a part of your life."

I had wanted him in my life too. So much. "Was it real?"

"It *is* real. I love you, Maisy. The only thing I kept from you was the past but everything else was real."

The lump in the back of my throat swelled. I loved him too. Despite the lies and the omissions, I loved him too. "You should have told me right away," I whispered. "That was too much to keep secret."

He hung his head. "I know. I was a coward and you don't owe me anything, but can I explain?"

I took a breath. It was time to get my questions answered. "Start at the beginning."

He ran a hand over his hair, brushing back some of the strands that had fallen out from his bun. "A few years after my mom died, Dad started dating. He was a doctor too so most of his dates were with women who worked with him at the hospital. That's where he met Nell. She was working in the cafeteria, Dad met her at lunch one day, and four months later, they got married."

I reached for my wineglass, frowning when I remembered it was empty.

"They got married fast, mostly because I think Dad was desperate to fill the hole Mom had left when she died. So I inherited a stepmom who was more than happy to quit her shitty job and spend Dad's money along with a stepbrother who didn't like having a younger brother."

"You and Everett didn't get along?"

"No," he scoffed. "We hated each other. At first, I thought we could be friends. Dad worked so much, I thought maybe Everett could keep me company, but instead we fought."

"About what?"

"Everything. He picked on me relentlessly and I fought back. I was young, pissed that Dad had brought them into my life. I wanted to go back to the days of just me and Dad. Mostly, I wanted my mom back. I took a lot of my aggression out on Everett. He did the same to me."

"And Nell?"

"Nell treated me like a burden. Everett too. I meant what I said in court today. She doesn't have a motherly bone in her body. As soon as she got Dad's paychecks, she hired a nanny, not that we needed one. I was ten and Everett was fourteen when they moved in, but a nanny on staff meant she could ignore us."

"And your dad?"

"Dad took Nell being home as an excuse to spend more time at the hospital. He got a promotion, worked his way up to chief of surgery. He'd make it home once, maybe twice a week before I was asleep. It was only when we took our fishing trips that he really paid me much attention."

Which meant Hunter had grown up angry, sad and alone. "Why didn't you ever tell your dad how you were feeling? From what you've told me, he loved you. Wouldn't he have tried to make things better?"

Hunter sighed. "Yeah. He would have. But for all her faults, Dad loved Nell. Just not as much as my mother. Nell put in zero effort with me and Everett, but she was all about

Dad. Trying to make him love her more than he did a dead woman's memory."

I felt a small twinge of sympathy for Nell but it faded fast. "And she was so focused on your dad, she neglected her own son?"

"Pretty much. Honestly, I don't know how close they were before they ever moved in. They were both so greedy and selfish. I think it just became easier for Nell to ignore Everett once she got set up as a rich doctor's wife."

My insides twisted with mixed emotion. On the one hand, it was Everett. I loathed his memory. But on the other, I felt bad that he'd never had a loving and proud mother. "Should I feel sorry for Everett?"

"Fuck no." He turned to look me right in the eye. "Everett was a rotten kid and grew into a rotten adult. He made his choices, not Nell. She wasn't responsible for turning him into a drug-dealing psychopath. That was all him, the greedy motherfucker."

Clearly, even as grown men, they had still hated each other. "So I'm guessing you and Everett never became friends?"

"No. Things between us just got worse and worse. He'd come back from college and try and seduce my high-school girlfriends. He'd buy beer for my friends but only if they didn't tell me where they were partying. I am convinced that the only reason Everett became a doctor was because he knew I wanted to follow in Dad's footsteps and it would piss me off."

The more Hunter talked, the more I pitied his childhood. I couldn't imagine the stress of having that kind of animosity in my home. Of living in a house without love. I'd grown up with parents and brothers that had adored me.

"I'm sorry."

"It's okay. Everett was an asshole, but I grew up and got to the point where I just ignored him. Once I started college, I distanced myself, and then, thank fuck, he moved."

I wasn't as grateful about Everett's move to Prescott. The only good thing that had come from his time here was Coby. "Why did Everett come to Montana to smuggle pills from the county hospitals? If he was a big-city doctor, wouldn't he have made more money just working? Doctors in Chicago make good money, right?"

Everett had scammed his way into three different Montana hospitals, recruiting nurses to steal prescription pills that he later resold. I knew pills could bring in a lot of money, but enough to compete with a doctor's salary? It didn't add up.

"He made good money in Chicago but probably not as much as you'd think. Those pills set him up. But I think it was more than just the money. I think it was about power. He wanted to prove he was smarter than us all. And I think it was a big 'Fuck You' to me and Dad."

"Why is that?"

"When Dad died, Nell inherited his insurance payout. She got the insurance. I got everything else. His money. The house. Everything. Everett didn't get a dime. We got into a big fight after Dad's funeral and he took off. He said he wasn't going to work his whole life. That he would get rich faster than me or Dad ever could."

"And that's when he came here to Prescott?"

Hunter nodded. "For all his intelligence, he was a dumbass. He had so much fucking brainpower, but instead of using it, he was always plotting for a shortcut."

Everett's last shortcut had cost him his life.

"Okay," I said. "So fast forward to now. It's been years since Everett's death. Why did Nell come for Coby after all this time? Why did she wait so many years to file the custody petition?"

Hunter ran a hand over his hair again and when he looked up, I didn't like the tortured look on his face. "It wasn't just now."

My muscles tensed. "What do you mean?"

"The first time I saw you was the day you had Coby. I was sitting in the waiting room when Beau brought you to the hospital in Bozeman."

"What?" My chin fell. "Why?"

"Nell sent me to ask you for Coby. She wanted you to give him over to her. She was grieving. She wanted that piece of Everett but didn't want to be around you so I went in her place. The only reason I agreed to come to the hospital and ask you was because she said you'd sent her a letter and you were considering giving Coby up for adoption."

"That's a lie!" I shouted. "I would never give up my son."

"I know that," he said calmly. "I took one look at you and knew you'd never give him up, so I left."

"Why would you even think about letting her take a baby if she was such a horrible mother?"

He placed a gentle hand on my knee. "I told Nell I was coming to ask you, but really, I was coming to talk you out of it."

"Oh." I slumped against the door.

"After that, I told Nell to leave you alone and that I wouldn't support her case if she tried to get custody of Coby. Miraculously, she dropped it for a while and moved to Grand Rapids to get out of Chicago. I finished up my residency and took an attending position at the hospital where Dad had worked. I thought that was the end of it."

"But it wasn't."

He shook his head. "No. Nell decided to go after Coby again. I just happened to catch wind of it when I ran into one of her old friends at the hospital. I went to Grand Rapids to confront Nell that night."

"And you convinced her to drop it. Otherwise I would have heard from her, right?"

"Not exactly," he said. "She wasn't going to drop it so I moved here the first time. I wanted to be close in case she came to Prescott. And it was my silent threat that if she pushed a custody fight, I'd expose her secret."

More secrets? This was exhausting. Would we ever get through them all? "What secret?"

"That Nell had already blown through my dad's insurance money and was living on Everett's drug money."

Shocked, I blinked a few times as I replayed his last statement. "She knew about Everett's drug dealing?"

"No. Maybe. I'm not sure."

"I'm confused. How was she living off his drug money if she didn't know about it?"

"Everett only had one checking account when he died and the balance matched up to his hospital salary perfectly."

That made sense. He wouldn't have been able to hide his pill mill if he'd been keeping his money in plain sight. "So where was he putting his drug money?"

"In an account in Nell's name."

"So he'd hidden his money with his mom."

Hunter nodded. "That's right. Now, I'm not sure if Nell knew it was from drugs or if she just thought he was taking care of her since Dad was gone. Regardless, after he died, she would have been able to do the math and figure out where that money had come from."

"How did you find out?" If I were Nell, I would have kept all that information to myself.

"By accident. You see, when Dad died, I got our house but I didn't kick out Nell. I figured it had been her home too and Dad would have expected me to help take care of her. So she stayed in the house and I stayed in the pool house. I'd been living there during my residency because I hadn't felt like buying my own place until I knew where my career was going to land me."

"Okay." I was still following, but just barely. "So you're living next to Nell after your dad dies. Everett leaves for Montana, then he dies."

"Right. And how does Nell deal with her grief? Two days after Everett's funeral, she takes a three-month vacation to Mexico. She just up and leaves, leaving nothing but a note for me to find days later in the kitchen. Since I'm living there, I'm getting the mail. After a month, it was piled everywhere so I decided I'd better go through it all in case there's something important. I find these bank statements and get curious. Then I find one last envelope of cash and get really curious since it has a Montana postmark."

"Everett's last donation to his mom's secret account?"

"He must have mailed it the day he died. I started putting two and two together and realized where all that money had been coming from."

I tipped my head back to the now-dark sky and studied the stars while I let everything sink in. "Why didn't you turn in that money? Then Nell would have been broke."

"Because of you."

My head snapped straight. "Me?"

He nodded. "All I ever had to protect you and Coby was my knowledge about that money. You're right, if I'd turned that money over to the authorities, they would have cleaned Nell out. But that money is the one thing she wants more than anything else. Without it as leverage, I had nothing to keep her from harassing you. I'd have played all my cards."

"I guess they weren't very good cards to begin with. She still came after Coby."

"Yep," Hunter muttered. "I thought she'd stay away with me living here again, but I guess not."

"Why this time?"

"I don't know. Maybe the money's gone? Maybe she doesn't care anymore? I'm not sure."

"Are you going to turn her in now?"

He shook his head. "If she tries to take Coby again, I will. But I'm hoping she'll just disappear once and for all."

"Why didn't you tell the judge about any of the money stuff?"

"Stuart said it wouldn't matter. He figured the judge would still have ruled for some visitation in her favor. He agreed I should keep this quiet unless it was vitally necessary. Just in case I need to use it later."

I inspected my empty wineglass as I thought everything through. "No matter what you did, Nell had always planned to get back at me, huh? This was her way of punishing me for killing Everett. Which means you moved out here for nothing."

"No." Hunter's hand still on my knee gripped tighter. "Not nothing. I might not have realized it at the time, but I moved here for you. I was a different man when I sat waiting in that maternity ward all those years ago. I was focused on my career and didn't want anything more than to step into my father's shoes. But that all changed when I saw you. It took me a while, but I realized that I wanted different things for my life. I came here thinking I was looking out for you, when really, I was looking *for* you."

"Then why didn't you come find me the first time you lived here? And why did you move away only to come back?"

His thumb drew a circle on my bare skin. "I was still tied to Chicago. I only took a sabbatical from my job and the hospital here only hired me on a temporary basis. I didn't come and find you because I knew I'd be leaving again. Mostly, I didn't want to bring all this shit to your life."

"Why was it different this time around? What changed?"

"I hadn't planned on seeing you. I had planned to come back temporarily until Nell backed off, just like the last time. But the day I got to Prescott, I saw you downtown. From that moment forward, I couldn't stay away. Then you kicked me in the balls and I knew I was in love with you."

I smiled at his joke. If I hadn't felt that strong pull between us, I might have doubted his reasons, but as it was, I knew exactly how he'd felt.

"I need you, Maisy." He scooted closer. "Please believe that. I know I fucked this all up, but please know, I did it all for you. And I'd do it again."

"This *is* fucked up, Hunter," I whispered. "You're Everett's stepbrother. You're Coby's uncle. I just . . . I can't do all this crazy. I can't do all the secrets."

He took my hands. "I told you once, I'd only leave if you made me. I mean that still. I'm not going anywhere, but this is your call. I'll fight, don't get me wrong. I'm not giving you up easily, but if you really can't get past it, I'll go."

"I love you, Hunter," I admitted. "But I don't trust you."

"I'll win it back. I'll prove I am the only man you'll ever need and I'll never, *ever* keep anything from you again."

I didn't doubt his determination. I *did* doubt my ability to trust him again. "I need time."

"Take as much as you want. I'll be here when you're ready."

I nodded. "Okay."

He stood from the step, bending down to kiss my temple. "Good night."

I looked up at the stars as his footsteps echoed down the staircase and crunched on the gravel when he hit the last step.

"I love you, Maisy. Tell me you believe that."

I didn't break my gaze away from the sky. "I believe that, Hunter. I just don't know if I can believe anything else."

# CHAPTER NINETEEN

MAISY

"Why is your last name Faraday and not Carlson?"

Hunter chuckled into the phone. "Hello to you too."

I stayed quiet, waiting for him to answer.

Over a month had passed since Hunter's staircase confessional, and in that time, he'd given me space. And answers. Whenever a question popped into my head, I'd call and ask. Yesterday, I'd called twice with questions about his extended family. Today, I wanted to know about his last name.

"Faraday was my mom's maiden name," he said. "I changed my name from Carlson to Faraday before I started medical school because I didn't want to be riding Dad's coattails at his alma mater."

"So you were a Faraday but Everett was a Carlson even though he wasn't your dad's biological son?"

"That's right. Nell forced Everett to change his last name

when she married Dad. She wanted everyone in the house to share the same last name. Everett hated it until he got to college but then I guess he decided it wasn't so bad. He'd toss Dad's name around like candy at a parade. I don't know if it made a difference for Everett or not, but I didn't want any special favors from professors or the administration. So I became Hunter Faraday."

I liked Hunter's pride and that he had wanted to succeed on his own accomplishments. I doubted his teachers would have played favorites but it was admirable that he'd cared enough to succeed on his own merit.

"Where did you go to college?" I asked.

"Northwestern. Med school there too."

An image popped into my mind of a younger Hunter walking around campus. I bet the girls had been all over the aspiring doctor with the sexy hair. My smile dropped at the mental image of another woman's hands tugging on his strands. Hunter and I hadn't had the past-lover conversation because that was one area where I was one hundred percent not curious.

"Anything else?" he asked.

I was out of questions for now. "Um, no. Bye."

"Okay," he sighed. "Bye."

I hung up my phone and set it on the lobby counter. He sounded sad and lonely. Should I call him back? Maybe invite him for dinner? What had he even been eating lately? Was he cooking for himself or just making peanut-butter-and-jelly sandwiches?

Though I disliked the thought of him surviving on takeout and PB&Js, I didn't lift my phone off the counter.

As much as I missed Hunter, I wasn't ready to take him back.

I was still too angry and disappointed.

Every time I thought about him coming to my maternity ward and not warning me about Nell's obsession, I saw red. When I pictured Hunter living in Prescott for a year, working at the hospital with my friends without introducing himself, my hands balled into fists. When I thought back to all the nights he'd made love to me and curled me into his arms for sleep, the bitter taste of betrayal filled my mouth.

I couldn't let Hunter back into my heart until those feelings were gone, which was the reason for my Q&A phone calls instead of talking to him in person.

I loved Hunter. I missed Hunter. But he had hurt me, and now, I was keeping him at arm's length.

Once again, The Bitterroot Inn had become my savior from the emotional turbulence in my life. I'd spent the last month back in my pre-Hunter routine, busting my butt to finish out tourist season.

Looking over at my reservation book, I flipped through to the weekend's pages. For the first time in months, there were a couple of empty rooms. Summer was on its way out and fall was moving in. Vacationers were back to work, kids were back in school, and I was enjoying the early September lull in motel activity.

Hunting season would start soon and reservations would peak again, but until then, I had a couple of weeks to enjoy a marginally slower pace. I could meet Milo for our weekly gossip coffee. I could have long phone calls with Gigi in the evenings. I could take lunch breaks with Hunter.

Except, I wasn't seeing Hunter.

Would my resentment go away faster if we spent more time together? Would I ever find the trust I was missing? *Maybe*. I sighed and leaned against the counter, propping my chin in my hand. My conviction to keep some distance was waning.

"What do you think, Pickle?"

My growing puppy looked up from the rawhide he was chewing at my feet. His big brown eyes blinked once before he went back to his treat.

"You're no help."

Without thinking it through, I picked up my phone.

Hunter answered on the first ring. "Hi."

"I'm going to the football game tonight. It's the first one of the season and always pretty fun. If you're going to the game, you're welcome to sit with us. I know Coby would really like that."

"What about you? Would you like that?"

I nodded.

"I can't see you, Blondie. Are you nodding?"

I nodded again.

"I'm going to assume that's a yes and see you tonight. Bye."

When he hung up, I set down my phone and looked back to my dog.

"Happy now?"

He just kept on chewing. Pickle might not care that I had just opened the door for Hunter to come back, but Coby would be ecstatic.

My little boy was just as confused as I was. He didn't understand why the sleepovers had stopped or why Hunter wasn't at our dinner table. I hated that he had been affected by all of this, but to Hunter's credit, he'd done his best to lessen the impact of our break on Coby.

Hunter had been at Coby's birthday party the week of the court case. With very few of my family members speaking to him, Hunter had spent most of the party alone. But he'd stuck it out the entire time, for Coby. He'd stood stoically in the corner, watching me, and smiling whenever I'd make eye contact. He'd even made it a point to apologize to my parents and brothers. Finally, I had taken pity on him and wordlessly stood by his side as we watched Coby open gifts.

After that, Hunter had arranged for time alone with Coby a couple times a week. They went fishing in the new boat. They had their own dinner dates at the cafe. Hunter had even taken Coby camping in his backyard one weekend.

I'd done my best to explain this change as "grown-up stuff" but Coby wasn't buying it. He knew things were strained. I just didn't know how else to describe the situation in a way he'd understand. How do you explain to a four-year-old boy the importance of trust? Or how difficult it was to forgive? Or how much damage his biological father had done to my heart?

Another question popped into my head and I picked up my phone.

Hunter again answered right away. "Are you calling to take back your invitation to the game? Because if you are, I'm hanging up."

"No." I smiled but hesitated before asking my question. "I was, um, wondering if you knew why Everett wouldn't want to be a dad."

Everett had been so adamant about not fathering a child —so much so that he'd been willing to kill me. There had to be some motivation behind that. Something I was missing. Because who wouldn't want Coby?

Hunter blew out a long breath. "I don't know. I wish I had an answer for you, but I don't. Maybe because his own father had never been in the picture. Maybe because Nell was such a shitty parent herself. Maybe because he was so selfish. I don't know why he wouldn't want kids."

"Hmm." I wanted another answer. Something more definitive.

"Maisy, he missed out and he'll never know how much."

That was the truth. "Okay. I'd better let you go."

He stopped me before I could hang up. "Maisy?"

"Yeah?"

"I know."

"You know what?"

"I know how much I'd miss out if I didn't have Coby. Or you."

A lump balled at the back of my throat. Rather than try and clear it away to speak, I just hung up the phone.

Then I thought about Everett, about Nell and Hunter's childhood, hoping another question would pop into my head so I could call him back.

---

"MOMMY! MOMMY, THERE'S HUNTER!" Coby jumped up from his seat in the football stadium and started waving.

When Hunter spotted us from his position at the bottom of the stands, he waved back as he lumbered toward the crowded staircase.

"Did you know he was coming?" Gigi asked from her seat behind me.

I turned and nodded. "I invited him to sit with us."

She grinned. Gigi had been nothing but supportive of my break from Hunter. She knew I needed some time to get over all of his secrets, but after a month, she thought my time was up.

I turned back around to watch Hunter as he started up the stairs. We were about seven rows up from the railing that separated the stands from the track and field. High enough that it gave me time to do a thorough inspection of Hunter as he climbed.

He was wearing jeans and a navy sweater, an outfit so simple and boring it accentuated his sex appeal rather than detracting from it. He'd pushed up the sleeves of his sweater, revealing his tan and muscled forearms. His jeans were faded at the legs, and with every step up the stands, his thick thighs pulled at the denim, molding around his powerful quads. The three women climbing the stairs behind Hunter had their eyes firmly fixed on his gorgeous ass.

*Get your own, ladies, that one is mine.* Well, maybe.

Not that I could blame those women for feasting on his sexy body. I was feasting too. Something Hunter knew when my eyes traveled up his flat stomach to his smirking face. *Busted.* With a wink, he grinned wider.

Dropping my eyes to the purse at my feet, I pretended to reach for something until the temperature of my face went back to normal. How was it that I'd gone years without sex, never once missing it, and only a month without Hunter and I was as horny as a teenaged boy who'd just discovered *Playboy*? I crossed my legs, shifted a little, but the ache in my core was still there.

"Stupid hormones," I muttered to my purse.

"What was that?"

My head whipped up. Hunter had already reached my side. He must have skipped a couple of steps with those long legs.

"Nothing." I smiled and scooted down a foot to make room.

"Coby!" Hunter caught Coby as he went flying past my legs. In one swift motion, Hunter hoisted my son onto a hip.

"Hunter! Look at my new shirt." Coby leaned back and stretched out his new shirt.

"That's awesome. Did you just get it?"

Coby nodded. "Mommy bought it for me."

When we'd arrived at the stadium, the high-school cheerleaders had been selling T-shirts. There had been one kids' shirt in neon green with Prescott Mustangs written on the front and I hadn't been able to resist. Coby had whipped off the shirt on his back faster than I could get out my credit card to pay for the new one.

"I was thinking about getting some Mustangs gear myself. Do you want to go down later and help me buy a hat?" Hunter asked Coby.

"Yeah! Can I have a hat too?"

"Coby," I chided. "You shouldn't ask for presents, buddy."

"Your mom is right," Hunter agreed, "but we'll still get you a hat."

He set Coby down and sank to the bench, leaning over to kiss my cheek. "Hi. You look beautiful."

I was just wearing a dark green Mustangs zip-up and jeans, but I had taken the time to do my makeup and hair. "Thanks."

There were eyes on me from all directions, but I turned to the football field and ignored them. Everyone had showed tonight for the religion that was Prescott High football. The guys were complete team fanatics. The girls tolerated the game because we all loved to socialize and gossip.

The fact that I'd brought Hunter into this mix was more telling than he probably knew. I was letting him back into the fold and this game was a way to give my friends and family permission to let go of his mistakes.

"Hunter," Dad said, turning around and holding out a hand. "Good to see you."

Hunter took Dad's hand. "Thanks, Brock. Glad to be here."

"Hunter, did you play any football?" Beau asked as they shook hands.

"I played quarterback in high school."

"No shit?" Jess asked from behind us. "Were you any good?"

"I held my own. I had a couple offers from some smaller division-one schools but I didn't want to play college ball."

Silas nodded to Jess. "Good timing."

All of the guys traded a look before Beau spoke for the group. "We've been looking for a QB for our league team. There are only three teams total so it's not a long season or anything, mostly just throwing the ball around on the weekends before it snows. Are you interested?"

"I'm in." Hunter nodded before getting mobbed with backslaps and more handshakes, welcoming him to the team.

The loneliness I'd heard in Hunter's voice earlier was gone. Inviting him had been the right call. And the nerves I'd felt about him joining us tonight had vanished the moment he'd taken his seat next to mine.

"I'm hungry." Coby squirmed as he sat on Hunter's knee.

"What do you want?" Hunter asked.

"Can I have a hot dog?"

"Sure, buddy. What do you want?" he asked me.

"I'll have a hot dog too."

"Okay. Be right back."

"Can I come?" Coby asked.

Hunter answered by holding out his hand as he stood, then together, they walked down the stairs. All around me, the chatter resumed. The guys started talking football. Mom was talking to Sabrina about her pregnancy. Dad was talking to Alana about the vet clinic.

And I sat quietly, enjoying the view of Hunter and my son holding hands.

"There's something truly magical about a man falling in love with your child, isn't there?" Gigi whispered in my ear.

"Totally." It made staying away from Hunter nearly impossible when he looked at Coby the way my dad looked at me.

Soon they disappeared from sight, returning ten minutes later overloaded with junk food from the concession stand. The view of the pair coming back up the stairs was just as nice as the view going down had been. Coby's smile was as wide as it had been all week and the love he had for Hunter was written all over his little face.

Guilt clawed at my insides. I couldn't let Coby suffer through this limbo any longer. I needed to make a decision. Hunter was either in our lives or out.

When he reached our row, Coby handed me my hot dog. "Here you go, Mommy."

"Thanks, buddy."

"We got candy too," he announced.

Hunter dropped a bag of Skittles in my hand along with a Snickers bar. My two favorites. Considering I'd never told him what my favorite candy was, I was impressed.

"How'd I do?" he asked.

"Good." *Really good.*

Hunter settled into his seat and we all started eating as the teams took the field to warm up before kickoff.

"Do you want something to drink?" Hunter asked. "I forgot to get a water."

I nodded and swallowed my last bite of Snickers. "Dr. Pepper."

"Okay. Be right back."

He stood and jogged down the steps. My eyes instantly locked on his butt. The way his ass looked in those jeans should be photographed daily. So firm. So damn firm. It looked more like chiseled stone than rounded muscle. Marveling at how well the pockets of his jeans framed his luscious ass, I jerked in surprise when a hand appeared in my line of sight.

There was a hand on Hunter's ass. A hand that definitely wasn't mine.

"What the eff?" Gigi asked.

"Coby, stay here." I was out of my seat and down the stairs before anyone could stop me, moving straight toward Hunter, who stood by the railing trying to inch away from the woman who had just groped him.

"Oh, I'm so sorry," the woman said, smiling and laughing like the fool she was. "I just tripped." She held out a hand. "I'm Renee. I don't believe we've met."

I slid right into Hunter's side, knocking her hand away with my elbow. Then I held mine out in return. "Hi. I'm Maisy. Renee, was it?"

Her smile drooped as she faltered, but she recovered. "Yes. Renee. Nice to meet you."

She took my hand and I squeezed hers just a bit too hard. "Are you new in town?"

"I, uh, just moved here last month," she stammered, trying to get out of my vise grip.

"Welcome to Prescott," I said with false cheer. "These football games are a great way to meet people." I looked to Hunter and slid my hand in the back pocket of his jeans. "We'd better get going if we're going to get our drinks before the game."

"Sure, baby." Hunter's chest started shaking with silent laughter as he nodded good-bye to Renee. "Nice to meet you."

"Oh, um, you too." With beet-red cheeks, she disappeared back to her seat.

"Let's go." I marched toward the exit.

Hunter's arm came around my shoulders and he led me down the stairs and toward the concession stand. "Jealous much, Blondie?"

A flare of annoyance streaked through my body. Of course I'd been jealous. What did he expect? Why wasn't he more annoyed at that lady's behavior?

"She was rude and practically mauling you," I snapped and stepped away from his side. "But if that doesn't bother you, then fine. Maybe women throwing themselves at you isn't a big deal. I mean, you're single or whatever, so I guess you can do whoever—"

"What was that?" His hand grabbed my elbow and spun me in front of him, stopping my rambling rant. "Say that again. Single? You think I'm single?"

I shrugged. "I guess."

His jaw set in an angry lock. "Do you think you're single?"

"I, um . . . no."

"Then why and the fuck would you think I'm single?"

I threw my hand toward the stands. "You didn't get too mad about Renee's hand on your ass and we're not together—"

"Stop talking. Right now." He grasped my hand to drag me behind him as he turned in the other direction and stormed away from the concessions.

My legs couldn't keep up with his long strides so I had to jog to keep up. "Hunter—"

"Stop talking, Maisy."

I shut up for a second, but as he got closer to the stands and the exit gate, I couldn't stay quiet. "Where are we going? We can't leave. What about Coby?"

He didn't answer. He just kept pulling me along until we reached the gate, but instead of going through and out to the gravel parking lot, he followed the small section of chain-link fence toward the dark area underneath the stands. I thought he would stop there, in the shadow of the tall bleachers, but he kept going, stepping over a metal bar and walking underneath the towering metal seats.

"Hunter," I hissed and held myself back. "We can't be under here."

He just tugged my hand harder so I'd follow.

Above us, people were laughing and talking. A couple of spilled drink cups littered the ground. The benches above squeaked as people shifted to stand for the national anthem.

"Hunter, I think—"

He shushed me and kept pulling, all the way to the far back corner, which was nearly pitch black. On this side, the stands were held up by a cinder-block wall, not the open metal posts like where we had entered. When we reached the cement, Hunter pulled me in front of him, positioning my back against the cold blocks.

I opened my mouth but he spoke first.

"You are not single. Neither am I." Then his mouth slammed down on mine, ending any chance of a discussion.

While the speakers blared and the stadium above us filled with *The Star-Spangled Bann*er, Hunter filled my mouth. He slanted his head and his tongue dove in deep, exploring with hunger. Exploring like it had been years, not just a month since his lips had been on mine.

I stood stunned for a second, not having expected a kiss, but the shock didn't last long. My desire for Hunter's mouth burned it away.

My hands ran up his hard chest and up his neck, pulling him closer and deeper. He bent so I could get my arms wrapped around the back of his shoulders and my chest pressed flush to his.

I'd missed kissing this man. His taste. His smell. The way he'd groan into my mouth. I'd missed it all.

As our tongues twisted and dueled, his hands wrapped around my waist, sliding down to my ass to squeeze hard through my jeans. I moaned into his mouth, wanting more as he pulled me into his erection.

I slanted my head, wanting a new angle to suck on his bottom lip, but he broke away, leaving me panting as I wiped my lips dry.

"Turn around," he ordered.

I immediately obeyed, bracing my hands on the cold cement at my face.

Hunter's hands came to my jeans and popped the top button, then hastily unzipped the seam. With one jerk, he yanked down my pants and panties, letting the cool air bite into my bare skin.

His warm breath tickled my earlobe when he bent down

to whisper, "I'm going to fuck you right here so that you remember that neither of us is *single*. Got it?"

My pussy clenched. *God, I missed his dirty words too.*

"Got it?" he repeated, his hoarse voice vibrating against my neck.

I was so turned on, all I could do was nod.

It was noisy above us but I could still hear the sound of him unzipping his fly. His hands came to my hips, tipping them up so he could position that thick cock right at my entrance before he thrust inside on one hard stroke.

A loud moan escaped my lips as he filled me completely.

His arms left my hips to band around my chest. "Fuck, Maisy. You feel so good."

I arched higher.

"Harder," I pleaded. He was holding back, not giving me everything, and I wanted it all. I wanted him to come undone when I did and lose himself in my body.

"I'm not going to last long, baby."

I shook my head. "Me neither." Just the fact that Hunter was fucking me while hundreds of people were sitting above us had me trembling already. As soon as he unleashed, I'd go right over the edge.

He kissed my neck gently and stood back. His big hands came back to my hips and hoisted me up so my toes were barely skimming the ground as he hammered me in long, hard jolts. Perfect fucking.

The angle was so right, my head fell forward. "Oh, fuck," I breathed.

"You are all mine." Hunter's voice echoed off the cement wall at my face. "Got it?"

I nodded and turned my head so I could moan into my arm.

"Say it, Maisy."

"I'm all yours," I breathed.

"Fuck yes, you are. And who owns this cock?" He rammed it in hard and stayed rooted. "Who?"

I gasped. "I do."

"That's right." He slid back out and started pounding again.

Above us the stands erupted in cheers as the game kicked off. My orgasm hit at that exact moment so I could cry out as I came. Pulse after pulse, my hands fisted on the cement wall, my arms shaking as I exploded long and hard. With my pussy squeezing him tight, Hunter fucked me even harder.

"Maisy," he groaned as he came, his rough voice sending a tingle down my rubber arms. I sagged into the wall when he collapsed into my back. His arms left my hips and came back to my chest to hold me while we both recovered.

"Oh my god," I muttered. "I can't believe we just did that."

Hunter chuckled as he slid out. "You didn't like it?"

"You know I liked it." I straightened, yanking up my panties and jeans while praying that no one was behind us with a video camera. With my clothes back in place, I turned and peered behind Hunter to see we were alone. *Phew*.

"Come here." Hunter's arms wrapped around me and he pulled me into his chest.

I fell into him, still weak from my orgasm and using his strong body to prop me up.

"We need to get back." I took a long inhale of the cologne on his sweater.

"One more second."

"What about Coby?" I asked but didn't make a move to let go.

"He's fine. There are about twenty people up there watching him."

"My parents. Oh my god, my parents." My cheeks flushed with mortification, and this time, I did step back. "They are going to know we just had sex. And my brothers are up there. And all my friends. They're going to take one look at my face and—"

"Maisy." Hunter interrupted me and pulled me back into his arms. "Stop talking."

I huffed out a loud breath and sank into his chest. "I'm still hurt." He needed to know that, despite the hot football-stadium sex, I was still hesitant to jump right back into an us.

He kissed my hair. "I know."

"How do we move past it all?"

"One day at a time," he whispered. "And when you're ready to start again, I'll be right here."

# CHAPTER TWENTY

MAISY

"These are incredible."

I nodded as I looked over Beau's shoulder. "They sure are."

Beau was kneeling on the floor in the motel's lobby, looking through the canvases that were leaned up against the wall.

Today, all of the photographs that Hunter had taken had arrived, and when the deliveryman had dropped them off, I'd immediately started opening boxes, frantic to see all my photos on an actual canvas.

Craft paper and boxes were strewn all over the floor and the canvases had been stacked against the wall. With every box I'd opened, my smile had grown, until I'd opened the last box and it had disappeared as I'd broken down in tears.

In that last package were my postcards and a display rack for the lobby wall.

We hadn't talked about my postcards except for the first time, months ago, but Hunter had remembered. He had taken a dream, something I had always wanted but never thought I'd really get, and made it come true.

My postcards and these prints were so beautiful, so special to me, that I had been completely overcome.

Beau had walked into the lobby the moment when I'd been balling my eyes out. When he'd asked me why I was crying, all I'd been able to do was point at the pictures. My brother had pulled me into a hug until I'd finally gotten control. While I'd blown my nose and dried my eyes, he'd started inspecting Hunter's photographs.

"I love this one." Beau slid a picture out from the back.

It was a black and white that Hunter had taken of the sign out front. *The Bitterroot Inn* was front and center on the canvas with my beautiful motel faded to a soft blur in the background.

"You should hang this in here." Beau nodded toward an empty wall at the back of the lobby.

"Good idea." I rushed away, straight for my office to get a hammer and some nails.

He laughed. "Not right now."

"Yes!" I called from the office. "Right now and you're going to help. This artwork has to go on my walls immediately."

Two hours later, I had hung all but five prints that were for the occupied rooms. The pile of paper and boxes in the lobby had been cleared and only a couple more prints were stacked against the wall.

"Where does this one go?" Beau asked, holding up the picture Hunter had taken of me and Coby.

"Oh, um, that one is Hunter's. He wants it for his house."

He nodded and set it down. "How are things going with you two? Are you working it all out?"

I shrugged. "We're in a weird spot." I hadn't seen Hunter since the football game a week ago. We'd texted a couple of times but hadn't talked, mostly because I just didn't know what to say.

"You guys seemed fine at the football game last Friday," Beau muttered.

My face flamed bright red and I turned away from my brother, going to the mini fridge to hide my embarrassment. Everyone except the kids knew exactly what Hunter and I had been doing when we'd returned to the stands without the drinks we had left to collect.

"Want a pop?" I asked Beau.

"Sure."

I pulled out two Cokes and set them on the counter. Then I pulled up my stool and took a seat while Beau leaned his massive forearms on the counter.

"So what's up?" He popped his soda. "Why are you guys in a weird spot?"

"I don't know. I guess I'm just . . . scared." It felt really, *really* good to say it out loud.

"Scared of what?"

"Everything? I honestly don't know how to explain it. I just feel scared."

"Do you love the guy?" Beau asked.

I nodded. "Yeah, but he kept so much from me. How can we get past all that stuff?"

"Is he still keeping secrets?"

"No. Whenever I ask him something, he's really forthcoming." Ever since his past had all come to light, Hunter hadn't denied me any information.

He nodded and took a drink. "Are you scared because you don't trust him?"

"Maybe. No. I don't know." I slumped against the counter and started talking it all out. "I trust him with Coby. And I trust him to tell me the truth. When I think back, I see now that truth was never the problem. He never lied to me. He just left things out. Important things."

"But you know it all now."

I nodded. "I think so. And what I don't, I'm learning. I just hate that he didn't tell me sooner. I guess I'm scared something else is going to happen and instead of confiding in me as his partner, he's going to hide it."

"Listen, what he did was an asshole thing to do, but after you sat us all down and explained it, I can see why he did it. I honestly think that was a one-time deal. If he's open with you now, why do you think he'd start keeping things from you again?"

Now that Beau had asked the question point-blank, I didn't think Hunter would keep secrets from me again. "Do you think I'm being stupid? Dragging this out for no reason?"

Beau's face softened. "No, of course not. We all get this can't be easy. You're being careful and thinking about the future. The rest of us are following your lead. If you don't think you'll ever move past it, we'll be right there. If you want to let him back in, we're all good with that too."

I smiled at my brother. "Thanks." Not all that long ago, I was the one giving him relationship advice when he'd been trying to win Sabrina. Now that our positions were reversed, I couldn't think of anyone better to confide in.

"I don't know if I'm really all that hurt anymore," I

admitted, "but I still feel mad sometimes. When I think about how many opportunities he had to fess up, I just feel that anger start to bubble. What if that never goes away?"

"Do you want to know what I do when I get pissed at Sabrina?"

"What?"

"I tell her I love her."

"When you're mad?" I cocked my head. "Why?"

"Because she always says it right back and then I don't feel so mad anymore."

My heart melted. "Aww. That might be, like, the cutest thing you've ever said."

"Hey!" He frowned. "It's not cute."

"Oh, it totally is."

He kept his frown and lifted up his Coke, but before the rim touched his lip, I saw the beginning of a grin. After a long drink, he set down the can and turned back to the photographs still on the floor behind him. The one at the front of the stack was the one of Coby fishing.

"It's okay to be scared, Maze, but don't let that fear keep you from being happy."

---

I STEPPED out of my car and took a deep breath as I stared at the hospital.

*I love you.*

That's all I had to say. I just hoped that Beau's tactic with Sabrina would work for Hunter and me too, because after an afternoon talking with my brother and voicing my fears, I was ready to be done with this separation from Hunter.

With one last fortifying breath, I opened the back door to the 4Runner and pulled out Hunter's canvas. When the door slammed shut, my feet started across the pavement. A small twinge of anxiety raced up my spine, a mix of residual fears from the Everett disaster and nerves about seeing Hunter. It didn't stop me though. I marched right through the sliding glass doors and let the hospital smell hit me in the face.

Sara was working at the ER counter and when she spotted me, she came rushing around the corner. "Hey! It's so good to see you here." Because she'd filled my vacant nursing position after she'd moved to Prescott with Milo, Sara had never seen me inside the hospital before.

"Thanks." I smiled and gave her a quick hug, her warm embrace settling my nerves a bit. "Do you know if Hunter is busy? I wanted to drop this off." I held up the picture.

"That. Is. Gorgeous. Did you take that?"

I shook my head. "No, Hunter did."

"He's a photographer too?" she asked. "Good catch, girl."

He was a good catch. And it was time for me to reel him back in and take him home.

I smiled. "Thanks. He actually did a whole series of photographs for the inn. You'll have to stop by and check them out."

"For sure." She turned and pointed down the back hall. "I saw him a minute ago walking toward the staff lounge. He might still be in there. Do you want me to page him?"

"No, that's okay. Would it be okay if I just popped back there and checked?"

"Of course."

"Thanks." I waved good-bye and then started off toward the staff lounge.

I hustled, hoping Hunter was still in the lounge. It was actually one of the few places in the hospital where Everett and I hadn't spent any time together, either personal or professional. In there, my reconnection with Hunter wouldn't be tainted by the past.

With fast strides, I crossed through the ER and back to the lounge. The second I walked through the door, Hunter stood from the fridge, water bottle in hand.

He turned toward the door with a jerk and squeezed the open water bottle too tight, sending a huge spurt right onto his shirt.

I scrunched up my face. "Sorry to startle you."

He shook his head and started laughing as he reached for a paper towel. "Don't be. This is actually a nice change of events. When you scare me, I just get wet. When I scare you, I end up bleeding or writhing on the ground in pain. This I'll take."

I smiled and stepped further into the room.

"What's up? Is everything okay?" he asked, blotting his shirt dry.

"Yes, I just wanted to drop this off." I held up the canvas.

Hunter set down his water and tossed his paper towel into the trash, then crossed the small, colorless room.

Taking the picture from my hand, he inspected the piece. "They did a good job on the canvas. How did the others turn out?"

"Ah-mazing. I've hung all but five and the postcard display. Thank you for that. You didn't need to get that too."

"Sure I did." He set down the picture on one of the small tables. "That was your dream, right? You can't have the pictures without the postcards."

I smiled and looked at the wet spot on his baby-blue

button-up shirt. He'd rolled up his sleeves in typical Hunter fashion to show those sinewy forearms and today he was wearing gray chinos instead of jeans.

My fingers brushed against the wet spot. "You look nice today."

"Thanks. These were the only pair of clean pants in the house. I need to do laundry."

I frowned. Before everything had gotten so mixed up, I had been doing Hunter's laundry. You'd think that with doing my own laundry, Coby's, plus everything for the inn, I would be sick of washing clothes, but right now, I missed doing Hunter's laundry. I missed cooking for him. I missed how we'd take care of each other.

And now was my chance to do what I'd come here to do.

"I love you." I looked up from his shirt into his beautiful caramel eyes, waiting for him to say it back so I could be done being mad.

He grinned. "I love you too."

*Huh. It worked.* I owed Beau a batch of his favorite cookies. "You can go ahead and kiss me now," I whispered.

Hunter's smile came down slowly on mine. His soft lips brushed against mine in a lazy tease as he whispered, "Say it one more time."

"I love you."

"Glad to hear it, Blondie."

Then right in the middle of the staff lounge with the door open for all those passing by to see, Hunter and I kissed like we were alone in my bedroom. When we finally stopped, I walked out of the hospital with the biggest smile I'd had in months and the first thing I did when I got into my car was text Beau.

*You were right.*

---

BY THE MIDDLE OF OCTOBER, over a month after my impromptu trip to the hospital to reunite with Hunter, life was good.

I was happily back to doing Hunter's laundry and cooking. He was back to giving me nightly foot massages and orgasms. And Coby was just overjoyed to have us both.

*Gosh, I'm happy. Like, really happy.* Standing at the stove in Hunter's dream kitchen, I stared at a simmering pot, unable to recall the last time I had been this happy. Not that I'd been unhappy before, but this was more than just easy contentment. This was the kind of happiness people craved deep in their soul. The kind people searched for but rarely found.

The kind that hadn't come easy and made me appreciate it even more.

"Hey."

I looked up from the pot and smiled as Hunter walked into the kitchen. "Hi. How was your day?"

Coby and I had come up to his house and gotten an early start on some laundry and cooking dinner.

"I'm good," Hunter said though his eyebrows were furrowed. "Are you okay? You were all spaced out just now. Was it another flashback?"

"No, I was just thinking about how . . ."

*Huh. Weird.*

I hadn't had one of my Everett flashes in months. Not since the night at my parents' house, in front of Hunter. I'd been so busy that I hadn't even noticed but I'd never gone this long without one before.

"Maisy?" Hunter asked. "What?"

"Oh," I shook myself out of my head, "sorry, I'm good. It wasn't a flash and I was just thinking it had been a long time since I've had one."

His shoulders and face relaxed. "That's a good thing."

"No kidding. Why do you think they stopped?"

"I don't know." He tossed his keys onto the counter. "Why do you?"

Was it because I knew so much more about Everett now? Or maybe because I wasn't nearly as stressed as I used to be? Or was it because Hunter made me feel so much more grounded and safe? I searched my gut for that unsettled feeling I'd had for years, but it was gone. Whatever the reason, I was grateful.

Everett had haunted me enough.

"I'm not sure why," I said, "but I won't miss them if they never come back."

Hunter came around the island and kissed my temple. "If they do, promise to tell me, okay? I still think it might be good for you to talk to someone about it all."

"I promise."

He walked to the fridge and pulled out a soda. "Tell me about your day."

Before I could answer, his phone rang. When he looked at the screen, his entire frame tensed.

"It's Nell." He put the phone to his ear and answered as he walked into the living room.

Nell?

I shut off the stove and followed.

"Yes. She's here," Hunter said into the phone, then paused. "No, you can't talk to her until you tell me what you have to say."

Nell wanted to talk to me? Why? She had my number; why hadn't she called me directly?

My stomach tightened. Nell had basically disappeared since the custody hearing. As far as I knew, she hadn't been calling Hunter and I certainly hadn't heard from her. I liked it that way. Nothing good could come from her call.

"I'm sure she would agree to that," Hunter said.

"Agree to what?" I whispered.

He held up one finger for me to wait. "That's fine. I'll text you the details after I talk to Maisy." He hung up and came right to me, resting his hands on my shoulders.

*Uh-oh.* My arms wrapped around my stomach. "What?"

"She'd like to meet Coby."

"Oh, shit." My heart dropped. I had no desire for that woman to be around my son, but I was also required to let her have her visits. "I can't say no."

He shook his head and rubbed my arms. "No, you can't."

During the court case, I'd been thrilled at the idea of weekend visits from Nell versus months of no Coby. But now? After I'd learned so much about her from Hunter, I had no desire to see that woman's face ever again.

Unfortunately, I didn't have a choice.

"Okay. When does she want to meet him?"

"This weekend. She said she'd fly in from Grand Rapids to Bozeman on Friday. Then drive here Saturday."

So much for a nice fall weekend. "All right." I nodded. "What should we do with her? Bring her here? Or to the motel? Maybe we should do this in public. Would that be better? Oh my god, this sucks!"

Hunter's arms pulled me into his embrace before I could completely flip out. "Relax. You're in control of the visits, remember? Let's start with a brief meeting. Maybe have her join us at the café for lunch or dinner. If that goes well, the next time she can come here."

"Lunch could work. I know you don't like her so if you don't want to come—"

"Stop. I don't like her, but I do love you. There is no way I'm letting you deal with her on your own."

I relaxed into his body, winding my arms around his back. "Thank you." Could I do this without Hunter? Yes, but I really didn't want to.

"You're welcome." He kissed my hair. "Now give me a smile so I know you're okay."

I leaned back and gave him the biggest, cheesiest smile I could stretch, showing him all my teeth.

"You have spinach in your teeth from lunch."

My lips closed as my tongue immediately started feeling around.

He chuckled. "Just kidding."

I laughed and pinched his side, making him yelp.

"There. There's my smile."

I smiled wider. "I'd better get back to dinner."

"Okay." He kissed me and went off to play with Coby before it was time to eat.

I went back to the stove and resumed my cooking, thinking about what this weekend would entail. Nell's call had rippled the waters, but with Hunter by my side, I knew we could deal with it. He wouldn't let his crazy family ruin our happiness.

How ironic. Everett had set out to destroy my life, but in the end, he'd just made it all better. I had Coby. I had Hunter. All because of him. Maybe that was why my flashes had stopped. I'd stopped being scared of Everett, instead simply being grateful for all the good he'd unknowingly provided.

Now I just had to deal with his evil stepmother.

# CHAPTER TWENTY-ONE

MAISY

"Nell." Hunter stood from our booth at the café and greeted Nell as she walked through the door.

"Hunter."

They didn't hug or even touch. They just nodded at one another.

No wonder Everett had been so cold. This woman was frigid. The minute we got home, I was asking Hunter what his father had seen in Nell. From what I'd learned, Hunter was a lot like his dad and I couldn't imagine Hunter falling for someone like Eleanor Carlson.

Hunter swung out a hand and gestured Nell to our table.

I smiled and waved from my seat while tucking Coby even closer to my side. Earlier today, Hunter and I had sat him down and explained to him about his other grandmother. Thankfully, he hadn't asked any questions about Everett. He'd just wanted to know why Nell hadn't sent him a birthday present if she was a grandma.

God bless my son for his resilience.

"Hello, Nell," I greeted when they reached the booth.

She just frowned.

*Super.*

Hunter slid into our booth first, followed by Nell on his side. She was wearing all black again, this time pants with a light turtleneck sweater. She actually reminded me of an older Audrey Hepburn with her hair in a French twist.

When she sat, Nell's eyes studied the table, the water glass and the silverware. She adjusted everything at her place setting until it was precisely the way she wanted it, and the entire time, she didn't bother to look at me or Coby.

Not that Coby cared. He just started bouncing on his knees in the padded seat, ready to get this show on the road.

"Hi, Grandma! Mommy and Hunter says you're my new grandma and that means you have to get me a Christmas present. I like trucks and tractors. And Legos. And I saw this thing on my iPad for making Play-Doh dinosaurs."

I pulled in my lips to hide a smile. *Seriously, this kid.* He was completely oblivious to Nell's attitude.

Eleanor's eyes finally left her place mat, and when they landed on Coby, she flinched.

My eyes snapped to Hunter and we started a silent conversation.

*What was that, Hunter?*

*Fuck if I know?*

*She'd better be nice.*

*If she's not, we'll leave.*

"Do you want to play tic-tac-toe?" Coby asked Nell, who was still staring at him with wide eyes.

When she didn't answer, Coby got up on his knees and

leaned across the table. "Grandma? I'm talking to you." He waved a hand in her face.

"Coby—" I started to tell him to sit back down but Eleanor interrupted me.

"Everett. Sit. Down. It is rude to lean on a table."

*What the hell?* Everett?

"Nell, this is Coby," Hunter said, then looked to Coby. "On your butt, little man. We don't want to spill any waters."

"Okay." He immediately obeyed.

"Why don't you color Nell a picture?" I asked, sliding over the crayons.

He nodded and started in on the kids' menu pictures.

"Everett, stay inside the lines," Nell said.

Coby kept coloring, ignoring her completely because he didn't know *Everett*.

My eyes went back to Hunter but he was staring down at his stepmother in complete shock.

"Coby," he told her. "His name is Coby."

She flicked her wrist to brush him off. "That's what I said."

"No," Hunter insisted, "you said Everett. Twice."

"Don't correct an elder, Hunter," she snapped. "It's rude and I raised you better than that."

He huffed. "You know what else is rude? Calling someone by the wrong name."

"It's fine." I held up my hands so they wouldn't argue in front of Coby. "Let's move on."

Hunter opened his mouth but I gave him a *Do not make this worse by fighting with your stepmother!* look.

He frowned and took a drink of his water to stay quiet.

And quiet it was.

Nell stared at Coby during the entire meal. She didn't

eat. She didn't drink. She'd respond to questions with one-word answers as she dutifully stared at my son.

I was so creeped out by the time our check arrived, I didn't wait for Hunter to pay before I slid out of our booth. "Thank you for meeting us today. Coby, it's time to go."

"Okay," he muttered, still moping. He'd gotten excited at the prospect of another grandma, and though she'd been staring at him through lunch, she'd hardly said a word. He might only be four, but he knew a rejection when he saw one.

For disappointing my son, I disliked Nell even more.

"Meet you at the car," Hunter said, nudging Nell out of the booth. "Nell, I'll walk you to your car."

"Come on." I bent to hold Coby's hand. "Let's go home and make cookies."

He perked up. "Triple chocolate chip?"

"You got it, dude."

I waved good-bye to our waitress and hustled outside, buckling Coby in his seat, then hopped in to wait for Hunter. When he slid into the driver's seat, his worry lines were much deeper than they had been at lunch.

"What?" I asked quietly.

He shook his head. "Later."

Later came three hours later after a double batch of cookies, serious playtime in the bathtub and five stories as Hunter and I both tucked Coby into bed.

"Well?" I asked him as I closed the door to my bedroom at the loft.

He stripped off his shirt and jeans, tossing them into the hamper. Then he climbed into bed and rubbed his hands over his face. "Something's wrong with her."

"What do you mean?" I stripped down and tugged on some pajama pants and a tank top.

"She is more than her normal level of crazy. When I walked her to her car, she started telling me how much Everett needed to learn manners. How much Everett needed a haircut. How much Everett needed to eat more vegetables. Everett, not Coby."

I sank down on the side of the bed. The last thing we needed was another crazy Carlson in our lives. "This is not good. What should we do?"

"I think she needs some help. Maybe she's never really dealt with Everett's death or something, I don't know. But that was not normal."

"You think?" I said dryly, then crawled into bed and curled into Hunter's side. "We can't have her around Coby if she's going to call him Everett."

"I agree." He hugged me closer. "I'm going to call the staff at the Grand Rapids house and see if there is more going on than I know about."

"I think that's a good idea."

Because if Eleanor had snapped, she wasn't getting anywhere near my child, court order or not.

---

"HOW DID SHE SOUND?" I asked Hunter the second he opened the door to my car and sat in the driver's seat. He'd been outside, pacing in front of the hood while talking on the phone with Nell.

"Off."

I frowned. "Just off? I need more than a one-word answer."

"She was distracted," he said while starting the car. "I invited her to come with us today and she declined. She said she had plans."

"Plans? What plans?" After our lunch yesterday, Nell had returned to Bozeman, where she was staying—she hadn't asked for a room at the Bitterroot and I hadn't offered. I had hoped after visiting Prescott and meeting Coby, she'd be on the first flight back to Grand Rapids. I had a niggling feeling about her staying in Montana with "plans."

"I don't know," Hunter answered. "She hung up before I could ask, but let's not worry about Nell today, okay? Let's just have fun."

"Okay." I smiled and reached over to take Hunter's free hand.

He reversed out of the parking lot at the inn and started driving us toward the corn maze. Today, we were taking Coby to Howell Farm to explore their famous corn maze and pick some pumpkins from their patch. The three of us had been taking as many outdoor adventures as we could to enjoy the last days of fall. By the end of October, winter would be right around the corner—or already here.

"Is that it?" Coby asked from his car seat thirty minutes later. Hunter had just pulled off the county road onto a gravel drive that led to the farm.

"Yes." I turned back to smile at Coby. "It looks like fun, doesn't it, buddy?"

"Yeah! I'm gonna get the biggest pumpkin ever!"

"Not if I get it first," I teased.

"What if we all got one? How many pumpkins will we need if we get one for all of us?" Hunter asked Coby through the rearview mirror.

"One," Coby counted and pointing to us as he went. "Two. Three."

"That's right! Good job! You're getting so good at counting."

Coby beamed at Hunter's praise.

Parking in the long gravel lot, Hunter did a quick survey of the farm. "This place is awesome. Do they do this every year?"

"Yep." Howell Farm had always been one of my most favorite places. "When I was a kid, it was just the pumpkin patch and the maze, but they've expanded it over the years."

The Howells had turned a mildly profitable farm into a wildly successful public venue. Each fall, families from all over Jamison County came to visit. Kids ran through the cornfield maze, adults sampled the hard apple cider, and everyone left with pumpkins. A huge attraction for local residents, it was even starting to pull visitors from out of town.

The Howells' most recent expansion was into the wedding business. They'd cleaned up their barn behind the pumpkin patch and now rented it out for wedding receptions. It had been too small for Beau and Sabrina's wedding party, but for something small and intimate, it would be perfect.

Maybe Hunter and I could get married here.

"What's that smile for?" Hunter asked.

"Huh? Oh, nothing." I unbuckled my seat belt and got out of the car before he could see my blush. Maybe it was presumptuous to think we'd get married, but I couldn't imagine myself with any other man.

The seed had been planted, and as we walked toward the admission booth, I couldn't stop thinking of wedding stuff. My eyes were locked on that barn, mentally assessing its potential for a winter wedding. We could bring in heaters if it was too cold. The path could be lined with lanterns so guests could find their way in the dark. The rafters in the barn could be strung with twinkle lights to give the room a golden glow.

I was getting completely ahead of myself but couldn't help it. I could see it all perfectly. Me in a long-sleeved lace dress. Coby in a little suit. Hunter looking gorgeous in a tux.

"Mommy!" Coby smacked my leg.

I snapped out of my wedding planning and looked down. "Yeah?"

"I said, it's time to go in the maze."

Hunter chuckled. "You've got stars in your eyes, Blondie. Is there something you want to share?"

"Nope!" I blurted, then cleared my throat to talk at a normal decibel. "No. Just, uh, thinking. Ready to go?"

Coby ran right for the entrance to the maze. Hunter just grinned and put his hand on the small of my back. Did he know what I had been thinking? I swear that grin was knowing.

"You need to wait for us!" I shouted as my son laughed and disappeared around a maze corner. "Coby!"

I jogged to catch him. The second I turned, he popped out and yelled, "Boo!"

I jumped, clutching my chest, then frowned at him kneeling on the straw walkway. "No scaring people today."

Over the last month, Coby had discovered a new "fun" activity. Someone—dear Uncle Michael—had taught Coby how to scare people. I'd lost track of the times he'd scared me. For a little boy who talked incessantly, he had mastered silence and patience in his effort to make me scream. And no matter how many times I told him to stop, no matter how many minutes he spent in the time-out corner, he wouldn't listen.

I was about two scares away from giving him a swat on the butt.

"Everything okay?" Hunter asked when he caught up.

"Yeah," I muttered. "Come on, Coby. Lead the way."

"Okay!" Coby jumped up off the ground and started running through the maze.

And then more scaring commenced. My warning had been for nothing.

"Coby!" I scolded for the fifth time. "I said, no scaring people. That is not okay."

He'd just jumped out at a group of little girls who were now running away, squealing.

He laughed. "It's fun!"

"Coby, you need to listen to your mom." Hunter was standing over him with a scowl.

"Come on. It's time to go," I announced. We were in the middle of the maze but with Coby's behavior, I was ready to change activities.

"No!" Coby protested.

"Yes. We're all done with the maze. If you can't listen to me about scaring people, then we can't stay. Let's go do pumpkins."

"Okay!" Coby shouted, happy again as he ran off.

Not one minute later, Hunter and I had lost him in the maze.

"Damn it," I muttered. "Where'd he go now?"

"I'm sure he'll—"

"Boo!"

Ahead of us, Coby jumped out from behind a row of

thick cornstalks and scared a mother with an infant in her arms.

"Oh my god," I said, rushing up to grab my son. "I'm so, so sorry." I started apologizing profusely to the mother who, thankfully, was laughing it off.

"Coby Holt!" I turned, hands fisted on my hips to start my lecture, but Hunter beat me to it.

"Coby, that's enough." Hunter's voice was as stern as his pointing finger. "If you do it again, we're leaving. And you listen to your mother. Understood?"

Coby's face paled as he looked up at Hunter. Tears welled in my son's eyes and his chin was quivering uncontrollably before he lost it and face-planted—wailing—into my legs.

I blinked a couple of times before reaching down and patting Coby's shoulders. Besides me, no one had ever really disciplined Coby. Mom and Dad would occasionally scold him, but for the most part he was a good kid and didn't need much more than a gentle reminder to shape up. Hunter disciplining Coby hadn't just shocked my still-crying son, but me too.

"I'm sorry," Hunter said, running a hand over his hair. "I didn't mean to step on your toes, but . . . shit."

"Hunter, it's—"

He interrupted me and started rambling. "This is going to happen, you know? I feel bad, but we're both going to have to discipline him. I'm not auditioning for his favorite uncle here, Maisy. I'm trying to be a dad and he needs to know I'm going to get after him from time to time. Please, don't be mad at me for this."

He wanted to be Coby's dad.

My shock evaporated and I took his hand. "I'm not mad.

Not at all."

"You're not?" he asked over Coby's crying. His face was still twisted in pain as he looked down at Coby. Hunter was learning that parenting wasn't always easy.

"I'm not mad." I couldn't imagine Coby having a better father than Hunter, and if he wanted the job, it was his.

"Oh." The worry disappeared from his face and he bent down to pry Coby off my legs. "Listen, bud. I don't like to scold you, but you have to listen to us. Okay?"

Coby nodded and fell into Hunter's chest. Hunter still looked miserable and Coby was still crying, but I couldn't help but think this was a good thing. This was part of them forming a father-son bond.

Staring down at them, I came to a realization. I had done it. I had found the best possible father Coby could ever want. We weren't alone anymore. I wasn't a single parent. Hunter and I were a team and, with Coby, a family.

Tears of immense joy flooded my eyes but I blinked them away. "Should we go get pumpkins now?"

Hunter leaned Coby back and wiped the tears from his tiny face. "No more scaring people, okay?"

"O-okay," Coby stammered.

Hunter gave him a sad smile. "Should we go have fun?"

Coby nodded and fell back into Hunter. They hugged for another moment until Coby had pulled himself together. Then, hand in hand, they walked together through the corn rows while I followed.

"Whoa. It got really crowded," I said as we emerged from the maze.

The number of people had quadrupled while we'd been in the maze. There was a line at the lemonade stand ten people deep and a thick cluster of people by the straw-bale entrance to the pumpkin patch. Adults were all standing around visiting while the kids ran everywhere.

"Can I go play?" Coby asked Hunter.

He nodded. "Sure, buddy. Don't go too far."

And off he ran, his punishment forgotten.

I slid into Hunter's side and hugged his waist.

"That sucked," he muttered.

I laughed. "It's not fun to be the bad guy. Welcome to the club."

"Maisy!" I looked up to see a high-school friend walking over.

"Hi!" I waved and let Hunter go, taking his hand to lead him over for introductions.

For the next twenty minutes, I introduced Hunter to a whole slew of people as they came to greet us. People I knew from my parents' church came to say hello. Friends from high school wanted to meet Hunter. Fellow business owners that I worked with at the chamber of commerce asked how things were going at the inn.

"You really do know everyone," Hunter said as the people we had been talking to walked away.

"Most everyone," I teased. "Get used to it, Dr. Faraday. You're part of the community now. Everywhere we go, you'll know someone too. Your days of being just another handsome face in a Chicago crowd are over."

"I like that." He smiled and my knees wobbled.

Would that smile always make me dizzy?

Just as much as I loved the smile, I loved that he was by my side. That he was mine. That people in our town would forever think of us as a unit.

Hunter, Maisy and Coby.

My eyes went to the pumpkin patch at the thought of

my son. I'd been checking on him periodically, watching from afar as Coby ran around to inspect all of the pumpkins. Except this time when I scanned the rows, I didn't see Coby.

My smile fell and I walked from our spot toward the patch. My eyes swept back and forth across every row, but my son wasn't anywhere in sight. "Coby!" I called, surveying the entire area again. My heart was racing and my eyes searched frantically.

Hunter came to my side. "Coby!" The panic on his face and in his voice matched mine.

"Coby, where are you?" I shouted.

I walked out of the pumpkin patch and started looking at the other areas of the farm. I didn't see him by the barn or the row of porta-potties. He wasn't by the lemonade stand or by the gift shop. And I didn't see him by the entrance to the maze.

"Coby!" I was screaming now. Other faces were staring but I didn't focus on them. I was too busy looking for my missing child.

How could this happen? He was just here.

"Coby!" Hunter shouted again.

"Who are you looking for?" a man asked at my side.

"My son." I didn't look at him while I talked but just kept searching. "Have you seen a little boy? Brown hair. He's wearing a neon-yellow shirt and jeans."

"No, but I'll help you look."

In the background, I heard him describe Coby to other people who then started their own search.

*Please god. Let me find him. Where is he?*

"Coby!" Hunter and I both called, over and over with no response.

"I'll check the maze," Hunter said. "You go check by the barn."

I nodded and started running toward the barn, searching frantically for my boy. The blood rushed in my ears as I searched in a complete panic. Terror coursed through my veins. Nothing, not even the night Everett had kidnapped me, could compare to the fear of losing Coby. My legs and arms tingled as I searched the barn. My system was so hyped on adrenaline I stumbled a few times as I ran. "Coby!" I shouted his name, over and over, but he didn't show.

He wasn't hiding again, was he? He wouldn't be trying to scare me now, not after Hunter had scolded him, would he?

No. No way. I knew my son, and he knew me. If he could hear the panic in my voice, he would not have stayed hidden.

I came barreling out of the barn and nearly crashed into a couple of women coming in with their kids. "Have you seen a little boy in a neon-yellow shirt?"

When they both shook their heads, I pushed past them and sprinted back to the main area. Other people were calling Coby's name as they looked around hay bales and building corners, but he was nowhere.

Ready to scream at the top of my lungs, I opened my mouth but stopped when a light flashed on the far side of the gravel parking lot. It was fast, just a neon-green flicker, but it caught my eye. I knew that light. It was the flicker of Coby's light-up shoes, the ones my parents had bought him for his birthday.

"Coby!" I screamed and started running. "Hunter. He's in the parking lot!" I shouted over my shoulder as I kept running, my tennis shoes kicking up small rocks as I moved.

Hunter caught up to me fast, his long strides sprinting past me on the gravel. "Coby!" he yelled.

Why wasn't Coby answering? He should be shouting "Mommy" or "Hunter" and be running back to us as fast as he could. Where was he?

I rounded the back of a large truck just as my son's yellow shirt disappeared into the backseat of a black sedan.

Just as Eleanor Carlson slammed the door and ran around to the driver's seat.

Just as she drove off with my son as Hunter sprinted through a cloud of dust, trying to catch them with no success.

# CHAPTER TWENTY-TWO

HUNTER

By the time we ran to Maisy's car and sped out of Howell Farm, Nell was long gone. We'd followed her trail of dust on the gravel, but when she hit the paved county roads, her trail disappeared. Anywhere else, and we would have been able to track her down, but the roads that led to Howell Farm formed a more complicated labyrinth than the corn maze.

I made a guess, choosing the road that led back to town, but Nell must have chosen a different route because her black sedan was nowhere in sight.

Coby was gone.

All I saw was open road as I flew back toward town. Open road, and Maisy shaking in the passenger seat. The color had vanished from her skin and her eyes were vacant. When I clutched her hand, it was ice cold.

"We'll find him." I squeezed her hand before letting it go and digging out my phone. My foot pressed harder on the accelerator as I flew toward town, calling 9-1-1 as I drove.

By the time we'd made it to the sheriff's station in Prescott, the place was swarming. The minute a call had come into dispatch that a child had been taken, every deputy had abandoned their Sunday-afternoon plans and raced for the station.

Jess had been waiting for us. He'd shuffled us into a conference room and started asking questions. Maisy and I had given him a recap, describing Nell's and Coby's clothes and Nell's car, then he'd left us to kick off the AMBER Alert and give his team orders.

Leaving Maisy and I alone, forced to watch the activity in the bull pen through a long window.

Deputies all dressed in plain clothes were buzzing around the open room, most of them on the phone. They'd been making calls to other county justice departments, enlisting support to set up roadblocks. They'd also been notifying airports and Amtrak of the situation and passing on Nell's and Coby's descriptions.

All the while, Maisy and I sat helpless.

Sitting in black swivel chairs, we sat fucking helpless.

"We'll find him." I slid her chair as close to mine as it could go, the wheels touching, and slid my arm behind her neck.

She nodded but didn't say a word. The shaking in her hands was getting worse, so with my free hand, I held them both in her lap.

"Okay," Jess said, coming back into the conference room and taking the seat across from us. "The AMBER Alert is going out shortly. We're making calls to every known transportation hub in Montana. We've got patrols stationed on all of the roads going into Wyoming and Idaho. Half of my deputies are going to start combing the old county roads. We'll get him."

"What can we do?" I asked.

He shook his head. "Hate to say this, but just sit tight."

*Sit tight.* The last thing I wanted to do was fucking sit tight.

"Maze, Gigi is coming down. Want her to bring anything?"

She shook her head and dropped her glassy gaze to the table.

"Maze, look at me," Jess murmured. Her eyes left her lap and locked on Jess. "We'll get him."

A tear slid down her cheek and the pain in my chest squeezed tight.

*Fuck.* I couldn't see her like this. I couldn't just sit here and do nothing but watch her suffer. Would she hate me for this? She should. I'd brought Nell into her life and now her son was gone.

The panic I'd felt earlier was starting to morph into blinding rage.

Nell—my own stepmother—had stolen Coby. She'd taken him from right underneath our noses.

What the fuck was wrong with her? What was she doing to him right now? If she hurt one hair on that boy's head, I'd strangle her myself. The idea that she could be hurting him made my stomach roll.

*Don't picture the worst. Don't picture the worst.*

Gruesome images flooded my mind despite my will to keep them out. I'd spent too many nights in a Chicago emergency room not to know what the unthinkable looked like. What it looked like when an adult tried to break a child's bones. Or what happened when a human body was thrown from a moving vehicle.

My stomach rolled again as the images played on a loop. The blood drained from my face as the bile rose, but I swallowed it down.

I had to stop thinking the worst. I had to stop thinking the worst and be the strong one, because Maisy needed me.

*Stop. Just. Fucking. Stop.* He'll be okay.

*Please. Please, let him be okay.*

A lone cry from Maisy's mouth interrupted my silent pleas. She slapped a hand over her mouth and squeezed her eyes tight, causing a few more tears to fall.

"Take a breath, baby. Just breathe." My hand slid down her back and rubbed gently. "Just breathe."

The hand on her mouth dropped. "He's *my* son. He's mine. My baby. I'm his mom and he needs me. I'm a good mom. A really good mom. And he needs me."

"You are a good mom. The best." I swallowed hard. "We'll get him back."

My throat was burning as it threatened to close tight. Maisy was breaking down and there wasn't a fucking thing I could do to stop it. So I just *sat tight*, watching as the love of my life, the strongest woman I'd ever known, completely fell apart. Her shoulders collapsed as she cried into her hands, folding in on herself in that black swivel chair.

"Baby. Baby, please, breathe. Just breathe."

It only made her cry harder.

Not knowing what else to do, I lifted her out of her chair, set her carefully on my lap and held her tight. She buried her face in my neck and kept on crying. Her entire body shook, every muscle, and no number of calming words or gentle whispers could make it stop.

My eyes shot to Jess, whose own face was creased with worry.

"Go. Find him," I mouthed.

He nodded once, then left us alone, returning to the bull pen to talk with his deputies.

"We'll get him back," I whispered into Maisy's hair. Not even her sweet lilac smell was a comfort, but I kept on whispering. "I promise. We'll get him back."

My phone dinged on the conference-room table at the same time Maisy's did in her purse. It was a loud, shrill alarm, not my normal ringtone. I picked it up even though I knew what the screen would say.

*AMBER Alert: Jamison County.*

My heart plummeted. No parent should ever see their child's name in an AMBER Alert. No parent should ever have to feel this kind of crippling powerlessness.

"We'll get him back," I repeated it again. Over and over, because it was the only power I had. I made a vow because I couldn't do anything else.

No matter how long it took, I would get Coby back. I'd look forever to find my son.

He was my son.

Everett might have donated the sperm, but Coby Holt was mine, just as much as he was Maisy's.

"We'll get him back."

Time passed too slowly as we sat and waited. And waited. And waited.

What felt like days were only minutes as the clock on the wall ticked with a deafening noise. The entire time, Maisy sat shaking in my lap. Her crying had stopped, only to make the shaking worse.

"Gigi's here," I said when I spotted her friend rushing through the bull pen.

Maisy didn't move. She just kept shaking. The shock had settled into her bones and she was shutting down. The fear of losing Coby had rendered her paralyzed.

"Hi." Gigi crossed through the door. She didn't say anything else, just came to the chair that had been Maisy's and scooted it close. Then she took Maisy's hands in hers and bowed her head to pray.

Felicity and Emmeline came in next, standing at our backs while their husbands joined the crowd in the bull pen. When Beau and Michael came in, they nodded at me and merged with Jess's remaining deputies to make phone calls. Maisy's parents came in last with Sabrina, the three of them taking the chairs across from us at the table. They looked distraught when they walked into the conference room, but at the sight of their daughter, distraught turned to petrified.

They looked as bad as I felt.

An hour went by. Then another. The thoughts I'd tried to banish—the ones where Coby's tiny body was lying lifeless along a gravel road—wouldn't stop plaguing my mind.

*Please. Please, bring him back alive.*

I hated being stuck here—helpless—when all I wanted was to be out searching for my child. But I didn't dare move. Maisy's shaking had stopped and now she was practically lifeless. A couple of times during the last two hours, I'd held my hand to her chest just to make sure she was still breathing. So as much as I wanted to help the search, I couldn't leave her alone.

More time passed until Jess appeared in the doorframe

of the conference room and caught my attention. He jerked his chin and I sat straight. All eyes were on Jess but he didn't say a word. I looked across the table to Brock, then down to Maisy. Her dad immediately stood and rounded the table, taking the seat at my side. With as much care as I could, I handed Maisy over to her dad, watching as she curled into his lap like she'd done it a thousand times.

"Be back." I bent to kiss her hair, then rushed out of the room.

"Did you find him?" I asked Jess the second we were out of earshot.

Jess nodded. "Yeah, we found him."

I let out a breath but didn't feel that flush of relief. "Is he okay?" My voice cracked. "Tell me he's okay."

"He's a little banged up, but he's okay."

"Banged up? What's that mean?"

He shook his head. "I don't know the details but was told nothing serious. Bottom line, Faraday, he's okay."

I steadied myself on Jess's arm as the relief nearly took me to my knees. *He's okay*. My son was okay.

"We need to go get him and get him checked out," Jess said. "Are you coming or should I call Dr. Peterson?"

"I'm coming." I turned back to the conference room and looked at Maisy.

"Go," Brock mouthed as he comforted his daughter. As much as I wanted to bring her along, she was too fragile. Instead, I'd bring Coby back to her.

I nodded to Brock and then followed Jess out of the station.

"Ambulance will meet us there," Jess said as I climbed into his truck.

"Right. Drive fast."

Forty-five minutes later, Jess pulled his sheriff's truck with lights flashing into a small airstrip one county over.

The grass around the rough runway was brown and untrimmed and the lines on the pavement had long since faded to near invisibility. The tin hanger that had once been gleaming silver was now spotted with brown rust. A worn, three-seater airplane was parked in the middle of the runway.

And Nell's black sedan was crashed into a row of sand barrels at the far end of the runway. It was surrounded by three of the neighboring county's cruisers.

Jess pulled up to the cluster, and before he'd even put his truck in park, I was out the door, racing toward the little boy who was sitting on the hood of a cop car.

"Coby!" I shouted.

He slid off the car in a flash, darting past the cops to race my way. "Hunter!"

I ripped the knees of my jeans when I landed, skidding to a stop to wrap my boy in a hug. He fell into my chest, his arms looping around my neck as I enfolded his small body.

"You're okay," I breathed. "You're okay. I've got you."

And I'd never let go.

He started to cry and I hugged him closer. While I'd been living a parent's nightmare, Coby had spent three hours in terror. His shoulders heaved as he cried and clung to me with every ounce of strength in his skinny arms.

"I want Mommy," he cried into my neck.

"Okay. We'll go get her." I pried him off my chest and did a thorough inspection, feeling my way along every inch of his arms, legs and torso. "What hurts?" He had a small cut on his forehead and another on his arm.

"My head hurts here." He pointed to the cut. "And my hand."

"Show me."

He pointed to his left wrist. I palpated it carefully, doing my best not to move it too much in case it was broken. "I think you just sprained it. Once the ambulance gets here, we'll get it all wrapped up. Okay?"

He nodded as more gigantic tears slid down his cheeks.

I pulled him back into my arms at the same time the ambulance's siren sounded in the distance. I held him tighter, turning to whisper in his ear, "I love you, Coby."

"I love you too."

I vowed right then to tell him every day. I'd never feared that my dad hadn't loved me, but he'd rarely said the words. Coby would know without doubt.

"How is he?" Jess asked, coming to my side.

I scooped up Coby and stood. His legs wrapped around my waist and his arms around my neck gripped even tighter, nearly choking me. "Scared mostly. A couple cuts and probably a sprained wrist. It might be broken. What happened?"

Jess had been so focused on speeding to the airstrip our trip here had been in complete silence. Now that I had Coby back in my arms, I was ready for answers.

"Pilot called it in." Jess pointed toward the deputies who were standing around a cruiser and talking to a man in a tan jumpsuit. "He saw the AMBER Alert come through, and when she showed with Coby, he stalled her. Deputies got here and she tried to make a run for it. Guess she grabbed Coby and got him back in the car. They blocked her in but she tried to bust through the barrier. Got stuck instead."

I pried Coby off my chest a bit. "Does your head hurt?

Are you dizzy? Do you see any white spots when you look around?"

He shook his head.

I was going to have him checked for a concussion regardless as soon as we got back to Prescott.

Nell was sitting in the back of a cruiser. Her handcuffed wrists were in front of her face as she pressed a white gauze pad to her forehead.

"Can I see her?" I asked Jess.

He hesitated.

"Please. I just need to ask why."

"It's not protocol and this isn't my crew." He blew out a loud breath. "Tell them you're a doctor and that you want to check that cut on her head before the ambulance gets here. Better hurry."

"Okay." I peeled Coby away again. "Hang with Jess for just a minute, okay, buddy?" He resisted but I transferred him to Jess anyway before walking to the back of the cruiser.

I nodded to the deputies, told them I was a doctor, and was waved on. I crouched down low in front of the open door at the back of the cruiser.

Nell dropped her arms, the gauze pad coming down too. The cut on her head—likely from hitting the steering wheel—would need about seven stitches but it had already started to clot.

Her face was pale and splotchy. Her hair, which had always been so sleek and straight, was a frizzy mess. She looked heartbroken. She looked nothing like the beauty my dad had married or the woman I'd grown up with.

"Why, Nell? Why did you take Coby?"

"Hunter." She reached for me with her handcuffed wrists. "I can do better this time. I can do a better job with

Everett. I just need some time and you'll see. He'll see. I can be better."

"Nell, that's *Coby*. My son."

She shook her head frantically, the clip in her hair now falling out completely. "I just need to try again. Everett will love me. I'll make him love me and he'll be okay."

"Nell—" I stopped myself. Nothing I said would matter.

Nell's sanity was gone. Something had happened in the last year that had completely cracked her mind. All the anger I'd had for her evaporated. In its place a deep pity settled, pity beyond any I'd ever had for another human being.

"Okay, Nell," I said gently.

Her frantic nodding stopped as a tear slipped down her cheek.

"You go with these nice men, okay? They'll get your cut all fixed up."

"But then I can try again?" she asked. "I can try again with Everett?"

I smiled and patted her knee.

Then I stood and nodded at the deputies, walking right back to claim Coby from Jess's embrace.

"Come on, buddy. Let's go home and get Mommy."

# CHAPTER TWENTY-THREE

HUNTER

"Is that all, sir?"

I nodded. "Yes. Thank you."

The man nodded back, then closed one of the big doors on the moving truck, waving good-bye as he climbed up into his driver's seat.

When it pulled away from the curb, I was left standing, staring at an empty house. All of its belongings were now on their way to storage. All of the things of my father's and mother's that I wanted to keep had been boxed and loaded into the back of my truck. All of the loose ends were now tied tight.

It had been two and a half weeks since Nell had kidnapped Coby. Two and a half weeks since I'd left Prescott. Two and a half weeks of working my ass off to close the book on my previous life.

Now that my job here was done, it was time to go home.

Home. A place I hadn't really had since Mom had died. A place I had now, thanks to Maisy and Coby.

Smiling at the thought of my family, I pulled my phone from my jeans.

*Me: All done. Coming home.*

Her response was instantaneous.

*Blondie: We'll be waiting.*

I slid the phone back in my pocket in exchange for my truck keys. Then, for the hundredth time today, I reached into my other pocket. Tucked away at the bottom was the best surprise I'd found all week. Assured that it was safe and secure, I slipped my hand from my jeans and went to my truck.

Then I went home.

---

MAISY

"I missed you," I told Hunter for about the thousandth time since he'd stepped foot in his house. Like every time before, he pulled me into his arms and said it back.

"I missed you too. I'm glad to be home."

I kissed his chest over his T-shirt and then let him go to finish cooking our meal.

Coby and I had come up to Hunter's house earlier today to get started on cooking a nice dinner. I knew that Hunter would be tired, driving all the way from Grand Rapids by way of Chicago over the last two days, so we'd come here to make sure he had a proper welcome home.

In the nearly three weeks that had passed since Coby's kidnapping, I hadn't let my son out of my sight. At first, he'd clung to me too, but after weeks of watching me clean rooms and fold sheets, he was getting bored. He'd been begging me to take him back to Quail Hollow, but I hadn't been ready.

Now that Hunter was back, I could get answers to all of my questions and, hopefully, put that horrible afternoon weeks ago behind us. Maybe if I could make sense of Nell's actions, I wouldn't have such a hard time letting Coby go back to his normal routine.

"So? How did everything go?" I asked.

Hunter and I hadn't had a chance to talk much while he'd been gone and I wanted to get more than the details he'd delivered through fast text updates and brief phone calls.

But before Hunter could tell me about his trip, Coby came flying into the room. "Hunter, look!" Under his arm was the remote-control car that Hunter had brought back as a gift.

Coby set down the car and stepped back, positioning the remote in his hands. Then he started pressing levers and buttons until the car jolted to life. He hadn't gotten the hang of driving it yet so it bounced off the fridge and spun in the other direction, and since Coby's hand was still on the trigger, the car came crashing right into my bare feet.

"Owie, bud." I bent down to massage my wounded little toe. "Let's not run that into people, okay?"

"Sorry, Mommy." He came after his car and set it up to go the other way.

Hunter smiled as Coby raced it through the living room. "That car is perfect for this house."

Even with the house fully furnished and décor complete, there was still a ton of wooden floor space for my men's car races.

"Anyway." I nodded for Hunter to tell me about his trip.

He pulled up a stool and sat at the island, rubbing his tired eyes. "It was a long trip but I'm glad I went. It was the right thing to do."

"How did Nell settle into the new place?"

"Good. Better than I expected. We decided to commit her for three years, and after that, we'll reevaluate."

I sighed. "Good."

Nell couldn't bother us again for three years. She'd be spending that time as the newest resident of Shimmering Waters, a private mental health facility outside Chicago.

The day she had kidnapped Coby had been the worst day of my life. I'd never felt paralyzing fear like that before. I hoped I'd never feel it again. Only when Hunter had brought Coby back from the airstrip had I snapped out of my trance. Falling to my knees, I'd held my son in my arms as my entire family had converged, surrounding me, Coby and Hunter in an enormous group hug where everyone shed tears of relief.

When we'd finally broken apart with wet faces, Jess had asked for a moment with Hunter and me to explain our options for dealing with Nell.

With Coby sitting just outside the conference room with my parents, Hunter had told me what Nell had said when he'd talked to her in the back of the police car.

The woman hadn't been in her right mind. We could have pushed and demanded she spend time in prison, but Hunter hadn't felt right about having her sent to a place where her mental state would just deteriorate further. She was his family, after all.

So rather than press criminal charges, we'd taken pity on her and agreed to get Nell into a mental institution. She needed help. Something had broken in her weak mind and she needed professionals with tools to help her put back the pieces—if she ever recovered at all.

"Are you feeling okay about it?" I asked. "No regrets?"

He shook his head. "No regrets. This is the best. At least, that's what I keep telling myself. The place she's at is really nice. Her doctor seems like a good guy and the staff is very professional."

"Maybe in a few months, you can go visit. I'm sure she'd like that."

He shrugged. "We'll see."

Was I still angry that Nell had taken Coby? Absolutely. But I just couldn't find it in myself to hate her any longer. She had no one in the world to care for her except Hunter. She'd lost it all: her money, her home and her mind.

Nell had hurt Hunter so badly by taking Coby; I was just proud that he'd been able to set that pain aside and care for her as a fellow human being. His father would have been proud too. I wasn't going to push Hunter to see her if he didn't want to, but I also wouldn't object if he decided to visit. It was his decision and I'd support him either way.

"Did you find out why?" I asked.

The timing of all Nell's actions was still bothering me. I had no doubt that Everett's death had been the catalyst for Nell's mental break, but why now? Everett had been dead for years. Why did she suddenly go crazy this year?

"It was my fault," Hunter said. "She snapped because of me."

"What do you mea—ouch!"

Coby's car slammed into my bare foot again.

"Sorry, Mommy, sorry!" he called before I could scold him.

I frowned. "Shoo. Out of the kitchen."

He came and scooped up his car, then went rushing out.

"Okay." I turned back to Hunter. "Continue. Why is it your fault that Nell snapped?"

"Because I moved here."

My eyebrows knitted together. "I'm not following."

"Remember I told you that I was living in the pool house at Dad's house?"

I nodded. "During your residency."

"Yes, and afterward too. I lived there until I moved here for the first time. Even after I left Chicago, I kept Dad's old house. Nell had already moved to Grand Rapids but she'd left almost everything in the Chicago house. She spent most of Dad's life insurance on a new house and new furnishings. All of that stuff, I just left. When I moved back to Chicago after I'd been here the first time, I moved right back into the pool house since most of my stuff was still there."

I was still confused at how his moving the second time to Prescott had sent Nell over the brink, but I stayed quiet as Hunter got up from his stool to get a glass of water, then sat back down.

"When I moved back here, I decided to sell Dad's house. I left not knowing how long I'd stay here, but . . . call it a feeling. I just knew it was time to clear out all of the stuff and let it go."

Hunter shook his head and yanked out his hair band, fixing his bun to trap some of the hairs that had fallen loose.

The suspense was killing me but I just stood quietly and

waited for him to keep explaining. Hunter had stopped keeping secrets, but one thing I had learned about my man was to be patient. When things were hard for him to talk about, he needed some extra time.

I could give him all the time in the world.

I'd give him anything.

"I hired a company to go through the house and pack it all up," he said. "Everything got shipped to Nell because I figured she had nothing else to do, she could sort it all out. I took my personal stuff, what I could fit in the truck, and she got the rest."

He took another drink of his water and paused his story while Coby came running back in to demonstrate how he'd just learned to do his car in a spinning circle.

"Good job, buddy," Hunter said. "Can you go into the living room and play for a sec while Mommy and I finish talking? Then I'll come in and we can practice it together."

"Okay." Coby smiled and off he ran.

"Coby?" I called before he disappeared. "I love you." I'd been saying it as much as I could.

He kept running. "Love you too! And Hunter!"

"I missed him," Hunter said when he disappeared.

"He missed you too."

Coby had asked after Hunter more times in a day than I could count. Now that he was back, the three of us would be spending some quality time together. And I would finally get some sleep. When he was gone, the bed was too cold and empty. I'd been tossing and turning for weeks.

"Anyway," Hunter said, continuing his story. "Everett had an old diary in his room. None of us had bothered cleaning out his room because it had been so empty, but when the movers had come to box up all of the stuff, they found an old diary in his closet. They sent it along with everything else."

"And Nell found it."

He nodded. "It was by her bed in Grand Rapids. When I got to her house, I started packing things up, looking for reasons why she would have flipped and taken Coby, and I found that diary."

"What was in it?"

He sighed and shook his head. "It was filled with page after page of hateful things about her. I had no idea Everett hated her so much but he had written it all down. What an awful mother she had been. How he thought she was ugly. All of this horrible stuff."

I'd never heard of a boy keeping a diary before but I guess it wasn't impossible, especially if he was young. "How old was he when he wrote it?"

"That's the crazy part. He was just a kid, an angry preteen whose mother had just married a new guy, and he'd gotten a younger brother he hadn't wanted. A lot of it was how he wanted things to go back to just the two of them."

"So Nell found this diary and started to question herself as a mother."

"Exactly," Hunter said. "I think my statement at the custody hearing reinforced some things already going through her head."

I knew all about Mommy guilt. If Nell had been reading that diary over and over, I could see how it would have made her crazy. She'd seen Coby as her second chance at motherhood and had taken him to try again.

"I get it." I nodded. "I don't forgive her for taking Coby, but I get it."

"Yeah. Me too." Hunter hung his head. "I wish I had

known about that diary. Maybe I could have stopped this from going so far."

"Maybe. Maybe not. I think if Nell had been in her right mind, she could have seen past the diary. I think there was more going on in her head than you'll ever know."

Hunter sighed. "You're probably right."

"Do you think that's why she filed for custody of Coby? Because of the diary?" At the time, I'd thought it was only a way to punish me for killing Everett, but now, I wasn't so sure.

"Partly. I think the things we talked about before are still true. She wanted her revenge. I mean, she wanted him before the diary. Maybe just finding it made her push harder. And then when she actually saw Coby . . ."

"She snapped."

He nodded. "I found an old picture of Everett at her house. They look so much alike at this age, it's uncanny. I think when she saw him in the café, it was the last straw."

Not for the first time, I pitied Nell. She hadn't been a great mother, but she'd clearly had her regrets, and she'd never get the chance to make amends with Everett.

"It was so sad going through her stuff." He'd sold everything of hers in Grand Rapids, other than her personal belongings now stored away. "She really loved Dad. She sent him love letters and kept them all. She kept every birthday, Valentine's Day or anniversary card he ever gave her. And I think in her own way, she loved Everett too. She was proud. She kept boxes full of his art projects and report cards."

"Then why would she be so cold?"

He shook his head. "I don't know. I don't know if she's ever really been all there mentally. She put on such a good show of confidence, I think her mind was a lot more broken than any of us ever knew."

I sighed. "Then it's good she's at Shimmering Waters. Maybe they can help her put the pieces back together."

"Maybe."

I went back to cooking, filling a pot with some water for gravy. I didn't know what would happen with Nell after she left the mental institution. I might never forgive her for threatening my child, but thankfully, I didn't have to make that decision today.

And if I ever did have to confront Nell, I'd have Hunter by my side. I wouldn't be fighting battles alone anymore. I wouldn't be relying on my own strength to move forward. I wouldn't be the only one finding the courage to forgive.

Hunter and I would tackle life together.

"Have you thought about anyone who could move into the loft?" Hunter asked.

"No. Not yet. Why?"

He grinned. "I called Beau on the drive back from Michigan and asked him how hard it would be to move Coby's bunk. He said we could do it tomorrow."

The whisk in my hand dropped to the counter. "What?"

"I called Michael too. It turns out that Alana really wants to move out of her parents' basement. I guess Michael is getting sick of sneaking in and out at night." His eyebrows waggled and I faked a gag. "Alana could take the loft."

My heart raced when I realized what he was saying, but I tried to play it cool by tapping my chin. "Where on earth are Coby and I going to live?"

He chuckled. "I've got an idea."

I lost control of my smile and it stretched wide. "Are you sure you want us here?"

"I'm sure I want you here."

"Okay." Easy as that. Now we all lived here together.

A sexy, wide grin split his face. "I'm going to tell Coby." Hunter slid off his chair and winked at me before walking into the living room.

My fingers scrambled for my phone so I could immediately text all of my friends to tell them that Hunter had just asked us to move into his home. When the dings started to chime back with *Yay!*, *Congratulations!* and Gigi's *I'm totally going to win our bet. He's going to ask you to get married way before Michael and Alana*, I giggled.

My laugh was cut short when Coby's car came crashing back right into my foot.

"Gah! Coby," I growled. "We're taking a timeout from this ca—" I bent to pick up the car and stopped mid-sentence.

Tied to the car's antenna was a ring.

A ring that had not been there before and was definitely not something that could have mistakenly come from the toy store.

I stood, car in hand, as Hunter and Coby peeked out from behind the couch.

"Mommy, will you marry Hunter?"

Hunter slapped a hand over Coby's laughing mouth. "I told you, I was going to ask, you little monster!" He started tickling my son—no, *our* son—until tears ran down Coby's cheeks and he begged Hunter to stop.

Tears were running down my face too. Because Hunter asking me to marry him through Coby?

*Best. Proposal. Ever.*

With Coby still laughing on the floor, Hunter stood and came into the kitchen. His jeans hung perfectly down his legs—legs I would tangle with mine every night. His T-shirt was stretched across his wide chest—the chest I would use as my favorite pillow. His heels thumped on the floor as he padded toward me with bare feet—feet that would keep mine warm when they got cold.

My fiancé.

"What do you say, Blondie?" Hunter took the car from me and set it on the counter. Then he framed my face with his hands. "Will you marry me?"

"Yes."

His lips were on mine before the word had time to even settle in our ears. We kissed, using our mouths and tongues and teeth, until Coby broke us apart.

"You guys," he groaned. "Can I have my car back?"

I laughed into Hunter's mouth as he chuckled into mine.

"Sure, buddy." Hunter broke us apart to untie the ring from Coby's toy. "This was my mom's ring. I didn't think Nell had kept it, but she had a whole box of Mom's jewelry stashed away in Grand Rapids."

Breathing in choppy gulps, I fought to rein in my happy tears as he slid the ring onto my finger. The diamond was no more than a carat and the gold band was simple. Bracketing the diamond solitaire were two ovals, each inlaid with another small diamond. It was a classic ring. It was unassuming.

It was just right.

Hunter stepped closer, pulling me back into his arms as my eyes stayed locked on my ring.

It meant the world to me that it had been Hunter's mother's, and I would wear it with pride until the end of my days. If Hunter ever offered an upgrade for an anniversary or birthday, I would politely refuse. This ring was the only one I'd ever wear on my left hand.

"Hey! Give me back my car!" Coby shouted, trying to squeeze between us to get his toy. Hunter and I both started laughing as Coby yanked the car off the island and took it back into the living room.

Smiling, I pressed my cheek into Hunter's chest and wrapped him up tight. "I love you."

His soft lips brushed against my hair. "I love you too."

We held on to one another for as long as Coby let us, finally breaking apart when he demanded Hunter play with him and grumbled about being hungry.

While they raced the car around the furniture, I went back to cooking dinner, texting my friends an update between mashing potatoes, microwaving peas and whisking gravy.

It wasn't fancy, but it was everything I had ever wanted for my life.

A happy life.

A life filled with more love than some people found in a lifetime.

A life with a man that would forever make me smile.

# EPILOGUE

## MAISY

S*even years later . . .*

"Fuck, baby, get there. Fast," Hunter growled, then bit the side of my neck.

The zing of pain went straight from my neck to my clit. When Hunter sucked the same spot he'd just bitten, my already-tingling legs began to tremble.

My back was pressed against the cool marble in our shower, my legs were around Hunter's hips, and my husband was pounding his cock into me with no restraint as the water poured down his back. With the sound of our skin slapping and water rushing, his mouth trailed openmouthed kisses up my jaw to my waiting lips.

My hands started clawing at his back, urging him to go harder and faster. With a rumble from deep in his chest, he obeyed, fucking me as hard as he could without dropping me on my ass.

"I'm so close," I said against his lips. "I need—"

I didn't have to articulate. After years of sneaking in shower sex while our kids were napping, he knew exactly what I needed. After one slow lick across my bottom lip, he sucked it into his mouth and my orgasm hit. He kept it between his teeth as I cried, my back arching away from the tile as my inner walls clenched around his thrusting cock.

"Squeeze me. Just like that." His words were barely audible over my strangled sounds echoing off the shower walls. "Just. Like. That." With each word, he thrust harder, finding his own release. His groan drowned out mine as he let go of my lip and tipped his head back.

I leaned forward and licked the water off his corded neck, making his fingers dig even harder into my thighs as he let go of his release.

When we were both wrung out, he let go of my legs and set my feet back on the tiled floor. I kept a grip on his shoulders until the white spots in my vision cleared and I regained my balance.

"Whoa," I said, breathless. My arms and legs felt like rubber and now I could use a nap myself.

Hunter chuckled. "You'd better hurry or we're going to be late."

I swatted his arm. "If we're late, it's your fault. You interrupted my shower, Dr. Faraday."

"Are you really complaining, Blondie? Because I'm pretty sure your pussy is glad the doctor showed up."

I pulled my lips in to hide a smile, then I smacked his ass and stepped past him to get my shampoo.

He laughed again and took the bottle out of my hand, just as I'd expected. One thing Hunter always did during our dirty showers was wash my hair. And then I'd wash his.

It was a simple gesture, washing each other's hair, but it meant everything to me.

It was the care Hunter took with me. It was the way his fingertips would dig in a little, rubbing any tension away. The way he'd bend down and kiss my shoulder when I was all lathered up. The way he'd tip me back under the water, supporting my weight with one strong arm as the other kept the water from running into my eyes.

And for all the care he gave me, I gave it right back.

I'd worship his hair, combing it out gently with my fingers before rinsing it clean. All these years and I was still as obsessed with Hunter's hair as I'd been the first day he walked into the inn's lobby.

We washed and finished our ritual before Hunter left the shower to get ready for the party. I rushed to shave my legs, miraculously not leaving any nicks, then dashed out to spend a little extra time—not as much as I had planned—in front of the bathroom mirror on my hair and makeup.

I tugged on jeans, a nice black sweater and a scarf to cover up Hunter's love bite. With my knee-high boots pulled over my dark-wash skinnies, I did one last inspection in the full-length mirror in our walk-in closet before leaving the bedroom in search of my family.

I found Coby in his room with Grayson, right where I'd left them for their mandatory hour of "quiet time," since both were too old to nap these days.

Grayson was on Coby's bunk, watching something on his tablet. Coby had his nose in a book. While reading still wasn't my favorite pastime, it had become Coby's latest obsession. He and Hunter had bonded over the first Harry Potter and now my son was rarely seen without a book or two under his arm.

"Okay, boys. You need to get dressed to go."

"We are dressed, Mom," Coby said, not tearing his eyes away from his book.

"Bud, it's too cold for shorts. Would you please put on some jeans or something?"

He frowned and set down his book, then climbed down the stairs from the top bunk. Even at eleven years old, Coby still loved his bunk. It was a little more cramped on top than it used to be, but when Hunter had offered to take it down, Coby had adamantly refused.

It was his special space.

And Pickle's, who was currently napping in the corner next to Grayson.

"Gray, you too. Climb on down from there."

My youngest son nodded, rubbed Pickle's ear and set down his iPad.

I ruffled his light brown hair when he hopped off the last step. It was too long, but when I'd tried to have it cut, he'd refused. Grayson was in a phase where he did everything his dad did. And since Dad had long hair, he had long hair. If he could have grown a beard, he would have.

"Do I have to change, Mom?" Grayson asked. He looked so much like Hunter except for his eyes—he'd gotten them from me.

"No, you're good." He was wearing jeans and a long-sleeved thermal, just like Hunter had been earlier. The minute we'd gotten home from our family sledding expedition today, he'd changed to match his dad. I had no idea why Coby had traded his warm clothes for shorts, considering it was barely above freezing outside. "Go grab your shoes, bubba."

"Okay." Grayson ran out of Coby's room toward his own down the hall.

"Mom, do you think Dad would take me shopping for a new book tomorrow?"

"I'm sure he would if you asked. Now get dressed." I stepped out so Coby could have some privacy to change and then continued on toward Layla's room. My three-year-old daughter was resting on Hunter's chest, rubbing her eyes and yawning, still groggy from her nap.

I crossed the room to the white rocking chair and pressed a kiss to her white-blond hair. "Did you have a good nap?"

She nodded and curled further into Hunter.

While five-year-old Grayson took after Hunter, Layla took after me. We had the same eyes and hair. The same shape to our face. The only difference was the shape of her nose, which was more like my mom's than mine. When the three of us were out together, there was no mistaking her gene pool.

"Does she need to change?" Hunter asked.

"Yeah." Layla was still wearing the leggings and Mustangs football sweatshirt from our sledding trip.

I walked over to her closet and inspected my options. While I had kept the boys' rooms tasteful and not age-specific, I had lost my mind decorating Layla's room. The walls were pale pink, even the inside of the closet. The white trim was perfectly matched to her four-poster bed and scalloped dresser. The pink floral rug in the center of the room was centered directly under a crystal chandelier.

She'd hate this room when she got a bit older, but for now, it was just right for my princess.

Pulling out a cream cable-knit sweater and some jeans

embroidered with matching flowers, I set them on the bed. "Here you go. She can wear her UGG boots."

Hunter smiled as he kept rocking his baby girl and I slipped out of the room to get our party contributions from the kitchen. Gathering up a plate of cookies and the Tupperware bowl of Hunter's pea salad, I had everything ready by the time the boys came storming down the stairs, followed by Hunter carrying Layla.

"All set?" Hunter asked.

I smiled. "All set."

Then the Faraday family set off for the party I'd been looking forward to for over a month.

---

"JESS IS TOTALLY GOING out of his mind," I told Gigi as I came out to the farmhouse porch and handed her a refilled glass of wine.

"Why do you think I had to come out here?" Gigi asked. "I'm afraid if I don't intercept poor Mason Drummond, Jess will scare him off before he can even knock on the door."

Jess was pacing the living room, watching the windows and waiting for Rowen's first date to arrive. His face was a mix of gut-wrenching anguish and cold-blooded murder.

It was kind of adorable.

I laughed and sat next to Gigi on their front porch swing, shivering as I scooted close to take a corner of the blanket she was offering to cover my lap. "This is fun. I'm glad you planned this party."

"Me too."

Gigi had planned this party for Jess, not Rowen. All of

our friends were here in an effort to distract Jess from the fact his little girl was going to her first dance.

"Can you believe my baby girl is sixteen and going on a date?" she asked.

I smiled and took a sip of my own wine. "They aren't babies anymore. When did that happen?"

"When we blinked."

A lot had happened when we'd blinked.

Marriage. Babies. Life.

Hunter and I had had our winter wedding not long after he'd proposed. I'd enlisted all of my family and friends to help plan it and we'd pulled off my dream wedding within a month. With Hunter's support, I'd been able to put Coby's kidnapping in the past, and we'd gotten married in the barn at Howell Farm. I'd had my white, long-sleeved, lace dress. Hunter had looked as gorgeous as ever in his tux. And Coby had been the most handsome best man in the history of the world. It had been a night filled with friends, love and laughter.

Like most of the days since.

One month after our wedding—the day Hunter's adoption of Coby had been approved— Coby and I had both changed our last name to Faraday.

Two months later, I'd been pregnant with Grayson.

Two years after he was born, we'd had Layla.

Then I'd blinked and they were both out of diapers. Grayson was in Emmeline Slater's kindergarten class, and before too long, Layla would be too. She wouldn't be my little princess, spending the mornings at Quail Hollow and then afternoons with me at the motel. She'd have her own life, her own friends and her own winter formal dances.

"I can sit out here and watch for Mason," I told Gigi. "Don't you want to go in and help Roe get ready?"

Gigi shook her head. "No, that's okay. I got emotional earlier when I helped her into her dress. I don't want to wreck her night by turning into a basket case because she's growing up. Jess is losing it and one of us has to stay calm. A little time out here in the cold air will be good for me to settle down."

"You can cry when she leaves and then get drunk. I brought more wine."

"And that," she clinked our glasses together, "is why we're best friends."

"Roe looks so pretty." I had snuck a peek into the bathroom where Felicity had been doing Rowen's makeup. Roe had chosen a deep-blue strapless gown, the color perfectly matching her eyes, and Gigi had curled her long hair into beautiful waves that hung down to her waist. Since Felicity was the master makeup artist in the group, she and Roe had quarantined themselves in Jess and Gigi's upstairs bathroom so that all of the other kids wouldn't bother them. The only other person allowed in the bathroom was Adeline, who adored her big sister just about as much as she adored her aunt Felicity.

Everyone else had been banished to the main floor.

"This farmhouse barely holds us all these days," I told Gigi. All of our friends had come over tonight except for Michael and Alana, who were on vacation for their anniversary, and Milo and Sara, who were at home with their two-week-old newborn.

We both looked over our shoulders to peek inside. Kids were playing everywhere. Dads were drinking beer and laughing. Moms were sipping wine and smiling.

"Yeah, but I like it full," she said. "Besides, if we run out of space, I'll just have Jess build another addition onto the garage."

"Good plan. Maybe a construction project will keep his mind too occupied to plot Mason Drummond's murder."

We both laughed and kept spying on everyone inside.

"Grayson looks more and more like Hunter every day," Gigi said.

My son was sitting next to his daddy at the dining room table, playing cards with Silas and Silas's son, Liam. "He sure does, but all the boys look like their dads."

It was the one thing I always got a kick out of in our group. All of the boys were spitting images of their big, strapping fathers, and for the most part, the girls took after their mothers.

Gigi giggled. "Strong genes."

"That's the truth."

We turned and relaxed into the swing, watching the dark sky as we waited for Rowen's date to arrive.

"How is Nell working out?" Gigi asked.

I sighed. "So far so good. I check on her every day but she seems to be doing fine. She's actually really good at cleaning."

"I still cannot believe the woman who kidnapped your son is now working for you at the motel."

"You and me both."

Eleanor Carlson had spent six years, not three, at the mental institution, repairing what had been broken in her mind. And when she'd emerged, she'd come out a different person. She had been humbled. She had been given the chance to grieve. She had been given a second chance.

In Prescott.

Because she hadn't had anywhere else to go, Hunter had invited her here. Nell was living in my old loft, cleaning for me at the inn so I didn't have to work as much. Her relationship with Hunter was stronger than it had ever been, and most importantly for her, she was building a connection with Coby.

She was becoming Grandma Nell.

Some days were better than others, but she was trying hard to forgive herself for the way she had treated her son and mine.

And thanks to help from the therapist I'd seen for three years after Coby's kidnapping, I'd been able to put it all in the past. Everything. I had moved past the kidnapping. I'd moved past the flashbacks. And I hadn't pinched my leg in years.

Everett was nothing more than a distant, unpleasant memory.

Headlights bouncing down the gravel lane to the farmhouse interrupted our conversation.

I took a deep breath as Gigi chugged the rest of her wine. "Here goes." I stood at the same time as Gigi, whipping off the blanket and leaving it on the swing.

Just in time, Gigi intercepted Jess as he came barreling out the farmhouse door. "Sheriff," Gigi warned, "take a breath."

His broad chest puffed up and he opened his mouth, but she stopped him with one finger pressed to his lips.

"This is her special night, Jess."

All of the air puffed out of his lungs, and in a pained voice, he whispered, "Fuck, this is hard, Freckles." Then he pulled his wife into his arms and held on tight.

I slipped past them and went inside to find my kids.

Coby was watching a video with Ben on someone's phone. Layla was following the other girls around with a beaming smile. And Grayson was still with Hunter at the table.

"Is Mason here?" Hunter asked.

I nodded. "Yep. I'm going to go up and tell Roe."

As I started up the stairs, the rest of the party congregated in the living room and the men all went for their "props."

Silas had brought a rope.

Nick, a pipe wrench.

Beau, an ax.

Hunter, a bone saw.

And of course, Jess came back inside with his gun firmly secured to his hip.

*Poor Mason.*

It was a good thing he was such an awesome teenager with a sturdy backbone. Picking up Roe with five big, overprotective men in the room would not be easy.

I hit the master bedroom in the farmhouse at the same time Rowen came gliding out of the bathroom.

"Well?" She twirled around, the smile on her face bright and beautiful.

How was this gorgeous young woman the same little girl I'd babysat during Jess and Gigi's first date? "You're stunning," I said, choking back tears. "He's here."

"Goodie!" She smiled brighter, clapping as she rushed over for a hug and then disappeared down the steps.

Behind her, Felicity came out of the bathroom, wiping her eyes dry, with Adeline racing past to follow her sister.

"Ready for this?" I asked.

She shook her head. "I'm so glad Victoria has a few more years. I don't think I could take it yet."

I nodded. "You and me both." Layla would be lucky to convince Hunter to even let her go on a date at sixteen. He was quieter in his protectiveness than Jess, but no less fierce.

I looped arms with Felicity and we walked downstairs, where our friends were fawning over Rowen and the men were looming over Mason.

And bless Mason's heart, he didn't even notice the men. His eyes were fixed on Rowen in a way that made Jess's already-distraught face fall even farther.

Jess saw it. We all did.

At sixteen years old, Mason Drummond was in love with Rowen Cleary. No matter how many angry men stood close by with their weapons of choice, it wasn't going to scare him away from his girl.

"Oh, lordy, Jess is in trouble," Felicity whispered.

"I think we're going to be seeing a lot more of Mason around."

She hummed her agreement when we hit the bottom step. Rowen gave one last hug to her mother and a kiss on her daddy's cheek before she breezed out the door with Mason in tow.

"Let's eat!" Gigi announced, sniffling as she led the way to the kitchen.

"I think I'd better open another bottle of wine," Sabrina mumbled, following Gigi. "Or three."

The party resumed as we spent the evening eating, drinking, laughing and counting down the hours until Rowen came back home.

At nearly ten, the party was still going strong except for Layla, who had fallen asleep on the couch in Hunter's lap.

"Do you want me to go lay her down?"

He shook his head. "I'm good. Would you bring me another beer?"

"Sure." I went to the kitchen for his drink, then brought it back just as Nick joined him on the couch.

"Where'd Gigi go?" I asked Hunter.

"Outside, I think."

It was freezing cold, and if she was outside, something must be bothering her. "I'll go check on her."

He gave me his signature wink, the one that still made my heart skip. "Okay, baby. Love you."

"Love you too." I bent down to brush my lips to his smile and then wandered out to the porch. I shivered and rushed to the swing to crawl back under Gigi's blanket. "Hey. Are you okay?"

She smiled and nodded. "Maybe a little tipsy but otherwise fine. I was just thinking about when Roe and I moved here. That was the beginning of our happy."

I smiled.

We all had our special places.

For Jess and Gigi, it was the farmhouse.

Nick and Emmeline's was the chapel where they had gotten married.

For Silas and Felicity, it was their ranch.

Beau and Sabrina would forever cherish the outpost where they had spent their first months together.

And for me, my happy started the day Hunter Faraday walked into The Bitterroot Inn and changed my life forever.

---

THE JAMISON VALLEY series continues with *The Candle Palace.*

# AUTHOR'S NOTE

I started writing *The Coppersmith Farmhouse* in July of 2016. One year later, I finished the last sentence to Hunter and Maisy's epilogue. There isn't any other word to describe those twelve months other than surreal. You see, I never dreamed of being a writer. My mother passed down her love of reading to me, but writing? I was the science and math nerd. I found my career in technology. I couldn't write a book. Could I? Maybe I could. So I started down this path as an experiment. I wrote *The Coppersmith Farmhouse*, knowing very little about creative writing but determined to finish just one book. Even if it was for my eyes only, I wanted to finish just one book. At the time, I had recently become a stay-at-home mom, abandoning my fast-paced career for cartoons, puzzles and toys. I'll admit, even though I loved the added time with my boys, I felt a little lost. I was living completely for my kids and hadn't figured out how to incorporate "me time" into our lives. I'd started to go stir-crazy, needing just a little something for myself, but I didn't want to jump back into another job that would demand relentless hours and all of my attention. So I started writing, not sure of what I'd find but hopeful it would be the one thing I could do for myself. And I found what I'd been missing. I found my characters. They found me. There is a little piece of me in each of the women in this series, and for what they've done to change my life, I will forever be grateful. These books led me to something new. To a place where I had never dreamed I would go. Thank you for taking this journey with me.

# ACKNOWLEDGMENTS

Thank you for reading *The Bitterroot Inn.* I would be nowhere without my amazing readers.

To all of the bloggers and my fellow authors who have helped spread the word about this series, thank you for your incredible support. To Kaitlyn, Jenn, Ana, Karen and all the members of Perry Street, thank you for being the best fangirls I could ever wish for.

Thanks to my proofreader, Julie Deaton, for putting the finishing touches on each of my books and making them shine. Thanks to my cover designer, Sarah Hansen, for creating my beautiful and unique covers. Elizabeth Nover, my immensely talented editor, I can't thank you enough for the many, many hours you put into reading, critiquing and editing my work. For all you've taught me this past year, I will be eternally grateful.

And lastly, to my family and friends. Without your love and encouragement, there would be no Jamison Valley series. Thank you for believing in me.

# ABOUT THE AUTHOR

Devney is a *USA Today* bestselling author who lives in Washington with her husband and two sons. Born and raised in Montana, she loves writing books set in her treasured home state. After working in the technology industry for nearly a decade, she abandoned conference calls and project schedules to enjoy a slower pace at home with her family. Writing one book, let alone many, was not something she ever expected to do. But now that she's discovered her true passion for writing romance, she has no plans to ever stop.

Don't miss out on Devney's latest book news.
Subscribe to her newsletter!
www.devneyperry.com

CPSIA information can be obtained
at www.ICGtesting.com
Printed in the USA
LVHW051624120523
746848LV00003B/353